FIGHTING FATE
Copyright © 2024 by Charli Cotner

ISBN 979-8-9891566-1-0

Cover Design by Brittany Evans

Edited by Represent Publishing

FIGHTING Fate

FIGHTING *Fate*

CHARLI COTNER

Represent
Publishing

On the List

- "EARNED IT" BY THE WEEKND

- "STRONGER" BY MANDISA

- "FADE INTO YOU" BY MAZZY STAR

- "FIGHT SONG" BY RACHEL PATTEN

CHAPTER 1
MILLI

You'd see how a true man treats a lady.

SIX MONTHS AGO . . .

Ever had that weird mix of annoyance and attraction toward someone? Like, one second they're under your skin, and the next, you're daydreaming about them in a way that's, well, not exactly PG-rated?

So, yeah, that's me with Miles Chasen. It's been Miles-this and Miles-that since forever. And there he is, looking like a walking temptation, while I'm here trying not to drool like a lovesick puppy. Awkward much?

Who's Miles Chasen, you're wondering?

He's the guy who could make those old ladies at the park drop their knitting. Those deep blue eyes? Hypnotic. And when he's warming up for a game, let's just say his legs alone could start a scandal.

But, hey, it's not weird to think this way about your best friend, right? No rules against having a major crush on him, I hope. Because if there were, I'd be six feet under, completely buried. No chance of escaping them, anyway.

Get it together, Milli. We're here for Luke, your brother, remember?

Dodging thoughts of Miles? Might as well try to ignore the blazing sun overhead. Our roots tangle back to the sandbox era, our dads' bonds forged in college and solidified on NFL fields. Miles—there's something about him, a confidence, a charm that's indescribably magnetic. It's just so . . . Miles.

He's the epitome of "sexy" without even trying, and believe me, it hasn't slipped past me. But I'm keeping that card close to my chest.

So here I am, sinking into our usual front-row seats at the game. The day's perfect for football—sun's shining, sky's crystal clear, and there's that intoxicating smell of spring and fresh grass in the air.

The stadium's alive, vibrating with chants of "Let's Go Panthers," and it's hard not to get swept up in the fervor. The dancers are killing it on the sidelines, and part of me is just a tad envious of their front-row view to the action . . . and naturally, to Miles.

Graduation's just around the corner, and I'm still figuring out my next step. But part of me imagines attending here, cheering on Miles every weekend. Those little glances he throws my way during games, and watching him—Mr. Greek God in Cleats—from the sidelines would be something else.

Just a daydream, right, Milli?

Just as my mind drifts away, a familiar deep voice pierces through. "Didn't expect you'd show up for the game." And there he is, leaning against the fence, looking infuriatingly handsome. Just his smirk alone should be illegal.

Maintaining a casual demeanor, I respond, "You know how it goes—family always comes first. Luke's on the field, so naturally, here I am."

"And when did you start playing by the rules?" he teases, those eyes twinkling with mischief.

Rules? They're not just in my playbook; they're etched into my very core, a part of who I am. I don't just adhere to order because it's expected—I revel in it; it energizes me. Yet, if he could only see how being here, observing him in his moment, is anything but a chore for me. Witnessing Miles fully embrace who he is sends an exhilarating charge through me every time, making my heart leap in ways I don't care to admit to those around me.

Would I rather be buried in a book? Usually, yes.

But watching Miles? That's a chapter of its own.

Picture this: a steamy romance novel, the kind with a cover that makes you blush. That's like the secret story of me and Miles. Only, he's clueless about our "involvement"—which, honestly, is mostly in my head. And me? Well, let's just say my knowledge of the more . . . intimate stuff is purely academic.

"Seriously, Milli, what's the real reason you're here?" Miles digs that sharp, probing look in his eyes.

I arch an eyebrow, throwing his question back at him. "And you? Chatting me up when there's a game on the line? Seems like a weird time for small talk," I retort, trying to sound nonchalant.

Miles flashes his confident grin. "Winning this game? Piece of cake," he boasts. "But, couldn't miss a chance to see you, Baby Sutton."

Every time I hear "Baby Sutton," it stirs something deep within me. What began as an adorable nickname has morphed into something far richer, something tender. Now, whenever it's uttered, it feels like a soft caress against my heart, sending waves of warmth through me and making my heart dance with an unspoken joy. It's not just a nickname anymore.

Our eyes lock, and I can't help myself—I take him in, every bit of him. There he is, all cool confidence and those sneaky smiles, like he knows something I don't. I'm usually on top of my game, keeping it chill, but this? Feels like he's egging my thoughts on, tempting them to jump into the deep end.

But who am I kidding? I never even try to fight off those thoughts.

Sure, I blame my overactive imagination and the romance novels I devour. But is that all there is to it? Especially when it comes to Miles? Did I mention those fantasies where I'm wearing his Panthers' jersey and . . . well, let's leave it at that. Maybe it's because we've known each other forever, or maybe it's just Miles being Miles—effortlessly attractive.

But I know, deep down, these are just fantasies, not real feelings. I mean, he's a college junior, and I'm a high school senior. To him, I'm just his nerdy bookworm friend, always lost in novels or dancing to Billie Eilish. Not to mention the college girls and . . . ugh, the cougars drooling over him. That's just . . . no.

Why would he look twice at "Baby Sutton" when he's got all that attention? Still, part of me hopes maybe one day, he'll see me as more than just a friend.

"Where are your parents?" he suddenly asks, scanning around.

Caught off guard, I'm jolted back to reality by his question. He's smirking as if he can read my thoughts. "You've got something right here," he says, pointing at my lip.

Shit. I did not just drool.

Stay cool, Milli. It's just a bit of spit, nothing more.

I quickly wipe my lip.

"Gotcha!" he says, flashing a wink as he walks backward. "But hey, it's flattering to be on your mind."

Heat creeps into my cheeks. "Keep dreaming, Sunshine," I retort, struggling to maintain my cool.

His laughter rings out as he points at me. "You got it, Baby Sutton. That's where you'd see how a true man treats a lady."

Did he really just say that?

Yes, he did, and so nonchalantly.

And sure, Miles has this way of "flirting" with me. In my mind, it's flirtation. To him? Likely just his style of playful teasing.

I watch him run off to the field, rolling my eyes. He might not be as affected by my presence as I am by his, but deep down, I relish that he sought me out first. It's a small victory, having Miles Chasen's undivided attention, even if just for a moment.

I shift my focus from him back to the field, catching Luke and his teammates head-butting their helmets in a pregame ritual. Out of the corner of my eye, I spot Mom and Dad heading my way. Despite the storm brewing inside, I muster a polite smile and wave.

Chill, Milli.

"Yeah, yeah," I mutter under my breath, barely listening as Mom chimes in.

"Oh, Milli, don't act like supporting your brother is such a chore. He's always been there for your dance recitals, hasn't he?" She settles next to me, laying on the guilt.

She's not wrong. Luke's been my steadfast audience, except when football interfered. I should be grateful, right? But here I am, benched at a football game as a "punishment" for being ten minutes late—and for what? Tutoring, of all things. Seriously, aren't parents supposed to be thrilled about that kind of thing?

And yes, I'm that girl—a dancer and an English tutor,

dreaming of a future where I teach both. I want to give back, to offer kids from less fortunate backgrounds the chance to dance and to learn, just like I did. Dance has shaped me, but it's not cheap. I can't even count the dollars poured into classes, costumes, shoes . . . you name it. That's why I'm set on making it accessible for those who can't afford it.

As I'm lost in thought, Dad leans in, whispering, "Don't mind her, Milli. Think about it—you've only got one more year to cheer for Luke. Then, it's all history."

He obviously forgets his own NFL dream is now Luke's. *Like father, like son,* they say.

Dodging that conversation, I nod along. "Right, Dad," I reply, eyes drifting back to the field, catching Miles in action.

He's something else—those arms, that build . . .

Focus, Milli.

But how? You'd think I'd be immune to his charms by now. Yet, the more I see him, especially after some time apart, the stronger the pull. Just one look at him, and my freaking heart races, my core tightens, and my legs instinctively squeeze together to ease the lingering discomfort. His magnetic presence makes my body react beyond my control.

Clearly, I need to deal with this issue.

Don't do it, Milli. Resist the urge.

I mockingly challenge my inner thoughts, thinking, *Resist? Yeah, right.* I purposefully grab my purse from the ground, intentionally averting my gaze. But just as I do, a hand lands on mine.

"Nope, not here. We're here to support your brother, end of story," a voice interrupts, grounding me in the moment. I exhale, annoyed, and slide my book back, just as Dad squeezes in between me and Mom, urging, "Focus, both of you."

Yeah, Dad, I had no idea this game was such a big deal.

The spring game is mainly a chance for the players to strut their skills for the fans, set the tone for the season, and maybe even predict how the team will perform.

Oh, by the way, did I mention that my football knowledge is basically unrivaled?

The best decision maker on the team? Quarterback.

Second most important offensive position? Left Tackle.

Those blockers protecting the quarterback? Guards.

And the guy running the ball and catching passes from the quarterback? Well, that's your Tight End, of course, aka Luke's position.

See? I know my football. Just because this game is technically my punishment, and I don't necessarily enjoy attending these so-called "games" (from the stands at least), doesn't mean I can't grasp it. After all, it's hard not to understand football when your father was a football legend, and your only brother is following in his footsteps. Football runs deep in the family, hence why The Suttons are known as a "football family"—insert eye roll.

"Got it, Dad," I respond quickly.

As I look back to the field, Mom nudges me. "Milli, have you seen Miles play yet?" Here we go again. Mom's got this thing for Miles, like he's some golden boy. Sure, I get it; I feel the same—but she doesn't need to know that.

She fans herself, lost in thought. "Your dad says he was on fire in practice. Can't wait to see him today." She sighs, then hits me with, "I don't understand why you two don't just date. It's so obvious. You're perfect together. What's stopping you?"

Oh, if she only knew.

Mom's always been the kind to just say whatever pops into her head, no filter. Rolling my eyes, I mull over her latest remark.

Well, let's see, Mom, why don't Miles and I date? Maybe because we're best friends? Or because he's in college, and I'm still in high school? Oh, and let's not forget how he's Mr. Experienced with the ladies, and I'm . . . not. Yeah, I'm pretty sure I'm out of my league here. But of course, Mom's not ready to let that go.

I offer a casual shrug, keeping my tone nonchalant. "Mom, between studying, college applications, and dance practice, there's just no space for—"

"And yet, you have all the time in the world for your precious books," she retorts with a tinge of annoyance.

Well, books are different. And besides, it's not like Miles is into me. Can't she drop it already?

I shrug again, brushing off her persistence. But she's not done. "At least your 'punishment' at the game lets you ogle some athletic eye candy. I told your dad this is hardly a punishment. Real punishment would be a week without your books."

She wouldn't dare. Would she?

And what's with her comment about athletic men? Is she trying to fit in with the cougar crowd, dreaming about guys half their age? I shake my head, eager to change the subject. "Maybe we should just focus on Luke?"

"Of course," she replies, slightly taken aback. "We did see him before the game. Looked ready, right, hon?" She turns to Dad.

Dad, ever the superstitious sports fan, claps his hands together, his gaze fixed on the field.

"Yep, he's going to show those recruiters what he's made of," he says with conviction.

Jeez Louise. One would think our futures are already scripted by them. It just makes me more determined to forge my own path. Luke, on the other hand, breathes football. The

NFL would be his ultimate dream—and our parents' too, apparently.

The loudspeaker announces, "Touchdown, Miles Chasen!" just as my phone buzzes. Glancing up, I catch Miles' signature smirk and that playful point he shoots in my direction. My heart leaps against my will.

"Milli, did you catch that?" Mom's overflowing with enthusiasm. "That touchdown, his pointing—it's as if he's signaling it was all for you." It feels far-fetched, yet a piece of me hopes there's truth in it. I dismiss her speculation with a shake of my head and turn my attention back to my phone.

PAYSON

Club Zero tonight. You in?

My eyes return to the field briefly. I bite my inner cheek, considering whether this is something I want to do.

But, I'm grounded . . .

Milli . . . you don't go against the parents' wishes.

But, what if, just this once, I want to let loose a bit? I mean, I'm nearing the end of my senior year of high school, so maybe this is a good time to celebrate? Just a month early.

Yeah, I think I could use some celebration.

Besides, the Chasens and Suttons always meet up at Glasshouse after each game, and my parents usually join Mr. and Mrs. Chasen at a bar afterward. So, the chances of them even noticing I'm not home aren't that high.

Quickly, I type back.

MILLI

Count me in!

PAYSON

Awesome! How about we gather at Brooke's at 8:30 to prep? Get that party ass ready!

MILLI

smh Sounds good. See you guys then!

A night out with my two best friends is exactly what I need.

And maybe a couple of vodka waters, too.

CHAPTER 2
MILES

Milli - 1 / Miles - 1

"So, Milli, how's high school wrapping up for you?" my mom inquires, her attention shifting across the table. My gaze momentarily wanders to the captivating strawberry blonde seated opposite us at the Glasshouse, our post-game retreat. The restaurant is a fancy yet ever-changing scene. It can be a hubbub of college students, a gathering spot for the older crowd, or a celebration point for families like ours.

Milli Sutton, affectionately known in my mind as Mills, Best Friend, Baby Sutton, is nothing short of breathtaking. With her commanding presence, long, elegant legs, blue-green eyes, and hair that perfectly marries shades of red and blonde, she's a vision. I've always had a handle on myself around women, but as she grew up, lost the braces, and her hair became less wavy, her presence is like a drug. Addictive and always craving more.

Though she might not realize it, our relationship, teetering between friendly flirtation and something deeper, has always remained purely platonic.

"It's been awesome," Milli responds with a smile that

could light up the room. "Super excited about the summer and starting college."

"That's fantastic! College is such an exhilarating experience," my mom says, her eyes lighting up with the memory. "I still remember moving Miles into his freshman dorm. Right, Sherry? We all squeezed into that old minivan with our boys."

Mrs. Sutton glances at her, nostalgia twinkling in her eyes. She nods and smiles. "Yes, it was one of the proudest moments of my life."

I notice Milli's eye roll and the way she starts tapping on her phone. Not really a surprise. The Suttons have always treated Luke, their eldest, like he's on top of the world. Milli's not one to show it outright, but I see those little signs—the slight curl of her lip, the way her fingers nervously twist a strand of hair. It's like a silent language, revealing what she feels inside.

I get where she's coming from. Being the sole heir to a family legacy, especially with a dad who's an NFL legend, I've felt my own share of that pressure. It was always about matching up to his achievements, like chasing a shadow that's always a step ahead. When I was younger, it felt like I was in a never-ending race to live up to his past.

But you know, times evolve. I was only seven when I began to forge my own way. And luckily, Mom has been my steadfast supporter, backing my decisions while pursuing her own ambitions in the high-end real estate market.

As Milli continues texting on her phone, curiosity gets the better of me. Who's on the other end of that conversation? A friend? Is she making plans for a get-together? Or could it be a guy? That last possibility sends a twist through my gut— she isn't mine, after all.

I know, I know, I silently scold myself.

But still, every time we're together, time just races by. I

always end up wanting more before we have to part ways. College life for me and high school for her puts a gap in our usual routines. I miss those impromptu midnight swims, sharing my mom's homemade chocolate chip cookies while swapping stories, or just walking side by side to class or on the football field. It's these simple moments I find myself longing for, more so now that they're not as easy to come by.

I quickly grab my phone, firing off a lighthearted text.

MILES

Your phone's stealing all your attention tonight, huh, Baby Sutton?

She looks up from across the table. A soft blush creeps over her cheeks just as she dives back into typing on her phone.

MILLS

Have to find some entertainment . . .

Our eyes meet once more, and instinctively, I arch an eyebrow. Is she challenging me, or is she just that fed up with these family dinners as much as I am?

I get it, though. Our parents can be overwhelming, always stuck on football and local hometown Stoneton gossip. But these dinners are my excuse to hang out with Mills, something I always look forward to.

MILES

Maybe I've got a better way to keep you entertained than scrolling through your phone . . .

She looks up sharply, surprise flickering in her eyes.

A part of me is thrilled by the reaction.

But then the reminder hits—*she's your best friend, Miles. The one line you've sworn not to cross. Reel it in, buddy.*

I suppose I shouldn't be too surprised by Milli's reactions anymore. Our dynamic has always been one of playful, slightly edgy flirtation. As we've grown, it's intensified, mostly with me trying to provoke her, but lately, she's become more than just Baby Sutton in my eyes. There's this feeling in my gut that if we spent time together, just the two of us, stepping out from behind the whole "just friends" facade, things could really escalate. But I've been holding back because Milli . . . she means more to me than just a fling. She deserves someone who truly understands her, you know?

It's not that I'm incapable of being that guy for her, but blending our dynamic could complicate things, especially considering our families. So, I've opted for caution, maintaining a respectful distance, in line with what her dad, my dad, and her brother Luke would expect.

Looking down, I catch her fingers moving swiftly again, and almost immediately, my phone buzzes with her reply.

MILLS

Oh? So, you think you've got something more interesting than my phone?

"Miles, what do you think about Guton's game strategy tonight?" Mr. Sutton's voice drags my attention to the other end of the table.

Before I have the chance to respond, my phone vibrates once more. I look at the screen and, for a moment, I'm taken aback.

MILLS

Go on, enlighten me. Make my night, Sunshine.

Wait, seriously? She's actually expecting me to make her night?

Hold on, could this be a setup? Maybe one of her friends is pushing her to test if I'll take the bait?

And then, my phone buzzes once more.

MILLS

Your face right now is priceless . . .

Damn, keep it together, Miles. Your poker face is slipping.

MILLS

How about a game of Words with Friends?
You know I always enjoy beating you at that.

Our eyes meet, and she bites her lip in a way that drives me crazy.

Clever girl, Milli.

Then, a sharp nudge against my shin under the table nearly makes me jump. *Fuck.* Milli subtly gestures toward her dad.

Right, Mr. Sutton. He asked a question.

"Shit, what did he ask again?" I mutter under my breath.

Luckily, Luke's deep voice comes to my rescue. "I mean, Guton's performance was solid," he comments, throwing me a lifeline with a look that says, "You got this?" "He really nailed it with his strategy and skill."

Ah, right, Guton.

While Mr. Sutton's eyes bore into me, my cheeks heat up a bit. Time to wing it. "Yeah, I think it was kind of risky, but it really worked out for their team," I say with a shrug. "We pulled off the win, sure, but Guton's guys were on fire. They showed some serious grit out there. It's a killer start to the season."

Out of the corner of my eye, Milli is stifling a giggle. What's she finding so funny? That text she sent? Or my all-over-the-place reaction? Yeah, I'm rattled, and no, that text was anything but amusing. I was expecting something a bit more . . . risqué, but she's just talking about Words with Friends.

Who even does that anymore?

Milli does, Miles.

She's always been good at getting a rise out of me, pushing my buttons ever since we were kids. It's like we're both addicted to this back-and-forth teasing that started around puberty.

Mr. Sutton nods at my comment, taking a sip of his scotch. I guess I can be pretty quick on my feet, even when there's a major distraction like Milli around. He glances between me and his daughter, a curious look in his eyes. But what's there to wonder about? He knows we are just friends . . . If he only knew half of what I think about her, he wouldn't be so quick to label me the "brotherly best friend."

MILES

Giggling at me over there, Baby Sutton?

Milli shoots me a look that's a mix of amusement and exasperation, the kind that says, "Seriously, with the nickname again?" accompanied by her signature eye roll. But what can I do? Baby Sutton just fits her, and honestly, it just sounds right when I say it. It's got a ring to it that I can't resist.

MILLS

Actually, I'm feeling a bit of secondhand embarrassment for you. I mean, who knew Miles Chasen could get so worked up over a text about Words with Friends?

MILES

Hey, it's no big deal, Baby Sutton. Not really embarrassed, just . . . your text got me thinking. Thinking about how we could spice up this evening a bit more . . .

With you . . .

The thought alone—of us, tangled up, the heat, the whispered words—fuck, it sends my pulse racing and my cock twitching.

Chasen, man, pull it together.

Inhaling deeply, I slide my fingers through my hair, tugging at the strands gently to ground myself in the present. Yet, it's challenging, more so when a quiet gasp close by jolts me back to the moment. A smile involuntarily forms on my lips as I look at Milli, observing her blush deepen to a more vivid shade of red across her cheeks.

Message received, loud and clear.

Looks like she's the one getting flustered now.

Game on, I guess.

Milli - 1 / Miles - 1

We're definitely playing some kind of game here, but what is it exactly?

Cat and mouse?

Just two old friends seeing who can out-flirt the other?

I'm snapped out of my thoughts as Milli slips away from the table, heading toward the restroom. Interesting timing . . .

Our families are lost in their own worlds. The dads are buried deep in football talk, and our moms? They're off in their own universe, chatting about who knows what. They jump topics faster than a game of hopscotch. And then there's Luke, doing his best Casanova impression with our waitress. Come on, man, at least wait till our parents aren't around.

Without thinking twice, my legs start moving, following in the direction Milli went.

Chasen, what's the game plan here, man?

Honestly? Not a clue.

Stepping into the restaurant's restroom area, I almost collide with Milli.

She seems a bit out of it, so I reach out, steadying her with a hand on her waist. Our gazes intertwine, and, in that moment, the world around us seems to vanish, leaving just the two of us. Our hearts beat in unison, their rhythm silencing all else.

She looks away, but not before I catch a spark of intensity in her eyes. *Is she experiencing this magnetic pull as well?*

Or is it only me? I can't ignore the feelings that have been quietly building. And really, who wouldn't be drawn to Milli? She exudes a Sarah Michelle Gellar but with an added layer of her unique Milli Sutton charm.

It's been months since we really hung out, just a few texts and FaceTime calls. I let my hand drift along her arm, and her reaction is instant—those wide eyes, the goosebumps. What's she thinking?

As she attempts to step back, I instinctively tighten my hold, surprised by how her hips fit just right in my hands. Instead of stepping back again, she moves in, closing any space left between us. My heart kicks into overdrive, mirroring the intensity of a game's final moments. Then, there it is—the familiar look in her eyes, brimming with a challenge.

The urge to lean in, draw her near, and press my lips to hers swirls tumultuously within me.

But then she steps back, allowing me a moment to catch my breath and collect myself. "I was just on my way to the restroom. Lucky I caught you, or that could've been a nasty fall."

She points at my chest, her touch firm. "The only reason I almost fell is you and your sudden linebacker build," she teases, her fingers pressing against my chest. "What's up with that? You weren't this bulked up last summer?"

A little more observant, aren't we, Mills?

I can't help but laugh, shaking my head. Milli, who used to be more on the reserved side, has really started pushing my buttons as we've gotten older. And I'm here for it, especially when her "compliments" come wrapped in a bit of sass. It's like she's dipping her toes into uncharted waters, and honestly, I'm ready to dive in after whatever she's tossing my way.

Her hand meets my chest with a light push, making me grin. It's clear, even in these small moments, that I'm getting to her somehow, and that's oddly satisfying.

"Can you," she starts, pushing against me, "just get," another shove, "this ridiculously huge," and one more, "body out of my way?" She keeps trying to push me back, but honestly, she might as well be pushing against a wall. She's strong with that dancer's build, but I'm standing my ground. Not to brag, but I've worked hard on this physique. It's a well-sculpted eight-pack with a little trail leading down to . . . well, you know.

I've had my share of battles, scars and all, but there's something about Milli's comments on my body . . . it's an undeniable high. "You looking to handle all this, Mills?" I tease, smirking and arching an eyebrow, a blend of pride and something else. Not that I care what she thinks.

Sure you don't, Miles.

Just as she's about to sidestep me, she presses her finger harder against my chest, stirring something inside me.

"Calm down, big guy," I whisper to myself, trying to keep it cool.

Milli's laugh breaks through; that real, unguarded one not many get to hear. "In your dreams," she fires back.

I catch her finger, pulling her close enough to whisper, my lips barely brushing her ear. "Nah, it's you who's dreaming, Baby Sutton."

She halts, tilting back slightly, our faces just inches apart. Her eyes lift to mine, widening momentarily. In them, I catch a spark, a hint of mischief. "Maybe," she answers with an effortless ease, and then glides by me as if our exchange was the most natural thing in the world.

What on earth was that about? Doesn't she realize she can't drop comments like that without making my cock harder than a shot of straight whiskey?

Feeling the need to adjust myself again, I notice an elderly lady watching me as she exits the restroom. *Great.* I wave awkwardly, and she blushes, fanning herself. Milli, of course, finds this hilarious.

I shoot her a look and silently mouth, "You're dead," with a mock throat-slash gesture. Her laughter only grows. The elderly lady appears taken aback, shaking her head and murmuring, "Kids these days." Despite myself, I find Milli's laughter infectious and join in.

Fucking hell, this woman. Her teasing has definitely kicked up a notch tonight. Not that it's a hardship; more like a turn-on. Before heading into the restroom, I throw over my shoulder, "Oh, and tell Payson I can't make it tonight."

Her eyes narrow, wondering how I'm privy to her plans at Club Zero. I'm always in the loop, forever on the guest list. With an eye roll, she turns and walks off, leaving me admiring her perfect dancer's ass as she returns to our table.

CHAPTER 3
MILLI

I'm all yours tonight, aren't I, Sunshine?

When Payson said we were hitting up Club Zero, I had a picture in my head, you know? Payson's the type to have her quirks; pretty set in her ways and all that. Clubs, I get it, they're usually all about the buzz and chaos, but I wasn't prepared for this scene. Instead of the whole shebang—bright lights, blasting tunes, a crowd getting down—it's just a few people milling around, chatting in little clusters.

I pull a face as I knock back the last of my vodka water. It's got this weird tang, sorta bitter, kinda like seawater with a kick. But hey, it's my go-to. It doesn't wreck me the next day, and with college dance tryouts in June and it already being late April, I need to keep my head in the game, both mentally and physically. I haven't nailed down a college yet, but I'm eyeing two, and they're both scouting for top-notch dancers.

Right up my alley.

Waving over the bartender, I flash my ID again. Okay, it's not really mine, unless you squint and say Chasandra Iden's my twin. The bartender didn't even double-take when I showed it. How did I get it? Let's just say it kinda fell into my lap when I hopped into Payson's car. She flicked it my way as I got comfy. Deep down, I know it's dicey, but hey, you're only a high school senior once, right? Gotta grab life by the horns or something—however that quote goes.

The bartender pushes another vodka water toward me, offering a wink. His gaze lingers on me a tad longer than comfortable, dripping with an attempt at charm, making me feel a bit uneasy. A little less try-hard would be nice, right?

Swiveling toward my friend Brooke, I ask, "So, this is what clubs are these days, huh?" She's lost in her phone, probably texting Jordan. They're like that picture-perfect couple, glued together since freshman year. Saw them once in the rain, him being all knight-in-shining-armor, holding her books and an umbrella. Totally melted my inner romantic.

Their thing is straight out of some love story book, maybe a bit PG, but who's to say what happens when no one's watching, right? Suddenly, I'm caught up in a daydream, imagining landing a guy just like that . . .

Snap out of it, Milli. You've got a laundry list: Graduation. Studies. Dance. College is breathing down your neck. Romance can wait.

I look around and say, "Where's the crazy lights, thumping music, and a packed floor with people dancing their hearts out?" We both eye the place, more bar-vibe than club, with couples nursing drinks and chit-chatting.

Brooke just shrugs. "I mean, Payson said this place was unique, but didn't click until now. She almost had to haul me here, betting you'd ditch."

My eyes pop. She really thought I'd bail?

Look, compared to my besties, I'm Miss Goody Two-Shoes. Straight As, dance ace, tutor, basically the poster kid for good behavior. And, I get it. But that's on me, my goals, my sweat. It's never been about pleasing Mom, Dad, or Luke. My game, my rules.

Luke's chill as a cucumber, just rolling through days without sweating the small stuff, while I'm like a walking planner. Got that from Mom, always super on top of things when I was a kid. Me, I'm all about lining up my week—class, dance, homework—like some kind of life Tetris.

Not every kid's got it smooth, especially with dyslexia. As a little one, that hit me hard. I was lost, trying to figure out why reading was like climbing a mountain, why words just danced around, why I felt so small in class.

How does someone with dyslexia become an English tutor you ask? Well, it wasn't easy, I'll tell you that. But I decided to turn my challenge into a way to assist others facing similar struggles. When I told my parents I needed a tutor who understood dyslexia, they were initially puzzled, but then they found Jane. She'd navigated the same complex path. Jane wasn't just a tutor for academics; she was like a beacon of support, guiding me emotionally as well.

She sparked my dreams, nudged me toward dance. Thought I was doomed to be bad at everything 'cause of the reading hassles, but, boy, was I wrong. Dance became my world, my light. Nailed my first routine at nine. And that thrill, that joy? Unreal. That's when I knew dance was it for me.

Brooke pipes up, eyebrow arched, "You have to admit, she's got a point. Didn't think you'd show tonight. Isn't your dance thing coming up?"

I nod, sipping my drink, feeling it hit a bit harder. Maybe it's the second round, or maybe I'm just a lightweight. "Yeah, there is," I say. Every year since ninth grade, Jazzy Jensen's Dance Studio puts on this big year-end show. Senior year being my last one, it's kinda bittersweet.

My phone buzzes in the pocket of my leather jean jacket as I add in, "Yeah, we're seniors, and this year is slipping away from us. That means fewer moments with my girls here in Stoneton and less opportunity to do all the usual senior year things," I gesture around at the surroundings of this so-called club, "whatever that is."

Brooke cracks a smile. "Milli, you're like a lost puppy in here."

True, clubs aren't my usual jam, but I'm all for a change of pace, showing my best friends I can let loose, at least once in a blue moon.

I dig out my phone and see a new text.

MILES

Playing it cool with the goodbyes tonight, huh, Mills?

MILLI

Oh, what, my hug didn't cut it?

MILES

No, I mean . . . yeah, your hugs are top-tier.

That gives me a little flutter in my chest.

MILES

But hey, weren't we supposed to duke it out in Words with Friends before you split? Thought we were doing the whole friendly rivalry thing.

I let out a snicker. Friendly rivalry, my ass. Miles is as competitive as they come; neck and neck with Luke.

MILLI

Last I checked, we don't need to be face-to-face for a word battle. So what's the real deal? My hug not up to scratch? Because I know my hug game is strong.

MILES

> Okay, maybe I just wanted more hang time,
> kill me? Missing you, Mills.

My heart's already in butterfly overdrive, and before I can even text back, Brooke says, "Crap. Isn't that your brother?" Her eyes are glued to the door.

I'm rooted to the spot. Seriously, Luke!? Of all nights, he picks this one to crash? Feels like some cosmic prank for ditching my grounding. Weren't he and Miles supposed to be heading back to college? Something about needing to be back for practice?

Brooke's still staring at the entrance, and I'm so stiff, it takes her nudging me to snap out of it.

Crap, crap, crap . . .

In pure reflex, I duck under the bar. "What? Luke's here? Why? Doesn't he have to get back to college? Shouldn't he be—"

Brooke cuts off with an, "Oh, shit," then claps a hand over her mouth.

I raise an eyebrow. "What's up, B? Spill it."

Her look says it all. If Luke's here, then it means . . .

She tries to play it cool. "Not a biggie, but your crush might've tagged along." She winces. "With, uh, three other girls."

Classic Miles, always the ladies' man. And yeah, guilty as charged, I still have a thing for him, regardless.

Didn't he suggest he was skipping out tonight? That's the impression he gave at the restaurant, yet how he was in the loop about tonight's plans is beyond me. Despite this, I find myself wrestling with a pang of jealousy at the sight of him with other girls, even though he's not mine to claim.

But who am I kidding? It's always been tough, right from our high school days. Envy used to hit hard every time some girl fluttered around him. I got better at dealing with it when he left for college—out of sight, out of mind. But when he's back, it's like, can't these girls take a break?

"Okay, so don't panic," Brooke says, which, obviously, sends me into full panic mode. Who says that and expects calm?

I arch an eyebrow, bracing for Brooke's next words, but she barely starts, "They're comin—"

My nerves kick in and I interrupt. "Where are they? What do the girls look like?" Brooke's just smirking at me. "C'mon, B, spill it," I demand.

Just as she's on the brink of laughter, a familiar voice from behind me slices through the air. One I'd recognize anywhere. I swivel around, and there's Miles, leaning down to my level, those mischievous blue eyes of his twinkling. "Milli, fancy seeing you here," he says, all grins.

"Talk about a small world," I mumble, thrown off by this twist. I mean, I'm not mad about Miles being here—the opposite, really. But him and Luke together? Not great with Luke being Mr. Overprotective Big Bro.

As I lock eyes with Miles, we both stand up. He's quick to steady me, hands on my waist, and it's like being zapped back to earlier tonight at the restaurant. My heart's doing the samba, my throat's all dry, and there's this buzz all over me, like excitement and nerves all mashed up.

"Is it just me, or did it get way hotter in here?" I whisper, fanning myself. Great, now I'm channeling my mom's vibes around Miles.

"Have you been drinking?" he asks, eyebrow cocked. It's not his usual flirty look, more like he's actually worried.

I catch my lip between my teeth, and his eyes follow the movement, then slowly drift over me.

When did this kind of tension start with us? Sure, there's always been something, but is it the booze making me see that Miles is really looking at me? I'm not even dressed up—just this black leather jean jacket, a white bodysuit that's a bit daring (thanks to Payson's advice), mom jeans, and Converse. Nothing fancy, but maybe Payson was onto something.

Just then, Brooke gives a little cough, and Payson joins in. "She's just living it up tonight, senior style. Got a problem with that, Miles?" She puts a bit of sass in his name, hips swaying just so. Miles clenches his jaw, clearly bugged.

"Yeah, didn't think so," Payson finishes with a wink.

My best friends, seriously, they're the best. Unbelievable, totally awesome. I try to look anywhere but at Miles, eyes darting around for Luke. Getting busted by him here would be a disaster. Sure, Luke was no angel back in the day, but there's this double standard, right? If I were him, I'd just be a cool guy having fun, but me? I'm just the rebellious, careless teen sister.

And it's not like Luke never pulled a Houdini himself. Guess who showed me the ropes? Big bro, leading by example.

"You know, Mills," Miles says, eyes catching mine, that smirk of his nearly making my knees give way. Good thing I'm leaning on the bar. If I ever hit the floor in front of Miles, trust me, it won't be because of a smirk. "If you were curious about who I came with, you could've just asked."

Not that I care about the girls eyeing him or how they look.

Yeah, right, Milli . . .

And just like that, here comes one of them. A tall, stunning blonde, wrapping around Miles like she's made for it. "Luke and the others are inside the club," she says.

Great, she's gorgeous. Athletic, flawless, the full package. And me? Thinking Miles might see me as more than a friend? What a joke. Is this the kind of girl he hangs out with at college?

"Wait," Brooke interjects, glancing at Payson, "this isn't the actual club?"

Blondie laughs. "Nope, this is just the waiting area."

A waiting area for a club? Since when? Both Brooke and Payson are blushing, and I'm sure I'm a tomato by now.

"We totally knew that." Payson tries to save face, elbowing me a bit too hard.

Miles raises an eyebrow, clearly not buying it.

But you know what? Screw it. Tonight's about wild, care-free Milli. Who cares about anything else? I've got just a month of high school senior freedom left.

Miles, with that teasing glint, goes, "Does Luke know you're here, Milli?"

I roll my eyes. "Like it matters. He doesn't, and what I do is my business, not his, definitely not yours."

It's not often I get riled up, especially around Miles, but watching him with Miss Blondie Bombshell is like a punch to the gut. It's one thing to know he's popular with the ladies, another to see it up close and personal. My friends are giving me those wide-eyed looks, probably because I don't usually snap back like this, especially not at Miles.

But tonight, I'm not holding back. It's my senior year, and I'm all about living it up, breaking out of my shell, and maybe, just maybe, letting Miles see a side of me he's never seen before. The side that doesn't just roll over and play nice, the one that's got a bit of fire.

Miles is there, all grins, with Blondie right in his space, whispering sweet nothings that get him to loop his arms around her, and a storm of envy brews inside me.

I let out a shaky laugh, pulling myself together, feeling a bit bold from the drinks. "You heard Blondie," I say, nodding toward her. Payson and Brooke snicker at my nickname for her, ignoring the scowl she's probably shooting my way. With a wave, I add, "Better not keep Luke hanging. You know how he gets with waiting."

Miles looks kinda puzzled. "Why don't you all come along?" He looks at Payson and Brooke. "What do you say?"

I'm about to shut that down when Payson's already pulling us along. "We'll just freshen up, then head in," she says.

My friends, always the best, right?

As we slow down near the bathroom, I turn to them. "Seriously, Payson?"

"You wanted to go clubbing, so here we are. What's the big deal?"

She's got a point. I did agree to this. But the thought of bumping into Miles all night, with that blonde glued to him, or any other college girls fawning over him? Yeah, that's definitely not what I had in mind.

I'm scrambling for a Milli-style excuse. "Look, Luke's in there. If he sees me, it's game over. He'll be on my case, and then it's goodbye to drinks, dancing, and, well, any sort of fun."

Brooke jumps in. "Since when are you into wild stuff, anyway?"

I shoot her a look. "That's not the point."

Payson's lips tighten, and her hands find their way to her hips. "So, what is the point?"

I sigh. "I just wanted one night of no rules, no worries. How can I let loose with Luke around?"

Payson's eyes gleam with a clever spark. "Don't worry about Luke. We'll handle it."

Miles

Tonight has me feeling all sorts of twisted up and really I've got no one to blame but myself for landing in this mess.

You see, I had a hunch of where Milli was off to after dinner. She left her phone behind, dashing to the bathroom—not her usual move. Guess I threw her off balance. Out of habit, I flipped her phone over, respecting her privacy and all. But then, right on cue, a message pops up from Payson.

Payson Pennington—she's a whole other story. Not exactly the world's best influence, always coaxing Milli into skipping school, fibbing to her parents, and don't even get me started on those wild, blind dates. Still, she's the one who roped Milli into hanging out tonight, so I can't be all mad at her.

After the restaurant, I casually mentioned to Luke that I was heading back to campus tomorrow. He was curious about my plans, but I wasn't about to say I was hoping to spend time with his sister. We're just friends, right? But when I dropped Club Zero's name, suddenly he's all in. Classic Luke—the place is right up his alley.

Did I want Milli to tag along when I asked? Hell yeah, I did.

But seeing her here, flirting with other guys, wasn't part of the plan. And that familiar tight knot in my stomach from the restaurant? It's returned with a vengeance.

Milli's out there, dancing like she doesn't have a care, chatting up guys left and right. And me? I'm trying to focus on Blondie here, but my eyes keep drifting back to Milli. I'm a moth, and she's the flame.

Downing my drink, I welcome the pleasant buzz that starts to settle in. Signaling the bartender for a new one, I pride myself on my ability to drink without facing a brutal hangover the next day. There's team lifting tomorrow, but I'm not worried about it.

Fresh beer in hand, I take in the scene. Club Zero's is

usually chill, but tonight, with spring breakers around, it's a whole new level of wild. The place is electric—strobing lights, bodies everywhere, the music loud and pumping.

"Got anything good?" Blondie—Sharon, Shayen, whatever—sidles up to me, all purrs and smiles as she eyes my drink. I can't even remember her name, and I feel a bit guilty about that.

"Nope," I say, giving her a casual brush-off. Not my style to be cold to girls, but she's clinging like crazy.

She huffs, muttering as she heads off for a drink. Can't blame her, but my mind's elsewhere. On Milli. She's looking all over the place, probably for Luke. And Luke? He's in his element, surrounded by a couple of brunettes, loving the attention.

Shaking my head, I steal another glance at Milli. It's like our eyes have radar for each other; hers find mine across the crowded room. I take a swig of my beer, peering over the rim. The moment she spots me, there's this tension that ripples through her, but it's fleeting. Soon enough, she's back to dancing with this guy, his hands all over her, gripping her waist like he's got some sort of claim on her.

As he twirls her, her body molds closer to his, his hands wandering with a boldness that stirs unease within me. She leans into him, her head tilting back to rest against his chest, while her captivating gaze locks onto mine. In her eyes, there's an unmistakable desire that sets off something deep in me—a kind of raw, *primal urge.*

She arches an eyebrow, all playful, her hands moving up to the guy's neck. The dude's clearly enjoying it; way too much. But it's not his reaction that's got me. It's Milli, the way she's just so alive, so aware of every move she makes, and fuck, how she holds my gaze as her fingers trail down the guy's neck, torturing me with every slow, deliberate touch.

What the hell is she playing at? And why's it getting under my skin so much?

My hand, not holding the beer, curls into a fist just as Milli tilts her head toward the guy, breaking our eye lock. He leans in, his lips way too close to hers for my comfort. And before I know it, my feet are moving, like they've got a mind of their own.

What the fuck are you doing, Miles?

But I'm already halfway to making a choice. I've got two ways to play this:

1. I could go over there, yank the guy away, and make it clear she's off-limits.
2. Or, I could grab Luke and let him handle his little sister.

Either way, I'm in deep. I know I should just let it be, but watching Milli like this, something's snapped inside me. I need to do something, anything, before this night spins way out of control.

As I scan the club, Luke's still caught up with a pair of brunettes, oblivious to everything else. Deciding on option one, my heart races, my hands a little sweaty, as I head toward Milli. It's a mix of nerves and excitement. I've known Milli forever, seen her grow from a quiet kid into this . . . this woman who doesn't need my say-so, like when she's dancing with some random guy.

You don't need her approval, do you, Miles? My inner voice mocks me.

I stride over, eyes fixed on Milli and her dance partner. I nod at the guy, telling him to scram. I'm taking over. "The hell, man, I was here first," he protests, his grip on Milli tightening. I see a flicker of worry in her eyes. Milli's not a chess piece, not someone to be shuffled around. She's a person, not a problem to be solved with brute force. She deserves finesse, understanding, and respect.

"I'm not asking twice," I say, voice low, fists clenched. He sees the barely contained anger in my stance, gets the message, and backs off, hands up like he's surrendering.

He steps back with a muttered, "She's all yours," leaving space for me to step in. Instinctively, my hands settle on her waist for the second time this evening, and I immediately notice her sharp intake of breath, her body stiffening at my touch.

But before I can get too hung up on her reaction, she's giving me this cheeky smile, slinging her arms around my neck all easy-like. "So, I'm all yours tonight, aren't I, Sunshine?" she ribs.

Hell yeah, you are.

I groan, both at the implications and her nickname for me. She's called me that forever, a nod to how I've always tried to stay positive, even when things got tough.

Cute, sometimes . . .

I lean in closer, my breath brushing her ear, watching a ripple of goosebumps dance across her skin. *Has she always reacted this way to me?*

"Looks like it, Mills. You good with this switch?" I murmur, feeling confident about her response, given the way her body's reacting.

Without a word, she grabs my hand, leading me deeper into the dance floor, away from Luke's line of sight. Not that he'd mind us dancing. It's not like he has ever told me to stay away from Milli; we're friends and all. But if he knew what I am thinking right now, he'd lose it. No doubt about it.

The DJ's seamless blend into "Earned It" by The Weeknd feels like it's echoing inside me, a cue I didn't know I was waiting for until it happens. As the song's smooth rhythm fills the space between us, I find myself drawn closer to Milli, almost instinctively. There's a brief shadow of hesitation in her gaze, a fleeting uncertainty that dances away as quickly as it came—probably chased off by the cocktails she's been sipping. That liquid bravery, it seems, has smoothed the edges of her usual caution. Without it, she might have hesitated, especially considering Luke could be watching, lurking somewhere in the shadows of this crowded place.

In a sudden move, I spin her around, her back pressing against my chest. My arms encircle her, feeling the warmth of her body against mine. My mind races with possibilities for how we can savor this closeness. She leans back into me, her cheek resting against my neck as the bass of the new song adds a more sensual rhythm to our movements.

The air between us vibrates with energy, a live wire sparking through my veins. Milli fits against me just right. She feels incredible. Almost too incredible. My chest is all lit up with this blend of wanting, excitement, and a rush of adrenaline.

"Miles," she breathes out, her voice barely above a whisper. Our eyes lock, a fleeting connection before she lets her eyelids flutter shut.

One hand stays anchored on her waist, while the other ventures up, my fingers tracing the delicate skin of her neck. She shivers under my touch, her breathing growing heavy. The dance floor lights flicker and dance, creating a dreamlike world around us.

In this moment, it's just me and Milli, lost together, utterly absorbed in the dance.

As the music slows, I turn her to face me. Our movements are perfectly in sync as we draw closer, our lips mere inches apart. That spark's there, no mistaking it—the kind of pull between us that feels like some unseen force is drawing us together.

I'm not entirely sure what this "it" is, this force that's

pulling us closer, but I'm powerless to resist. Gently cradling her jaw, I lean in, our lips meeting in a tentative, teasing brush. For a second, I question if this is right, but then her hands weave into my hair, pulling me closer, and her tongue finds mine.

In this kiss, there's a question and an answer, a dance of desire and uncertainty, but all of that fades into the background, leaving just the two of us, here and now, lost in each other.

I growl softly as our kiss deepens, feeling the heat between us intensify. My yearning for her overshadows everything else—it's like a heady, overwhelming rush. My hands find their way to her legs. I lift one around my hip, and the other naturally wraps around me. There's no mistaking the way she reacts to the pressure of my arousal against her; she lets out a soft whimper as our bodies press closer together.

A husky groan escapes me, drowned out by the thumping bass of the club's music.

She looks down at me; her legs intertwined with mine, her arms wrapped around my neck. Bathed in the club's lights, she looks ethereal, almost angelic.

My angel, I think fleetingly, despite knowing it's a stretch.

Dream on, Miles.

She seems to catch my thought and lets out that adorable giggle of hers. She tilts her head back, exposing her slender neck, and I can't resist the temptation. I trail kisses down her throat, gently nipping at her skin.

"Miles," she breathes out gently, her voice stroking the air like a feather, and fuck, the sound of my name on her lips sets off a tidal wave of anticipation inside me. Every inch of me feels hot, every fiber tense and ready, every muscle wound tight, ready to burst any second now.

I continue my exploration, my lips moving along her

collarbone, tracing the scar from our childhood backyard football games. Her soft whimpers fill my ears as I kiss up to her jaw, finding her ear and playfully biting it. Our kiss resumes, filled with her sweet murmurs.

I've always wanted her like this, but it's only now, in this charged atmosphere, that it feels like the universe is giving its approval. If there's even the slightest chance she wants this too, I'm not holding back. This moment, right here with her, feels too right to ignore.

"Miles," she moans into our kiss, and as I pull back to look at her, I'm completely lost in the moment.

Abruptly, I'm jerked back, Milli torn from my grasp as a fist lands solidly on my face. The force feels like being hit by a train, knocking me off my feet. My sight goes fuzzy, and as I crash to the ground, I look up to see Luke looming over me with a glare.

"Fuckkkk . . . " I mumble, the room spinning, with echoes of Milli's moans still playing in my head.

Luke's eyes are filled with a fury I've only seen on the football field. "What the fuck is going on?" he snarls.

I open my mouth to respond, but words fail me. Then Milli steps in, tugging at Luke's hair to get his attention. "Luke, seriously, it was just dancing."

Payson, ever the protective friend, jumps in. "She's just having fun, Luke."

"I wasn't talking to you, Pennington." Luke dismisses her with a wave, his irritation clear.

The tension builds as Payson huffs in frustration. I let out a sigh, berating myself internally. *You knew better, Chasen.*

Milli, ignoring her brother, turns to me, concern in her eyes. "Miles, you okay?" she asks, biting her lip.

I just nod, not trusting my voice, and wipe the blood from my lip.

"Deserved it, man," Luke mutters, shaking his head. "Now, get out of here, Milli, before I decide to tell Mom and Dad."

This is escalating fast.

Milli glares at Luke, her frustration evident. "You will not," she asserts, then helps me to my feet, her eyes briefly lingering on the blood on my lips.

Whirling to face Luke again, she jabs a finger into his chest. "I'm not a kid, Luke! I can have a night out without you going all caveman on me!" Her hands fly up in exasperation, frustrated by his overbearing behavior.

With her back to me, she mutters, "I'm going home."

"I'll drive you," I offer quickly, reaching for her arm.

"YOU," Luke snaps, pointing a finger at my chest, "are not driving her anywhere. I've got it. You've done enough for tonight. Just go back to campus, man."

Defeated and filled with self-reproach, I watch as Milli and Luke vanish into the club's shadows.

"Damn it, Chasen," I mutter under my breath, raking a hand through my hair in frustration. "What the fuck were you thinking?"

CHAPTER 4
MILLI

You know I`m more of a lace guy.

SIX MONTHS LATER . . .

"Isn't this just a blast, Milli? God, look at how big this room is! Makes me wish we had this kinda space back in my college days." Mom laughs, her eyes taking in every inch of my new dorm.

Here I am, standing smack in the middle of my very own college room. As a dance student, I got the early bird special —on campus two weeks before classes kick off. The jocks in football and hockey, they get hauled in a month early. But for dance? Just a fortnight. So, here I am, about to live the real NorthRidge student life, not just as someone's little sister tagging along. I've got two whole weeks to wander around this campus, make this place my own, you know?

The room radiates a sleek, contemporary feel—two beds, a desk, a super comfy couch, and even a mini-fridge. I'm already plotting it out in my head: my little corner with a cozy bookshelf overflowing with all my go-to romance reads, my bed looking all inviting with a fluffy white comforter, and the perfect egg chair for kicking back with a tea and a great book. And right there on my desk, a snapshot of me in full dance mode, like my own little pep squad for those marathon study nights.

I grin ear to ear, turning to my Mom. "Yeah, it's awesome. Can't believe this is actually happening."

I always knew I'd head off to college, but picking the right one? That was a headache. UC Irvine was top-notch for dance, perfect for my post-college dreams. Then there was USC's Glorya Kaufman School of Dance—solid program, big on performance and choreography. Both amazing but no scholarships, and I didn't want Mom and Dad breaking the bank for me. I wanted to do this on my terms, financially and all.

Then bam! NorthRidge University comes outta nowhere with a full ride for dance. Wasn't my first pick, especially with Luke already there. But a full ride? Couldn't just ignore that. Still, the thought of being around Luke again—should I stay or try my luck elsewhere?

Relax, Milli. You've got your two ride-or-dies right here with you.

And it's the truth. I'm thrilled at the prospect of having Brooke and Payson nearby. From the get-go, they both aimed to end up here—a common path for Stoneton High alums. Ultimately, it comes down to the financial backing your family can provide, the scholarships you manage to secure, and matters like that.

Mom whirls around, her eyes twinkling with excitement. "I swear, Milli, this is a dream come true! You're going to adore it here!" she exclaims, barely containing her joy.

I muster the brightest smile I can.

Easy there, Mom.

I had this picture in my head—quick hug, peck on the cheek, Mom darts off to Luke's football stuff. But nope, I guessed wrong. Here she is, fawning over my room like it's her first college visit. I mean, it's not, but I'm not about to burst her bubble. I appreciate her dropping me off before rushing to hover over Luke. He doesn't need it; he's a big boy. But Mom loves her "favorite" child visits.

Living in Luke's shadow has been my life story. His football wins were my cues to knock something out of the park—acing a test, nailing a dance. Don't get me wrong, I love English and dance, always have. But there's always been this itch to one-up Luke, just once.

So, here I stand, on the threshold of college life—my spotlight moment, my opportunity to truly discover and express myself. Within the confines of my dorm room, a surge of exhilaration and liberation washes over me. This is it—my turn to make a mark, to be who I really am.

I wander over to my bed, flop down, and soak in the sun pouring through the window. I stretch out, taking a deep breath, feeling the bed give a little as Mom sits down, clearing her throat.

"Milli," she begins, her voice tinged with hesitation. "Um," she pauses briefly, then continues, "You know college is about finding yourself, exploring new horizons, right?"

Oh man, not this chat . . . not again. We almost dove into this whole spiel back home, but my phone buzzed, and bam, conversation over. Dodged a bullet there. Seriously, this is more cringe than the talk we had when I got my first period, and trust me, that was a whole saga . . .

I'm half-looking at my mom, trying to figure out how deep she's gonna dive this time. I know when parents say "exploring," they're usually hinting at, you know, sex stuff. And here's Mom, bringing it up again. Seriously?

"Uh, yeah, Mom, I get it," I say, trying to sound nonchalant about it.

Mom's voice goes all gentle, like she's trying to be cool. "I just want you to know it's okay to be curious, to explore your sexuality and all."

Inside, I'm groaning. Can't we just have a normal, quick goodbye? Is that too much?

"And hey, Luke and Miles are here, right?" she says, kinda laughing. "They'd totally deck a guy for kissing you without asking."

I let out an awkward laugh because if only she knew how painfully true that statement was six months ago when Miles kissed me that night at the club and Luke knocked him on his ass. That memory is etched so deep within me, I swear it'll be buried with me.

Sitting there on my bed, I start feeling all weird and open. I like my privacy, always have. The thought of Mom poking around in my personal life? Yeah, not great. We usually keep our chats pretty light. Maybe that's on me, maybe her. I mean, she grew up without a mom. Her mom left her and Grandpa when she was young. Makes me wonder if that's why we don't go deep in our talks, or if there's something else. But I can't shake this feeling, like we're missing out on something, some deeper connection.

"Anyway." Mom slaps her hands together, and I catch her eyes starting to get all watery.

Oh no, not the waterworks. I can't deal with crying. Just can't.

She understands; it's clear as she hastily dabs away a tear and rises to her feet, casting a sweeping gaze across the room. Her attention settles on Payson's side, and there's a familiar crinkle of her nose—reminiscent of Luke's nervous gesture, yet hers is tinged with distaste. Payson's belongings are strewn about. Chaos in the form of a barely concealed box of condoms peeking from under the sheets, a lacy bra draped over a pillow, and remnants of her wild night scattered around.

She just shakes her head, and I'm biting back a laugh. She's never been Payson's number one fan, but she's never tried to mess with our friendship, either. That meant putting up with Payson all these years, just like I've had to play Miss Perfect at her Stoneton committee gigs.

Raising an eyebrow at me, I jump in before she can say anything. "Payson's here early because she's an RA," I explain. That's Resident Assistant—basically an older student who helps out in the dorms. Payson's always been set on North-Ridge, and with her parents knowing the dean and all, she wrangled her way into the RA gig. She's convinced it'll look great on her resume for her dream job as a therapist. Once Payson's got a plan, there's no stopping her.

She lets out this big, dramatic sigh. "Well, good for her." She nods toward Payson's bed. "Just make sure she doesn't drag you into all that, okay?"

I stand up, facing her squarely. "Yeah, I know, but trust me, I'm not into that sort of thing," I say as firmly as I can, trying to nip this talk in the bud.

She looks at me, her eyes filled with doubt, as if she can't quite take my word for it. "Really? Not even a tad curious?" she challenges, those eyes sharpening with intrigue. It's strangely amusing—ironic, almost. She was the one who told me to let it go, and yet, here she is, seemingly unable to shake off the very thing she dismissed.

I give my head a firm shake, striving to maintain composure. Drawing in a deep, calming breath, I extend my arms wide. "Look, Mom, I'm in college now. It's all about exploring, figuring out who I am, one step at a time, okay? And if that means some adventures happen on that bed over there?" I nod toward my bed, a half-smirk playing on my lips, embracing the moment's awkwardness. "Well . . . it's a possibility."

A chuckle escapes me as her face scrunches up in dismay.

"Milli, was it really necessary to plant that picture in my mind?"

"My point is that you don't need to worry about me. All I care about is my studies, my dance, and making friends besides the ones I already have. Those three things will make my college years great."

"And don't forget, Luke's around too," she throws in, one eyebrow going up. "If you need anything, he's just a call away."

Oh yeah, Luke, my very own superhero . . .

I wave my hand, trying to wrap up this chat. I've got a mountain of unpacking to tackle, plus I have to meet with my advisor before classes start. And I'm itching to slip into my Target pj's and get lost in my book, *Educational Temptation*.

Yep, it's about a professor and one of his students . . . What can I say? It's hot and spicy, igniting all those sensations in just the right spots.

"Mom, I appreciate this conversation, truly, but I've got to get started on unpacking and meeting with my advisor," I say to her.

She gazes at me, her eyes glistening, then gives a nod. "Alright, sweetheart. Just don't forget, your dad and I are always here for you."

I give her shoulders a hug. "I know, Mom. And hey, think about it—you've got your own adventure ahead. You've been supermom for so long, and now with you and Dad as empty nesters, it's your chance. Maybe even take over Joy's spot on the committee."

She laughs, kissing my cheek. "Not a bad idea, baby girl."

Pulling away, my mom's eyes take another sweep of the room. There's a softness in her gaze, a mix of pride and a hint of sadness. "Alright, I'll leave you to it. Just call me tonight, okay? I want to hear all about your meeting with the advisor."

I offer her a smile, bright and comforting. "Absolutely, I

will. Mom, you know I love you." Those words are filled with a sincere warmth, a connection that spans the gap between my fledgling college days and the home I've just stepped out of.

She hesitates at the doorway, casting a glance back with a soft, affectionate smile. Her eyes glisten with unshed tears. "I love you too, Milli," she murmurs, floating a kiss in my direction before she vanishes through the door.

～w/w～♡～

LATER THAT NIGHT . . .

Every muscle in my body screams as I collapse onto my bed. "I am officially out of juice," I mumble, eyes closing from sheer exhaustion.

The moment Mom left, I couldn't resist the pull of my book. I thought I'd wait till later, but the temptation was too strong. My advisor meeting got pushed, so I figured, why not a little reading break, right?

A "light" reading break, Milli?

Who am I kidding? It was like stepping into a whirlwind of passion and intensity, each page fueling a fire inside me. It took every bit of my discipline, every fiber of my dancer's willpower, to finally snap the book shut. With a reluctant sigh, I put it aside, knowing I had to get my room in order, especially with dance practice looming in the morning. I got most of it done, setting things up just how I pictured, except for some pillows for my egg chair, still MIA.

Suddenly, the door bangs open and Payson struts in. "You better grab some shut-eye or something, 'cause Alpha Rho Tau is throwing their kick-off bash tonight, and you don't want to miss it," she announces, the door thudding shut behind her.

I let out a groan, feeling every bit of my tiredness. "Do I really have to go?" I grumble, rubbing my eyes. "Aren't you supposed to be, like, the responsible RA, guiding the newbies, not hyping up parties?" I tease, cracking one eye open just a sliver.

She gives a nonchalant shrug. "Well, there's no one to 'guide' yet," she says, making air quotes. "I showed up early because RAs have to learn all the mentor-y things." She waves her hand dismissively, as if the responsibilities of an RA were nothing more than a minor inconvenience. "Which means I'm totally free to hit the party tonight. You're coming, right?"

The energy in the room shifts, a blend of Payson's infectious enthusiasm and my own weary reluctance. It's the start of something new, a college adventure just waiting to unfold, with every choice shaping the journey ahead.

But, the thought of heaving myself out of this comfy bed to go party with a bunch of frat guys? Yeah, not exactly my idea of a great time right now. I had my heart set on diving into my new book and slipping into silky pajamas. Isn't that the ultimate college girl's dream night?

"No, Milli, not everyone kicks off their college life buried in a book," Payson remarks.

Crap, did I say that out loud? But wait, it's not really my "first" night of college, right? That's when classes start, isn't it?

Payson's head pops up from her closet. "You didn't say anything, but come on, I know you. Straight into nerd mode with your steamy books, right?"

I roll my eyes internally. Yeah, I'd rather live vicariously through "slutty" books than be "slutty" in real life. Payson turns, holding up two dresses; her face lit up with excitement. "Which one for the party?" she asks.

I scrutinize them—one's a daring, tight number with a

neckline that dives south and a slit that's more like a reveal. The other, more subdued, flowy, but still subtly sexy.

Eyeing Payson up and down, it's clear—she'd look killer in either. "Well," I start, weighing my words, "the first one's definitely gonna turn heads."

She bites her lip, a flicker of uncertainty in her eyes. "Yeah, but is it too much?"

"You'll look amazing, Pay. Trust me, you'll be the center of attention," I assure her, but inside, I'm not keen on the idea of being part of that scene tonight.

Her face breaks into a grin. "You're right," she says, dropping the dresses on her bed. Then, in a swift move, she's grabbing my hands, pulling me toward my closet.

"Whoa, what're you doing?" I protest.

"Finding you something for the party," she declares, like it's the most obvious thing.

I shake my head firmly. "No way. I'm not going. I'm beat from unpacking and I've still got stuff to sort out tomorrow."

What stuff, Milli? That inner voice taunts me.

Payson's gaze sharpens, irritation coloring her expression. "Are you even listening to yourself? This is college! Our time to shine. We've got, what, four, maybe five years to live it up to the fullest."

Five years?

She exhales, a hint of desperation in her voice. "Just come out tonight, Milli. Please?"

I hesitate, her pleading look making my resolve waver.

"Pleaseee," she begs, big pouty lips and all.

I let out a heavy sigh, pointing a finger at her. "Fine, but no hangovers. I've got dance practice tomorrow, and I need to be on point."

Payson's hand smacks my ass, making me jump. "Deal." She grins. "We'll keep it chill."

Her eyes then sweep over my wardrobe with a look of

playful disdain. "This, though, we need to work on. Looks like it's plan B for you tonight."

Plan B? My mind races. *What the hell is that?*

Payson whirls around, brandishing what looks like a microscopic crop top paired with a skirt. Sure, the skirt seems manageable, but the crop top? It's practically a glorified bra.

As my phone buzzes on the desk, I head over to check it, calling behind me, "There's no way I'm wearing that." My dancer's physique might be petite, but, "I'm pretty sure I'd be spilling out of that outfit in all the wrong way," I tell her.

I glance at my phone and see two new messages just as I hear Payson's voice. "That's exactly the point." I shake my head, a little smile tugging at my lips as I open the texts.

LUKE

Hey sis, everything good?

MILES

Hey Mills, need any help unpacking? I think I can handle the bra and underwear drawer.

A chuckle escapes me. You'd think things with Miles might've turned weird after that club night, but nope. It actually brought us closer. We chalked it up to too much booze—though, for me, it wasn't just the alcohol. But I didn't want to lose him over something that might mess everything up, including our families' ties.

The best thing was, our friendship didn't skip a beat. The jokes, the laughs—all still there, and that means the world to me.

I respond to Luke first.

MILLI

All good over here! How was practice?

LUKE

Tough start, but that's the usual drill at the beginning of the season, even after a month. How about grabbing coffee tomorrow? I'd love to hear about your first dance practice.

MILLI

Sounds good! Talk to you then! Have a good night. Love you.

LUKE

Love you too, sis.

To Miles, I say:

MILLI

Haha, very funny. I'll leave the sock drawer to you.

I look again at the outfit Payson's holding out—this lacy crop top with a snug, satin skirt. It's definitely a statement piece, one that'd highlight every curve and edge of my dancer's body. But is this really me? I came here to study, dance, find myself—not to play dress-up.

But then again, what's one night of letting loose?

MILES

HAHA, who's the funny one now? You know I'm more of a lace guy.

Tell me, Baby Sutton, do you have any lacy underwear?

A gentle wave of warmth floods me, but I dismiss it with a chuckle.

"Who's making you laugh over there?" Payson asks, looking at me with a raised eyebrow of interest. However, she jumps in with her assumption before I get a chance to answer. "Let me guess, Miles?" Her tone suggests it couldn't be more apparent.

I just give a noncommittal shrug as she adds, with a hint of sarcasm, "Big surprise there." Choosing to overlook her comment, I turn my attention back to responding to Miles.

MILLI

Maybe . . . Maybe not. Buh bye, Sunshine

I close my text messages and lift the outfit Payson has selected, pausing briefly.

Is this what I meant by the college experience I described to Mom? Venturing into new friendships, embracing new experiences?

Seizing the clothes, I move toward the bathroom, but not without shooting Payson a cautionary glance. "I'm trusting you—this better not turn into regret."

CHAPTER 5
MILES

Understood, Mr. Protective.

Coach Jensen's voice thunders across the field. "Chasen, let's run that play again!"

We're drilling the same old play we've been perfecting since I was a freshman. Sure, it's a killer on the field and has bagged us some solid wins; I could run it in my sleep at this point. But there's always some freshman who hasn't learned the hard lesson about partying during the week.

I bet a few of them are nursing hangovers from last night's Alpha Rho Tau bash. I was all set to go, decked out and everything, but then I thought better of it. Senior year's about getting priorities straight, after all.

I line up, ready for action. Bensen snaps me the ball—did I mention he's the top center in the nation? The guy's a beast, both on the field and off. As I call the signals, the ball thuds into my hands, and I scan the defense.

The sun's beating down, casting these long, stretching shadows over the field as we run through the play. Our O-line is like a fortress, giving me the protection I need.

"Keep the rush off, guys! Tighten it up!" I yell, watching

the defense try to break through. We move like a well-oiled machine, me faking a handoff, looking for an open man.

Our receivers are sprinting, juking, doing everything to shake the defense. The tight ends and slots are hunting for any gap they can find. I dodge a linebacker, buying myself a precious second. A receiver breaks free, waving for the ball. I let it rip; the spiral cutting through the air, just as a defender nearly gets me.

I imagine the crowd going wild as my receiver snags the ball and makes a beeline for the end zone. It's a thing of beauty, exactly what we aim for every game.

"Touchdown!" Coach bellows. "Excellent work, team! Let's do it one more time! Sharpen up!"

Seriously? Again?

Luke chats away as we head to the showers in the locker room. "This week's practice, man—brutal. Makes those insane two-a-days in the summer seem easy."

I just nod. Coach has been on us, hard, pushing us past our limits. But something's been off for me. The usual football aches and pains have been there, sure, but there's this dizziness, like everything's narrowing down to a point. My teammates have been checking on me, and I keep saying I'm fine. Practice seems smooth enough, but deep down, there's this gnawing worry.

Is it the late summer heat? Maybe I'm dehydrated? Or is it something else? The thought twists in my stomach, but I push it away and focus on getting to the locker room.

As I try to keep my thoughts on track, memories of my childhood have a way of seeping in. It's like being hit by a wave of anxiety that stops you cold, bombarding you with endless what ifs. You'd imagine that surviving cancer would banish those fears, but they stick around, lurking in the dark, ready to leap out over the smallest worry. Yet, I've always been a fighter, never one to get bogged down by fear. Pushing forward with optimism has been my mantra because, honestly, what's the alternative? Living in constant fear? That's never been who I am.

Though, Coach Jensen's relentless training regimen doesn't help. In all my years with him, I've learned that "intensity" is his middle name. His idea of a light day is still a workout that would make most people's muscles scream.

Josh, our star receiver, pipes up, "Brutal? More like merciless." He's right. Josh is a force to be reckoned with on the field, and his NFL prospects are as bright as Bensen's. They're both incredible athletes, destined for greatness.

Luke's nodding, adding, "Yeah, but that's senior year for you. Coach is pushing us to the limit, especially for those of us with an eye on the draft."

He nudges me, and I muster a small smile, hoping it masks any concern. The last thing I need is for Luke to sense something's off. I keep telling myself I'm fine, pushing aside any nagging doubts.

"Hey, wanna grab coffee at Scholar's Brew after?"

Luke's suggestion catches me off guard. We're more kitchen raiders than café hoppers. Scholar's Brew isn't our usual hangout.

He chuckles, seeing my surprise, and heads for the showers. "Milli had practice today," he explains under the cascading water. "Just wanna see how she's doing."

I get it. Luke's always been the protective type, but sometimes it's too much. Milli came here for her own space, her own life. I get the whole sibling protection thing, but there's a line, and sometimes Luke crosses it without realizing.

"Sure, I'll join you," I say, deciding it might help balance things out if we both show up. Maybe it'll feel less like he's hovering and more like friendly support.

"Cool," Luke says, and soon we're walking into Scholar's Brew.

Milli's on the phone, and Luke gives her a wave. I notice she doesn't have a drink, so I silently ask if she wants something. Luke's already at the counter, charming the barista without even trying.

I wait, hoping Milli will catch my eye and let me know if she needs a caffeine fix. It's a small gesture, but sometimes it's these little things that can make a person's day just a bit brighter.

"Really, Sutton, get a room." Payson's voice sharply pierces the air, her stare intensely fixed on Luke as he blatantly flirts with Toriey, the barista. I can't help but let out a chuckle. Caught in the act, Luke spins around only to catch Payson lifting his coffee order right off the counter, a look of both annoyance and a touch of amusement crossing his face.

He strides over to her, a playful smirk on his face. "I've got a room, Pennington, and let's just say it's well-used," he quips, grabbing his coffee back.

Payson rolls her eyes dramatically. "Is that your roundabout way of admitting you're a player, Luke?" she shoots back, snatching the coffee again and heading for the door, clearly not planning to return it.

Luke just shakes his head, resigned. "You're welcome, by the way."

Payson arches an eyebrow, tossing her hair back with a dramatic flair. "And why exactly? For gracing you with my presence? I'm aware it's quite irresistible," she remarks, a cunning grin on her lips. Before she leaves, she drops a hint to Milli about something from the night before.

Last night? My curiosity piqued, wondering what might have happened.

Before I can dwell on it, Milli gestures toward the menu, signaling for a matcha latte. I order up a storm, compensating for our missed kitchen raid—coffee, bagels, pancakes, eggs, fruit, orange juice. I'm pretty sure the cashier is silently thanking me for my generous contribution to their daily sales.

Returning to the table, Milli is still on the phone, probably with her mom.

"Hey, Mrs. Sutton," I chime in, noticing Milli's grateful glance for the interruption.

"Oh, Miles," her mom responds with her usual upbeat tone. "We were just talking about Milli's advisor meeting—or lack thereof."

Milli rolls her eyes, mouthing, "Thank you," and taking a sip of her latte.

"We've still got a week, Mom," Milli says, trying to keep her cool.

"Don't worry, Mrs. S., I'll make sure Milli doesn't slack off," I say, throwing a wink at Milli, which only makes her cheeks turn a deeper shade of red. Did I just make things awkward? Maybe I'm still a bit frazzled from practice.

As I start on my feast, Luke joins us, a slip of paper tucked into his sweatpants—Toriey's number, no doubt.

Mrs. Sutton's voice interrupts my thoughts. "Why didn't you call me last night, Milli? You were supposed to."

Milli hesitates, her expression troubled. "I got busy," she says vaguely.

Busy doing what, exactly? Payson's cryptic comment about last night gnaws at me. Something's up, and I can't shake off a nagging feeling of concern.

Miles, she doesn't need overly concerned men in her life, let alone at college.

Luke leaps into the conversation. "Busy with what?

Weren't you just supposed to unpack and get some rest for the dance?"

Milli looks trapped, her eyes darting between her phone and Luke. It's clear why she was hesitant about coming to NorthRidge—this kind of scrutiny from her own family.

Acting on impulse, I cut in, "She was with me, Mrs. S. I was giving her a tour of the campus, showing her all the important spots, you know, dance studio, library, that kind of stuff."

Luke's gaze snaps toward me, his eyes briefly ablaze with irritation, a storm that quickly clears as Milli interjects, "Yeah, I just wanted to get familiar before today. No biggie."

A twinge of frustration knots in my stomach—"no biggie" that I'm in the dark about her escapades last night. My hands ball into fists beneath the table, a silent battle raging within me as I remind myself that Milli's life isn't mine to control. Yet, that doesn't strip away my role as her steadfast friend, our history of shared secrets, a testament to our bond.

Luke watches me intently, his eyes narrowing slightly as I dismiss Milli's comment with a shake of my head, then he refocuses on his meal. His protective stance is understandable; since that charged night at the club, he's been clear about boundaries, marking Milli as forbidden territory. Not just because she's my lifelong friend, but also because of our friendship. The thought of crossing that line with Milli is like flirting with chaos, but in the secrecy of my heart, I'd brave any storm for another chance to taste those soft, tempting lips.

Miles, stay grounded.

"Oh," her mother interjects, her tone laced with curiosity. "That's wonderful, Milli. And thank you, Miles, for being there for her. I'm sure she appreciates having you and Luke by her side."

"Yeah, so much love," Milli mutters under her breath, a

comment lost on Luke. "Anyway, Mom, I should get going. Got things to wrap up here," Milli says.

"Alright, honey, have a great day. Call me later this week, okay?" Mrs. Sutton's voice is warm and motherly.

"Sure thing, Mom," Milli replies, her smile tight but genuine.

"Love you, Luke. Can't wait for your game next week."

"Love you too, Mom," echoes Luke.

"Love you too, Mom," Milli whispers, though Mrs. Sutton has already ended the call.

Milli's head falls forward onto the table, a sigh escaping her lips like a deflated balloon.

"That tough of a practice, huh?" Luke inquires.

She lifts her head, the previous shadow of disappointment in her eyes now replaced by a flicker of excitement, igniting a spontaneous smile on my face. It's remarkable how Milli's mere happiness can illuminate my world.

"No, it was really good, actually," she says, her voice dancing with enthusiasm. "The studio was a dream—polished hardwood floors, those amazing full-length mirrors . . . " Her voice trails off into a whimsical sigh, her eyes reflecting her daydream as she cradles her chin in her hand. "I even had the chance to meet my dance partner. You know, I usually do solo dancing, but I have a feeling I might come to enjoy this, especially after today's practice." She shrugs, adding, "And, on top of that, I was assigned to work with the young dancers I volunteer with—they're sisters, and it was just a perfect match."

Luke nods, his attention split between his meal and her words. For the next half hour, Milli is a beacon of light, her eyes shimmering with passion as she recounts her dance practice and outlines her plans for the upcoming school year. While I bask in the glow of her joy, a persistent nag gnaws at me, a searing curiosity about her night—whether it was with Payson, someone else, or something entirely different.

Miles, it's not your concern.

But my heart disagrees violently; when it comes to Milli, everything about her becomes my concern. It's like a relentless wave that washes over me, refusing to recede.

That night, my fingers are almost trembling as I reach out to her.

MILES

You gonna tell me why I had to cover for you with your mom and Luke?

MILLS

I'm not sure what you mean . . .

MILES

Really, Mills? You're going to make me say it? Why did I lie, saying I showed you around campus last night, when you know it like the back of your hand?

MILLS

Oh, that.

MILES

Yes, that.

MILLS

It was nothing, just caught up with stuff.
Don't sweat it.

But her casual dismissal is like a splinter under my skin, gnawing at me for the truth.

MILES

Since when do we keep secrets, Mills?

MILLS

eye roll

sigh . . . a long, weary sigh

A small grin tugs at my lips as I recline into my pillows, a bittersweet triumph blooming in my chest. I can feel it; she's on the cusp of breaking. Our history of honesty is about to pay off.

MILLS

Alright, I caved and went to the Alpha Rho Tau party. Happy now?

She was at that frat party? The one I was supposed to be at? The one I avoided? My freshman teammates were probably all over it.

The voice in my head taunts me. *Look who's playing the overprotective brother now.*

I shove the mocking thought aside, focusing on her.

MILES

You were at that party?

The very thought stirs a storm in me. That party is infamous, a hallmark of wildness, only second to our post-game celebrations. I'm part of that fraternity, but it doesn't mean I revel in every raucous night. I skipped it, opting for solitude, a choice now laced with regret and worry. What if something happened to her?

MILLS

Yeah, is that an issue, Sunshine?

Every instinct screams, *Yes, it's a damn issue!* But I hold back the tide of concern.

MILES

> No, it's fine. Just . . . stay safe at those parties, okay?

I watch the screen, the typing indicator flickering like the slow beating of a heart. Time stretches, thin and taut, until finally she replies.

MILLS

> Understood, Mr. Protective. Next time, do I get to drag you along as my bodyguard?

My mind races with unspoken promises. *Oh, I could be so much more . . .* But I choose to steer us back to safer waters.

MILES

> You damn will, Baby Sutton. *winky face*

However, I choose to send a winky face because it's Milli, and I need to remind myself that she doesn't need yet another overly protective person in her life, especially in this new phase where she's exploring her identity.

CHAPTER 6
MILLI

I lock eyes with Payson as she settles into the seat across from me at a library table; Brooke follows closely. I watch, slightly amused, as Payson meticulously unpacks her bag, spreading her study materials with a precision that speaks of her meticulous nature.

"Alright, study buddies it is," I whisper, more to myself than to them.

A gentle smile plays on my lips. It's not that I mind them joining; it's just that Payson's idea of "studying" often involves a whirlwind of gossip, laughter, and shared secrets. I adore these moments with my besties, but college has upped the stakes. With my dance practices now demanding more of me, there's a delicate balance I'm still learning to navigate.

"Think tonight will be a success?" Payson asks, her voice laced with curiosity.

I remove one AirPod, responding, "The game? Absolutely. It'll be intense, but aren't those the kind that really get the heart racing?"

Payson begins scribbling in her notebook, and I can't help but tease, "Looks like we're actually going to study today."

"I wasn't talking about the football game, Milli," she shoots back, her words pulling me back to the reality of my own challenge.

I swallow, feeling a lump in my throat. The truth is, I'm a whirlwind of emotions about my first dance performance at NorthRidge University Stadium. Excited, yes, but also a bundle of nerves and fears. In my head, I try to lighten the mood with a bit of sarcastic humor, but it doesn't quite mask the jittery feeling in my stomach.

Just remember, Milli, dancing is like life—it's best when you follow the rhythm without overthinking the moves! My thoughts sway with a touch of irony.

"Yeah, I'm ready," I say, trying to sound more confident than I feel. Nervous? Absolutely. It's a huge crowd, and being on scholarship means I've got to prove I'm more than just a high school star.

Inside, I'm battling a storm of doubt and pressure. But I also know my worth, my talent. It's just the weight of expectation that's heavy on my shoulders.

"That's great to hear," Payson says, her cheerleader spirit surfacing with a little hand wave that makes me smile despite myself.

"You know we'll be there, cheering you on, right?" Brooke adds, her eyes shining with unwavering support. That's the thing about my girls; they're always there, a solid, unbreakable circle of support and love.

I smile, genuinely touched. "Yeah, I know," I say, just as Payson asks, "What are the plans for after the game tonight?" Her gaze shifts between mine and Brooke's.

Brooke shrugs. "Well, I think Josh might be visiting. We haven't seen each other since—"

"Since the other day?" Payson interrupts, rolling her eyes.

Did I mention that Payson can't stand Josh? I mean, she'd gladly kick him in the nuts any chance she got. But I actually like him; I think he's good for Brooke. Payson, on the other hand, thinks he needs to dial down his constant need for attention. But isn't that the point of dating? Wanting to be around that person, sharing your ups and downs? I mean, I'm not exactly an authority on relationships—I've only had one in high school, and it crashed and burned before it even began. But every time I've imagined having a real boyfriend, it's always been about cuddling, hand-holding, forehead kisses, someone who grabs my waist, and someone who craves my attention, my presence. I want someone who will fight for me, someone who sees me for who I am, flaws and all.

Is it too much to ask for, even if that *someone* happens to be Miles Chasen?

God, Milli, are you even listening to yourself?

But deep down, I sense there's a hidden turmoil in Payson, a storm brewing beneath her cheerful exterior. I suspect she's nursing a quiet hurt, feeling slighted by him for swaying Brooke away from rooming with her. Payson had originally planned to share a room with Brooke, but when she learned I was coming, she gracefully stepped back, allowing me to take her place. Her random roommate search landed her with Gracie, a charming southern belle from Alabama. Yet, I can't help but feel Payson's warmth masks a lingering resentment over the whole affair.

Suddenly, Payson's hands crash down onto the table, her energy a blazing inferno of excitement. "Did you guys hear about Barrett and Professor Scooty last year?" she exclaims, her eyes sparkling with the thrill of scandal. "A freshman and a professor—can you believe it?" She laughs, the sound rich with delight, as if this gossip has just made her day brighter.

I watch her, my eyebrow arching in skepticism, a silent

testament to the relentless tide of rumors that wash over NorthRidge.

She flings her hands in the air, exasperated, "What even is this place? NorthRidge is supposed to be prestigious, and here we have professors and students in illicit affairs!"

Brooke chimes in, a devilish glint in her eye, "I mean, it's kinda hot."

Payson retorts, "Sure, if you're into the whole cougar thing."

I shake my head. In the midst of academic halls, our conversation has veered into the realm of forbidden romances.

Brooke leans in, her chuckle infectious. "Think about it—the secrecy, the age gap. It's like something out of one of Milli's romance novels." She winks at me, fully aware of the steamy, heart-racing narratives hidden within the pages of my books. True, I've read tales of forbidden love, but they're more than just erotic escapades; they're stories of deep emotion and enduring love.

I shrug, trying to appear nonchalant, but their laughter is contagious, and soon, we're all giggling just as the librarian passes by, shushing us with a stern finger to her lips.

Payson, always the maverick, responds with a twinkle of mischief in her eye, "Ease up, we'll tone it down when midterms hit."

Brooke and I exchange a look, fighting back more laughter to avoid further reprimand. But Payson's right; the librarian does give us some peace for the next hour, allowing us to actually focus on our studies.

My phone buzzes in my pocket, and as Payson shows Brooke the latest viral TikTok, I sneak a peek at my phone.

MILES

Come outside real quick.

I glance up, my heart skipping a beat as I scan the library, but my chosen spot is far from any external distractions.

MILLI

Why? I'm busy.

MILES

Aren't you going to see your favorite person?

You know, the one who'd help sort your most intimate drawers?

A chuckle breaks free, and a smile finds its way onto my face, despite my efforts to remain concentrated. The memory of Miles jesting about my lingerie collection sends a warm rush through my veins, sparking a flame inside that I find hard to suppress.

Calm down, Milli.

But inside, my heart races with the thought of seeing him, even if just for a moment.

MILLI

Shame the drawer's all neat and tidy now . . .

MILES

Oh? And can I be the one to verify that, Baby Sutton?

My smile broadens, and I catch my lip between my teeth, aware that I would undeniably allow him to do that and . . . more.

But no, Milli, that's off-limits.

The thought lingers, tempting and taunting in equal measure. It's ludicrous, really—the idea is so far from acceptable it's almost laughable.

Miles has this peculiar obsession with socks—everything has to match: colors and patterns in meticulous order. He'd probably have a meltdown if he saw the chaotic state of my sock drawer.

I sigh, packing my things with a sense of excitement. A break would do me good, especially with the game looming over me.

"Tell Miles I said hi," Payson calls out, barely looking up from her phone.

I exchange a knowing look with Brooke.

"Break a leg tonight," she says warmly. "We'll be right there cheering you on. Don't forget to come see us after!"

With a wave, I head out to find Miles. He's there, exuding a casual confidence, idly kicking at the ground. He's the picture of ease, effortlessly charming in his game day attire—that leather jacket with the number #7, his panda shoes, jeans, and a backward hat. He's everything vibrant and lively, a stark contrast to my more reserved nature.

"I'm here, Sir Sunshine," I quip, greeted in return by his signature smirk and a light, playful shove.

"Don't push it, Mills," he jests, "or you might regret it."

Internally, I wonder if regret is really what I'd feel.

"What's the big emergency?" I ask, curiosity piqued.

He chuckles, a hint of shyness peeking through his usual bravado. Then, he hands me a book, and my heart leaps. It's our game day tradition, one we haven't done in person for years.

Our fingers brush as he hands me the book, a jolt of warmth shooting through me. It's just a touch, but it feels like so much more.

Milli, keep it together.

He clears his throat, the smug Miles reemerging. "Can't break tradition, right?"

I bite my lip, feeling like I'm in some sort of romantic haze. He's thoughtful enough to bring me a book on game day—a romance, no less. It's a gesture not many would think to make, especially with the pressure of a game on the horizon.

I look down at *Crimson Desire: Tempestuous Hearts of the Forbidden Isle*. My heart flutters. I'd forgotten our tradition, guilt washing over me for not having something for him.

He reads my expression, his shrug casual but his eyes understanding. "Don't sweat it, Mills. You've got a lot on your plate. I figured a book might help you relax."

A part of me wants to say he'd help me relax, too, but I bite back the words.

Instead, I nudge him. "You're sweet for getting me this. But you know I've already read it, right?" His face falls for a second before I burst out laughing. "Kidding. Never heard of it."

He relaxes, joining in my laughter.

I tuck the book away, regretting not having his gift. "I'm sorry I didn't get you anything for game day."

He smiles, that boyish charm never fails to quicken my pulse. "It's fine, Mills."

But, before he can finish, his friends barrel in, roughhousing in that typical guy way. "Lay off, Cam," Miles grumbles, fixing his now messy hair.

I secretly admire the look—the tousled, just-got-out-of-bed style suits him. Should I tell him?

No way, Milli. Not a chance.

Yeah, you're probably right. It's for the best.

"Okay then, I'll see you later. On the field tonight, right?" His eyes connect with mine, a twinkle of shared excitement evident. The idea of both of us on the same field tonight ignites a flutter in my chest, an innocent giddiness like a child's laughter.

It's just a sporting event, Milli.

Yet, it feels significant, more than just a mere game. This thought warms me from within, gently soothing the fluttering nerves. This comforting sensation only amplifies later that afternoon when I leaf through the book from Miles and discover a neatly folded, crisp white note.

"Baby Sutton, can't wait to see you kick ass tonight. Make sure the dancer's outfit is appropriate for all eyes. Except mine, of course."

CHAPTER 7
MILES

E-x-p-l-o-r-i-n-g

It feels like fate is playing some twisted joke on me, like I'm trapped in this surreal echo from six months ago. Except now, it's not me hounding her for her whereabouts or sneaking around just to catch a glimpse of her flawless self.

It's as if the universe is taunting me with a cruel joke: "Look, but don't touch, buddy." I got burned pretty bad last time, and I'm pretty sure Luke hasn't forgotten it either. Whenever we'd talk about Milli coming to The NorthRidge University, he'd give me this knowing look, a warning glare that silently screamed, "hands off."

Completely off-limits.

Watching her at the game tonight—or should I say, our game?—she was like lightning, igniting the sidelines and the halftime show with her energy. My gaze couldn't help but gravitate toward her, as if I was spellbound. Yet, incredibly, this didn't distract me from delivering one of my best performances on the field. The sound of my dad's cheers, his fist punching the air, my name on his lips, was the sweetest form of validation. I was more than just on my game; I was dominating. High completion rates, controlling the offense, and nailing that decisive performance that clinched our win with a solid two-touchdown advantage. It was a night where everything clicked, on and off the field.

So, yeah, the game was epic, and I can't decide if it was Milli's magic in the air or just that she did remember our first game day ritual after all. Walking into mine and Luke's place from the library, I spotted it—a note chilling with a stash of Powerade. "Forgot your gift, but thanks to DoorDash, crisis averted ;) Stay hydrated, Sunshine." That note, with its cheeky charm and the thoughtful stash beneath, had me grinning like a fool. It wasn't just her words that got to me, but the care tucked between those lines. Milli's always there, making sure I'm looking after myself—well, next to my parents, but that's a given. Her gesture was a small reminder of how well she gets me, and just like that, my day was made.

But, as I stand here, seeing Milli at one of my frats parties, again . . . is well . . . unexpected. I heard from Luke that they were throwing one due to our celebratory win, and I was all in for some celebrating. One thing I wasn't expecting tonight? Milli to be here, because she doesn't do parties. And the way she is dressed . . .

Fuck, I'm getting hard just looking at her.

Milli, Miles, just Milli.

I commit it to memory, repeating it several times internally, making sure the message is unmistakably received by every part of me. Luke would likely flip over her outfit and then hold me responsible for not extricating her from this situation. Yet, I find myself irresistibly drawn to my best friend.

The shy, nervous, down-to-earth Mills I know? Nowhere in sight, because right now, Milli looks incredibly seductive. I spot her across the room, standing by the drink table, casually chatting with some familiar faces from last year's classes.

She's breathtaking in her form-fitting, black cropped top and tight skinny jeans, hugging her curves in all the right places. Loose waves frame her face, and her minimal makeup accentuates her natural beauty. I try to compose myself, but my palms grow sweaty.

It feels wrong to be so affected, but it's beyond my control. She has this unique power over me, making me feel like an awkward teen all over again . . . and here I am, twenty-one years old.

Get it together, Chasen.

It's a whole lot harder than it sounds. Every time I see Milli in a place like this, it's like the devil himself is taunting me, reminding me of that night at the club. That kiss, her against me, those moans . . .

Suddenly, I'm jolted from my thoughts by a sharp nudge.

"Hey, what the hell, man," I snap, turning to Cameron, our freshman linebacker. The guy's a beast on the field, but he can be a real pain. We've been acquainted since the summer training camp.

He nods his beer at her. "Who's that? She's smokin' hot." His words linger in the air, heavy and crude.

I follow his gaze, and there's Milli, laughing like she doesn't have a care in the world. It's a side of her I rarely see, except maybe when she's in her element, dancing or helping someone with their homework. Or that night six months back.

But what's got her laughing like that?

Not Payson; she's busy giving some guy a lap dance.

Is it that guy? Alex Bruden, our lineman. I doubt he's her type, but she's looking at him like he's the next big thing in ballet. I know a ballet dancer when I see one, don't ask how. Watching her with him, I feel this twinge of jealousy.

Let it go, Miles.

But I can't help myself. I turn to Cameron, who's now

loitering on the stairs, and give him a heads-up. "Man, don't even think about it. She's . . . not the one you want to mess with."

He looks intrigued. "Why's that? She taken?"

"Something like that," I grumble under my breath.

But, only to me.

"College just started, and she's already off the market?" He squints at some guy who's getting a bit too cozy with her. "Is Alex her boyfriend or something? Sure looks like it with him nudging her hip and caressing her arm every two seconds."

Shit. Is he? Here I am, supposed to be celebrating our win against the Chargers, and instead, I'm all worked up over Milli. Cam's gaze flicks between them and me, then he nudges me again, already half-drunk. "Ohhh, she's with you, isn't she, Chasen?"

I down the rest of my drink and mumble, "Fuck, I wish," under my breath. Instead, I say, "Nah, she's just my best friend."

He looks at me, disbelief written all over his face, and bursts out laughing. "Who the hell has *that* hot of a girl as a best friend?"

Well, apparently, I do. Didn't realize that was such a hardship?

"Well, you see, Cam, some people can just be platonic friends," Gunner, one of our freshman tight ends, chimes in. "Guys and girls can have conversations, share interests and hobbies without it being about sex."

But then Jebs, our backup QB and one of my frat brothers, has to go and stir the pot. "But come on, you can tell he's into her. That's Luke's sister he's been eyeing all night. You're more than just friends, aren't you, Chasen?"

A few guys chuckle, and Cameron's eyes nearly pop out of his head. "Damn, can I be her best friend, too? She's got that sexy librarian look, and it's doing things to me," he says, adjusting himself.

I shoot him a glare that could freeze hell over, but he just laughs it off, giving my shoulder a squeeze. "Chill, man, I'm just messing with you."

Yeah, well, not everyone's laughing, especially not me.

"But, you know, if she ever wants me to give her a test run . . . "

"Dude, do you ever shut your mouth?" Gunner snaps, silencing Cam with the impact of the punch.

My hands ball into fists, a wave of protectiveness washing over me. Milli's not some prize for Cam to take for a "test run." But losing my composure here isn't on the table—I need to keep my cool, can't let the guys catch me slipping.

I fake a chuckle, tossing out a line to put him in his place. "Try anything, and Luke will have you running for the hills, man. He doesn't play when it comes to his sister."

And believe me, I've had my fair share of run-ins with Luke over Milli.

The team, a mix of rookies and vets, let out uneasy laughs. They all know Luke's reputation—cross him and you're in for a world of hurt. They don't know the half of it, though.

"Yeah, just kidding," Cam backpedals, then disappears into the crowd.

Rookies, I swear. They think they're all that until reality checks them. Milli's off the table, and these guys should respect that.

Cameron's words gnaw at me, stirring up feelings I shouldn't be having. The thought of anyone else getting close to Milli, making her laugh, or seeing her in that fucking outfit—it gets under my skin. I watch her from a distance, her laughter ringing out. Even Alex seems to be in her orbit now. Note to self: have a word with him at practice.

I know I shouldn't be so wrapped up in her, so fiercely protective, but it's hard. There's just something about Milli that makes me want to keep her safe from these college clowns. I didn't expect to feel this way when she first came to NorthRidge.

I find myself sinking into the only empty couch in the room, cracking open another beer. Perfect spot—out of Milli's direct line, but close enough to keep an eye on her.

And speaking of keeping eyes on things, I've got my three freshmen charges here tonight, making complete fools of themselves. Coach K thinks we're mentoring them, but sometimes it feels more like herding cats. We're supposed to guide these newbies, help them adjust to life at NorthRidge. They're fitting in alright, maybe a little too well.

With a sip of my beer, my mind drifts back to my freshman year. NorthRidge University, with its storybook campus, always had a way of drawing you in. The old brick buildings, the historic library—it's like stepping into another world. And now, here I am, a senior, trying to show these young guns the ropes. They've got a lot to learn, but they'll get there. Just like I did.

This campus, it's like something from a dream. The ivy-clad buildings, the bricks steeped in years of history; they speak to you. Every corner, every stone pathway here is drenched in memories. The main buildings, with their weathered charm, always make me think I'm stepping into a Harry Potter movie. And the library—it's like something out of a fairy tale, with its soaring spires and stained glass windows. Walking under these ancient trees, watching their shadows dance on the paths, there's a sense of magic in the air. But now, as a senior, there's this bittersweet tang, knowing my time here is coming to a close.

Mentoring these guys—Cam, Gunner, and Deven—it's a trip. They're good kids, full of energy and mischief. Like that time they hid my keys just for kicks, or swiped my towel, leading to my infamous towel-less strut to the women's locker room. I showed them who's boss, but I can't help but laugh at their antics. It reminds me of my own freshman year, which was a wild ride of parties, flings, and just scraping by academically. I was living like there was no tomorrow, making up for lost time after a childhood overshadowed by illness.

Life handed me a rough start, no doubt. Squaring off against brain cancer at just seven, my childhood felt like navigating a relentless storm—each day wrapped in uncertainty, every breath a fight for something more. College, though, was my horizon of freedom. I lunged at life with everything I had, determined to soak up every experience far from my parents' watchful eyes. Their advice on reigning in the partying or keeping my head in the game? It just bounced off me. I was too caught up in proving that I wasn't just a survivor—I was a thriver, ready to leave my mark, unfettered and unafraid.

But as you grow, things change. My dreams, my ambitions, they've taken a different shape. I always thought I'd follow my dad's footsteps straight into the NFL, aiming for the Texans. It was part of the plan, part of my identity.

Did I want it? Hell yes. But doubts crept in, whispers in the back of my mind. *Was I strong enough, fast enough, durable enough to make it?* Those thoughts could've broken me, but they didn't. They made me tougher, more determined. I had already stared down cancer and won; I wasn't about to let anything else beat me. Keeping that fire alive in my heart, despite the odds, has been my driving force.

So fourteen years ago, after I walked out of that hospital, I set my eyes on a single goal: to be the greatest NFL player there ever was. To a seven-year-old kid fresh out of a cancer ward, that meant embracing a life filled with the things I loved most: football, wealth, and women. It sounded like the ultimate dream.

But as the years rolled by, my perspective began to shift. People change, right? With each passing year, I found myself questioning, reassessing my dreams. One thing, though, remained constant—my desire to make a difference, to help people. My own battle with illness had shown me how crucial doctors and nurses were. Their impact on my life planted a seed, a purpose I hadn't fully grasped until recently. And then, like a bolt out of the blue, it hit me.

Here's the crazy part: I want to be a doctor. A total departure from my childhood dream, sure, but it just feels . . . right. The idea of saving lives, of being that crucial part of someone's survival story, it's indescribable.

So, since junior year, I've been hustling—studying hard, keeping my eyes on the prize of medical school. It's tough, but something inside me knows it'll be worth it. This new path has been my little secret; I haven't told my friends or family. They wouldn't understand why I'd want to give up an NFL career. But when I think of my future, it's always in blue scrubs, either in an operating room or teaching the next generation of doctors.

"There you are, handsome," Leah purrs, latching onto my arm as she sidles up next to me at the party.

Does Leah's constant attention bother me? Not really. It's convenient, keeps other girls at bay, and guarantees a bit of fun later. But my mind short-circuits because Milli's nearby, and the last thing I want is her catching me with another girl on my arm. Not that I owe her any explanations, but still.

I look around for her, but she's disappeared from where she was just moments ago.

Leah's hand creeps up my thigh, heading into dangerous territory, but instead of the usual thrill, I feel . . . off. With Milli somewhere in this room, everything's different. I gently but firmly hold Leah's hand in place, stopping her advance. Her eyes flash a brief flicker of surprise and maybe disappointment, but then she's back to her usual self, trying to inch closer again.

But I'm not feeling it, not tonight, not with Milli around. It's confusing and frustrating. I need to find her, see where she went. Maybe then I can figure out what the hell is going on with me.

"I figured you'd be dragging me home by now," Leah teases, her voice a silky whisper.

I let out a sigh, rolling my eyes slightly. It's like a script these girls follow—the star athlete, the frat boy charm; they eat it up. But honestly, I'm past that stage now. Seeing my freshmen behaving like they've got no care in the world, especially with an early morning waiting, just makes me shake my head.

"Nah, I'm just chilling with the guys tonight," I reply casually, nodding toward the two remaining of my trio. Cam's vanished into the crowd again.

Then, a sudden burst of laughter catches my attention. It's Milli, perched on the kitchen counter, the center of a chaotic scene of party debris. And there's Cam, leaning in toward her with a look in his eye that sets off every alarm in my head.

A belly shot. Of all the shit . . .

I'm up on my feet before I even realize, leaving Leah stumbling beside me. "One sec, I've gotta handle something." I stride toward the kitchen. "Or someone . . . " I mutter.

It's like I'm on autopilot, my focus entirely on Milli and Cam. I push past Cam, my hand moving instinctively to tug down Milli's top, covering her.

"Chasen, what the hell, man?" Cam protests, annoyance flaring in his eyes.

I fix him with a hard stare. "Back off, Hines."

I'm on the verge of pulling Milli away from here, but just

as I'm about to act, she gazes up at me, her cheeks rosy from laughter, her eyes alight with vivacity. It catches me off guard —she appears so . . . vibrant.

"So, you're stepping in if you're sidelining Cam?" She cocks an eyebrow, her lips curved in a mischievous smile.

"Oh, just fucking great," I mutter.

There's a palpable tension in the air as I try to figure out my next move. Milli, who's usually more reserved, seems to be enjoying this daring departure from her norm. Cam, on the other hand, is grinning like a Cheshire cat, obviously getting a kick out of the situation.

I take a moment to steady my nerves. "Milli, I don't think this is a good idea," I say softly, trying to sound reasonable yet firm.

Her eyes lock with mine, a blend of defiance and playfulness. "What's the matter? Scared, Sunshine?" she goads, her tone laced with a challenge that unexpectedly sends a shiver through me. I'm aware that I should be putting an end to this —that I need to remind myself this is Milli. Yet, there's something about her boldness, her spark, that's undeniably captivating.

Out of the corner of my eye, I see Cam smirking, silently mouthing, "Sunshine," and barely holding back his laughter.

Fuck this.

Closing the distance between us, I fix her with a steady gaze. "I'm not scared," I state firmly, my voice a low rumble. "But maybe you're the one who should be."

Her eyes, initially wide with surprise, soon gleam with a mischievous and enticing light. In a playful retort, she coyly lifts her top just enough to display her toned abdomen. Fuck, her skin is flawless; beckoning me toward her. It's not like I haven't seen her like this before, but each time feels like the first, stirring a deep, possessive feeling inside me.

I close my eyes for a split second, trying to regain control.

Get a grip, Chasen. You know how last time went when you touched Milli.

The warning echoes in my head, a reminder of the line I'm about to cross again. "Last time was a mistake," I whisper to myself, feeling a knot of tension in my gut. "This is a really, really bad idea."

But then my eyes lock onto Milli once again, and everything else fades into a blur. I'm drawn in, despite every screaming instinct telling me to back off. I pour the tequila, watching it settle in her navel, and I'm hit with a wave of déjà vu, thinking of that night at Club Zero.

Milli arches slightly, ensuring the liquid doesn't spill, and fuck, every part of me reacts. My body is betraying my mind's frantic warnings.

This shouldn't be happening, but it is.

Cam's whistle slices through the air, a sharp reminder that all eyes are on us. "Show 'em how it's done, Chasen!" he shouts, a grin in his voice. The crowd's noise swells like a wave, eager for a show, but they fade to nothing more than a dull roar in my ears. In this charged moment, it's just Milli and me; everything else blurs at the edges.

As I hover above her, the world shrinks to this intimate bubble we've created. The heat from her skin under my lips sends a jolt through me, more potent than any drink I've ever had. The taste of tequila on her is a sweet burn, igniting a fire within that roars for more. Her gasp, delicate yet laden with unspoken promises, has my heart slamming against my chest. Her fingers tangle in my hair, a silent plea that anchors me to the here and now.

"Miles," Milli whimpers. She pushes herself up higher to watch the show. And god, if that whimper of hers doesn't make my balls tighten as I try not to come in my pants like a fourteen old boy.

I push her back, laying her down. Her sweet moans echo

in my ears as I trail kisses up her neck, my hands venturing under her shirt. The crowd's cheers and jeers fade into nothingness.

Then someone mentions Luke's name, and it's like a bucket of ice water dumps over my head. Reality crashes back in a brutal wave. I pull back abruptly, my heart racing, my mind a chaotic storm. What the hell am I doing? This is Milli, Luke's sister, my best friend. The memories of our last mishap flood back, a stark reminder of the consequences.

She looks at me, her lip caught between her teeth, her eyes blazing with something that stirs a conflict deep within me. But I know I need to end this, now.

"Alright, that's enough!" I snap at the onlookers, pointing at them with a stern finger.

I zero in on Cam and Gunner, who are barely holding back their amusement. "This stays between us, you got that?" My voice is hard, my usual easygoing demeanor gone.

Cam looks at me, his expression shifting from amusement to surprise. He's never seen me this serious outside the football field.

"But Chasen," he starts.

But I'm not having any of it. "You didn't see a thing," I insist, my tone brooking no argument.

I need to get out of here, clear my head. I can't let things go any further. Not with Milli, not like this. It's time to put a stop to this madness before it spirals out of control.

Cam gives me a nod, his eyes flickering with understanding, as he states, "It stays between us." I just stand there, letting his words linger in the air. He awkwardly attempts a salute, some sort of Boy Scout gesture.

"Good," I reply, my voice firm. I try to keep my expression neutral, but a scowl inevitably forms. "Just remember what it feels like to have your balls intact."

I throw one last look at Milli. She's no longer biting her

lip; instead, her eyes are narrowed, a storm of anger and something else swirling in them. I can't deal with this right now—I came here to unwind, not get tangled up in whatever this is. Frustration boiling over, I make a beeline for the door.

Pushing through the throng of partygoers, I finally reach the exit. Stepping out into the cool night air, I take a deep, calming breath. But before I can fully escape, I hear her voice.

"Miles, wait."

"Not now, Milli," I mutter, not stopping as I descend the steps.

Her hand catches my arm, halting me. She's looking at me with confusion, maybe frustration. "What was that back there?"

I reply with heavy sarcasm, "Oh, you know, just your typical belly shot."

Her hands land on her hips, her expression exasperated. "I know what a belly shot is, Miles. What I meant was, why did you do that?" She's poking my chest now, each word punctuated with a jab. "Why did you pull that stunt?"

Catching her finger, I notice her sharp intake of breath. "First, I wasn't about to let Cam, or anyone, get that close to you. Second, it was just a bit of fun," I say, trying to lighten the mood.

"Just a bit of fun?" She rolls her eyes. "You always tell me to break out of my shell, to have some fun. So that's what I was doing. And you just had to step in."

She's right. I'm the one who's always pushing her to loosen up. But watching Cam hover over her, I couldn't stand it. "I know, and you're right," I admit, my eyes dropping to the ground. "It was hard watching him, or anyone, disrespect you."

She steps closer, giving me a push. "Disrespect? Miles, what you did wasn't any different. You stepped in his place. Does that mean you disrespected me, too?"

I look back at her, my voice softer. "No, Milli, I didn't mean it like that. You know I would never disrespect you. You're my best friend."

Her eyes seem slightly shocked by my words, perhaps even hurt, as she mutters, "Best friends, right?"

"So, what was all that about?" she probes, arching an eyebrow. "You can't just keep every guy away from me because you think they'll 'disrespect' me, Miles. I'm allowed to choose who I interact with; it's part of the college experience. E-x-p-l-o-r-i-n-g," she emphasizes, drawing out each letter.

Not if I can help it. Guys in Alpha Rho Tau, especially, have a reputation for preying on freshman girls.

I exhale deeply, my fingers weaving through my hair. "Mills, it's not about controlling you. I'm just asking you to be careful. Not every guy who shows interest has good intentions."

She rolls her eyes. "Oh, please, Chasen. Just trust me, will you? I'm not a child anymore."

I'm painfully aware of that.

"I understand," I say, my voice laced with earnestness. "But can you at least try to see it from my perspective? Luke would never forgive me if anything happened to you on my watch."

And neither would I.

She glances down, a sigh escaping her lips. "Fine, but next time we're at the same party, can you not . . . do what you just did?"

I frown slightly, unsure of exactly which "thing" she's referring to, but I nod, fully aware that it's a promise I might struggle to keep.

Especially when it comes to Milli.

CHAPTER 8
MILLI

Bingo, Baby Sutton.

"So, nothing else happened? No goodnight kiss or anything?" Brooke probes as we walk to our classes on a crisp new Monday morning.

I reply with a casual shrug, trying to mask my real feelings about the weekend's events. Honestly, the last thing I want is to dive into a detailed analysis of my encounter with Miles—especially the part where he simultaneously made my heart race and then treated me like I was some fragile thing in need of protection.

And that moment with him . . . Why did it have to be so complicated? Why couldn't we just either forget it happened or . . . or maybe explore what it could lead to? I'd be lying if I said I wasn't curious.

Strolling through the campus, the smell of autumn leaves fills the air. NorthRidge University is stunning this time of year, with its top-tier facilities, the modern library, and the gym that's always buzzing with activity.

A year ago, I wouldn't have pictured myself here. North-Ridge was far from my first choice, but a promise to my mom led me to take a tour. And what do you know? The dance team felt like destiny calling, and the campus—with its picturesque landscape of towering trees, undulating hills, and vine-covered brick buildings—had this unexpected tranquility about it. Watching students hustle to their classes, I'm reminded why I chose to be here.

Brooke raises an eyebrow, her skepticism clear. "Just talking, huh? You know you can tell me if there's more."

I wish there was . . .

"Really, Brooke, it was just a game of belly shots, then some talking," I say, trying to sound convincing.

Navigating that conversation with Miles was like walking through a minefield of awkwardness.

"Actually, it was kind of nice. Setting boundaries, you know?" I gesture vaguely, half trying to persuade her, half trying to reassure myself. "Miles and I, we're clear on where we stand."

Which couldn't be further from the truth. I'm as confused as ever about my feelings for him.

"And, well, I don't want to go down that road with him again," I add, recalling how things turned sour last time we got too close.

But a part of me had relished that closeness . . .

Brooke nods, understanding yet playful. "I get it. But remember, a little bit of exercise is good for the heart."

"Right," I laugh, giving her a friendly nudge. "I'll keep that in mind. Thanks for the advice, B."

As Brooke and I walk into our statistics class, I'm relieved that it's finally starting. The delay, courtesy of our professor's vacation followed by an illness, had put a pause on this course. Not that I minded the extra free time.

Brooke's gaze suddenly shifts, her eyes widening with what seems like surprise. Before I can ask what's up, an uncomfortable feeling settles over me. Scanning the room, my eyes inevitably land on Miles, just a couple of rows ahead, surrounded by a group of freshmen I recognize from the Alpha Rho Tau party. They're all engrossed in some joke, laughing and goofing around.

Miles in my statistics class? That's unexpected. There he was, effortlessly cool in a plain white Tommy John tee that hugged his athletic frame just right, making a simple statement that somehow amplified his charm. His outfit, understated yet striking, played up his casual allure. The backward cap, a faded baseball hat with hints of gold, sat on his head with that signature ease of his. It was obviously a well-loved piece, lending a laid-back vibe to his overall demeanor.

His familiar grin, confident and a bit smug, especially around girls, lights up his face. From the outside looking in, you'd never guess the battles he fought—the childhood cancer, the challenges he's overcome. He has this air of someone who's never been touched by worry or pain, but I know better.

Trying to avoid his gaze, I remind myself not to get caught up again in his orbit. The last thing I want is for him to think I'm still hung up on our recent, complicated interaction.

But deep down, I know I am.

Fate, however, seems to have a different plan, and our eyes meet. His smirk, that signature Miles expression, sends my stomach into a series of flips. He's always had this effect on me, but now, seeing him regularly instead of just during occasional breaks, it feels like a constant test of my self-control.

"What's up, Baby Sutton?" he calls out casually, as if we were just old friends catching up.

Brooke elbows me gently. "You good?" she whispers.

I roll my eyes to mask the turmoil inside.

Yeah, just internally freaking out. Pull it together, Milli.

Shrugging nonchalantly, I try to sound indifferent. "Just Miles."

Brooke's skepticism is clear as day, her grin accompanies a doubtful, "Mmhm, right."

Miles gives me another glance, his eyes briefly flicking to the empty seat beside him, as if inviting me over.

I swallowed hard, trying to appear unaffected.

Professor Huggins starts the lecture, and Brooke, naturally taking charge, ushers us to the front row seats. Fantastic, just what I needed. The spotlight seems to shine directly on me, vulnerable, an unease magnified by my dyslexia—a sensation I'm far from fond of. With a sense of reluctance, we take our places.

Throughout the lecture, I can feel Miles' gaze on me, making it hard to concentrate. I find myself sneaking peeks at him, drawn in by some invisible force. Each time our eyes meet, it feels like the world around us fades away, leaving just the two of us locked in this silent, intense connection.

"Milli, you heading to practice later?" Brooke's voice snaps me back to reality.

Caught off guard, I stammer, "Huh?"

She nudges me, whispering, "Please tell me you weren't just staring at Miles this whole time?"

Trying to brush it off, I mumble, "No, just zoning out."

Brooke's raised eyebrow tells me she isn't fooled.

I risk another glance at Miles. He is still looking at me, his expression intense and unreadable. As class ends and everyone packs up, Miles stands and nonchalantly makes his way toward us.

My heart pounds as he joins us outside Willowbrook Hall, his gaze never leaving me.

"Hey, Brooke," he greets casually, then turns to me. "Milli," he utters in that deep, husky tone that sends heat from my breasts straight to my core. "Where are you heading next? Mind if I tag along?"

I pause, thoughts swirling. Part of me knows I should refuse, label it a bad idea. Yet, it's only a walk, isn't it? A harmless trek to the campus dance studio with my best friend. Besides, there's something in his look that renders me utterly incapable of saying no.

God, did he always have that penetrating gaze? The one that seems to extract my words, my emotions, before I even manage to react.

Yeah, who am I fooling? He's always had that effect on me.

Furthermore, we are just friends—no more, no less. I need to reign in my tendency to overanalyze. It was just an innocent peck on my stomach, a moment of playfulness, right? He's probably long since moved on. After all, he quickly got over what happened that night at the club. And from what I can tell, he appears to have left the "incident" at the party in the past.

Before I can react, our group halts in the heart of the campus. Suddenly, Brooke grabs my arm and draws me aside, saying, "Sorry, Miles, but Milli and I are grabbing lunch together. Maybe another time?"

"Hey, look who's here," Payson exclaims, joining us and enveloping both me and Brooke in a hug. She then turns her attention to Miles. "Chasen, good to see you, and your tongue, are still intact, huh? I half-expected it might have disappeared into Milli's belly after the other night."

What the heck? I playfully elbow her, maybe a bit harder than usual, and nervously chuckle.

Can she be any less subtle?

She tilts her head back and laughs, "Oh, but wait, it did."

I let out a sigh and mutter, "Give it a rest, Pay."

Even as her eyes danced with playfulness, she pinned me

with an intense look. "Seriously, it's true. Everyone at that party saw right through you two." Dropping her arm, she fanned her face. "Whew, just reminiscing about it is enough to make me all flustered."

"Real mature, Payson," Miles quips.

A shadow of disappointment clings to me following Miles' indifferent reaction; it is clear our previous encounter hasn't touched him at all. I want to speak up, to defend myself somehow, but before the words can form, Brooke changes the subject. "Hey, how about we talk about something else? Like what we're doing this weekend?"

Payson shrugs. "Sure, we could hit up that new club downtown. I heard they have a killer DJ."

Rolling my eyes once more, I interrupt the conversation. "As enjoyable as this chat has been, I won't be hitting any parties this weekend." Miles seems to relax a bit, his eyes softening—almost a hint of relief? I go on, "The football team has a bi-week and then the following week is their first away game, which translates to more dance practice for me. Speaking of dance practice . . . " I say.

"Let me go walk with you," Brooke offers, grabbing my arm again.

I brush her off. "I'm good, really. Thanks, though."

"Milli, at least let me walk you to the studio. It's right on my way," Miles insists, his gaze holding mine with a gentle intensity.

Man, why does saying no to him have to be like climbing Mt. Everest?

I still manage a nonchalant smile and say, "Yeah, sure."

After farewells to Brooke and Payson, we start off. My heart is doing somersaults. Miles' presence is like a warm blanket on a cold night, and his scent, a mix of musk and sandalwood, is downright heady. It sends my feelings into a tailspin.

"So," Miles begins, slicing through our quiet bubble, "what's your plan for the rest of the day?"

"Not much. Just one class today. Last week was hectic with three, so it's nice having a lighter week. But I've got dance practice later. Coach is having us try on new uniforms for the next game. Seems we're updating to match the new university colors."

"Oh," he trails off.

"Just 'oh'?" I tease, eyebrow arched.

His grin is infectious, a laugh booming out that could shake leaves from trees. "Just imagining 'Little Milli' all decked out in her Panthers' gear. The old ones looked great on you, though," he adds with a wink.

He isn't wrong. The old uniforms feel new to me. Miles' reaction at that first game had been . . . memorable, much like the look he is giving me now. Warmth climbs up my neck, my cheeks likely flushing a deep shade of red. "You'll catch the new ones at the next game," I manage to say, fighting back a grin.

Not that it is a secret—we'll be side by side all season.

His smug smile weighs on me, even as I force my gaze forward.

Reaching the dance studio, Miles' fingers graze my arm ever so slightly, the faint contact sends a ripple of goose-bumps across my skin. You'd think I'd be used to his touch, but nope, not happening.

"Your plans for today?" I ask, poking fun. "Let me guess: Football?"

He mockingly gestures a win. "Bingo, Baby Sutton."

His usual spark seems dimmed at the mention of football. Something is up. "You okay? You don't seem up for football today."

He pauses, then says, "Nah, I'm good. Just not feeling great."

I raise an eyebrow, but don't push. I nudge him. "Never pegged you as the midweek party type, especially with football and senior year."

He chuckles. "Not hungover, just exhausted. Coach's been drilling us hard, plus my classes are a beast this semester. Cut me some slack, will ya?"

His words seem to echo with a hidden depth, hinting at more than just fatigue. But I know Miles; he'll open up when he is ready. Until then, I'll simply be there, as I always have been.

I nod, understanding his unspoken message. "I get it, but remember . . . " I start, only to be momentarily distracted as a student bustles past us, interrupting our little world.

A brief, awkward silence falls between us. Eager to dispel the tension, I quickly add, "Just so you know, I'm here if you need anything."

Miles' response is a playful smirk. "Oh, really? In what way?" he jokes, his tone light. "I could use a good massage, right about here . . . " His hand starts to drift toward his inner thigh, a mischievous glint in his eye.

My eyes widen in mock horror.

A blush creeps up my cheeks. No way, not happening—my mind needs to be on dance, not on . . . other things. It feels like the universe should be sending me a lifeboat right about now. I hurriedly open the studio door, throwing a look over my shoulder. "Catch you later, Sunshine."

Miles winks back, unfazed by his own cheekiness. "See ya, Mills."

And there it is—Miles, the master of charm and flirtation, in all his glory.

CHAPTER 9
MILES

Describing college football practices could only be summed up in one word: unbelievably gruesome. Growing up with a dad in the NFL, I witnessed the sport's physical demands from a very early age. I still vividly recall the sight of him returning home with bruises and cuts, struggling to walk after a brutal game. The intensity of it all was etched into my memory. Every season, my mother would urge him to hang up his cleats, but it wasn't until I hit rock bottom, battling cancer, that the gravity of sacrifice truly hit home.

During those dark times, when I wasn't sure I'd make it, my dad started missing more practices and games to be with me. But what I have been going through in college football is a whole new level of intense. The non-stop hits, grueling workouts, and the pressure to perform at the highest level are overwhelming. I often wonder why I am putting myself through it. What is the point? If I have to guess, it is my way of giving back to my dad for all the time he'd sacrificed for me. He retired from football early to be there for me, and now, I want to make him proud in the same sport.

The sun is beating down, casting a golden hue across the field as I grip the football tightly, feeling its familiar texture against my skin. Confidence pulses through me, a natural rhythm that comes with leading this team. With a determined focus, I survey the field, mentally mapping out each play before it unfolds. My teammates surround me, a united force ready to execute our strategies flawlessly.

At Coach K.'s signal, we dive into a drill. I drop back, my movements calculated and precise, scanning for our open receiver, JJ aka Jordan Johnson. The ball leaves my hand in a perfect spiral, sailing through the air.

JJ sprints ahead, reaching out with arms extended as the ball descends. A rush of excitement floods through me as the pass links up flawlessly, prompting the team to explode into a chorus of rowdy, "hell yeahs." It's a hell of a fine-tuned symphony, a perfect blend of coordination and sheer effort.

"Great job, everyone," I call out as we gather together, my voice filled with a sense of unity and togetherness. "Let's carry this energy into our next game against the Thunderhawks. We're a team, and together, this season we will be unstoppable." Time becomes a blur as the drills continue. Each throw, each decision, is a testament to my dedication to the game.

The team disperses, and I stand in my same spot on the field, letting the moment sink in. I take a breath, trying to capture the essence of this place, this moment. The realization hits me like a sudden gust of wind—with each practice that passes, it's a step closer to the end. Each repetition, each throw, brings me closer to the final chapter of my time on this field.

I close my eyes, allowing the memories to flood my mind—the victories, the defeats, the laughter, and the camaraderie. It's bittersweet, but I'm grateful for every instance I've had on this field, knowing that these experiences have shaped me into the player and person I am today.

Thud.

What the fuck.

I grab the side of my head, watching the football hit the ground after smacking me right in the head. Glancing over, Luke is grinning while Cam and the other guys burst into laughter, nudging each other and pointing at me as if I'm the laughingstock of the day.

I throw my hands up in frustration. "What the hell, man?" Irritation laces my voice.

Luke starts to make his way over to me. "Hey, don't blame me. Coach said to get your attention."

Asshole.

"Listen, my whole aim was to grab your attention in a manner that would make you take notice of us."

I roll my eyes and retort, "Ever heard of a simple 'Hey, Miles, over here'? That would've worked just fine."

He gives a shrug, his face breaking into a sly grin. "I'm not too certain, buddy. You looked completely absorbed in your own little universe."

I shake my head, releasing a sigh.

"What's eating at you, huh?" he probes.

It's the looming end of my football career, but I don't say it.

"Is it the new professor, Mrs. Abben?" Luke suggests with a wink, hinting at her attractiveness. "She's quite the looker."

I internally cringe. How does Luke manage to excel in football and academics when he's so fixated on women and flirting? I readjust my helmet, giving it a couple of taps, trying to refocus.

"Dude, you sure you're up for finishing practice?" Cam asks, concern in his voice. "You're looking a bit pale."

I quirk an eyebrow at the suggestion. Pale? Really?

Luke throws an arm around my shoulders, a bit more forcefully than necessary—or maybe I'm just more sensitive today. A sharp pain shoots through my temple, making me wince.

"Yeah, he's fine. Just not his best day." Luke quickly covers for me.

Cam lets out a snort. "That's an understatement. You've been off your game for the last thirty minutes."

Shaking my head, I try to dispel the fog clouding my mind, forcing myself to focus. The heat, the sweat, the echo of practice around me—I should be in the moment, yet my thoughts are elsewhere. I grit my teeth, fighting the headache that's setting in.

"Chasen, everything okay?" Coach's voice pulls me back, and I turn toward him, trying to appear unaffected.

What's with all these questions? I'm standing, aren't I?

"I'm fine, Coach. Just need a moment."

He gives me a nod, though his concern is apparent. I can't stand this feeling of vulnerability, of weakness. It's a place I never want to be in.

I push the frustration aside and inhale deeply, forcing myself to refocus on the practice.

Panthers' Day is looming, and the stakes are high, especially with a father like Drew Chasen. His expectations have always been sky-high, leaving no room for anything less than perfection. With his dream of me entering the NFL almost within reach, the pressure is suffocating.

If I don't snap out of this soon, I risk being benched.

I can almost hear his criticisms: "What was that out there, son? You know better than to drop passes like that," or "Those throws won't land you a spot in the draft, let alone the top picks."

Don't get me wrong, I love my dad. But at times, his intensity is overwhelming, as if he's trying to relive his own dreams through me. It's a heavy burden, but in the end, he's sacrificed a lot for me. Now, it's my turn to step up.

I understand that my dad's harsh coaching and demanding words are his way of showing support, his attempt to secure an NFL opportunity for his only son. Yet, back then, what I truly needed was simply a father. Not a coach, not a mentor, and perhaps, even just having him as a friend might have made a bigger difference in my recovery.

Brushing my fingers through my hair, I make my way into the locker room and lean against my locker, its echo filling the silent space. Opening it, I notice my phone illuminating with my dad's name. Predictable. This has become his ritual ever since training camp started, phoning after each practice to dissect feedback and scout evaluations. A pounding headache grips me, zapping all my energy, making the thought of enduring another one of his exhaustive debriefs unbearable. Choosing to ignore the call becomes my only moment of relief.

A gentle tap on my shoulder makes me spin around to find Luke looking at me, worry etched across his face. I arch an eyebrow in curiosity, giving him the floor to speak. Yet, he hesitates, leaving a silence that nudges me to break it with a, "What's going on?"

"You looked a bit off today," he notes with concern.

I give a nod, right as I'm hit once more by a stabbing pain in my head, mimicking a drill twisting into my skull, dispersing my thoughts into chaos. The chatter of my teammates fades into a vague hum behind me. I want to request some room to breathe, yet the words stubbornly refuse to materialize. Gritting my teeth, I fight through the agony.

"Someone get him water," Coach commands sharply, and instantly, a teammate dashes off to comply.

I shut my eyes, trying to escape the relentless noise and pain. It feels like forever before a water bottle is thrust into my hand. I drink eagerly; the coolness offers some relief to my dry throat, but it does little to quell the pounding headache.

"Maybe we should take him to the hospital." Luke's voice reaches me, tinged with worry. I understand his intentions are pure; he's always been one to care deeply. But the last thing I need is for my coach and teammates to think I'm weak just because I'm battling a bit of dehydration and fatigue.

"No," I croak out, dismissing the suggestion. A hospital is the last place I want to be.

Stepping back from my locker, I wave my hands around, trying to reassure everyone. "See? I'm fine."

Cam smirks. "Is that your best stripper impression, Chasen?" Some of the guys laugh.

Coach, familiar with our banter, rolls his eyes but still looks concerned. He suggests, "Maybe you should see the nurse, just in case?"

I shake my head. "I'm just tired from the workload this semester."

It's partly true; I am taking a heavy course load. But that's not the whole story. Coach, sensing there's more to it, doesn't press further, which I appreciate. He nods and heads off.

The others disperse, but Luke hangs back, eyebrow raised. "How many credits are you juggling?"

I slump onto the bench, taking in the familiar surroundings of the locker room. The beige and white checkered floor, the panther blue walls, and the spacious, high-end lockers all speak of NorthRidge University's excellence in sports and academics.

"About 25 credits," I reply, avoiding his gaze.

Luke's eyes widen, taken aback, and I get it. Most college students only take around 12 credits and that's full time in a semester. But then again, he doesn't know the full extent of it. This intense academic focus is essential for my dream of becoming a doctor. It's a hefty load, but necessary for my goal of getting into top medical schools like Harvard, Baylor, or the University of Pennsylvania. These are the institutions I've aspired to since I first dreamed of becoming a doctor.

And really, it's easier said than done. Getting my grades back on track isn't exactly a walk in the park, especially after I slacked off during my first few years of college. But I've learned from those mistakes. I'm determined to become a doctor, no matter what it takes.

"Man, Chasen, why are you piling on so many credits?" Luke inquires.

I offer a casual shrug. "Well, for one, I plan to graduate with you guys, obviously."

He gives me a skeptical look before suggesting, "You know you could still make it to the NFL, even without finishing your degree, right?"

I roll my eyes and reply, "Yeah, I know, but what's the point? I'm close to graduating and I'd prefer to have a degree, just in case life has other plans for me."

Like becoming a doctor . . .

I have no doubts about my NFL prospects. Dad's training and guidance, especially since my recovery, have been invaluable. Surviving a health scare at seven and bouncing back only fueled my drive to excel, to never show weakness.

Luke nods, seeming to understand as he opens his locker.

Just then, Cam's voice echoes from the shower area. "Hey Chasen, you hitting up the Alpha Rho Tau party tonight?"

I shake my head, amused. Trust Cam to be thinking about parties straight after practice. I recall my own early days in college, just as eager for the social scene.

Approaching Cam with my sweat towel in hand, I twirl it and playfully snap it against his thighs.

He yelps dramatically. "Dude, what the hell? That's going to leave a mark," he complains.

I chuckle. A little bruise is nothing for a college football player. He could even spin it as a battle scar from practice to impress a girl. Which is what I would have done, but that's not my scene anymore. There's a new focus in my life now: Football. Graduation. Medical School.

"Sorry, man. Just felt like messing around. You were conveniently there," I respond with a shrug.

Cam shoots me a look. "You walked over here to hit me. I didn't exactly get in your way."

I turn back to the others, an amused grin on my face. "Guys, was Cam in my way?"

They all nod enthusiastically, chiming in with a resounding, "Hell yeah!"

Luke chimes in, "Cam, you've got one of the best damn mentors this year, but I'll warn you—he won't hesitate to pick on you for the fun of it, no doubt about it."

Luke's comment fills me with a sense of pride, and for a fleeting moment, I entertain the idea of a real bromance. But I quickly shake off the thought, smirking as I playfully gesture toward him and retort, "He's right, you know, you were in my way, Cam."

Cam rolls his eyes and mutters, "Oh, screw off," but we all end up laughing, easing into our usual post-practice routine.

I rush through my shower, my mind already on my studies. Since our freshman year, Luke and I have been roommates, first at Alpha Rho Tau. I stuck with the fraternity, knowing it could bolster my medical school applications. Holding the presidency twice was a point of pride. Now, though, Luke and I live off campus in a sturdy brick and wood house we bought together. It's an older place, full of character and potential as a future rental for other students— our so-called "Football House."

I quickly gather my things, slinging my bag over my shoulder. As I pass by Cam, I drop a piece of advice, "Best to avoid those Alpha Rho Tau parties on weeknights, especially if you want to stay on top of your game."

He looks puzzled, so I break it down further. "Think about it. Drinking and then trying to perform at practice? Recipe for disaster. You don't want to risk getting benched, do you?"

With that, I head out to the parking lot, making my way to my Chevy CK. Some might wonder why, with my dad's resources, I'm driving this old truck. It was my grandpa's, and the hours we spent fixing it up are some of my fondest memories. Every repair was a lesson, a bonding experience. He used to say, "If you can fix a car, you can fix anything." Driving it now is a tribute to him, a way to keep his memory alive.

Just as I'm about to get in, a laugh catches my attention.
Milli.

Her laugh, unmistakable and full of life. It stands out even in the busy parking lot.

I sling my bag into the truck and spin around, catching sight of her leaning against her white jeep, exuding a natural glow. Her strawberry blonde locks fall in gentle waves, catching the last rays of sunlight. Clad in a dance leotard of deep panther blue that hugs her form perfectly, contrasted with casual gray sweatpants, she epitomizes an effortless mix of athletic grace. Laughing with some guy, her eyes light up, brimming with happiness.

Who the hell is he?

Jealousy sparks inside me as I watch Milli, curious how he elicited such an authentic laugh from her. Another sharp pang of pain hits, momentarily clouding my sight. I shake my head in an attempt to dispel the haze. The thought nags at me, whether this will be a recurring theme of my senior year:

standing by as Milli captures the interest of guys across campus.

It's nothing, Miles.

But it doesn't feel like nothing at all.

I start a mental countdown from five, a technique I picked up during my cancer treatment in the hospital. I remember Kins, my nurse, always encouraging me through the pain.

"Miles!" she would call out, her face struggling to mask her worry with a smile. I could see her efforts to stay strong for me, just as I tried to be strong in return.

I take a deep breath, recalling her words. *"When you feel pain, try this technique."*

I had listened intently, a seven-year-old desperate for any relief. My dad was often busy with football, and my mom, though trying to be supportive, was occupied with her real estate dealings. Kins was a constant presence, understanding and patient.

"Pinch your thumb and pointer finger together, close your eyes gently, as if you're settling into a peaceful sleep," she had instructed. *"Then breathe deeply in and out, counting down from five. Do it five times. It'll help you focus and shift your mind away from the pain."*

I had nodded, eager for any respite from the agony.

It's a method I've relied on ever since, and it's always brought some relief. Like now.

5, I inhale deeply and exhale slowly. 4, I focus on my breathing. 3, the world around me starts to fade. 2, my mind begins to clear. 1, the final breath brings a moment of calm.

As I walk toward Milli, I try to steady the whirlwind of emotions inside me. With each step closer, a blend of eager anticipation takes hold. I'm determined to keep my composure, but being near her stirs a storm of feelings that's sometimes hard to contain.

Get a grip, Chasen. You can't afford to mess this up.

Mills.

Luke's sister.

Remember, just best friends.

With a mental switch to "best friend mode," I approach her Jeep, greeting her casually, "Hey."

"Hey, stranger," Milli responds, her laughter lingering from whatever the guy beside her just said.

It irks me more than I care to admit.

"So, who's this?" I ask, nodding toward the guy. His expression tightens at my choice of words, as if I've slighted him. It's not like I know his name.

Milli catches the edge in my tone and the way I'm eyeing him, a flicker of surprise in her eyes. I've never been territorial like this. But she quickly hides any sign of discomfort, her face lighting up again. "Oh, this is my dance partner for the year," she explains.

Oh, so this is the "partner" she mentioned to me and Luke. He's a guy? I don't have much time to ponder over it though, as Milli's enthusiasm is unmistakable while she discusses their routine for the home game. Despite her excitement, she seems to be holding back some details, probably out of politeness.

"Hey," I reply, struggling to sound welcoming, but I can't shake off a sense of envy. This guy gets to be close to Milli—touch her—all under the guise of dance.

Why am I even bothered? It's not like she's mine.

He offers his hand, and after a moment, I shake it. "You're Miles Chasen, right?"

No fucking kidding.

I narrow my eyes slightly, and he laughs. "Man, you're a campus celebrity. Hard not to know you. I'm Wyatt."

Great, Wyatt. Don't care.

His recognition of my campus fame is the least of my concerns. It's the way he looks at Milli, and his casual remark, that irks me.

"Nice to meet you, Wyatt," I say, forcing a laugh. "Yeah, guess I'm a bit known around here." I let go of his hand and turn back to Milli, who's watching me with an unreadable expression.

What just happened here?

Milli averts her gaze, breaking our eye contact. "You two seem to be getting along well," I comment, aiming for a casual tone.

Twirling a pebble with her shoe, Milli replies in a hushed tone, "You could say that."

Wyatt casually drapes his arm around her shoulders. "Just finished dance practice with Mills. Couldn't have asked for a better partner this semester," he says with ease.

Hearing the nickname "Mills" directed at her jolts me, prompting an involuntary tightening of my jaw. It's a term of affection I reserved exclusively for her. A surge of irritation and confusion hits me, but I try to mask it.

"Well, that's great, *Mills*," I echo, the name feeling strange and forced coming from my mouth. I take a moment to collect myself; Milli deserves better than my irrational jealousy. Forcing a smile, I add, "Glad to hear you're enjoying it."

Wyatt smirks at me. "Yeah, Milli's got some impressive moves," he says, his gaze lingering on her a moment too long. Turning back to me, he suggests, "You should check out our practice sometime. We're quite the duo, right, Milli?"

I raise an eyebrow, struggling to keep my cool. "Maybe I will," I respond, my words strained.

Suddenly, a sharp pain in my temple makes me lurch forward. I steady myself against Milli's jeep, shaking my head to clear the pain and force a smile.

Milli rushes to my side, her eyes meeting mine with a mix of confusion and concern. "Miles, are you okay?" she asks softly, her hand comforting on my arm.

I nod, not wanting to burden her with my issues. "Yeah, just tired from practice," I assure her.

She gives me a sympathetic look. Wyatt, oblivious to the situation, chuckles. "Well, see you tomorrow at practice, Milli."

Milli, still holding my gaze, replies, "Yeah, see you, Wyatt," and then likely smiles at him over her shoulder.

Wyatt glances between us, his smirk still in place. "Catch you later, Chasen."

I turn my focus back to Milli, carefully tucking a loose curl behind her ear, and watch as a blush, my favorite kind, spreads across her face. "So, he's your dance partner?" I ask, trying to sound merely curious.

She raises an eyebrow. "Jealous, Sunshine?"

With a playful scoff, I reply, "Nah, just making sure he's up to your standards."

Her eyes narrow slightly. "No worries, Miles. He's a star athlete, top of his class, and a Dance/USA Champion."

She glances at him, adding, "And have you seen him? Impressive, right?"

Inspecting guys' physiques isn't exactly my hobby . . .

I'm torn between thinking she's either messing with me or genuinely smitten. Either way, it's doing nothing for my growing headache. If it were anyone but Milli, I'd have bailed already.

"Most of the dance partners I have been with were way too skinny, and could barely lift me without causing a panic."

"But," I chip in.

She pauses. "But not Wyatt, he's . . . "

Rolling my eyes feels almost reflexive. She barely knows him, and yet here she is, going on like he's some kind of godsend.

Turning back to me, she says, "He's different. He's got this energy, this . . . fire. When he touches me, it's electrifying."

Hearing about their physical closeness irks me more than I care to admit.

"Also," she continues, eyes following him.

Is she seriously ogling him?

What's so special about this freshman?

He's probably clueless with women. Now there, I have confidence in my abilities. Milli deserves someone skilled.

Not that you'll find out, Miles.

"He's built, but not intimidatingly so. You feel safe in his arms. And his dance moves? They're like silk, pure fluidity. Dancing with him feels like we're one entity."

Milli bites her lip, lost in thought, while I'm about to burst with frustration.

Get it together, Chasen.

"So, he's good?" I ask.

"He's remarkable," she declares, her smile glowing. "I had my doubts about teaming up, but it feels like destiny. You can call it fate or whatever you prefer, but it's . . . great, fun."

Fate? Hardly. I nod, speechless. What the fuck am I supposed to say?

Oh, that's awesome, Milli. I'm so happy you have found someone who gets to rub themselves all over you every day.

Something I've only dreamed . . .

She lets out a sigh, the tension melting away as she speaks. "Yeah, with Wyatt and the Hanmann sisters around today, I'm feeling pretty fortunate." Excitement twinkles in her eyes, and my annoyance fades a bit. Her happiness isn't just about Wyatt.

I gently brush away a stray curl clinging to her lip. She watches me closely as I slowly glide my thumb over her lip, her gaze following my every move. The urge to kiss her, to erase Wyatt from her thoughts, is overwhelming. But the soft sound she makes brings me back to reality. I tuck the hair behind her ear and say, "That's awesome, Mills. I'm really happy for you." And I mean it. If anyone deserves a great partner and adorable little sisters as dance students, it's her. She deserves everything and more.

She chuckles softly, looking down. Something's on her mind.

"What's going on?" I ask.

Looking up, she confesses, "I'm just surprised at how well I'm adjusting to all this. I was worried I might not like it."

I raise an eyebrow.

"Because of Luke and everything."

Ah, Luke . . . He's not so bad, just overprotective, which I get. But as much as I want to shield her, especially from college guys, I have to step back. I need to focus on finishing my senior year strong and getting into a top medical residency program.

She exhales. "I envision these next four years as a journey of self-discovery, of embracing risks and savoring every single moment. And I sense, deep down, that I'm beginning to embark on that very journey."

A smile crosses my face. It's common for freshmen to view college as a new beginning, a time to redefine themselves, and she's embracing that. We talked about this when she considered NorthRidge University. I promised to support her transformation, and seeing her start this journey is truly heartening.

"You're making a great start. Don't worry about Luke; he's just being a big brother," I reassure her.

Her smile, thankful and bright, lights up her face. "Thanks, Sunshine. That means a lot." Her voice quivers slightly as she adds in, "I'm, uh, glad we could move past the other night."

Oh, that night, the one where we got closer than ever? Far from forgotten, Mills.

We hold each other's gaze, the magnetic pull between us

intensifying with every second. My heart races, my palms begin to sweat. She steps closer, narrowing the gap between us until we're inches apart. I catch the faint scent of her perfume, like honeysuckle, utterly captivating.

Instinctively, I reach out, my thumb caressing her cheek. "Me too, Mills," I whisper.

She presses gently into my touch, a soft sigh escaping her lips. Her eyes flutter shut, then open, brimming with the same longing that undoubtedly mirrors my own.

I lean in slightly closer, and—

"Now I get why you're skipping the Alpha Rho Tau party tonight."

Damn it. Cam.

Milli leans against her jeep, catching her breath, hands on the vehicle as if to maintain a semblance of distance between us. Her glance flickers from Cam to me, an unspoken question in her eyes.

I step back, trying to defuse the tension. "What do you mean?"

Cam smirks. "Oh, come on. It's obvious. But hey, your secret's safe." He taps his head knowingly.

"I don't follow," I reply, aiming for nonchalance.

Whatever's going on with me and Milli, that's our business.

Milli coughs lightly, then says, "He was just asking about dance practice."

Cam rolls his eyes. "Right, and I'm the Pope."

Noticing Milli's discomfort, I interject, "Just commenting on your off day catching the ball, Cam."

Which was true enough, despite his readiness for the party.

Cam retorts, "Seems like you're the one off your game, Chasen."

Milli's gaze, a mesmerizing swirl of blue and green, holds

mine, filled with silent questions. Cam's doubtful eyes are on us, making openness a challenge. He signals a warning with a sharp gesture, his tone laced with caution. "Be careful. We both know someone's not going to be happy about this."

A tension grips me, my jaw tightens, and my hand forms a fist without my consent. Was that a thinly veiled threat? Did he really just try to intimidate me?

Shaking my head, I close the distance between me and Milli, fighting the impulse to draw her into an embrace. I halt, giving her a smile meant to comfort. She looks from Cam to me and back again, then places her hand over mine, giving it a gentle squeeze. It's a small gesture, but it washes away the tension in my jaw and hands, a relief I hadn't realized I needed until this moment.

"See you later?" she asks, hope tinting her words. She waves at Cam. "Nice running into you, Cameron."

Cam gives her a playful Boy Scout salute, his signature move. I used to find it amusing, but now it seems more like a mask for something else.

"Take care, Milli."

As she drives away, Cam nudges me. "You're in deep, man."

Don't I know it. Fuckkk.

Pussy Panthers

MILES

All in favor of me killing Cam?

GUNNER

I'd be okay with it.

DEVON

Count me in.

LUKE

Why are we killing it Cam, again?

CAM

What the fuck, bro? You do realize I am in this chat, right, Chasen?

MILES

Oh, right, I forgot. Maybe it's better you know before it happens?

DEVON

Alright, now that this is unfolding, are we going Dexter style?

GUNNER

Absolutely, we could sedate him, wrap him in plastic in his dorm room, and transport him to our "kill room"—our football house.

LUKE

You absolutely will not do any such thing, especially not in my house. That's where I draw the line.

CAM

Seriously, guys, you don't tell someone you plan to murder what you're planning to do to them. *Sigh* *Eye roll*

Miles exited the conversation.

CHAPTER 10
MILLI

Can't a girl catch a break?

"Alright, Milli, can you start next Sunday?" Mrs. Raker's excitement is evident as she leans forward across her polished desk.

I nod, replying warmly, "Yes, I'm free. I have dance practice in the afternoon, but I'll be there for tutoring sessions every Sunday."

Mrs. Raker claps her hands, her hot pink reading glasses catching the light. "Perfect, absolutely perfect." She beams.

Rewind a couple of weeks, while in the library, I spotted an ad pinned to the cluttered student bulletin board. It was shouting out for an English tutor, needed specifically for Sundays. Now, isn't that a stroke of luck? Sundays are my days of rest, and English? Well, that's where my passion and expertise lie. Fast forward to today, and you'll find me, heart pounding with anticipation, on the verge of interviewing for that very role.

"So, you have dyslexia? How long have you been managing it? Do you think it could affect your ability to tutor others with dyslexia in English?"

I feel a flicker of irritation, but keep it in check. People often misunderstand what it's like to live with a "challenge" like dyslexia. Instead of snapping, I answer calmly, "Yes, I have dyslexia. But no, I don't think it'll be a hindrance. If anything, it might help me build a stronger connection with my students. I understand their struggles and can tailor the material in a way that's more accessible to them."

She gives a nod, a hint of satisfaction crossing her features at my response. I let out a breath I didn't realize I'd been holding, the tension slowly unfurling from my shoulders. This interview has stretched on, now reaching the ninety-minute mark, leaving me in a limbo of uncertainty— whether this is a good sign or bad.

As her fingers dance across the keyboard, my eyes wander through her office. There's an unexpected coziness to it, unusual for a workspace, particularly one that belongs to someone in her sixties. The bookshelves are overflowing with volumes of every size and color, giving the room an inviting, homely atmosphere. Odd little trinkets—a playful desk organizer here, a whimsical figurine there—inject a dose of personality into the space. A plush rug lies beneath my feet, softening the hardwood, while the gentle patter of rain against the windows offers a serene backdrop, revealing a tranquil view of the campus. It's a space that feels welcoming, almost like a warm embrace.

Mrs. Raker finally looks up. "That concludes our interview."

I take a deep breath, our eyes meeting.

"I'm delighted to welcome you to our library's tutoring team, Milli," she says, her smile bright as she stands and extends her hand.

Under my breath, I murmur, "About time," while gathering my belongings, a wave of relief washing over me.

Just as I'm about to leave, she adds, "Oh, and there's a 'special' student who might need your help."

"Special?" I ask, eyebrow raised. What does she mean by that? Difficult, or dealing with specific challenges? I'm keen to work with students who face struggles like mine, so I'm curious about her use of "special."

I question, skeptically using air quotes, "When you say 'special' student, are you referring to someone with dyslexia?"

Mrs. Raker chuckles, shaking her head. "Oh, no, dear, nothing like that."

I'm a bit startled by her dismissive attitude toward dyslexia, as if it's a grave issue. She explains, "This student is simply struggling in a class and needs to catch up before semester ends."

Truly? A twinge of frustration stirs within me. I had expressly stated my desire to work with students with dyslexia, but now it appears I may be redirected. Given my already bustling agenda filled with classes, dance rehearsals, games, and offering complimentary dance classes, this potential shift threatens to tip my balance into chaos.

Just fantastic.

Before I can express my concerns, Mrs. Raker interjects, "You'll meet him soon. He's a senior at NorthRidge, and I think you'll get along well. It won't interfere with tutoring dyslexic students."

Relief floods through me, yet the wink and smirk Mrs. Raker throws my way sends ripples of confusion through my mind. Could she be insinuating there's more to discover with this guy? The thought feels like a stretch. As it stands, my love life is entangled with fictional beings and my one-sided crush on Miles, a journey that feels like it's going nowhere fast.

I manage a smile, polite but strained, as I mask my swirling confusion. Stepping back into the sanctuary of the library, with its towering bookshelves and students lost in their own worlds of studying. Turning a corner, a book titled *The Art of Movement* catches my eye. Authored by a renowned choreographer. Unable to resist, I scoop it up and claim a quiet nook by the window. Outside, the rain whispers against the glass, and a gentle breeze carries the promise of fall, setting the perfect stage for losing myself in the pages.

Engrossed in the book, time flies by. The techniques and philosophies within its pages resonate deeply with me. My concentration breaks when I hear a familiar voice.

"Looks like some things never change."

Catching sight of Miles, smirking in that effortless way of his, hat flipped back, and dressed in his laid-back combo of black sweatpants and a "Touchdown Against Breast Cancer" tee that hugs his frame a bit too well, I bite back a sigh. Our campus shrinks every time we bump into each other—fate's little nudge, perhaps. But between us? I secretly relish these accidental meet-ups. A glimpse of him, even just weekly, has become a highlight for me.

As our eyes lock, my heart starts its own erratic ballet of emotions. My cheeks warm as I observe him, oozing charm without even trying. It's not just me who's caught in his spell —other women also stop to appreciate, greet, or strike up chats with him.

I grumble silently, *I'm right here! Find someone else to admire.* I can't exactly shout it out; after all, there's no "Miles Chasen's girlfriend" label attached to me. I don't have exclusive rights to his attention.

When his gaze meets mine again, I force a neutral response, keeping my annoyance at bay. "What's up?" I ask, striving for a calm tone.

He chuckles, oblivious to my inner turmoil, and pulls up a chair next to me. Before sitting, he gives me a quick once-over, biting his lip slightly.

And I know why he's looking—it's the outfit. The white bodysuit is snug, paired with a blue skirt featuring a daringly high slit. It's bold and maybe a bit revealing, but it boosts my confidence.

I had doubted Mrs. Raker would hire me in this attire, but then, my childhood tutors advice echoed in my mind: *"Milli, you can wear the finest clothes, but it's your confidence and personality that truly shine."* That advice emboldened me to stop worrying about others' opinions on my style. People should appreciate me for who I am, not for my clothes, my family's fame, or anything else.

With our eyes still locked, Miles sports his trademark smug grin, a gleam in his teeth and a twinkle in his eyes that remind me of sunlight breaking through storm clouds.

This guy . . . Can't a girl catch a break?

Before either of us speaks, a cough interrupts us. Luke is standing nearby, his gaze sharp. Miles quickly retracts his hand from behind my chair, nervously rubbing his neck, before turning to Luke. "Hey, how's it going?"

He blinks. There's a flash of curiosity in his eyes that quickly disappears as he says, "Heading out from the library. Figured we'd do a bonfire at the house now that the rain's given up."

He's right on point. Since I settled here with my book, the rain has stopped, leaving behind a sun-kissed, cooler evening —perfect for a bonfire. Nostalgia hits me suddenly. Bonfires were our thing back in the day when Luke and Miles were just high school kids. Over time, they turned into something we'd do only during breaks or summers, when we all had a chance to get together again.

Miles throws a quick, probing glance my way, and I wonder if he's looking for my reaction or if he's thinking about something else entirely.

I arch an eyebrow just as Miles' chuckle resonates, a deep

sound that vibrates through my very being. "Come on, Mills, lighten up. It's going to be fun. You need a night out," he urges, his voice laced with a persuasive tone.

He's not wrong. A night like this could be a perfect escape from the week's chaos, a chance to reset for what's coming. Closing the book, I stand up and head toward Luke, my bag swinging over my shoulder. Miles stands, too, falling into step beside me.

I reach out, looping my arm around his arm, feeling a familiar ease. "Alright, show us the way," I say, a smile in my voice.

Miles

"Pennington, step aside. You don't know the first thing about lighting a fire," Luke chides, playfully pushing her away and taking over the fire-poking duties.

Payson, hands on hips, looks ready to launch into a full-blown rebuttal. This back-and-forth has been a staple of our gatherings since we arrived over an hour ago.

As I lounge in my usual chair, surrounded by friends at one of our typical bonfire sessions, there's a comforting sense of home tonight. The weather is perfect, and the crowd is just right—our teammates, Milli, Brooke, and her boyfriend Josh.

My phone buzzes. I don't need to check to know it's my mom.

Mother Dear: Miles, did you see Dr. Reynolds yet? They told me you haven't been scheduled.

I fight the urge to roll my eyes. She's been on my case about this since summer camp. I meant to go in early

August, but it slipped through the cracks. I'm fine, though, really.

I appreciate her concern, but my attention shifts as Milli steps out onto the patio, drink in hand. Under the warm glow of the patio lights, her innate sweetness shines. My pulse quickens at the sight of her.

MOTHER DEAR

Miles, please make it a priority to go in sometime soon. Please, for your mom, it will give me a peace of mind.

I send a quick text back because she won't quit unless I agree. Looking back toward Milli, our eyes meet. She bites her lip, glancing around the bonfire where everyone is absorbed in their own world. I nod at her, signaling her to join me. She scans for a spot to sit, finding none except, perhaps, my lap.

She hesitates, then makes her way over. I pat my thigh invitingly. If Luke weren't caught up in his own banter, I'd have pulled Milli onto my lap without hesitation. Instead, I coax her with a playful, "Come on, Mills, I don't bite."

She edges closer, sipping her drink, her cheeks flushing a deeper shade. "I'm not so sure," she teases.

I raise an eyebrow. "Only if you ask me to."

Her reaction is instantaneous. She almost chokes on her drink, coughing and laughing simultaneously.

"Everything good?" I say, flashing a grin. With Luke out of my immediate concern, I draw her onto my lap. She shifts a bit, settling in. "Comfier now?" I tease, lifting an eyebrow.

As she takes another sip, Luke throws a glance our way but is quickly distracted. Milli, sensing his diverted attention, shifts boldly, her shapely curves moving from my thigh to the very center of my lap, and I can swear my cock jumps with excitement.

She wriggles a bit more, and I can tell she's doing it deliberately because when she glances over her shoulder, the mischief in her eyes gives it all away. She's teasing me, clearly enjoying herself. What she doesn't realize is that I'm more than willing to play along. It brings back memories of our time at the restaurant months ago.

I tighten my grip around her waist, and she startles, but I keep her in place.

I'm acutely aware we're skirting the edge of something dangerous, but it's thrilling. "Everything okay?" I ask her, keeping my voice light. She's still facing the fire, but I can almost feel her effort to stay silent. Part of me wishes she wouldn't—I know what sounds she's holding back.

The echo of her moan, lingering in my ears from before, ignites a tingling sensation across my skin. It's a memory that's been on a loop in my mind, refusing to fade.

"Okay, friends, gather up. Let's play a game!" Payson declares, her voice ringing out, red solo cup in hand, basking in the bonfire's glow.

Luke gives an exaggerated eye roll, briefly locking eyes with me. He mouths, "Friends?" I stifle a chuckle. Milli, catching his reaction, laughs out loud for both of us.

Turning back to Payson, Luke teases, "Is there ever a time you're not game for games, Pennington?"

Payson shoots a glare at Luke and flips him off, undeterred. "Let's kick things up a notch with a round of truth or dare," she announces, her enthusiasm undimmed by Luke's sarcasm.

"We're not kids," he grumbles, but the others are already showing interest.

Payson smirks at Luke. "Not just any game—Dirty Truth or Dare."

The suggestion rouses a mix of cheers and chuckles.

Leaning toward Milli, I whisper so only she can hear. "You game for this, Baby Sutton?"

For a moment, she tenses, but soon she melts into the warmth of my breath. Her smirk tells me everything—I know she's more than okay with it.

"Since when do you enjoy such games, Mills?" I can't quite figure out if this daring side of her is going to be my undoing or not.

Payson claps excitedly. "Here's the twist: truths have to be intimate or risqué, and dares, well, they should be bold and flirtatious."

Intrigued, I settle in. The first few rounds bring out some eyebrow-raising confessions. But as we dive deeper, the mood shifts. It's my turn to ask, and naturally, my choice is Milli. The way she's been tonight, I'm betting she'll be bluntly honest or her body language will reveal everything. Sipping my beer, I mull over my question, opting for truth over dare, mindful of Luke's watchful eye.

"Mills, what's one fantasy of yours?" I lean in, my voice low but clear enough for her. Our gazes meet, and she catches her lip between her teeth, igniting a surge of desire within me. "Come on, Baby Sutton, those romance novels must've sparked some wild ideas."

I'm using every bit of self-control not to draw her in, to thread my fingers through her strawberry blonde curls, to trail them down to the nape of her neck. The urge to press my lips to hers, to let our bodies merge into one in that electrifying moment, is almost overpowering.

Stay cool, Miles, I tell myself.

Her reply, "Getting fucked in a truck," sends my self-control into overdrive to maintain composure. The group erupts into hoots and hollers, with Josh, Brooke's boyfriend, even cheering, "Hell yeah." The tension thickens, her words hanging in the air like a charged, unspoken invitation.

"Why the truck fantasy?" Payson quiets some of the team-mates with a gesture, her curiosity directed at Milli.

Milli shrugs, casual but thoughtful. "It's the thrill of the unexpected, the intimacy of being in close quarters, and the adrenaline from doing something bold."

Luke grimaces. "Milli, I don't need to hear this."

"Relax, Sutton. She's in college. Let her have her fantasies," Payson chides.

"And don't forget the thrill of possibly getting caught," one of my teammates adds, egging her on. But I'm barely paying attention to the banter. My focus is entirely on Milli, feeling her body pressed against mine. Luke's concerns about our closeness seem irrelevant right now. From where he's sitting, across the flames, he can't see everything.

"Alright, my turn," Brooke pipes up, leaning in to kiss Josh. His encouraging words, "Go for it, babe," barely registers with me. Just then, Milli leans in closer, her breath mingling with mine, her eyes a mesmerizing swirl of green and blue. "They didn't let me finish that fantasy," she murmurs, her voice a tantalizing whisper.

My eyebrow arches in surprise.

"Getting fucked in a Chevy CK," she confesses, her gaze intense and inviting. The bonfire's flicker in her eyes adds a layer of depth to her words.

Holy shit, she's serious. I'm momentarily speechless; my mind reeling from her bold admission.

Brooke's voice cuts through the tension. "I dare Miles to kiss Milli."

A new round of cheers erupts, but I barely have time to react before Luke intervenes. "That's enough. I'm not watching this."

"Lighten up, Sutton. It's just a game," Payson says.

"It's not just a game. It's your excuse for us to cross lines," Luke counters, his tone hardening.

Payson smirks. "Scared of a little dirty play, Sutton?"

Luke lets out a sigh, the air around him practically vibrating with frustration. The tension between them is palpable, hinting at an impending clash. Despite the distraction their disagreement provides, I can't help but mourn the interrupted moment with Milli.

"I'm not scared of playing dirty, Pennington," Luke retorts, his voice firm with challenge. The group's attention is now on their brewing standoff.

"Prove it," Payson challenges, her grin tinged with mischief.

I lean in toward Milli, whispering, "What do you think is about to go down?" Her fingers intertwine with mine on my thigh, a gentle reminder of the tension between us, a tension I'm struggling to keep in check.

She leans in to whisper, "Definitely something's up. Payson's got that gleam in her eye, the one that screams trouble's on the way."

As Luke moves closer to Payson, there's a shift in the atmosphere. The crowd around us starts chanting, echoing those teenage games of daring. Payson and Luke, caught in their own world, seem to forget everyone else.

"Do you even know what 'playing dirty' means?" Payson goads him.

Luke steps closer, towering just above her. Yet, despite her smaller frame, she remains unflinching. "Why don't you spell it out for me?" he retorts.

In a sudden move, they kiss—a fierce, passionate kiss that seems to stop time. It's intense and unapologetically bold, drawing gasps from some of my teammates.

Milli groans. "Okay, that's enough." As if on cue, they part, both looking slightly stunned by their own audacity.

The game continues, but the mood shifts back to a more casual tone. The crowd grows as more friends join, including

Cam. His surprised look at seeing Milli in my lap barely registers with me. I'm too caught up in the moment—Milli curled against me, her head on my chest, enveloped in a blanket.

Being this close just feels natural, like a glimpse of what could be. Luke hasn't said anything about us being this intimate. To him, maybe it's just friendly comfort. But to me, it's more. It's the warmth of her against me, our entwined fingers, a tender touch that feels like coming home.

Milli has been my steadfast support, particularly through my ordeal with cancer. Her constant presence was a guiding light in those bleak periods. *"We'll tackle it together,"* she consistently assured me.

Now, as she looks up to lock eyes with me, her soft, "Thank you, Miles," resonates with immense gratitude, highlighting the strength of our connection. In this instant, all else dims into the background.

As she lets go of my hands to encircle my waist with a comforting hug, I murmur gently, "What for, Mills?"

Her smile wraps around my heart like a warm hug, easing that unique tightness she alone can cause. "For everything, but especially for persuading me to be here tonight. After such a tough week, this . . . it's exactly what I needed."

Before I can respond, she yawns, the fatigue of the day evident. She snuggles her head back against my chest, her voice soft and reflective. "I can't believe I was so close to picking a different college than my best friend."

Best Friend.

That term strikes a chord deep within me, almost like the universe knew I needed that wake-up call. Softly, I plant a kiss atop her head, pulling her into a firm hug. "Yeah, me too, Mills," I whisper back.

CHAPTER 11
MILLI

Go big or go home, right?

The next two weeks are a whirlwind of activity. Between classes, perfecting a new dance routine for the upcoming home game, helping out the Hanmann sisters, and adjusting to my new role as a tutor, time flies. However, the "mystery" senior I am supposed to tutor still hasn't shown up. It seems odd to me—if I were in their shoes, I'd be all over arranging sessions, especially if I was a senior struggling in a freshman class. But then again, not everyone operates like I do.

"Finally, our monthly margarita night is back!" Brooke exclaims, her voice tinged with nostalgia for our high school tradition. Since freshman year, we've had these DIY margarita nights, always timed for when our parents were out. It was our little secret indulgence.

"RIGHT?!" Payson's voice is loud with excitement as she settles onto her bed. I'm lounging in my egg chair, while Brooke makes herself comfortable on my bed, forming a cozy circle.

"I still can't believe we skipped it last month," Payson says, and I feel the same. Skipping our monthly margs is unusual for us, but we had all agreed to focus on settling into our new routines first. Now, with October rolling in and Halloween around the corner, we decide to spice things up with a Spooky Citrus Margarita. And it's a hit.

"This is amazing," Brooke declares.

I laugh and raise my glass. "Definitely a 20 out of 10 on this one."

"We're like the perfect team," Payson muses. "I'm the tequila, Brooke's the lime juice, and Milli, you're the orange juice. Separately unique, but together, we're a killer combo."

I can't help but smile. "Why am I orange juice, though?"

Payson takes a sip of her margarita, grinning. "Because orange juice is sweet, just like you, Milli Sutton."

Our banter is interrupted by the TV announcer's voice. "Let's appreciate the Panthers' strong start this season."

Payson groans. "Football on margarita night?"

"Well, I can't make it to the game to cheer them on—it being an away one and all," I explain. "This is the next best way to show my support."

"Can we at least turn it down?" Payson asks, and I quickly agree. The constant talk about the season and NFL draft picks is starting to encroach on our girls' night vibe. Sure, I should probably be more invested, considering Luke and Miles' prospects, but missing out on the game chatter for one evening won't hurt.

After we turn the volume down, our chat drifts from football to more personal topics. We spend the hour catching up on recent happenings, not just the usual high school and family updates. Payson has us in stitches with her story about her RA duties, especially the part about walking in on a freshman in a compromising situation. We all knew Payson's time as an RA would be filled with such weird and funny encounters.

Then Brooke surprises us with her news—she's joined a

sorority. Payson and I are taken aback; it is so unlike her. But she explains how a chat with a classmate led her to try it out, and now she is part of Aurora Theta Gamma, known for their charity work. It seems like a perfect fit for her.

When I mention my new tutoring role, Payson and Brooke exchange looks that say, "We knew you'd do it." Our conversation then shifts to our classes and coursework.

"So, he's in your stats class?" Payson asks, refilling our margaritas. The drinks are hitting the spot, the tequila making its presence felt.

"Yeah, he's either retaking it or left it for his senior year," I speculate.

Brooke chimes in, saying she had the option to take it later, too, but Payson quickly changes the subject.

"So, when are you and Miles going official?" she blurts out.

I roll my eyes, taking a sip of my drink. Clearly, her curiosity traces back to the bonfire night. Just thinking about that evening, Miles' touch, his kisses on my forehead—god, I crave more of it.

I shoot back playfully, "What about you kissing my brother, huh?" I want to flip the script a bit.

Brooke spits out her drink, laughing. Payson tries to deny it, but her blush says otherwise.

"You did enjoy it," Brooke teases.

Payson huffs. "I just made him back up his words."

"You looked pretty keen on his 'words'," I quip, earning more laughter from Brooke.

Their kiss was unexpected; they are so alike but can't stand each other. I steer our chat to our upcoming plans, including the Halloween party—our first in college.

Before I know it, our margarita night is winding down and all I want is to cap the night off with a shower, even though I miss my nightly baths dearly. Back home, it was my favorite routine—homework, a relaxing bath, and then slipping into bed with a romance book.

The sound of the shower kicks in, the warm water working its magic on my tired dance-sore muscles. As I stand under the steam, my phone pings on the bathroom counter. Without another thought, I open the shower door, sneak to the sink, grab my phone, and make a mad dash back to the shower—phone and all.

Kill me, why don't you?

Leaning my head against the tiled wall, I unlock my phone to find a few new messages.

> **LUKE**
>
> Better wish me luck.

> **MOM**
>
> Hey, sweetie, how's everything? Call me when you get the chance.

> **MILES**
>
> We just freaking kicked Thunderhawks' ass. Did you see my last throw to JJ? And #50 thought it would be cool to kick me in the freaking head without a helmet?

"Wait, he got kicked in the head? Is he okay?!" I questioned aloud in concern.

Milli, he's fine. He's texting you, isn't he?

"Yeah, I'm sure he is," I answer, feeling a bit relieved, but a pang of guilt strikes me. I hadn't watched a single second of the game as I was immersed in my girls' night. Despite that, I need to make sure he is alright without appearing overly concerned. Miles has a habit of accusing me of babying him at times, but honestly, the guy has given me more than enough reasons to worry about him.

When he fell off our four-wheeler, when he broke his thumb playing badminton (don't even ask how), or that time he came running into our house in tears after a tough day with chemo.

"Milli, Luke, Milli, Luke!" someone yelled from downstairs. I thought it was Mendy, our nanny, returning for something she forgot. But then I heard it again, sounding more urgent this time. I quickly left my book and jumped out of my chair. Opening my bedroom door, I heard the cries growing more frantic. "Milli, Luke, where are you? I need you."

It was Miles.

I shut my bedroom door and dashed to the big staircase, looking down to find him. His face was worried, and there was blood on the tissue he held against his nose. It was his first day of chemotherapy, something he talked about the night before. I thought we might not see him for a while, as his parents and nurse said he might not feel well for a few days. But seeing him with his voice weak and his eyes asking for help was really scary.

Without thinking twice, I rushed down the staircase, taking two steps at a time until I was in front of him.

"Milli," he said, sounding strained. "I-I don't feel good," he continued, reaching out to me with a shaky hand.

I quickly grabbed his cold, sweaty hand with mine and gave it a gentle squeeze. "I'm here, Miles. What can I do for you?" I asked softly, feeling sad to see him hurting.

"I don't know," he said, his nose still bleeding. "I suddenly got dizzy, and then my nose started bleeding."

"Okay, let's clean you up and get you sitting down," I told him, leading him to a nearby couch. I grabbed a bunch of tissues from the coffee table and started wiping his nose.

While I helped him, I noticed how much weight he'd lost in the last few weeks. His cheeks, which used to be round, were sunken now. His eyes seemed tired and puffy, and his skin was pale and almost see-through.

"Thank you, Milli," Miles said, sounding a bit stronger.

The memory lingers as I return to the present, my phone chiming with new messages. The vivid recollection leaves me with goosebumps and a racing heart. That night had been one of the toughest, a memory etched deeply in my mind.

Shaking off the powerful flashback, I refocus on Brooke's message. She and Payson decided to hit a party. I don't feel like joining, but I send them well wishes and turn my attention to texting Miles.

MILLI

Wait, you got hit in the head, are you okay?

MILES

Yeah, all good, Baby Sutton.

MILLI

You sure? Need anything?

I let the water cascade over me, wondering if I am being too nosy or if he'll even reply.

MILES

Well, if you're offering to drive your sweet ass to Timberdale Junction for a massage and some Jack Reacher, then yeah.

His text brings a reluctant smile to my face, but also a flutter of something else when he mentions my "sweet ass."

Quickly, I type back.

MILLI

Big fan of those crime-solving adventures, huh, Sunshine?

But sorry, can't do that favor for you.

MILES

Don't hate on my shows. You watch them too.

> Why not? I'm your best friend, Mills.
> Shouldn't I be at the top of your favorite list?

His response makes me laugh. He knows I can't resist a good crime-solving show, even if it is just an excuse to spend time with him.

MILLI

> Right now, I'm busy doing a favor for myself.

MILES

> Now I'm intrigued. What's Milli Sutton's idea of self-care?

I grin, my thoughts drifting to my pink vibrator waiting in the drawer.

If only he knew.

But before I can respond, another message pops up.

MILES

> Let me guess.

This should be interesting. Miles usually has a knack for guessing my habits.

MILES

> A relaxing shower, a bowl of strawberry ice cream (because of your hair, obviously), and a good romance novel?

I laugh out loud. He is close, but not quite. The accuracy of his guess is endearing, though. It reminds me just how well he knows me, down to my favorite ice cream and reading habits.

MILES

> Or is it romance novels of the steamy variety these days? ;)

A giggle escapes me, nearly causing me to drop my phone in the shower.

I send a reply, the tequila lending me a dash of boldness.

MILLI

> Almost there, but not quite on point. I did opt for a hot shower, though I'm more of a bath person. And yeah, I might indulge in some strawberry ice cream later. But for the book, let's just say it's going to be a little more . . . spicy.

After hitting send, I feel a rush of nerves. What if he thinks I'm being too flirtatious? Suddenly, another message flashes on my phone.

MILES

> Alright, spicy, I like it. But spill the beans, Mills—what kind of spicy book are we talking about here?

> Is it one of those enemies-to-lovers stories? Or a fake relationship plot? Hey, maybe it's an F/F romance? Those can be pretty hot, not gonna lie.

Oh. My. God.

Chill, Milli, it's no biggie. He's just chatting.

I roll my eyes at my inner buzzkill, trying to mess up my vibe. Taking a breath, I keep typing, adding a bit more flirt than I'd usually risk.

MILLI

> And how exactly would you know they're hot, Sunshine?

> But to be clear, it's an F/M romance in a Mafia Forced Proximity Marriage. Let's just say, it's definitely not PG-13.

MILES

Let's just say I might have a clue ;) But sounds intriguing, maybe I should give it a read?

Definitely not. That's my boundary, firm and clear. The thought of Miles flipping through one of my spicy romance novels? Unthinkable. I can practically hear the relentless ribbing I'd be subjected to. Nonetheless, his response draws a chuckle from me. Smiling, I type out my reply.

MILLI

I'll consider it. But only if you swear to return it intact.

MILES

I cross my heart and hope to die.

My heart flutters and does a little swooning dance at his words, imagining Miles, with all his charm and strength, making such a promise.

MILES

Are you reading your book now?

I take a moment, re-reading his message.

I mean, at this exact moment?

Don't do it, Milli.

But could it be just a harmless, friendly text?

My heart pounds with a mix of thrill and nervousness, overpowering my hesitation. In a spontaneous move, I capture a photo of my legs against the cold, tiled shower floor.

And yes, my ass is sitting on the cold tile with my bare legs. A girl can only endure the ache between her legs for so long.

I press send, but what if he doesn't appreciate it?

MILES

Baby Sutton. What am I looking at?

A laugh escapes me.

MILLI

I think my legs?

I imagine he can hear the playfulness in my reply.

MILES

Such fucking hot legs, Mills

My heart skips a beat.

MILES

So smooth.

Soft.

Long enough to wrap—

A blush spreads across my cheeks, and it's not from the steam of the shower.

Is he flirting or just teasing me?

MILLI

Sunshine, you admiring my legs?

Dealing with this side of Miles is challenging. I'm constantly torn between enjoying our flirtatious exchanges and fearing it might mean nothing. It's an emotional whirlwind.

MILES

Absolutely, especially after that pic.

This whole situation is a wild step out of my comfort zone, yet it's electrifying, like I'm more alive than ever. It's a thrill that surpasses even the rush I get from my romance novels.

Visions of being with him begin to overwhelm my thoughts—his body close against mine, our hearts pulsing together, catching glimpses of his face at the height of passion. My heart races with a fervor I've never known.

MILES

Mills . . .

His message breaks into my daydream.

But what should I say? "Thanks for the compliment? I know my legs are great. Want to come test them out?"

I close my eyes, wrestling between my heart's longing and my mind's caution.

I should end this now before it spirals. Yet, how can I possibly do that when just his words ignite a warmth inside me, intensifying with each moment? I bite down on my inner cheek, my body alight with nerves. This is new, yet with Miles, it feels strangely safe. Comforting, even?

I type, my fingers quivering.

MILLI

Do you want to see more?

Go big or go home, right?

The wait for his reply seems endless, with my heart pounding. Is it our usual banter, our deeper moments, or the margaritas speaking? Whatever it is, I'm all in, embracing the now.

MILES

Milli, did Payson grab your phone?

I burst out laughing, a real, deep laugh, and then . . . oh no.

I glance down. A tiny yellow splash on the shower floor.

Did I just . . . ? Isn't that a post-childbirth thing, laughing too hard and . . . ?

I press a hand over my mouth, trying to contain my laughter. Who even does that?

I shrug it off. It'll just wash away, right?

Back to the messages. A picture? A text?

Miles probably has tons of options, and his experience? Probably vast.

Me? One awkward time with Zachary Patel, Chess Club president. Not exactly a high bar.

Taking a deep breath, I embrace this new college Milli, stepping out of my comfort zone. So what if it's with Miles Chasen? Friends help friends, right?

I stand up quickly, turning off the shower, grabbing a towel. I dry off, leaving my breasts slightly damp. If I'm sending a picture, they need to look their best.

Friends, Milli. Just friends.

But right now, I'm exploring. And that's okay.

Discarding my towel, I stand before the mirror, taking in my reflection. The scar just above my hip bone is a memento from rough football games with Miles and Luke. My fingers trace over it, a reminder of carefree days. I weigh the heft of my B-cup breasts in my hands, their bounce modest but enticing, the pink nipples yearning for a touch.

My gaze drifts to the drawer, the one whispering a tempting shortcut to release. But I resist, choosing instead my coconut-scented bedtime lotion. Originally meant for a soothing pre-sleep ritual, tonight it serves a different purpose.

I look at my body, reminding myself, "Friends."

Yet, I can't deny my own appearance. My dancer's physique, hard-earned and now a source of pride, catches my eye. My hands glide over my belly, a brief caress over my clit, a teasing promise of what could be. A moment of hesitation:

the vibrator, a solitary but effective relief, or continue this tantalizing exchange with Miles?

Choosing the latter, I revel in the thought of leaving him wanting more.

Comfort zone: 0 / New Milli: 1

Decision made, I reach for the razor and shaving cream. It's been a while, but I'm ready to channel my inner Nicki Minaj. Leaning over the sink, I carefully shave, the razor whispering across my skin. I imagine Miles waiting, wondering. The thrill of keeping him in suspense is sort of exhilarating.

After tidying up, I flash a grin at my reflection. Okay, I look . . . good.

MILLI

You're getting the best view, I hope you know.

MILES

Baby Sutton, I already knew that.

Empowered, I grab my cream white lace robe and approach the full-length mirror. I slip it on, initially to cover up, but then impulsively let the straps fall. The robe opens, revealing one leg entirely, the other partially hidden, a glimpse of my bikini line teasing the eye. My cleavage peeks out, nipples reacting to the cool breeze.

I know it's undoubtedly sexy, revealing more than I'm usually comfortable with, but not so much as to scare him away.

Doubtful, Milli.

Well, a girl's gotta take a shot, right?

Taking a leap of faith, I capture the moment in a photo. It takes me a full thirty minutes to gather the courage to send it.

MILLI

How's the new robe look?

My lips catch nervously between my teeth.

MILES

Fuck, is that supposed to be a robe?

You enjoying this, aren't you, Mills?

His reply has me unconsciously tracing my lips with my tongue.

I suppose, in a way . . . It's refreshing to be on this side of the dynamic. Typically, it's him who's doing the teasing and getting under my skin.

MILLI

Just a little.

MILES

God . . . you look fucking hot.

His words hit me, and I'm looking in the mirror again, eyes fixed on my perky breasts, feeling a surge of empowerment. My fingers graze my nipples, feeling them respond instantly.

I see an attachment with his message.

MILES

Hope this counts as teasing?

I brace myself, expecting—

Feet? I squint, narrowing my eyes to make sure I'm seeing what I think I am. There I am, staring at a photo of his freaking feet, nonchalantly sprawled across a hotel bed.

Just then, my phone starts to ring. Who could be calling now?

Incoming call. NO, FACETIME . . .

My heart skips a beat.

Miles.

Why is he FaceTiming me?

Panic starts to seep into my veins, a familiar, unwelcome sensation. I close my eyes and focus on my breathing, just as my old tutor taught me for managing study stress. Inhale. Exhale. Inhale. Exhale. Gradually, the rhythm soothes the edges of my anxiety, a gentle reminder of the calming power of dance and controlled breathing.

I open my eyes, looking into the mirror. "This is for me," I tell my reflection. "For the new Milli." It's a mantra, a declaration of self-reinvention.

I accept the FaceTime call, and Miles fills the screen. His shirtless appearance catches me off guard; his chest is a sculpted canvas of strength, each muscle defined and perfect. I've seen him like this many times, but now it's different— more intimate, more intense. The small scar above his belly button draws my attention, a memory of him proudly showing off his "battle wound" to me and Luke. We thought he was invincible then, a real-life superhero.

His blue eyes meet mine, bright against the backdrop of his messy brown hair. He offers a smile, and it illuminates his entire face, his teeth shining brilliantly against his sun-kissed skin. The difference from his days undergoing chemotherapy is truly staggering. One wouldn't even know he had cancer as a child.

"Mills?" he says, his voice snapping me back from my thoughts.

I'm transfixed by him. I continue to ogle at his body as if my eyes could make him materialize through the phone, right into my bed, and certainly on top of me.

"Baby Sutton? You've got something right here," he says, pointing to his mouth.

Drool? My mind barely registers his gesture, lost in fantasies of kissing those lips, feeling their warmth on my skin.

He glances back into the camera as he runs his fingers through his hair. He lets out a breath. "Not that I'm one to complain about an amazing rack," he shakes his head, "fucking amazing view, but you might want to put those things away," he says as his eyes drop to my chest.

I suddenly realize the camera angle and notice he has a straight shot to my freaking . . . boobs.

Well, just one. It's literally halfway hanging out of my freaking robe. I must have been so nervous and panicky with him calling me that my boob was like, "Hey, Milli, if we are going to answer, let's give him a show, yeah?"

Definitely not. Sending flirty texts and pictures is a whole different game. Why? Because:

1. You're shielded by the anonymity of your phone.
2. You don't see the immediate reactions—his deep breaths, the arch of an eyebrow, or that tantalizing lip bite. There's no lip-licking to distract you.

Texting is silent. No words, no sounds, only text. There's no pressure to decode the meaning behind each message.

It's just you and your phone. No awkward silences, no immediate judgments.

Seeing my robe again in the camera's frame, I quickly attempt to rearrange it. What was I thinking, daring to go this far? A wave of heat floods my cheeks. I'm aware I shouldn't be feeling self-conscious, yet I'm suddenly swamped with a sense of being too exposed.

I scold myself internally. I can't believe I had the audacity.

It's good for you, Milli, I try to reassure myself.

Miles is chuckling, a look of genuine admiration in his eyes. "God, Mills, you're so fucking beautiful."

His statement halts me mid-step. Did he really just say that? Aloud? And to me? I pull my robe tighter, a half-hearted gesture toward modesty. As our gazes lock once more, he lifts his hands, gesturing playfully for me to stop. "No, no, no, don't do that. I like what I see," he says.

The way his gaze lingers on me is intoxicating, and for a moment, I revel in it. "Mmhm, I bet you do, Sunshine," I retort. Shifting my position, I lie down on my bed, making sure the camera angle reveals nothing more.

"Sorry, that's exclusive content," I tease.

"And how does one gain access to such exclusivity?" he asks, a sparkle in his eyes.

"Sorry," I respond with a nonchalant shrug, "the member-ship fee is pretty steep."

He grins, confidence oozing from his reply. "Don't worry, I'm quite the expert at gaining access. Shouldn't be a problem for me."

My eyes drop to my bed, my cheeks probably blazing red, breaking the intense lock our gazes had. The suggestive undertone in his words sends a tremor through me, kindling a heat deep inside. I scold myself in my head—I may have initiated this flirtatious dance, but his bold remarks are knocking me off my feet.

"What's up with the selfie, Mills?" he inquires, pulling me back to reality. I ought to be cringing in mortification, yet, strangely, I find myself unaffected by embarrassment.

"Because I wanted to. Got an issue with that?" I retort, trying to sound casual.

He leans back, laughter resonating in a deep, masculine timbre. "Absolutely not. More, please."

I lift an eyebrow. "That's not happening, Sunshine."

He mirrors my gesture. "Oh, really? Why not?"

I shrug again, feigning indifference, and he just chuckles. "Okay, okay, I appreciate what I get."

A smile dances briefly on my lips. Miles clears his throat, and I blurt out without thinking, "Are you feeling okay? How's your head? I'm sorry I didn't check in earlier. Got caught up with the girls; margarita night. Time just flew. I totally missed the game."

He grins as I ramble on. "It was on TV, so I guess that counts, right? Caught some of the commentary—"

"Mills, relax, I'm all good. Look," he interjects, abruptly standing and twirling like a ballerina, then flopping back down. His lightheartedness sparks laughter, his effortless charm shining through.

Despite his reassurances, the worry for Miles' well-being lingers. After all the times he's shrugged off injuries, especially ones as risky as a head hit without a helmet, it's hard not to be concerned.

"Should've pointed those toes, Miles," I tease, trying to keep the mood light.

He responds with a chuckle, "I know, I know. A mistake, coming from a ballerina/hip hop pro like you. Shame on me." His tone is playfully self-deprecating. Relief washes over me. I was afraid this conversation would veer into serious territory, but Miles has this knack for keeping things easygoing and fun.

We're both just sprawled out on our beds, eyes glued to our phones, enveloped in a silence that doesn't bother me. Yet, something's shifted since I stepped out of the shower, a restlessness creeping in that's anything but familiar. My night was supposed to follow a well-worn path, a soothing routine that never fails, but now . . . now, this has thrown me off course.

It's funny, isn't it? How life throws you these wild, unpredictable moments.

I'm just about to fill the silence when a sudden commotion on his end catches my attention.

"Hey, Chasen!"

"Dude, why are you lounging in your hotel bed?"

The same question nudges at my thoughts. After any match, but more so after one on foreign turf, I've heard stories of their wild celebrations. Seeing him here, instead of living it up with his team or, at the very least, with Luke, throws me off a bit. Though, selfishly, I'm glad for it; it means more time with Miles for me.

"Yeah, you're our mentor, remember?" I hear Cam's voice, dripping with sarcasm.

I shake my head, a chuckle escaping me. His trio of troublemakers has just gatecrashed our moment.

Miles yawns, but it's a facade. I can tell. Years of harboring a crush turns you into a keen observer. I've watched him enough to know his genuine smiles from his forced ones, his real yawns from his fake.

"Dude, who's he talking to?" Devon's voice cuts in.

"Wait, is that a video call?" Gunner adds.

"No way, he's on a video call," Cam states, and I can almost picture his eyes stretching wide in surprise.

The phone shakes in Miles' hand, his voice tinged with nervousness. Clearly, his friends are trying to sneak a peek. I bite my lip to hold back laughter.

Miles clears his throat. "None of your business." He waves them off. "Now get out of my room. Wait, how did you even get in here? You don't have a key."

Keys jingle. "That's because I let them in, you douchebag."

That voice—I recognize it instantly.

Luke.

"What the hell, Chasen? You got a girl over there?"

"Something like that . . . " Miles mutters, so quietly it's almost just for me.

I shut my eyes tight, hoping beyond hope that Luke doesn't see me on the call. It's not that it's a huge deal, but more about the curiosity it might spark. Why is Miles on a FaceTime call with me, rather than out with the team?

Miles shrugs at his friends, playing it cool. "Maybe I do, maybe I don't."

The room erupts with their hooting and cheers.

"Oh, he definitely does."

"Go for it, dude."

"Who's the lucky lady tonight?"

I roll my eyes. Could they be more obnoxious?

And just like that, they remind of who Miles really is—always the center of attention, especially with women. I inhale deeply, trying to steady the fluttering in my chest. I feel this twinge of jealousy imagining him with other women, but I push it away. We're just friends.

"So, what's the plan tonight, guys?" Miles brings me back into the moment.

"Just the usual," Cam replies, with Luke adding, "Heard the coach gave Dorren the keys to a suite, told us to not go 'too' hard."

I smile, partly enjoying being on this side of their plans. I'd have thought they'd be reprimanded for such antics at an away game, but Coach Kraft seems more lenient than I expected, as long as they don't overdo it, I assume.

Miles nods. "Sounds like Coach. But I'll pass tonight."

"What?" they all exclaim. "You can't bail on us now."

"Sorry, guys, I've got . . . stuff"—his eyes flicker to the camera, meeting mine—"to take care of."

The room falls silent as his friends digest Miles' words. I can sense their confusion, the unspoken questions hanging in the air.

"Things?" Luke probes, a note of suspicion in his voice.

Miles pauses, and I can almost feel the tension radiating

through the phone. He takes a deep breath before saying, "Just some personal stuff I need to sort out."

Is it possible that he is dealing with something he hasn't mentioned to me?

Then again, I have to remind myself he's not obligated to share everything. But it stings a bit. I'd hoped the openness we had as kids would endure as we grew older. But then he went off to college, and our paths diverged. Our occasional check-ins felt hollow, leaving me longing for the closeness we once shared. Now, with college bringing us back into each other's orbits, I'd hoped for . . . more. Yet, here I am, feeling just as distant.

There's a pause, then Devon chimes in, "Gotcha, man. 'Personal' means private."

"Yeah, was kinda hoping you'd hang with us tonight, what with Panthers' Day coming up and all," Cam adds, his youthful naivety showing.

I roll my eyes. Cam, a *freshman*, doesn't know the half of it. Panthers' Day isn't a walk in the park. Miles shakes his head, slightly exasperated. "Guys, the season's no joke. We discussed this, remember?" His tone carries a hint of frustration, a mentor trying to instill some seriousness in his team.

Cam's retort is quick. "Hey, cut me some slack. It's my first year, just trying to enjoy it, you know?"

There's a flicker of understanding in Miles' eyes, a softening of some sort. "Yeah, I get it. Just don't show up hungover tomorrow, okay?"

The guys promise in unison, their camaraderie clear. Miles' usual, easygoing self reemerges as he jokes about their playing skills. The laughter is genuine, a moment of light-hearted banter before they sign off.

Finally, it's just me and Miles again.

But then Luke's voice breaks through. "You sure you're okay, man?"

I hesitate, wondering if I should end the call. But then I think, what if Miles really needs someone right now? Isn't that what friends are for?

I decide to stay, silently hoping Luke doesn't notice me.

Miles exhales heavily. "Yeah, I just need some time to myself tonight."

Luke's skepticism is evident. "You sure? You can talk to me, you know."

I find myself holding my breath, waiting for Miles' response. This is it—a glimpse into the personal side of Miles I've been missing.

As Miles hesitates, I recognize that look—a mix of internal struggle and reluctance. It's a look I've seen before, one that tells me there's more beneath the surface he's not ready to share. "Nothing to worry about, just personal stuff," he finally says, but the silence that follows tells me Luke isn't entirely convinced.

"Alright, but you know you can always talk to me, or Milli, right?" Luke's offer hits me unexpectedly hard.

What was I thinking, flirting with Miles like that? I'm supposed to be his steadfast friend, not someone blurring lines in a risky game.

Good luck keeping that boundary, Milli, my mind mocks me.

Miles acknowledges Luke's offer with his usual confident grin. "Thanks, man. Appreciate it."

Luke leaves, and we're alone again.

"Sorry about that," Miles says, a hint of sheepishness in his voice.

I force a casual shrug. "It's okay. Luke's my brother, after all. I'm used to it." But as he absentmindedly scratches his head, his muscles flexing, I find myself momentarily distracted.

Stay focused, Milli. Just . . . focus.

Miles' voice breaks through my thoughts, uncertain. "Guess I should let you go?"

I'm suddenly aware of the intensity of our earlier interaction, and I start pacing, phone in hand. "Yeah, we should probably end this call. And, uh, keep this between us, right?" I laugh nervously.

As my cheeks flush with embarrassment, I accidentally drop my phone. From the floor, Miles' voice floats up. "Mills, uh, you do realize I can see quite the view from here . . . "

I freeze, mortified.

Miles chuckles, trying to lighten the mood. "Relax, baby."

Baby? Since when did he drop Sutton?

My heart races as I pick up the phone, my voice barely a whisper. "I'm sorry. I don't know what came over me."

Miles' face softens on the screen. "Hey, it's okay. We were just having a bit of fun, right? Nothing wrong with that. We're adults."

But can it really just be "fun"?

"Thanks," I say, trying to sound reassured. "I just don't want things to get weird between us."

He nods, his eyes warm and understanding. "It won't get weird, Mills. We're friends."

I force a smile, agreeing, "Friends."

But as I hang up and collapse onto my bed, my mind is a whirlpool of uncertainty. How do we go back to being just friends after something like this? How do I just pretend I didn't nearly expose myself to my best friend?

Milli, the goal is simple: stay casual, no entanglements, no drama. Just two friends engaging in ordinary conversation about the day-to-day.

It should be straightforward, right?

CHAPTER 12
MILES

The Giving Tree

Yes, Mom, I'm here. Though it's more like I've been strong-armed into it. And yeah, I'll fill you in on what the doc says.

My thumbs fly across the screen, conveying my annoyance at being here, yet acknowledging her concern—all the while trying to mask the unease twisting in my gut about what my doctor might say. Being here, year after year, feels like a never-ending cycle. But, if something were wrong, I'd know, wouldn't I?

Miles, you've been feeling off, remember?

Ignoring that nagging thought, my phone pings with another message from my mom.

I know, sweetie, but you never go this long without seeing Dr. Reynolds. I just wanted to make sure you didn't forget.

Forget? I'm not sure that's possible; it's always on my

mind. Just because I've beaten cancer in the past doesn't mean those memories, appointments, and everything else aren't etched into my brain. Honestly, if it weren't for my own mother's constant texts, I might not be here just because it adds to those so-called memories.

MILES

> Yeah, I understand, Mom, and I appreciate your concern. I've just been pushing myself really hard with studies and football, leaving little time for proper rest and hydration, so it's been on the back burner.

> But hey, I'm here now. So, all good.

MOTHER DEAR

> Okay, baby, just keep me posted, please. Dad's also eager to know. So, don't wait too long to update us about any news.

MILES

> Always do, Mom.

I reassure her with a quick text, punctuating our conversation with a digital goodbye. I pocket my phone; a knot of apprehension tightens in my chest as I think about Dad. His priorities are skewed, obsessing over my ability to stay in the game rather than my well-being. It's always, "Can he play? Panthers' Day is a big deal this year. Everything for him hinges on this season." His focus isn't on my health; it's on whether I can keep throwing passes, keep scoring touchdowns, as if my career is the only thing that defines me.

Placing my phone on my lap, I glance at the nurse in front of me, sporting her stethoscope. She's checking the vitals of the patient seated next to me. It's a new week, Wednesday to be exact, and there's quite a crowd of patients. Busy day, if you ask me, but then again, dealing with cancer, it's not uncommon to see this many patients.

I'm not exactly a patient, but sitting here among these cancer patients feels quite similar. The routine is all too familiar. The reminder calls from the doctors every year at the same time. Then various tests on different days. A physical examination, vitals, blood tests, imaging studies, and sometimes an endoscopy, but not this year.

I glance over my shoulder and spot a little girl, about six or seven years old, smiling up at me. Her smile doesn't quite match her eyes, a mixture of happiness and sadness. She's clearly putting on a brave face, given what she's going through. She has a head wrap and wears a child-sized hospital gown.

"What are you reading over there?" I ask, nodding toward the book in her hand.

Her smile transforms into a genuine one, perhaps excited to have someone to talk to. I understand that feeling; I've been there. I was always desperate for a conversation with someone other than my nurses or doctors. My parents were constantly in and out of my room. I remember countless times sitting in this very chair, hoping to meet someone around my age who I could just hang out with. I longed to feel normal, if only for a day. So, I can imagine that this little girl is in a very similar situation.

She hands me her book, and I look down to see it's *The Giving Tree* by Shel Silverstein. I smile at her and ask, "One of my favorites. What's your favorite part?"

Looking up at me with big, bright eyes, she says, "When the tree gives the boy her trunk to make a boat. It's so kind and selfless."

I offer a soft smile and hand the book back to her. "You're absolutely right. That is a great part. You know, when I was in the hospital, my favorite book was *Matilda* by Roald Dahl. Have you ever read that one?"

Her eyes light up, and she shakes her head excitedly.

"No, but I've heard of it! Will you read it to me?" Her words tumble out in a rush of excitement, and before I can even nod, she's off like a shot toward the front desk, her voice trailing behind her as she requests the book. A chuckle escapes me, watching her energy infuse the room with life. I scoot my chair closer to hers, ready for our impromptu reading session.

There's a gentle hum in the air, the kind that comes from the quiet bustle of a hospital. As I settle in, I notice the nurse, a regular fixture in this world of white walls and beeping machines, approaching. She's here to assist the little girl, her movements practiced and gentle as she connects the IVs to her tiny arm. Our eyes meet for a moment, and her smile, warm and appreciative, speaks volumes. It's a silent exchange, a thank you for a moment of normalcy in a place often devoid of it.

Opening the book, I begin to read, my voice a steady rhythm in the hushed room. There's a strange comfort in the act, a soothing balm not just for her, but for me too. Hospitals have always been a source of anxiety for me, a fact I don't often admit. But here, in this small bubble of a world, with a story unfolding between us, that anxiety begins to ebb away.

Her reaction is immediate and heartwarming. As her smile grows and her eyes sparkle with the magic of the tale, it's like watching the sun break through clouds. It's a simple, fleeting moment, but it's enough. Enough to make my own troubles, my own fears, seem distant and less daunting.

As the final words of the story hang in the air, my regular nurse, Kins, appears. "Miles, you're up," she calls, her voice a familiar anchor in this sea of uncertainty. Standing, I turn to the little girl. "I'm Miles, by the way."

Her response is a hug, a small, warm presence against my leg. "I'm Harper," she says, her voice a soft melody of newfound friendship.

I respond with a playful nose boop, her laughter a bright note in the sterile environment. "Maybe we can read together again?" I suggest. Her tight hug is an enthusiastic yes.

As I follow Kins out, the memory of Harper's smile lingers, a reminder of the small joys that can be found even here. The hospital, with its endless corridors and pervasive scent of antiseptics, has been a backdrop to much of my life. It's a place of memories, some sharp with pain, others soft with moments like today.

Walking to my appointment, I remind myself, *Just a routine check-up, Miles.* It's a mantra, a way to push back against the tide of what ifs that always seem to accompany these visits. The hospital never changes, the same rooms, the same machines, each visit a mix of the familiar and the unnerving.

Dr. Reynolds, my doctor, and in many ways, my inspiration for pursuing medicine, greets me with a kind smile. He notes my missed appointment, but I brush it off. Football practice, a constant in my life, sometimes clashes with these necessary check-ins. Kins, always observant, gives me a look, but it's the truth. Football might not be my forever, but it's a part of me, a bridge between the past and my future in medicine.

As Kins takes my vitals, the brief sting of the needle is a sharp reminder of past struggles, of treatments, and fears.

"How are you feeling?" Dr. Reynolds asks, pulling me back from the edge of those memories.

"I'm good," I reply, the words a shield against the past. "No pain, no symptoms."

You sure about that, Miles? The question, unspoken but loud in my mind, echoes with doubt. I mentally shush the intrusive thoughts, focusing on the present.

Dr. Reynolds looks up from his clipboard, his expression a blend of professional concern and genuine interest. "That's great to hear. And how's your senior year of football going?"

A proud smile naturally finds its way across my face. "We're off to a solid start. The team's really coming together this year."

He mirrors my smile, a sign of shared happiness. "I'm glad to hear that." Standing, he returns the chair to its spot and gives Kins a nod. She squeezes my shoulder reassuringly before stepping out. We delve into the routine of the check-up, covering everything from my physical condition to any concerns since the last visit.

I'm upfront with him, mentioning the occasional headache from the rough football practices and reminding myself about the importance of hydration.

Dr. Reynolds doesn't let the hydration comment slide. He's stern yet caring as he emphasizes the need to look after my body. I listen, nodding in agreement. I know he's right.

His hand lands on my shoulder, a firm, grounding presence. "Miles, remember, you're a survivor, not invincible. Take care of yourself, all of you. And don't hesitate to reach out if you need help." His words are familiar, reminding me of the journey I've been on and the balance I need to maintain.

The check-up wraps up with him and he hands me a consent form for tomorrow's imaging tests. "Just routine," he reassures. I know the drill, but inside, a part of me tenses at the thought.

I force a tight smile, pocketing the form. "Thank you, Dr. Reynolds," I say, eager to step back into the flow of my everyday life. Football, studies, friends—they're all waiting.

Dr. Reynolds' serious look follows me. "Take care, Miles. And call if you need anything."

I nod, closing the door behind me; a ritualistic end to the visit.

Pulling out my phone, I quickly text my mom the update.

MILES

Everything's fine. Routine check-up.

The words feel hollow, a facade to mask the underlying fear, however small, of what might be.

As I turn to leave, Kins' hand on my shoulder stops me. She pulls me into a hug, a familiar and comforting embrace. In that moment, all the tension and worry dissolve. Her presence, her warmth, is like a shield against the world's uncertainties.

"It was nice to see you, Miles," she says, her voice radiating care. "Remember to take care of yourself, for your future patients' sakes."

I step back, surprised. "How did you . . . "

She laughs softly. "Miles Chasen, I've known you long enough to see your passion for medicine. And you'll be a great doctor. You've always had my support."

A wave of emotion washes over me. "Thanks, Kins," I manage to say. "That means everything to me." Her belief in me, in my dreams, adds another layer of strength to my resolve. It's moments like these that remind me of the support system I have, a foundation that keeps me grounded and hopeful for the future.

Even though I feel a bit exposed by how easily Kins can read me, I can't bring myself to be upset. There's a certain comfort in having someone who recognizes my dreams beyond the football field. I remember how she'd approach me after my dad made his football-centric comments. *"He's just looking out for you,"* she'd say, her voice laced with understanding. *"He loves you and wants the best for you."*

But I can't help questioning it sometimes. Is it really about what's best for me, or is it about what's best for my football career? These thoughts stir up a mix of emotions, a blend of gratitude and lingering irritation. Dad's words, meant to be encouraging, sometimes feel like they are boxing me in.

She gives me a gentle and knowing smile just as she says, "Now, go kick some ass at football practice. I'll see you tomorrow."

Returning her encouraging smile, I nod and begin my walk down the hallway, feeling a slight lift in my spirits. That's when Harper comes into view. I offer her a wave and, acting on a spontaneous urge, I make my way over to her. Crouching down to her level, I ask, "See you around?"

Her smile in response, radiant and brimming with joy, is utterly contagious. "Wait," she says, and I raise an eyebrow. She pulls out a Polaroid camera. "I like to snap a pic every day, to remember."

Her words send a jumble of feelings through me, a combination of warmth and an unexpected pang of vulnerability. But I keep those feelings tucked away, locked in a corner of my mind. I flash a grin, playing along. "Sure thing. I'd love to snap a picture."

And just like that, we capture a moment, our smiles wide and genuine. In that snapshot, we're just two people sharing a simple, happy moment, and for a brief time, it feels like everything in the world is damn great.

Pussy Panthers

CAM

Dude, Miles, what the fuck, why weren't you at practice today?

GUNNER

Yeah, man, we need our #1 QB.

DEVON

Boys, boys, settle down, he probably had some "personal" issues to take care of.

I silently shake my head, knowing full well Devon's hinting at my recent FaceTime call with Milli. Sure, it was personal, just like the reason for missing practice, but they don't need to know the details.

MILES

I know you missed me. I would miss me too.

CAM

Eyes Roll

Sighs deeply.

Dude, no need to boost your own damn ego. That's what women are for.

LUKE

Strongly agree with you on that Cam.

A grin sneaks onto my face, no matter how hard I try to keep it straight. Luke, well, he would agree. But, Cam? He's got a point, but really, I don't need girls fawning over me to feel good about myself. It's a nice ego boost, sure, and I'd be lying if I said I've never soaked it up whenever I could. But all the flattery from the girls at school? It's like water off a duck's back to me. There's only one girl who really gets to me, and she's off-limits.

I flop onto my bed, fresh from the shower, and flick open a new text.

MILES

Missing me, yet?

MILLS

As if, Sunshine.

Her sass leaps right off the screen, and damn, it makes me want to hear her voice. It used to be so easy, calling her up when I was in college and she was still in high school. But now? Times have changed. I feel it, this shift between us, subtle but undeniable. Still, I can't help myself; I need to hear her, especially with the stress of midterms and medical school applications.

My heart hammers a little as I dial her number, second-guessing my impulse. This is Milli's time to find herself, not to be tethered by my demanding need for her. But then her voice, sweet and familiar, flows through the line, calming the storm of my thoughts and quickening my pulse all at once.

"Sunshine, why on earth are you calling at . . . " Her voice fades into silence, and I can almost see her, casting a glance at the delicate gold watch on her wrist—a gift from me after my first game day. It was one of those special moments, with "Milli Girl" engraved on the inside, a nickname that holds weight only in our most tender moments.

"It's almost 10 o'clock," she finishes, her tone shifting as she closes a door, muffling other sounds.

"I just . . . wanted to hear your voice," I blurt out, feeling like a sap.

But then she softens. "Well, good because I wanted to hear yours, too."

We laugh, easing into a rhythm that feels both strange and familiar.

"This is weird, right? Talking like this when we're practically living in each other's pockets now," she says.

"Is that a bad thing?" I ask, a twinge of worry nipping at me, concerned that I might actually be bothering her.

"No, quite the opposite." She sighs, and I can almost see her smile. "It's comforting, like old times."

Right then, the day's heavy load—the endless cramming, that doctor's visit, the gnawing worry about my residency—starts to fade into the background. Talking to her, it's like a spell's been cast, each word from her knitting us closer, crafting this perfect vibe between us. This thing with her, it's been under the radar, kind of simmering below the surface, waiting for its moment. And lately, every second we're together, it feels like it's bubbling up, turning into something . . . something real.

But what exactly? That's the million-dollar question. Yet, it's there, growing stronger and clearer with each laugh, each conversation, each shared glance.

CHAPTER 13
MILES

Miles, come on, get a move on. Use those legs, the ones that carry you to touchdowns on the field, the voice in my head chides, prodding me to act.

Sure, it sounds easy. Just walk up to your best friend and interrupt her daily routine.

To say, "I need your help," and admit vulnerability.

And then steeling myself for that look of pity, the kind teachers often have when they notice a student struggling to keep up. But my challenge wasn't related to my battle with cancer; it was about needing guidance in a freshman course that was unexpectedly giving me a hard time. I mean, I'm aiming to be a doctor, but this class? It's a nightmare, even at freshman level. And Milli's help? That's a bonus I can't deny.

But, honestly, after getting my ass kicked at practice and then playing guinea pig with those hospital scanners, all I really want is to crash, forget the day, the week—hell, the whole damn month. But quitting is not in my playbook, not when graduation's breathing down my neck. And Milli?

Seeing her—even if we just spoke the other night—somehow makes it worth it.

I let out a breath and open the small Tylenol container I always carry in my backpack. Yesterday's game against the Lions was tough, but the victory made the aches worth it. The bruises, though, they're worse than usual—more noticeable, more painful. I'm popping these pills like they're candy. That can't be a good sign, can it? Lost in these thoughts, I'm still lingering at the library entrance when my phone vibrates with a new message.

MILLS

How did the doctor's appointment go? I know you said it was fine on the phone, but what about this morning? And don't even think about lying to me. You know I'll find out, so just spill.

I catch myself grinning as I glance over at Milli's message, even from across the room where she's stationed herself for our tutoring session. That caring vibe of hers, it's like her trademark—always on point with checking in post-appointments. She's invariably the first to hit me up, asking how things went, before launching into her spiel on self-care. You know, the usual drill: getting enough rest and remembering my vitamins—all the essentials.

Does it bother me? Not in the slightest. In fact, it's comforting to have someone like Milli caring, someone other than my parents looking out for me. Sure, my parents are always on my case about health, but Milli's concern? It's a different, a welcome kind of warmth.

MILES

Everything's fine, really. No need for the third degree. What's the deal, Mills? You aiming to be my personal health guru or something?

Seeing a glimpse of her across the room, a smile plays on her lips and her head gently shakes, while the guy next to her is deep in his textbooks.

MILLS

Ha, Sunshine, trust me, you wouldn't be able to afford me—or keep up, for that matter.

Is she for real? I'm pretty confident I could keep pace with her in more ways than one. But her keeping up with me? Now, that's an open question. I'm about to shoot back a reply when another message pops up.

MILLS

Just making sure you're taking care of yourself. I need you in top shape for the next game.

Chuckling to myself, I type out my response.

MILES

Yesterday's game wasn't a letdown, was it?

She shakes her head once more, yet a smile lingers, and she lightly bites her lower lip in the way that drives me crazy. As she tucks her phone away and leans over to help the guy she's tutoring, I notice her ample cleavage, more revealing than usual. The memory of that accidental reveal during our video call flashes in my mind—no figment of my imagination, but stark reality.

But they're totally out of bounds. It's like staring at a delicious cookie you know you can't grab.

I mean, they're just breasts, right?

But these are Milli's, and that changes everything.

I shouldn't be thinking this way, I know that. But come on, how can I not?

It's not just about physical attraction; it's Milli. Growing up together, those summer days by the pool, her in her bikinis—you'd think I'd be used to it. But there was never a moment to just . . . notice her like that. We were always in the thick of friends and family.

I remember stealing glances, but that was it. Luke was always more vocal about noticing girls while I just played along, my eyes always finding their way back to Milli's subtle, shy smile.

Now, watching her tutor, there's a twinge of irritation at the guy she's helping. He's nodding along, but his eyes keep wandering. This isn't some cheap entertainment—it's a study session. Show some respect, man.

And I'm telling myself the same thing. *Focus, Miles.*

As I'm about to step closer, perhaps intervene, I feel a presence beside me.

Luke.

"What are you looking at?" he asks, his tone sharp.

I play it cool, wondering if I should point out what's happening. Maybe it'd put an end to the inappropriate ogling.

Fuck. I shouldn't be this bothered.

Before I know it, I'm nodding toward Milli and the guy. Luke's expression changes as he observes the scene. His fists clench, and his anger builds up.

This isn't what I intended. I thought he'd just have a word and move on, not escalate things.

Anticipating trouble, I step in front of Luke, trying to diffuse the tension.

"Hey, ease up. Guys look. It's natural."

Luke's glare intensifies. *Okay, maybe that wasn't the right thing to say.*

Quickly, I try to correct the course. "What I mean is, let's not make a scene. I'll talk to Milli."

I snap my fingers before his face, an effort to reel his attention back to the present. "Leave it to me. If you step in, it'll just rile Milli up and prove her right about her concerns of being here."

Luke's stare flickers between me and the scene behind, and I hope I've managed to steer this situation away from boiling over. He finally exhales, a breath he seems to have been holding back for ages. "Concerns? She hasn't mentioned anything to me."

I laugh. "That's because you can be a dumbass sometimes, man."

"What the fuck, dude, that's harsh," he retorts, giving my arm a nudge that sends me a step backward.

"Just back off a bit, okay? She doesn't need her big brother stirring things up right now."

He looks at me, his expression softening as he digests my words, then nods in agreement. Luke claps a hand on my shoulder, his grip firm yet reassuring. "Alright, I'll lay off," he concedes, then pauses, "for now, at least."

I grin. "Trying to play the tough, protective big brother, huh?"

He chuckles and gives me a light jab in the ribs. I double over, feigning pain, as he says, "You'd do the same, wouldn't you?" It sounds more like he's probing for confirmation than making a statement.

"Absolutely," I reply, although my protective instincts toward Milli aren't exactly brotherly.

My mind chimes in, a reminder that Milli's in a college full of guys. It's a thought that only serves to annoy me further.

But why should it? Milli and I . . . well, our relationship? Friendship? I don't know at this point but it is complicated—at least for me. And that does nothing to ease the uncomfortable knot in my stomach or the tension coiling up my back.

Luke nods briefly and shifts the conversation to football, discussing strategies for the upcoming game before heading off. My gaze drifts back to Milli and that guy who's increasingly getting on my nerves. He's got his hand sneakily positioned behind her on the chair, trying to look smooth. Seriously, what is this, middle school?

"Looks like you're here for your session," a voice whispers from behind, snapping me out of my thoughts.

I turn to see Mrs. Raker, and I greet her with a warm smile.

Standing here, I must look pretty odd, just hovering around. Mrs. Raker, sharp as ever despite her years, probably noticed everything—my entrance, Milli's tutoring session, my chat with Luke, and now my awkward loitering.

"She'll be finished in about," she checks her watch, "ten minutes or so."

I smile, a bit lost for words. "Thanks, Mrs. Raker, but I can see the time. There's a clock right there."

"You've been waiting a while, I see," she continues, her voice filled with a hint of curiosity.

I don't mind her chatter; it's a distraction from what's really eating at me. Has it been ten minutes yet?

I shrug nonchalantly, trying to appear casual. "Yeah, just wanted to make sure I wasn't late. Missed a session last week, so . . . "

She widens her smile a bit, letting out a subtle, "Hmm," almost as if she senses there's more to the situation. And just maybe, there is . . . Perhaps I simply want to catch up with Milli and have a casual chat.

Yeah, right, Miles. Keep telling yourself that.

My eyes drift back to Milli. I watch how her face brightens when the guy next to her grasps whatever concept she's explaining. The gentle way she touches his arm, her excitement over the subject so genuine and passionate. It's fucking adorable, undeniably so, and I find myself wishing I was on the receiving end of her attention.

Soon enough, Miles.

Mrs. Raker's voice snaps me back to reality. "Smart to be early, I suppose."

I raise an eyebrow, curious about her tone. She chuckles, as if privy to a private joke. "Milli's been a bit on edge. She has no idea you're the one she's tutoring."

That's a surprise. Don't tutors usually know who they're tutoring ahead of time? Mrs. Raker, reading my confusion, explains, "Your name wasn't on the initial schedule. Coach Kreft added you last minute."

Awh, Coach knows I need a tutor.

"Yes," she confirms, tapping her temple knowingly. I chuckle—typical. Coach always has his finger on the pulse, not just about the game, but about us, his players, ensuring we're covered both on and off the field.

"Right," I respond with a nod of understanding.

She wishes me luck and heads off, but not before praising Milli's tutoring, especially given her dyslexia. Yeah, Milli's incredible, no doubt about that. And that's exactly why I need to steer clear of complicating things between us.

Miles, that ship has sailed.

Letting out a sigh, I take a seat close by, intending to dive into my medical school applications. However, it's a lost cause. My focus keeps getting hijacked by this guy who's now just blatantly ogling Milli's chest . . . Seriously, what the hell? As he finally gets up to leave, there's this brief exchange . . . the way he looks at her ignites a fury within me that's hard to tamp down.

"Same time next week?" he asks.

Milli gives him a genuinely charming smile, and an all-too-familiar feeling starts to stir within me. Jealousy. It's not the first time I've felt this intense, unsettling emotion. My stomach twists into knots, my throat dries up whenever I see her interacting with some other guy on campus. And whenever Luke casually brings up at home how Milli can't stop talking about how great Wyatt is, it's the same story—that sharp, uncomfortable feeling.

Holding her phone, she aims it at the guy. "Sure, just text me if you need any help during the week." The guy smirks and locks eyes with me, a challenge in his gaze. "I'll definitely take you up on that offer."

Inside, I bristle at his words.

What am I even thinking? Milli isn't mine, nor is she off-limits. She's free to text or hang out with whoever she pleases. Yet, I can't shake this growing irritation, and it's driving me nuts.

Catching my gaze, Milli's expression softens. "Hey, what's up?" she asks. I'm on the verge of making a smart remark about the sky, but she continues before I can. "God, this week has been brutally exhausting, right? And, dance, well, this week's practice is just killing me."

That catches me off guard. Just moments ago in the library, she seemed so composed while tutoring, but that's Milli for you—she's an expert at hiding her true feelings. Sometimes she's an open book, emotions worn plainly for all to see. Yet, at other times, like now, she takes me by surprise with the depth of what she's feeling underneath that composed exterior.

She continues, "You'd think I'd be used to a busy schedule by now. I'm up at 5:00 am for dance, then it's a rush to classes—no time even for a shower," she says, scrunching her nose in a way that's just too cute. "My days are packed with classes, then back to dance, and after that, these tutoring sessions."

She exhales a deep, weary sigh. "You know, tutoring on a Sunday wasn't really in my plans. But when Mrs. Raker mentioned they needed someone for this slot, what choice did I have?" She shrugs, a hint of resignation in her voice. "Sundays are usually my downtime."

A small smile finds its way onto my face. There's something about Milli's selflessness that always gets to me. Despite juggling a schedule that's already packed to the brim, she doesn't hesitate to squeeze in more—not just for her own sake, but to lend a hand to others. It's one of the many things about her that I've always admired.

Shaking her head, she adds with a tad bit of frustration, "Plus, this 'special' student better be punctual. He's already thrown off my schedule. I only found out I was tutoring him when I started the job. And I don't even know what makes him so 'special'."

And as for being "special"—just because I battled cancer as a kid doesn't define me. I just need to catch up on my studies. That doesn't make me any less capable. But that's a thought for another time.

As she tidies up the table, I listen to her vent. She's really fucking cute when she's like this, her lips moving rapidly as she speaks, her frustration almost tangible.

Stay focused, Miles.

"Moreover," she continues, "I don't even know what this guy looks like. How's he going to find me for the tutoring session?"

Hearing her groan, my instincts kick in. I feel an urge to comfort her, to just pull her into a hug and let her sink into the familiar warmth we've shared so many times.

Do not do it, Miles.

But, fuck it, this is my girl, and without thinking, I step forward and wrap my arms around her. She's momentarily stiff with surprise, but then she exhales deeply, melting into my embrace. It feels incredibly right, her body fitting perfectly against mine.

It reminds me of those times after my chemotherapy

sessions, when our hugs were a refuge, a way to escape the harsh reality for a moment. Now, it's my turn to offer her that same escape from her stress.

As she pulls back, her face tilts up to mine, our arms loose around each other. She nestles her face into my chest, and my heart thumps loudly.

God, this girl.

Looking up again, she searches my eyes, and I gently cup her chin, my thumb lightly grazing her lips. "I'm pretty sure he won't have any trouble finding you," I say, trying to lighten the mood.

Her gaze sweeps across the room, dodging any direct eye contact. "Well then, where is he?" she murmurs, her voice laced with a tinge of panic.

"I think he's already here," I say, hoping she'll pick up on the hint.

Her eyes finally settle on mine, a flicker of realization crossing her face. "You're my 'special' student, aren't you?"

Inwardly, I smile. If only she knew how special she is to me.

"Yeah, it's me," I respond, a sly grin spreading across my face. "Right here, your very own 'special' student."

She places a hand over her mouth to stifle a laugh, her blue-green irises dancing with amusement. I brush my thumb against her lip again, asking, "Ready to study, or what?"

Teasingly opening her mouth slightly, she playfully bites my thumb, her eyes locking onto mine with an unmistakable, unabashed hunger. My cock turns stiffer than the pencil in my back pocket. God, what would those lips look wrapped around my . . .

A little giggle finally breaks out, causing my thoughts to shift, and witnessing her giggle like when we were kids has my heart squeezing. Stepping back, she replaces my thumb with a pencil.

"Something on your mind, Miles?" she asks, her eyes briefly dropping to the noticeable outline in my sweats before meeting mine again. And, just like that, gone is the stressed Milli, and there's a new edge to her smile now, one I haven't seen before—it's more daring, more flirtatious.

Fuck if it's not a turn on.

She looks at me with confusion, probably wondering why I'm not responding to her teasing challenge. As much as I'd like to take this further, I know I need to focus. This moment isn't about giving in to impulse; it's about priorities, about staying on track.

All other thoughts need to be shelved for now.

Milli tilts her head, a questioning look in her eyes. "But why?"

It's a fair question. Miles Chasen needing a tutor? I've got the whole package—the charisma, the looks, and the skills on the field. Yeah, I'm as brainy as I am athletic, and that's a side of me everyone gets to see. Most people don't know about the struggles I've faced—needing a hand with football, fighting through cancer, struggling to keep up in school. I've been in a constant state of catch-up, always pushing to be better, to do better. Eventually, I got there. My football skills? Top-notch. My grades? Better than most. College was supposed to be my escape, a break from the pressures of my past. That's why a freshman class didn't get my full attention.

But now, I'm here, scrambling to pass statistics—a class I took in my wild freshman year.

Opting for Milli as my tutor? Never would've crossed my mind. It's not that I doubt her skills—it's just, she's my best friend. And lately, she's been more than that in my thoughts. Every little thing she does seems to resonate with me on a different level.

Adding her into my already hectic schedule means we're going to be spending even more time together. Don't get me wrong, I'm not complaining about that part. But sometimes, it's just too much. I need space to clear my head, to dispel these thoughts that keep surfacing.

I lock eyes with her, trying to explain. "I guess you're wondering why I need a tutor. Honestly, I'd rather not be here, seeing as how busy you are. I don't want to waste any of your time."

She stands there, hands on hips, giving me that look that always messes with my head. I adjust my stance, trying to play it cool. She notices, her eyes flicking down, then back up to meet mine.

I gesture toward the chair. "Mills, sit down."

She hesitates, but eventually does, still looking a bit guarded.

"Here's the thing," I start, and Milli's demeanor softens a bit. "I really need your help. You and Luke, you're the only ones who know how my freshman year went."

The mere mention of that year brings a nervous chuckle from me, and I catch a pained murmur from her, "Yeah, how could I forget."

I laugh, a bit awkwardly. Maybe bringing up that year wasn't the smoothest move.

But, before I can second-guess myself, I plunge ahead. "Mills, I need this. I promise, whatever happened between us, it won't get in the way of tutoring."

Her eyes narrow, a playful glint shining through. "What exactly do you mean by 'what happened between us,' Miles?" she inquires, her voice carrying a teasing lilt.

Is she toying with me? My cheeks flush with warmth, but I swiftly shove that feeling aside. "That's not what's important at the moment. The main thing is, I need to ace this class."

Her eyes widen slightly, as if taken aback by my more

serious demeanor. "You do realize you don't have to graduate to play professional ball, right?"

I glance around the tutoring center, thinking back to all the conversations I've had about this. Luke brought it up, and Dad even suggested skipping college for football. But Mom and I were adamant about getting that degree, not knowing then how crucial it would be for my med school plans.

Turning back to Milli, she's watching me, a mix of understanding and curiosity in her eyes. "I know that," I say, "but I want a backup plan. I need to prove to myself that I can do this."

Her expression changes to one of pride. "Okay, Sunshine, I'll help you," she agrees.

Relief washes over me, and I lean back, giving her a grateful wink. "You almost had me worried there."

She bites her pencil, and I have to suppress the urge to replace it with something else.

But I offer her a teasing smile instead. "You know you wanted to tutor me, right?"

She rearranges her books, trying to keep a straight face. "Don't get ahead of yourself. I choose who I tutor, you know."

I stand up, upping my charm. "Come on, who could resist tutoring me?" I ask playfully.

She shakes her head, a reluctant smile creeping onto her face. I pretend to climb onto the table, and her reaction is immediate. She grabs my leg, finally breaking into a full smile. "Get your ass down from there."

Yes, ma'am.

Her commanding tone is something I've rarely seen. It's usually Milli the Peacemaker, but this assertive side of her? It's unexpectedly fucking hot.

I maintain a smile and shake my head as I settle into my chair. Her hand is an inch from my now throbbing cock.

She nibbles her lip, glancing at her hand, then back at my

face, and then downward again. Eventually, she withdraws her hand, appearing a bit bashful with flushed cheeks, and murmurs, "Sorry."

This tutoring session might just be more interesting than I thought.

"But I love it when you touch me," I tease.

She gives me a shove. "You wish."

Oh, I do, Mills. I definitely do.

She claps her hands, snapping me back to reality. Leaning in, she rests her elbows on the table, and I can't help but notice how her . . . well, let's just say they're a bit distracting. She seems slightly anxious, her fingers fidgeting.

I show my open palms, raising an eyebrow in question. She sighs and reaches out, our fingers intertwining. A jolt of awareness surges through me.

Focus, Miles. Just friends, remember?

"Okay, first things first. Let's set some ground rules," she says, all business now, and it's cute.

God, it seems like everything she is doing tonight is fucking cute.

I nod, making an effort to keep my eyes on hers. "Alright, lay them on me. What kind of rules?"

She fixes me with a look of stern determination. "First, you've got to take this seriously. No slacking or goofing off. You want my help, you need to put in the work."

Yes, ma'am.

"Got it. What's next?"

She bites her lip, and I have to remind myself to stay focused.

"Second, no sexual innuendos."

I chuckle. "What if they're not sexual?"

She arches an eyebrow. "Miles, you know you can turn anything into that."

I bite back a smile. She's adorable when she's flustered.

Fuck, I'm dying to kiss her.

No, you're not, Miles.

"Okay, okay. I'm a guy, it's kinda in my nature," I admit.

She sighs, becoming all serious again. "Miles, I don't want to become a joke. I'm here to help you, not for you to sexually torture me."

I chuckle. "You really think I'm capable of sexual torture?"

She gives me a look that says she remembers exactly what happened during our video call.

"Oh, I know you are, Sunshine," she says, shaking her head as if to clear the memory.

Good luck, Mills. I can't even erase that memory.

That video call was one of the hottest moments of my life, and there wasn't even a single orgasm in sight. "Okay, I'm on board with those. Anything else?" I ask, ready for more.

"Don't be late," she points out.

"Roger that," I salute her, playing along.

She flashes a brief smile before shifting into a focused mode. "Let's map out a strategy for you to ace this class."

I scratch my head, waiting for her to elaborate.

"Take out your notebook and calendar so we can go over that now," she instructs.

I raise a brow and ask, "What's that?"

With a chuckle, she nudges me gently. "Pull it out, Chasen."

As I reach for my things, I turn my head over my shoulder and let a smirk slip past my lips. "You realize you just made a sexual innuendo yourself, right?"

Her eyebrows wiggle. "I said you couldn't make them, not me."

My eyes widen before I burst into laughter. "Bossy, Baby Sutton, I dig it." Flashing me a smile, she gives my shoulder a playful shove and we dive into planning my path to acing statistics.

CHAPTER 14
MILLI

"Let's take a quick break, Milli." I cast a glance over to where Wyatt stands, his expression lined with concern.

I exhale a deep sigh and stretch over to grab my water bottle from the side of the dance studio. Beads of sweat trace a path down my back. Dancing used to be my haven, a place to lose myself away from the world, but lately, it's like my mind is a magnet for worries and they're sticking to me, even here.

My thoughts drift to the tutoring sessions I've lined up. Just the other day, right after class, I had to dash off to help William, one of my students. He was freaking out about his upcoming midterm essay—understandable, especially for someone like me who grapples with dyslexia. It took some reassurance, but I managed to calm him down, promising to help him prepare this Sunday.

Then, there's the relentless pace of my classes. Will they be as demanding as last week, especially with midterms looming? Will our professors pile on even more work? And there's Jen, our dance coach, with her penchant for impromptu two-a-days. Any slight misstep from one of us can mean grueling extra practice for the whole team. Not that Wyatt and I really need it—we've been nailing every routine. We're already primed for game day this week.

But as I take a sip of water, the weight of responsibilities begins to suffocate me. Even in moments where I should be catching my breath, my mind won't stop racing.

Wyatt slides down beside me, extending his legs and interlocking his fingers before leaning back against the mirrored wall. His eyes, filled with empathy, remain fixed on me. He reaches out, softly taking my hand in his. "What's going on in that pretty head of yours?"

That's the million-dollar question.

How do I even begin to explain? One moment I feel like I'm in control, the next I'm drowning in assignments, my tutoring schedule, and dance rehearsals. I'm not just worrying about myself, but Wyatt, the Hanmann sisters, and everything else. I love it, sure, but it's overwhelming.

And then there's Miles. It's weird—I used to see him just on weekends and breaks, but now it's like he's always around. I crave his attention and then, suddenly, I need space. It's confusing, to say the least.

Get a grip, Milli. This isn't how your freshman year was supposed to be like.

EXACTLY! That's why I'm pushing myself so hard today. This week has to be different, better than how it started, I insist, the conviction in my voice strong.

I recall the conversation with Payson and Brooke after my tutoring session with Miles. Payson, with her usual candidness, had said, "Milli, this is your year. You're supposed to discover yourself; let loose. You're acting like a stressed-out senior." She had pursed her lips in that characteristic way of hers, indicating her disapproval, and added, "Remember our pact before school started, right? You owe it to yourself to fulfill that promise."

And she's not wrong.

Then Brooke, after giving me one of those essential best friend hugs, had chimed in, "Milli, I love you, but Payson's right. You need to dial it back a bit. Maybe reschedule some tutoring sessions, treat yourself to your favorite Sour Patch Kids, or just dance. Lose yourself in it. You know how much it grounds you."

And Brooke was spot on, too.

I take a long drink of water, savoring its coolness. I close my eyes and let out a deep breath, trying to shut out the chaos in my mind and just be here with Wyatt. He's been a constant, calming presence, reminding me of my previous tutor, who made everything seem so easy.

The first time I saw Wyatt, I was taken aback by his athletic build, so unlike the typical male dancer's physique. He could have easily been mistaken for a football player. But it was more than his looks—his energy, his fluidity in movement; he was like poetry in motion.

My phone vibrates on the floor, prompting a tired breath from me as I lower my head into my hands, peeking at the screen through the gaps between my fingers.

Mother: Milli, it's been a while since we heard from you. Give your mama a call when you get the chance. We miss you.

Just another thing to add to my ever-growing list of things to handle.

I hold back an eye roll. This marks the fifth "just checking in" text this week alone, mirroring every other week. Had I chosen a college out of state, without Miles or Luke nearby, her overprotective tendencies might have skyrocketed. Yet, I remind myself to be thankful for a mom who shows her care and concern, even if it feels overwhelming at times.

I'm about to decide whether to respond when another notification distracts me.

LUKE

Mom mentioned she hasn't heard from you lately. Maybe give her a call? Want to grab coffee soon? I kind of miss you, sis.

Wyatt, noticing my distraction, clears his throat, pulling my attention back. His hand finds mine again, offering comfort.

"I'm just overwhelmed," I confess. "Is this how college is supposed to be? Crazy schedules, non-stop family check-ins, tons of coursework? I thought it was meant to be about freedom and figuring things out."

He gives a small, understanding smile and gently squeezes my hand, his thumb drawing soothing circles. "The first year is full of new experiences," he says thoughtfully, his gaze drifting to our reflection in the studio mirror. "As freshmen, we're meant to take each day as it comes. We're not supposed to have it all figured out yet. That's for the seniors."

His words draw a rare chuckle from me, a welcome sound amid the chaos of my week. It's comforting, having someone to talk things through with.

When he asks if I really love what I'm doing—the dance, the tutoring, all of it—I'm initially puzzled. But as I think about it, a smile forms. I genuinely love these things, despite the stress.

He holds my gaze, his words resonating deeply. "If you truly love what you're doing, even if it's stressful, then it's worth it." His perspective strikes a chord. Dancing, especially ballet, challenges me but brings immense joy. Tutoring, too, while demanding, is incredibly rewarding when I see a student succeed.

I nod while Wyatt begins to gather his belongings. I take a moment to observe him, the worry lines on his forehead, the tiredness in his eyes. Initially, I hesitated to share my troubles, not wanting to burden him. But as time has passed, I find myself opening up more, much like I used to with my former therapist. It's a relief to have someone who listens without judgment.

It's a bit like what I used to do with my former therapist.

I remember how vital therapy was for navigating the challenges of my childhood and learning differences. Those sessions were a lifeline, helping me untangle my thoughts and build resilience. I've learned that bottling up my feelings is counterproductive. To move forward, I need to express them, and with Wyatt, I've found that outlet.

He's become an incredible friend, the kind you hope to find when you step onto a college campus for the first time. Will people judge me? Will I make a lasting impression? Will I find my new partner-in-crime or end up flying solo? These were the questions swirling in my mind.

Wyatt has his own challenges, like working double shifts at the local diner, the Golden Spoon, to make ends meet. He still finds time for his passion—dance. He never shows it, always wearing his Capezio gear, which doesn't come cheap. It's a reminder that we're all working hard in our own ways.

Seeing him in his dance attire—black hoodie, oversized tights, and tennis shoes—always brings a smile to my face. He's undeniably skilled, but it's a bit amusing seeing such a masculine guy in dance gear. Our practices often involve close contact, and I remember how, during our first session, I had to grab his rear end. He joked about it, saying, "Milli, it's a great ass. Grab it, hold it, squeeze it, feel it, do whatever you want, I don't mind," and winked. That moment clarified that Wyatt and I would always be just friends—especially since he's gay.

Oh, did I forget to mention that? He came out to me right after our first week of practice. It was a relief, knowing his flirtatious behavior was just playful banter.

As I mull over these thoughts, my phone buzzes with a call from Miles. My heart races momentarily, but I remind myself of my commitments—over an hour of dance practice and a tutoring session later. Miles will have to wait.

I send the call to voicemail, labeling it mentally as a "spam call," even though it's anything but.

Wyatt raises an eyebrow, but I brush it off.

Miles' text comes through next, mentioning a project he's submitted and asking if I've seen it. Guilt washes over me for not taking his call. But right now, my focus needs to be here, in the studio, on the dance floor, preparing for what's next.

With a deep breath, I refocus, turning to Wyatt with a renewed sense of purpose. It's time to embrace the here and now, to find joy in the present moment, and let everything else fall into place in its own time.

Milli, it's your time. He can wait.

I had already seen Miles' assignment since I'm his tutor. And judging by his answers, he's practically acing it. The whole idea of him needing my help seems a bit far-fetched now. It's like he just wanted an excuse to spend time with me. Or maybe he's seeking something more?

The idea ignites a flutter of excitement within me.

Wyatt, observing my reaction, gives a theatrical sigh and places a hand on his hip, much like Payson when she's frustrated. I shake my head, trying to dismiss the thought.

"Fine, keep your secrets," he says playfully, "but one day, I'll get it out of you."

I stand up, brushing off his comment with a light chuckle. "Really, it's nothing."

But deep down, I know it's not "nothing." Still, I keep it to myself, even from Wyatt. He comes over and gives me a reassuring hug, the kind that reminds me I'm not alone. As he walks away, I smile at his bold choice of tights.

Wyatt is unapologetically himself, a trait I admire. He embodies what we all strive for: to be fearlessly authentic, confident in our abilities, and fully present in each moment.

My phone buzzes again. It's Miles.

> MILES
>
> Milli Sutton
>
> Mills
>
> Baby Sutton.
>
> . . . I see I'm not important enough for you to answer your phone.
>
> . . . or a text message back.

I roll my eyes; it's hard to tell if he's genuinely annoyed or just doing his usual thing to mess with me.

Ping.

Good Lord . . .

> MILES
>
> Mills, if you don't respond, I'm coming to your dorm right now. Over and back.

I chuckle. His text reads like he's trying to dodge a cop radar with his "over and back" line.

But as I stare at the screen, I let out a heavy sigh. All these messages from him . . .

It's time for some me-time. Milli time.

Deciding I don't want any outside distractions, I opt not

to respond to Miles. If he wants, he can come to my dorm. It might be amusing to see him squirm.

You're bad, Milli.

Firmly, I switch my phone to "DO NOT DISTURB" mode and toss it into my dance bag. Leaping to my feet, I draw in a long, steadying breath and stride back to the center of the dance studio, my mind set on immersing myself in the routine.

Positioning myself in front of the mirrored wall, I extend my leg gracefully, pointing my toe as I inhale deeply. "Just be, Milli," I murmur to myself, allowing my mind to drift as I start moving in sync with the soft rhythm playing in the background. The music wraps around me, a comforting cocoon, pulling me away from the chaos of thoughts, into a world where movement and expression reign free. The tension melts away from my muscles as I dance, each movement fluid and natural.

In this space, I am truly alive, unencumbered by worries or expectations. The practiced routine flows from me as naturally as breathing. My body spins, leaps, and glides across the floor with an adrenaline-fueled grace. Sweat forms on my brow, my breath quickens, but I push on, relentless.

There's no stopping me now.

Not a chance.

I pour every ounce of my being into the dance, channeling all my bottled-up emotions—the frustration, fear, doubt, and insecurity—into each movement. It feels like a cleansing ritual, a way to rejuvenate and start anew.

As the music reaches its crescendo and then fades, I find myself standing still, panting and glistening with sweat. A smile of pure satisfaction spreads across my face as I wipe the sweat from my cheek. My heart gradually calms, and there's a palpable sense of relief, like shedding a heavy burden. Looking at my reflection, the familiar, confident, and passionate Milli is staring back at me, and it's a sight for sore eyes.

This is it—my moment to pause and truly appreciate the simple joys of life. To find my footing once more amidst the chaos, and honestly, it feels damn incredible.

CHAPTER 15
MILES

"Dude, you're totally coming off as a jealous boyfriend. You get that, right?"

My phone slips from my hand once more, adding to the gazillion times it's happened tonight. It lands with a soft thud on the jumble of study books scattered all over our well-used couch—the one Luke and I practically live on. The screen briefly lights up, throwing a faint glow that paints fleeting shadows across the messy pages of open textbooks and scrunched-up notes. Glancing over nonchalantly to the opposite side of the couch, there's Cam, unsurprisingly downing another gulp of our beer. I mean, seriously, it's only Thursday—smack in the middle of the week—and he's acting like it's just another run-of-the-mill moment.

Miles, pot calling the kettle

I shake my head, trying to brush off his comment that's clearly about Milli. My mind was all over the place during classes this morning, then during practice, and of course, Cam picked up on it because the guy's sharp as a tack. Then again, he doesn't know shit, especially when it comes to me and Milli.

"Remember when I mentioned that knocking back beers on a weekday, especially with a game around the corner and Panthers' Days coming up, might not be the best plan?" I remind him, half-heartedly.

He raises an eyebrow, offering a nonchalant shrug as he takes another swig from the beer he helped himself to from our fridge. Did I argue when he showed up unannounced? Well, no, because I've made it a point to have him and the other two fantastic freshman mentees over to ensure they're keeping up with what they should be doing—including my own responsibilities in mentoring them.

I'm aware I should've probably snatched the beer from his grasp, but I've been reminding the guy since he strolled into our apartment an hour ago that it's not the wisest move. Yet, all he's done is shrug, and I've let it slide. Though, at least he's here and not out painting the town red. I mean, if need be, I can ensure he gets home safely.

Cam rolls his eyes and reclines on the chair across from me. "Relax, dude. I'm just unwinding a bit. We've been practicing like crazy for weeks; a little booze won't do any harm."

I roll my eyes. I'm pretty certain his response is on autopilot because it's definitely not the first time I've heard it. "It's not your alcohol tolerance I'm concerned about. I'm worried you'll get too sloshed and mess up our chances of winning."

Cam snickers, completely unfazed by my comment. I let out a sigh, knowing this argument is going nowhere, and turn back to the TV. But my mind is elsewhere—on Milli. Why hasn't she responded to my texts since yesterday? I was only joking about showing up at her dorm, but now I'm seriously considering it.

Miles, get a grip.

I know it sounds like I'm acting all overprotective, but it's not like that. It's just this instinct to make sure she's okay. Milli's been my rock.

When I had that hospital stay? She was at my door the moment I got back, asking about every detail.

After the surgery or whenever I felt low? She'd show up with my favorite gnocchi soup and suggest we binge-watch *Goosebumps* reruns together. She wasn't much into thrillers, more of a chick flick kind of person, but she knew it was my ultimate favorite.

During chemo? She stood right by me, helping pick out hats to cover my hair loss that week.

It feels like there wasn't a single moment during those tough childhood years when she wasn't there for me, and just reminiscing about it has my eyes welling up with tears.

Fuck. Get it together, Miles.

I close my eyes, rubbing the bridge of my nose as a headache starts to build. Fucking headaches have been a constant companion since childhood, ebbing and flowing, but never really going away. The what ifs linger in the back of my mind, especially since Dr. Reynolds has yet to call.

"You sure me drinking is really the reason for your irritation right now? It doesn't happen to have anything to do with Sutton's little sister?"

I want to brush it off, tell him he's wrong. But deep down, I can't, because he's partially right.

Annoying little fucker. He's like a pesky fly you just want to swat away.

Still, I reply, trying to sound nonchalant, "Nah, why would it have to do with her?"

He shrugs. "I don't know, man. You just seem wound up lately. Maybe a beer would do you good."

And he's right. I am fucking tense. If he had the same pressure I do—the constant nagging from my dad about scouts, the upcoming Panthers' Day game, expectations of making it to the NFL, and acing senior year for med school —he'd probably be reaching for a beer, too. It feels like I'm back in those days of playing catch-up after long hospital stays.

Trying to manage the mounting frustration, I briefly close my eyes, taking a moment to compose myself. Then, I stand up and head to the fridge, grabbing a beer. Cam watches me with a smug look that says, "I knew it."

Taking a sip, feeling the chill of the beer calming my nerves, I address the unspoken tension. "I just can't afford distractions right now," I say, dismissing his earlier comment about Milli. "There's a lot riding on this year."

Cam nods, his attention already drifting. Then he drops a bombshell. "Did I tell you I saw Milli at the dance studio yesterday? Who's that guy she's dancing with?"

My blood starts to boil.

This is exactly what I don't need—thoughts of Milli with *Wyatt*. He doesn't fit the typical dancer's mold; he's built like he's training for the WWE, not freaking dance.

"Nah, you didn't mention it," I reply, struggling to keep my voice even.

Cam smirks. "She looked hot, man. And the way he was touching her . . . I wouldn't be surprised if there's something going on."

That's when Luke chimes in from his bedroom, grabbing a beer and sitting down on the couch. "Can we not talk about my sister with some dude I haven't met?"

Cam shrugs, unphased. "What can I say? Your sister's like a magnet for the guys on campus."

Luke turns his head to give Cam a glare.

Cam throws up his hands and says, "Hey, don't be mad at the truth. The truth is the truth, after all."

Luke sighs and leans back on the couch, resting his feet

on the table. "Tell me about it. I didn't think it would be this bad."

I mean, he must have seen it coming at least a little bit. Milli might be reserved, but she did have guys lining up in high school.

Luke grabs the remote and flips to an NFL game. He adds, "Chasen had to practically drag me away from a brawl with some dude she was tutoring." He chuckles. "Thank goodness he intervened, or Mrs. Raker might've chewed me out."

Cam looks at me, eyebrows raised in mock surprise. "Oh, Miles to the rescue?" His silent mouthed comment, "More like your rescue," doesn't go unnoticed.

I silently mouth back, "Fuck you" and flip him off, but deep down, he's got a point.

Cam just laughs and takes another swig of his beer. I've lost count of how many he's had.

Luke, still focused on the game, asks, "Have you seen any of this game?"

As if I have the time to sit through an entire NFL game on a Thursday night. I catch bits of games, usually on Sundays, after my tutoring sessions with Milli. But during the week? No chance.

Luke takes a sip of his beer, commenting, "Chicago doesn't stand a chance against Denver."

I nod absentmindedly.

"Hey, don't knock Denver. That's where my allegiance lies, you know? Orange Crush forever," Cam shoots back, his tone laced with humor and a mischievous grin playing at the corners of his mouth.

"How could any of us forget your hometown pride?" Luke mumbles, barely audible, and I suppress a chuckle.

It's true; Cam wears his Denver loyalty like a badge of honor. I recall our season opener when Cam, brimming with unabashed enthusiasm, got yanked off the field. Our coach's words still echo in my memory, *"Cameron, this isn't the NFL, and we're certainly not the Broncos."* We all struggled to keep our laughter in check for days after that.

Shaking my head at their antics, I glance at the TV, where the score flashes—Chicago leading by 10. But knowing Denver, the game's still up for grabs. They're famed for their dramatic second-half revivals. Plus, they've got Jakens, the rookie sensation. His game-changing plays, those needle-threading passes, and his uncanny knack for outmaneuvering defenses have revitalized the team. He's the reason Denver's not just a team, but a force this season. So yeah, Chicago might be ahead, but with Denver's track record, I wouldn't bet against a comeback.

I'm on the verge of escaping to my room when Gunner and Devon barge in.

How on earth did they get in? Luke and I are almost obsessive about locking the door. Then it clicks—Cam flashes a set of keys with a triumphant wink. That wink, it's so him —cocky, mischievous. I narrow my eyes, curiosity tinged with suspicion rising within me. But before I can delve deeper, Gunner and Devon slide what appears to be an invitation across the kitchen counter.

Join Us for a Noble Cause:

A Touchdown Against Breast Cancer

You're Invited to Make a Difference

In the spirit of teamwork and community, we invite you, our esteemed college football players, to a special gala event dedicated to raising awareness and volunteering for a cause close to our hearts, including Coach Kreft—Breast Cancer Awareness.

Event Details:

Date: Sunday, October 28th
Time: 6:00 pm - 9:00 pm
Venue: Gridiron Glory Hall
Dress Code: Black Tie

Please let us know if you can join us in this noble endeavor.

To confirm your attendance, kindly respond by
Sunday, October 10th to kreftpanthers@gmail.com

Agenda:

- Welcome Reception: Mingle with fellow athletes, organizers, and breast cancer survivors.
- Opening Remarks: Gain insights into the importance of our mission.
- Volunteer Training: Learn how to make a meaningful impact in the fight against breast cancer.
- Guest Speaker: Hear from a prominent figure in breast cancer research and advocacy.
- Gala Dinner: Enjoy a delectable meal, network, and connect with peers.
- Awards & Recognition: Celebrate and acknowledge the efforts of those dedicated to this cause.
- Fundraising Initiatives: Discover how we can make a difference through donations and pledges.
- Closing Remarks: Recap the day's activities and look ahead to future initiatives.

Your commitment to volunteer for breast cancer awareness is deeply appreciated. Your participation and support can truly make a difference. Together, we can be champions both on and off the field.

Note:
If you have any dietary restrictions or special requirements, please inform us when confirming your attendance.

Event Organizers:
Coach Kreft and Mrs. Kreft

Shit. How could that slip my mind? It's an annual thing, always around this time of year. I know too well the weight it carries, the financial burden it brings. Yeah, my dad was a pro footballer, but after he retired, and with my frequent hospital stays and rehab sessions, the bills just kept mounting.

Suddenly, I'm transported back to those tough times, to hushed conversations that no child should ever have to eavesdrop on.

"Goddammit, Denise, this is the second call we've gotten from collections about Miles' hospital bills."

Walking back and forth in our big kitchen, Mom looked really worried. She was like this whenever Dad started to get mad at her, saying things needed to be different. But how could they be? My sickness wasn't going away, and neither were the bills that kept growing.

I peeked from behind the big pole in our dining room, trying to hide. Mom sighed really loud. "I know, Sean. There's not much I can do, can I?"

She threw her hands up, and I knew what Dad was going to say. It was always the same. "Well, if I hadn't given up my job, we wouldn't be in this mess, right?"

I shut my eyes for a moment as Mom looked surprised, just like she always did when Dad talked about his old job. It was something he said all the time when money, promises, or the fact that he had to go to the hospital more often because of my pain came up.

Did he really think that ignoring the bills, skipping my rehab, or avoiding the hospital would make everything better if he still had his old job? Was I really such a big problem for him?

"You don't mean that, Sean. I know you don't," Mom said to him with kindness, moving closer and giving him a warm hug. He closed his eyes, feeling comfort in her embrace, while she gently rubbed his back. Her voice was soft, barely a whisper. "We'll make it through this, baby."

"We've got 'The Little Stars of Hope Foundation' coming up. You know how much it helps us, and we still have some of our savings," she softly reminded him.

He just held her a little tighter and nodded, his way of showing he appreciated her strength and support.

I've witnessed how the power of a united community can make a real difference in the lives of those fighting cancer, and it goes way beyond the football field. It's about standing together for a cause greater than ourselves, like Coach Kreft's wife and her battle with breast cancer. She's been in and out of hospitals, enduring what I went through. Coach even had to skip some games to be by her side.

"Chasen, are you in?" Luke asks, raising an eyebrow, snapping me out of my reverie. I shoot him a knowing look—he's well aware I never miss these events.

"Do we have to go to this thing?" Cam asks, reluctance coloring his tone. "It's on a Sunday, my chill day."

His words prick me with a hint of annoyance, yet I swiftly control the flare-up. Cam is unaware of the profound bond I have with this cause. He remains in the dark about my personal fight against cancer, a battle intimately known only to my family, the Suttons, and Coach Kreft. Gaining admission to NorthRidge necessitated a comprehensive medical examination, making it impossible to keep this chapter of my life concealed.

Grabbing the invitation, I place it front and center on the fridge. Turning to face my three mentees with a stern look, I point at them firmly. "You're all going. No excuses."

Expecting Cam to retort, I'm pleasantly surprised when they all nod in agreement, a wave of relief washing over me. The last thing I need is to coax them into attending when I just want to enjoy the event on my own terms.

Luke watches me, a slight shake of his head and a small smile betraying his amusement. He's familiar with the dynamics of mentoring, though his group is less rowdy than mine. He claims I complain more about my freshman than he does, but sometimes you just need to vent, right?

"In answer to your question, Luke, absolutely. I'll be there," I assure him.

Luke's smirk teases. "Always the early bird, aren't you?"

A chuckle escapes me, lightening the mood. Nodding, I know I'll be the one arriving early, setting up, not just making a grand entrance. I prefer being hands-on rather than just another face in the crowd.

"Always first in line," I affirm, ruffling Gunner, Cam, and Devon's hair playfully as I pass by them.

Cam appears slightly annoyed as he tries to smooth his hair back into place. "What was that for?"

I internally roll my eyes. First, he's grumbling about minor bruises, now he's fussy over a bit of hair ruffling. What minor inconvenience will he complain about next?

I simply brush it aside, observing as Devon and Gunner initiate a mock tussle, dragging Cam into their friendly chaos with light jabs and teasing remarks.

Retreating to my room, I flop onto my bed and pull out my phone, lost in thought. A dilemma plays in my mind.

Should I text her? Just a quick message to check in, or should I just leave it be?

Relationships, emotions, connections—they're complicated, especially when my future might lead me across the country in a year's time.

But this is Milli. *My Mills.*

Without much hesitation, I find myself typing a message.

Okay, no judgment—it's just going to help me feel better knowing she's alright.

Then it hits me—wouldn't Luke have mentioned if something was wrong? But he doesn't know Milli is tutoring me, so I can't just casually ask about her. I don't want to stir up unnecessary drama.

I imagine Luke's confused face, him wondering, "Why does she have your assignment?" That would lead to a whole conversation I'm not eager to have, with him possibly launching into his usual spiel about the NFL and education.

Opting against a text, I decide to call her instead.

After a few rings, her voice, sweet and familiar, fills the air, instantly setting my heart racing. "Sunshine, is this going to be a regular thing?" she teases about our calls.

I laugh. "You bet. Got a problem with that?"

Her laughter echoes mine. "Not at all, if you don't."

"I don't," I reply quickly.

"Good, me neither," she says, her tone soft and almost shy.

As we talk, my phone vibrates. I switch Milli to speaker and glance at the incoming text. A wave of unease washes over me; it's from my dad.

DAD

Hey son, just checking in. Ready for Panthers' Day?

Is he forgetting about our upcoming game, or is he more focused on the Panthers' game and the scouts it'll draw?

I let out a sigh, the weight of expectations heavy on my shoulders. I quickly text back, affirming I'm prepared, all while listening to Milli describe her dance practice with the Hanmann sisters.

DAD

Great. Lots of scouts will be there.

I roll my eyes slightly. I've been aware of the scouts' presence for some time. My focus is on the here and now, not just impressing scouts but also winning for our team and school. Still, his reminder adds to the pressure I'm already feeling.

"How was practice today?" Milli interrupts my train of thought.

I spill about the day's grind, guiding my trio of clowns, which cracks her up, knowing the kind of grief they toss my way.

DAD

> We should set up some one-on-one time with scouts after the game. What do you think?

MILES

> Sounds like a plan, Dad.

I respond quickly, a bit mechanically, recalling how often we've had this conversation.

12 YEARS AGO

"Okay, champ," my dad assured me, squatting down to meet me at eye level. "Coach Denton will be at your tryout." He looked straight into my eyes, making sure I was paying attention. "Remember everything you learned at football practice today," he said, a hint of excitement in his voice, emphasizing the importance of the skills I'd been practicing.

Like I could ever forget. It had been etched into my brain for as long as I could remember. My dad had been eagerly anticipating this day ever since I achieved remission. I went through all those medical evaluations, endured over two months of constant monitoring, had a team of professionals—doctor, nurse, and physical therapist—keeping a close eye on me. They wanted to make sure I was physically, mentally, and emotionally prepared for this moment.

Was I ready? Yeah, I suppose I was. I mean, it was what my dad left the NFL for, you know? There was no point in dwelling on it; I just needed to go out there, give it everything I had, and show him that he made the right call by giving up his career for me.

He continued, "Being a part of the Titan Tigers is a dream come true for you. We've got to show him that you're just like your dad, make him proud, and make your mom and me proud. Show him that you are true, Chasen."

I nod my head. "Sounds like a plan, Dad."

5 YEARS AGO

"Okay, Miles, today's the day. Coach Kreft, Coach Pen, Coach Attikins, and Coach Drane, they're all going to be at your college tryouts. This is the moment we've been waiting for. It's go time, son."

No pressure, Dad, none at all. It wasn't like I hadn't been preparing for this day. As he mentioned, we had been gearing up for this moment for a while, although it was mostly his moment, one he had been anticipating and training me for. And now, the day was finally here, but I couldn't seem to muster up much excitement. It was more a sense of pressure, of not letting my dad down when he had been looking forward to this day ever since I joined the All-Stars.

Dad gave me a few reassuring pats on my shoulder and looked at me with a mix of caution and concern, as if he wanted to make sure I was alright. But just as quickly, he returned to his stern and determined self. "Alright, you look great, kid. Let's go out there and show them you deserve a spot on their roster, yeah?" His face lit up with an enormous smile that could rival any in the history of mankind.

I offered him a grateful smile and nodded my head, responding, "Sounds like a plan, Dad."

Another ping from my phone pulls me back to reality.

DAD

> Remember, only 6ish months till NFL tryouts.
> You need courage, guts, dedication. It's a big
> leap from college football. Show those
> scouts you're up for it.

I mentally nod. Always ready, always a step ahead. I quickly type a response, hoping it conveys my confidence.

MILES

> I'm ready.

I catch myself holding my breath as Milli's voice comes through. "Sunshine, you still there?"

Shit, yes. But before I can reply, another message from Dad dings.

DAD

> How are you feeling? Watch for muscle
> soreness, fatigue, headaches.

The same routine questions, day in, day out. My irritation spikes, and I feel a flush of heat. But then Milli's voice interrupts my thoughts. "Miles?"

She seems about to ask something, but instead, she mentions needing to shower and hit the books, so she wraps up the call. A twinge of disappointment hits me, but it's quickly overshadowed by a buzz from my phone—a new message from her lighting up the screen.

MILLS

> You want to see me in the new dance
> uniforms? They're kinda skimpy.

I chuckle, feeling the tension ebb away. I can almost see her scrunching her nose adorably.

MILES

Will I have to knock out some of my
teammates for staring?

MILLS

Not to toot my own horn, but it's a very, very
big possibility.

MILES

Uh huh, and what about me? Will I get in
trouble for staring?

But it hardly makes a difference; I'm well aware of my
tendencies, and without a doubt, I'll find myself staring,
among other things.

MILLS

I might make an exception . . .

. . . for one person.

Well, fuck. This conversation could take two different
directions, and before I can even figure out which way it's
going, my phone goes off again, making me let out a low
groan. Is this woman trying to get my body to react this way?
To twitch and burn for a release?

MILLS

And we both know who that is.

Is it me? That's who she's referring to, right? Because,
God help me if she isn't.

MILES

Ugh, Mills, are you trying to finish me off?
And no, that's not an innuendo ;)

I text, remembering one of our rules of tutoring. I can
almost hear her chuckle, making me laugh inwardly.

"Miles, what's going on in there?" I hear Devon's voice from outside my door.

"Get lost, Devon," I snap back.

He just laughs, and I hear Cam whisper, "Probably getting a hard-on from that damn Emma Watson poster on his wall." Right on cue, my eyes find the image he's talking about, although it's not exactly a poster. It's a part of my Women of the World Calendar, and she happens to be on this month. No shame. She's attractive as hell, anyway.

My phone buzzes, jerking my focus back to the screen, and I audibly groan this time.

"Hey, Chasen, we get it. You're into Emma Watson, but can you hold off until we're out of here?" Cam says, undoubtedly smirking.

What a dumbass.

MILLS

I mean I have to wear the outfit. Whether it floats your boat is up to you.

The Saturday game against the Midtown Mavericks takes an unexpected turn when Milli shows up in her new dance outfit. She is breathtaking, and I am utterly captivated. After the game, in the showers, I can't hold back. My hands pump the fuck out of my cock. I don't want to get off—I never have before with Milli—but the way she moved, those suggestive glances, the deliberate teasing during team breaks—yeah, that got me going. It's the kind of torment that's both torturous and addictive. The sort that leaves you wanting more even though it's driving you nuts.

I have this deep-seated sense that what is unfolding

between us is the beginning of something. What that "something" is, I have absolutely no clue, but I am more than ready to dive in and explore every aspect of it.

CHAPTER 16
MILLI

"Come on, you can't keep feeding me that same old line," I remarked, my voice carrying a teasing edge.

Leaning against the time-worn barstool, Miles arches an eyebrow, that signature smirk playing across his face—a silent, knowing conversation in itself. The dim, nostalgic glow of Grub 'n Guzzle Tavern casts a comforting shadow over his relaxed posture. It is like he is a part of the tavern's fabric, blending into the ambiance of clinking glasses and soft murmurs, a place that feels like a forgotten snapshot from a simpler time.

I had only stumbled upon this tavern after a chance encounter with Wyatt post-dance practice. His suggestion to try it out for tutoring sessions had been an unexpected but welcome change. Sundays, he said, were calm here, a stark contrast to the lively college nights. And here I am, soaking in the mellow tunes from the jukebox, the hum of conversation around us, my eyes occasionally catching the movements by the pool table or the laughter at the bar. The aroma of comfort food fills the air, merging seamlessly with the sounds of a lazy Sunday evening.

Miles inches nearer, his elbow grazing mine in a silent communication. His eyes sparkle with that familiar mischief, one that usually precedes his attempts at charming his way out of something. But I am determined to stay on course, despite the distraction he presents.

Yet, in the midst of it all, a thought flickers through my mind, unbidden. Is this what it would feel like to be on a date with Miles? Not something grand, but simple, comfortable—something true to us. I wonder if the casual touches, the shared glances, are small gestures of something more, akin to the tender moments I have read about in countless romance novels.

"Give me a break, Mills," he implores, his voice a blend of playfulness and persuasion. He throws in a nostalgic reference; his eyebrow quirk in a way that makes my heart skip a beat. "Remember the good old days?" he asks, his words wrapping around me like a warm, familiar blanket.

His laughter, genuine and tinged with fondness, fills the air as he reminisces about our shared past. "You always had my back, even when I lagged behind in schoolwork. Remember how you'd make me sit and study, determined as ever, even though you were younger?" His voice softens with the memory.

I smile, thinking back to those days, our roles reversed, me trying to keep him on track through his struggles and hospital stays.

He reclines on his stool, a distant look in his eyes as he relives those moments. "And that time after Dad's relentless football drills, when I was completely wiped out?" he muses, a faint smile on his lips.

I nod, the memory vivid in my mind—him, exhausted yet

persistent, and me, lost in a book, oblivious to the world except for his presence.

He continues, a softness in his voice, "I remember finding you in your backyard, Luke lost in his games, and there you were, so absorbed in your book, glasses perched on your nose. You looked . . . fucking cute."

My breath catches; no, my heart skips a beat at his words, spoken so effortlessly. As if he's always seen me this way? Our gazes lock, and in that moment, the world around us fades away. His eyes are filled with a desire, mirroring my own.

God, I want him so damn bad it's almost unbearable. And there have been countless hints, haven't there? The party, the bonfire, those tutoring sessions—the signs are unmistakable. I'm certain he feels it, too. So, why the hesitation?

You're best friends, my mind chides me.

His throat clearing snaps me out of my daydreams. Miles begins, then his words taper off into a sigh. As he speaks, a faint blush colors his cheeks, and even the tips of his ears turn a telltale shade of pink. "I was scared to tell you about the stuff with my dad again. I didn't want to be a downer. That day, I almost didn't come over, but my damn cleat got caught in that old fence between our yards."

I bit back a laugh, picturing a younger, more vulnerable Miles caught in such a comical yet telling moment.

"Don't even think about laughing," he half-threatens, but the mischief sparkling in his eyes betrays him. My attempt to stifle it fails miserably; laughter escapes, resonating around the tavern. A few curious glances come our way, but I couldn't care less. I'm thoroughly enjoying this.

I mock salute him, encouraging him to continue. "Carry on, soldier," I say with a grin.

He rolls his eyes but chuckles. "You sound like Cam at football practice, always with that Boy Scout salute."

I tease him further with a bitten lip and another mock salute, but then, suddenly, his hand shoots out, gripping my wrist. Our shared laughter evaporates, leaving a thick silence buzzing between us. His thumb traces gentle circles around my wrist, undoubtedly feeling the rapid beat of my heart. He strokes a particular spot softly, his gaze locked on mine, deep and probing. "You feel that too?" he whispers, the line blurring between a question for me and a question for himself.

Time freezes around us. I'm acutely aware of every spark of electricity that zips through the space between us, but to confess that aloud? It's a hurdle too high, especially amidst the backdrop of the tavern's bustling energy.

Then, his fingers find their way to my fingers, gently intertwining with mine, setting off a storm of emotions and questions within me. Can this be happening? In the past, holding hands with Miles was a gesture of pure innocence, but now, it's heavy with the weight of unspoken promises. The intensity in his gaze, the firm set of his jaw—both betray a struggle within him as profound as the one I'm facing.

I am tempted, so tempted, to lean in closer, to claim this moment and him in a way I've never dared before.

To pull our joined hands into his lap.

To cradle his face, to trace the lines of his lips with my fingers.

To kiss him, right here, in front of everyone, declaring silently but unmistakably that he is mine.

But reality snaps back as he clears his throat once again, and I withdraw my hand, pressing it to my chest in a silent reprimand to my racing heart.

Not now, Milli, I scold myself inwardly, feeling the heat in my cheeks.

I take a hurried gulp of my Shirley Temple, seeking the brief respite it promises from the overwhelming flood of emotions.

Miles momentarily collects himself, diving back into his story. "So there I was, caught, remember? My foot snagged, and I'm wrestling to break free; felt like an eternity. And then, down I went, and you caught every embarrassing moment of it."

I nod, playfully mimicking my younger self's high-pitched, confused voice. "What the heck are you doing, Miles?" I scrunch up my nose, imitating my eleven-year-old self's bewildered expression.

His gentle nudge against my shoulder pulls my attention down, where I notice his shoe brushing against my calf with a delicate motion. Jeez Louise, is he unusually touchy tonight, or is it just my imagination playing tricks on me?

You wouldn't guess he's laid a finger on me by the way my body flips out around him. It's like every time, even if it's just a harmless hand grab, my heart does a little cha-cha, my skin gets all tingly, and I've gotta squeeze my legs together.

Focus, Milli.

I take in the tavern's buzz, the other patrons and staff moving in their own worlds, unaware of the spark flying between us. Meanwhile, Miles maintains that impish smile, his gaze never leaving mine. The slightest touch from him sets off tremors along my skin, amplifying the charge in the air between us.

Leaning back with ease, I place my hand behind my head in a relaxed gesture. My voice morphs into a light, teasing mimicry of a younger Miles, infused with a hint of roguish charm. "Oh, hey Milli, didn't see you there," I quip, embodying a nonchalant coolness.

He responds with a chuckle, nudging my shoulder. "Come on, you know that's not how it went down," he says, his eyes sparkling with humor.

I roll my eyes, a light-hearted dance in our banter. "Remember, Miles? That night, you were so lost, and I . . . I helped you see your dad's pressure differently. Not as hate, but his odd way of showing love." My eyes drift to our feet, tangled in a light-hearted shuffle, wrapping us in a cozy bubble. "I told you to get up, and I'd help with those catches before you hit the books."

His grin is contagious. "Yeah, something like that," he replies. Our eyes lock, and the unspoken tension since entering the tavern thickens with every silent moment.

Leaning in, his whisper sends a thrill through me. "Mills, I never really thanked you for pulling me back from the edge that night."

His intense blue gaze locks with mine briefly before drifting to my lips. My eyelids droop slightly, every fiber of my being suddenly hyperaware. Breath becomes a luxury I can't seem to afford, a dizzying sensation overtakes me, and I'm consumed by a desperate yearning that's been simmering since we entered this space.

Milli, focus. This isn't the time or place.

But what if it is? Just for tonight, can I let everything else go?

My thoughts are cut short as his phone rings. He holds up a finger, signaling, "just a second."

Miles answers, his expression flickering from joy to something else—sadness, or annoyance, perhaps. It's hard to read from here. But once he starts talking, his cheerful demeanor returns.

I overhear the familiar voice on the call. Peeking over, I see it's a FaceTime call.

The sight of him on video brings a rush of memories, stirring a warmth in my cheeks. Will every video call now remind me of our own? Of that accidental yet thrilling exposure? Miles always had this down-to-earth charm, his easy confidence captivating not just me but seemingly every woman at NorthRidge University.

"Miles, who's that?" his mom's voice interrupts from the phone.

Seizing the moment for a bit of fun, I lean into view. "Hey, Mrs. C., how's it going?" I flash a bright smile.

She returns the smile, a hint of surprise in her voice. "Hey Milli. I thought I recognized you. Miles, weren't you studying with your tutor?"

Wait—his mom doesn't know I am tutoring him?

Miles glances my way, a brief flash of embarrassment crossing his face before he masks it. He turns back to his phone, fingers brushing his face as if to smooth away any lingering discomfort.

"Yeah, Mom, Milli's tutoring me."

There's a pause, his mother sounding surprised. "Milli's your tutor?"

Does he feel embarrassed about me tutoring him?

Her face brightens, excitement evident. "That's wonderful! Hey Sean, did you hear? Milli's helping Miles."

In the background, his dad's voice comes through, a muted note of approval. "That's great, son."

Mrs. Chasen's expression turns thoughtful. "Does your mom know about this, Milli? Oh gosh, she's going to have a field day when she finds out."

I catch a glimpse of Mr. Chasen in the video, holding up a tie. "Which one for the gala?" he asks. Mrs. Chasen points to the light blue one, which indeed complements his eyes. The resemblance between Miles and his father is striking, especially those deep blue eyes.

He turns his head to give Mrs. Chasen a kiss on the cheek and says, "Miles, you never replied to my text the other night. Is everything okay?" His brows furrow with concern.

He mentions something about personal matters, but his words are shrouded in vagueness. *What's really going on with him?*

Then, Mr. Chasen mentions his doctor's appointment, and Miles' demeanor shifts subtly. He looks tired, almost defeated. I can't stand seeing him like this, especially when we're only halfway through our session. I decide to take the lead.

"Hey, Mrs. C., have you picked out your dress for the gala yet?" I stand up and add some dramatic flair by running my hands along my body. "I'm thinking of something timeless with a modern twist."

This is so far from my comfort zone—I usually can't stand discussing dresses, parties, and all that jazz. Just think back to how much I dreaded choosing an outfit for my first North-Ridge party with Payson. But I know it's something both Mrs. Chasen and my own mother love to chat about. If it distracts them from pestering Miles, it's worth it.

"Oh, I can totally see that," she says, her eyes practically painting the picture in her mind.

Miles swings the video screen my way, giving me a knowing smirk as he observes my little detour. I shoot him a wink because, why not? Our flirty banter doesn't just evaporate because his parents have joined the scene.

I keep it rolling. "Imagine this, Mrs. C., a soft pastel pink, a classic A-line shape that nips at the waist, off-the-shoulder with a sweetheart neckline, and a subtle V-neck back adorned with those dainty buttons."

Her eyes widen, and she clasps her hands over her chest.

Miles, wearing a sly grin, nods in agreement. "You've got that right!"

Sure, I might have pondered what to wear, but am I going to admit that to anyone? Not on your life. Yet, it's a gala for a cause that means a lot to me.

"Wow, Milli, that dress sounds like a total dream," she gushes.

"Total dream," Miles mouths behind the phone, teasing

me. And just because of that, I want to look absolutely stunning, a total dream to him.

I flash a grin as I settle back onto my barstool. "Thanks, Mrs. C., I'm honestly excited to find something like it."

But let's be real, what I'm really eager for is to see how Miles will react when he lays eyes on me in a dress like that.

Mrs. Chasen smiles. "I can't wait to see you in it. I'm sure you'll look absolutely stunning!"

With a smile of my own, I use my finger to signal Miles to shift the camera's focus back to him.

He swiftly complies, knowing exactly how to reassure his parents. "Mom, Dad, the doctor's appointment went well," he states confidently.

Despite his words, his expression betrays a hint of something else, and I file that away for later.

"He assured me everything's okay," Miles continues, and relief washes over his parents' faces. "I've got to go. Tutoring session awaits."

Their goodbyes are filled with love and warmth. Mrs. Chasen's parting words, "Can't wait to talk to your mom, Milli," echo with a hint of excitement.

Yeah, because tutoring Miles is the height of gossipworthy . . . Not.

"See you at the gala in two weeks," I respond, maintaining my cheerful facade.

As Miles ends the call, he seems to relax, the tension visibly draining from him. I reach over, offering a comforting back rub, and his signature grin reappears.

He teases, "There you go again, Mills, always saving the day."

I suppress a laugh, maintaining my composure. "What can I say? I'm the best."

His gentle push comes with a whisper, "Don't I know it,

Baby Sutton," accompanied by a wink that sends a warm tingle through my core.

And that flutter down there? Yeah, it's escalated into a full-blown sensation, pooling right between my legs. I'm kind of itching to do whatever it takes to earn another one of those cheeky winks.

CHAPTER 17
MILES

What are you doing, Miles?

Ever had one of those days where everything just feels misaligned, as if your body and mind are on completely different wavelengths? Today's that day for me, where not even my go-to songs can chase away the persistent gloom, and my thoughts are caught in a tumultuous storm of doubt.

I'm caught in a constant hustle, darting from one university class to another, finding fleeting moments of peace on the football field. But overshadowing this routine is the exhausting wait for updates from my doctors. The annual cancer screening has come and gone, leaving me in a limbo of silence that's excruciating. My thoughts are ensnared in a relentless cycle of what ifs. What if the cancer has returned? What if the scan results are unfavorable? Logically, I know I should be in the clear, but logic seldom soothes the gnawing fears.

Amidst this turmoil, here I am, in the heart of our football field, preparing for tomorrow's game. The sight is overwhelming—a grand symphony of senses. The colossal stands reach toward the sky, each seat silently awaiting its fan. The field stretches out, a vibrant green canvas under the open sky.

This moment is an adrenaline rush. It makes me wonder about the possibility of a life in the NFL—playing on different fields, soaking up each exhilarating second.

But is that really what I want?

At twenty-one, it feels impossible to have life all figured out. The pressure to choose between a potential NFL career and my dream of becoming a doctor weighs heavily on me. Medicine feels like a calling, but it's laden with high expectations from myself and others.

Then there's the allure of the NFL, a path my dad once pursued before his own sacrifices for my cancer battle. Stepping onto that field, experiencing the roar of the crowd, and honoring my dad's legacy calls at me.

With Panthers' Day, the gala, and the MCAT on the horizon, I'm swamped with a sense of being overwhelmed. The one silver lining this week has been acing my statistics midterm. Clearly, tutoring sessions with Milli are paying off. It's not that I ever doubted their value, but the relief of having one less stressor is palpable. Now, I just need to tackle the final exam and then move forward. It's like life itself, isn't it? We keep moving, taking a step forward each day. But amidst all this, I wonder how I'm going to manage the complexities of the real world when managing college life already feels like a high-wire act.

On top of these personal challenges, there's the societal pressure to have every aspect of your future mapped out—career, marriage, children. The very thought adds a layer of weight to my shoulders. I can almost see the excitement in my mom's eyes when we eventually delve into these topics. But for me, it's not just excitement; it's an ever-growing list of expectations I'm not sure I'm ready to meet.

"Are you just going to keep daydreaming, or are you going to run the ball?" Coach's voice pulls me back to the present.

I casually pivot my shoulder to check out the scene—him and the gang of teammates are staring at me like I've grown a second head. I shrug it off and say, "Eh, I don't know. It's kinda nice."

But the truth is, my vision's blurring again, making it hard to focus. I've been dismissing it as bad throws, but is that really all it is?

I close my eyes, taking a deep breath, trying to push away the worry. Coach joins me, his hand on my shoulder. "Not too bad, huh?"

And for a fleeting moment, the tension building inside me dissipates as I crack up at the sheer absurdity of the situation. I can only imagine what my teammates must be thinking, witnessing the two of us staring up at the sky as if we've just spotted a UFO.

"Seriously, though, no barking orders, no teammates complaining, and no fear of getting smacked in the wrong place by a rogue ball. Just me, chillin', soaking in that fall sky," I murmur more to myself, but Coach can hear.

His head dips, and I catch it out of the corner of my eye. He gives my shoulder a friendly squeeze. The rest of the gang saunters over, heads craned to the sky, as if they're trying to figure out what we see up there—which, in reality, is just a whole lot of nothing but the wide-open sky.

I let my head drop down, and about a dozen other guys are pulling the same stunt. Coach decides to break the silence, grumbling, "Okay, enough with the daydreaming, you bunch of dreamers. Let's refocus on winning that game tomorrow."

Cam jumps in, coming to our defense. "Hey, we were just following Miles' lead. He's my mentor, after all."

I roll my eyes as Coach puts on his best serious face, but

there's a hint of a smile hiding behind it as he shakes his head in response. "Smartass," he mutters before wandering off toward our linebacker coach.

The whole team bursts into laughter, whooping and hollering, and they start heading back into their positions for practice. I'm about to do the same when I hear a familiar voice. "You doing okay, man?"

I glance over and notice Luke beside me. We both gaze up at the sky once more, and that previously dissipated tension returns in full force. However, instead of dwelling on that, I make a decision. "Honestly, Sutton, I'm not sure," I admit for the first time.

His head snaps back into place so quickly, undoubtedly wearing a quizzical expression.

Where do I even begin? How do I put into words the myriad of challenges I'm facing? On one hand, there's the mountain of academic work piling up. On the other, there are these feelings for Milli that I can't quite shake off. After our night out at the tavern—our laughter mingling, her soft touches, and those looks she gives me, filled with desire and something more—I'm pretty sure there's something real brewing between us. It took every ounce of restraint not to lean in for a kiss or suggest heading back to my place with Luke. But deep down, we both know how that scenario might unfold.

And there's really one person I feel comfortable sharing most things with, but I can't rely on her indefinitely. After all, graduation is looming this year, and I'm about to dive head-first into medical school, complete it, then move on to the residency and who-knows-what-else phases.

Breathe, Miles. One step at a time.

Drawing a deep breath, I finally meet Luke's gaze and shake my head. "It's nothing major, just feeling the heat with finishing the semester strong and the upcoming Panthers' Day Game."

It's not a complete fabrication; those are genuine concerns, after all.

Luke gives me a skeptical look, one that says he's not entirely convinced, and advises, "How about taking things one day at a time?"

That suggestion resonates with me. One step at a time. It's like a gentle nudge to open up, a reminder to live in the moment.

I nod, taking in what he's saying. "Just concentrate on the game tomorrow, okay?" he concludes, adding, "And as for wrapping up the semester, there's time to stress about that later."

His words coax a chuckle from me. "Out of sight, out of mind," I mutter to myself.

With a playful slap on my back, Luke jogs back to the field, rejoining the others. I watch them, a sense of camaraderie in their laughter and banter.

Navigating through the storm—overcoming cancer, confronting my deepest fears—has led me to a profound sense of thankfulness. The times spent with my team, the shared laughter, and the unbreakable bonds we've formed, these are the moments I hold dear. They stand as vivid reminders of life's beauty, a life brimming with endless possibilities and fresh starts.

Stepping into the huddle, I'm enveloped by the team's collective energy and fervor for the game ahead vibrating through us all. "Alright, boys," I announce, a smile spreading across my face, "let's zero in on these play-action plays."

Their response is immediate—grunts, shoves, a readiness to dive in. We form up, each player in position, ready to dissect the details of our play-action strategy.

I run through the plays, ensuring everyone understands

their role, from the offensive line's blocks to the receivers' routes. Every element of our play-action pass needs to be precise, a well-crafted illusion to outwit the defense.

We delve into the specifics: my role as quarterback, the depth of the fake handoff, the offensive line's convincing blocks. Mastery here isn't just about knowledge; it's about execution under pressure.

Our wide receivers and tight ends dedicate themselves to running routes with crisp, surgical precision, while the linemen focus on perfecting their blocking techniques. I practice the fake handoff over and over, then set up to deliver perfectly timed, pinpoint passes. It's like crafting a symphony of movement on the field.

We go through the play-action plays repeatedly, refining our timing and coordination until it becomes second nature. The rhythm of the practice field mirrors the rhythm of a seamlessly executed play. There's sweat, there's the sharp sound of Coach Kreft's whistle, and there's a relentless drive to run it again and again until it becomes flawless.

The practice wraps up with a highlight—Will, my go-to receiver, pulls off an impressive spin move that earns a round of applause. I grin in admiration. Grabbing my water bottle and towel, I take a refreshing gulp, signaling the end of another brutal practice.

As I'm about to head to the locker room, Coach calls out. "Miles, heads up! The guys' showers are out of order. Use the ladies' across the hall."

"Got it, Coach," I respond, knowing I'll probably have the place to myself—most of the team prefers their own showers. Plus, I anticipate a scenario where, upon returning home, Luke and I would be vying for the shower. So, it makes sense to take care of it here. Besides, sometimes I hit the library to study, and everything I need is right on campus, so why bother leaving and returning?

Total waste of time, in my opinion.

As I begin my trek toward the locker room, a faint melody catches my ear. Not the usual locker room speakers, but more like a phone's speaker. I continue walking, and when I round the corner, our football team's locker room is on one side and a plain women's locker room on the other, typically used by female staff or managers. I know they're all out on the field right now.

It's probably just another player; some have already left, while others are sticking around to work on their drills. Returning to our regular locker room, I grab my shower essentials and head across the hall. With just a towel slung around my waist, I make my way, spotting only four open showers. I choose the one nearest the door.

Stepping into the shower, I carefully adjust the water temperature, blending the cold and hot water to my liking. I catch a glance at the neighboring shower area where the mirrors are fogged up. It's impossible to make out who's in there, and it seems pointless to disturb whoever might be inside—especially if they're engrossed in listening to, uh, Twilight music? The soundtrack sounds oddly familiar, like the one from when Milli convinced me to watch the movies with her. It sounds like "A Thousand Years", but there's a violin twist to it? Whoever it is, they clearly need their privacy.

I ease into the warm water, letting it wash over me, melting away the stresses and hits from the practice. However, it doesn't take long before I hear a frustrated muttering, "Shit, shit, crap. Stupid, dumb girl," someone murmurs.

Wait, what the hell? Who's calling someone stupid, and why did that voice sound oddly familiar?

I quickly wipe my face and reach for my towel to investigate the situation. But the moment my hand reaches for the towel hook, there's nothing there.

"Fuckkk me," I curse under my breath.

Leaving my towel by the mirrors now seems like a bad idea. What if there's danger lurking? I'd have to make a naked dash for it.

Shaking off these wild thoughts, I step out, instantly chilled by the air. As I rush for my towel, I collide with someone.

"What the hell?"

A flurry of curses fill the air, and before I can process it, I've instinctively wrapped my arms around the other person.

And judging by the breasts I'm currently bumping into, it's definitely a woman's body.

But not just any woman's body. I recognize those legs I've often pictured wrapped around my waist, this body I've longed to hold, and, well, that stomach, the one my lips and tongue have sensually explored. Even in this unexpected moment, there's a familiarity that sends my mind reeling.

I let my gaze wander lazily, starting with her feet on the floor, then tracing her toned legs and stomach, despite it being pressed right against mine. As my eyes rise to meet hers, I find my hands instinctively positioned on her shoulders, as if to steady us both.

Our eyes lock, and for a heartbeat, we're frozen in a mutual shock. The reality of the situation crashes over me—I'm completely bare, holding Milli in the same state.

Milli. My Mills.

She's right here, her body pressed against mine in the most intimate way possible.

Miles, get a grip, I mentally chide myself, but my thoughts are a whirlwind of disbelief and confusion.

Our eyes are wide, mirroring each other's shock as we

remain motionless, grappling with the reality of our closeness.

What do you even do in a situation like this? Holding your best friend, both of you, without a stitch of clothing?

The answer is simple yet feels monumental—you fucking let go.

Listening to my inner thoughts, I gently guide Milli back by an inch, attempting to create some distance between us. However, it only seems to intensify the situation. Instead of catching a mere glimpse of her fully exposed body, I find myself viewing it from a close and intimate angle. Not to mention, her incredible breasts. God, are they fucking delicious and practically beckoning me, whispering, "Reach out, indulge, savor the temptation."

I'm really craving it, I can't deny it. My tongue subconsciously moistens my lips. The temptation to reach out, to feel their softness against my calloused hands, is almost overwhelming. I wish I could make her sweet sounds, just for a moment. Maybe a playful flick of her nipple, or even a gentle bite with my teeth.

If there's a higher power listening, please let this be my stress relief right now. I promise to repay the favor somehow, but I'm just not ready for this to end yet.

Suddenly, a soft whimper jolts me from my daze. Confusion floods me as Milli tilts her head back, lips parted slightly in a vulnerable expression that's both startling and captivating.

"Oh god, don't stop, Miles," she breathes out in a hushed tone.

What the hell?

My eyes lower, and my heart stutters in my chest. My hand, seemingly moving with a mind of its own, comes to rest on her chest, right over her breasts. The very same ones

I've glimpsed only through our video calls, the ones I've secretly longed to touch.

This can't be real . . .

But it's happening, right here, right now. I'm caught in this surreal moment, witnessing a side of

Milli I've never seen.

She's your friend.

I know I should stop, but my body isn't listening. *Friends, friends, friends,* I internally chant, yet it does nothing to quell the growing tension within me.

My grip unconsciously tightens, and it feels undeniably right. Her form fits perfectly in my hand, almost too perfectly.

I close my eyes for a fleeting second, lost in the sensation. It's like the universe is teasing me, offering a moment I've fantasized about but shouldn't indulge in.

Then reality crashes back with the sound of Luke's voice. "Chasen, man, you in there?"

Panic sets in. I'm motionless, my hand still on Milli, and he is just a few steps away from walking in on us.

Milli seems half in a trance, her eyes heavy, teetering between apprehension and an undeniable pull of desire. She's no longer tilting her head back; instead, she's biting her lower lip, a subtle, contemplative gesture.

Her eyes flit about, taking in our proximity, then dart toward the door where Luke's voice emanates from.

"Man, you in there?" Luke's voice comes again.

Focus, Chasen. Think fast.

"Yeah, yeah, I'm here," I manage to say, my voice strained as I maintain my touch on Milli.

"I'm thinking of showering here since I'm meeting a girl on campus," Luke says, oblivious.

My mind is elsewhere, completely absorbed by the

woman in front of me, her presence overwhelming all other thoughts.

"It would just be a waste of time, don't you think?" Luke adds.

If only he knew. Right now, I wish for nothing more than for him to leave.

Right fucking now.

"Sutton, my man, you were awesome out there," I hear Cam say, and I can only picture Luke grinning like a Cheshire cat at the compliment about his skills on the field.

Cam's distraction is a godsend. You'd think Milli and I would scurry to our separate shower stalls, but we don't. Neither of us make a move.

Our eyes stay locked, our breaths all tangled up. My muscles tense as I fight the urge to just scoop her up and carry her out of here, even though I know it's a pipe dream with Luke waiting right outside the locker room. But for now, I can hold on to this moment as mine.

My hand finds its way to her hip, fingers tracing the trail of goosebumps along Milli's spine. Her eyes drift to my lips, only inches from hers, in a silent invitation.

"Miles," she breathes out, her whisper barely grazing my lips.

Luke's voice filters through again, his plans changing, the excitement palpable. He's always had a thing for impromptu plans, especially when it involves a girl.

Cool, Luke. Now, please, just get the hell out of here.

The fading sound of his cleats tells me we're alone. The tension slightly eases, but neither of us move away. Milli leans into my touch, her body melding into mine.

God, this woman. Memories flash in my mind—That night at the club? Unbelievable. My lips on her stomach during the party? Absolutely. Seeing her on FaceTime? Hard as a rock, no doubt.

Now, observing Milli's hard swallow and the faint motion in her throat, a shift occurs within me. An intense fascination takes hold. Our eyes meet, and I inch closer, feeling her breath tickle my lips.

"What are you doing, Miles?" she asks softly. Hell if I know, but one thing's certain—I don't want whatever is happening to end.

Words fail me. Logic dictates I should pull away, yet my body outright rejects the notion; I'm anchored in the moment.

Her gaze meets mine, filled with swirling questions. "This," I manage to say, just before my lips gently press against hers in a soft, searching kiss. That contact sends a zap straight to my cock, but her subtle pullback leaves a pang of disappointment in its wake.

But then, Milli surges back, her lips meeting mine with a desperation that sets my pulse skyrocketing. We become a tangle of eager hands and clumsy kisses, as if we're trying to make up for lost time, unable to satiate our hunger for each other.

Was our connection always charged with this much intensity? She opens her mouth slightly, her lips softly seizing my upper one in a kiss that's both gentle and fervent. I pour every repressed emotion into this kiss, releasing a flood of pent-up feelings. My hands find her waist, my thumbs caress her sides with the utmost care. Her foot slides up and down my leg, her movements pressing her against me in a tantalizing rhythm. As my tongue tentatively traces her upper lip, her response is playful, inviting a dance of mutual desire.

Cradling the side of her face, my fingers trail down to encircle her neck. Our kiss deepens, becomes more fervent, our tongues exploring in a synchronized ballet of passion. A soft moan escapes her, stirring a growl from deep within me. "Fuck, Mills."

In a fluid motion, driven by instinct, I scoop her up, her arms and legs encircling me in a seamless, intimate hold. I carry her toward the locker room vanity, setting her down gently. Our lips separate, but merely by a whisper's distance, her legs winding around mine, pulling us to the edge of a boundary I've only fantasized about crossing.

What would it be like to have my cock inside her? To kiss her sweet pussy, to discover her taste?

A faint blush dusts her cheeks as she looks at me, her gaze piercing, as if she's reading every unspoken thought.

Her finger beckons me closer, a silent invitation I'm powerless to resist.

I lean in, her hands finding a firm hold on my shoulders, ready to lose ourselves again in the heat of our connection. But then, the insistent buzz of my phone shatters the spell, vibrating obnoxiously on the sink beside us.

Fucking incredible timing . . .

Our foreheads meet, a shared sigh of frustration and resignation escaping us. The room is filled with the persistent buzzing, a stark reminder of the world outside this moment.

Reluctantly, I step back to check the message, a nagging intuition urging me to see who it is.

When I do, the message isn't what I anticipate.

Kins: Hey, Miles. We tried calling you earlier today, but you must have been busy.

Busy is an understatement, I muse to myself, reflecting on the intense, whirlwind moments that just unfolded.

Reading further, the message hits like a cold wave.

Kins: Dr. Reynolds wants you in for another scan.

That sinking feeling in my gut tells me this isn't routine. More scans usually mean they've found something in the initial one.

Milli's hand gently touches mine, drawing my attention. I

quickly hide my phone, hoping she hasn't caught a glimpse of the message.

I try to convince myself it's nothing, giving her a strained smile that I know doesn't fully light up my eyes.

I release her hand to grab our towels, which, to my relief, are placed side by side. A small favor from the universe in an otherwise unsettling moment.

Wrapping the towel around my waist, I take Milli's hand again. She seems to have withdrawn slightly, a change I can't ignore. The heat of the moment has cooled into a more somber reality.

Gently, I guide her to her feet, wrapping her snugly in the towel. My arms fold around her in a natural embrace, a silent promise of comfort. For a moment, a precious, fleeting moment, as she leans into the circle of my arms, the looming worries and the heavy silence between us lose their grip. It's her—her nearness, the soft heat radiating from her—that scatters the clouds of anxiety, wrapping us in a serene bubble of peace, if only for a heartbeat.

She retreats slightly, yet remains within the circle of my arms, and in this instant, she's more than just my best friend —she's a haven, a source of calm in the storm. It feels right, like a missing piece falling into place.

Casting one last look her way, my fingers delicately raise her chin. Our gazes lock, and as her eyelids flutter shut in expectancy, I lean forward but, at the last moment, shift to the left, pressing a gentle kiss near the corner of her lips. She responds with a soft, understanding sigh, a look of mingled emotions playing across her face. It requires every ounce of my resolve to erase that expression from my mind. But I do. I collect my belongings, and with a heart caught in a whirlwind of feelings, I take my shit and leave the locker room.

CHAPTER 18
MILLI

"So, he just left without a word?" Payson asks, her voice laced with disbelief. "No goodbye, no playful banter? You didn't even toss him a witty line like, 'Hope you enjoyed the show?'" Her chuckle is infectious.

Brooke, standing by the dance studio mirrors, joins in, her hands theatrically placed on her chest; a comical imitation of me. "Like, 'Thanks for getting cozy with my chest.'"

I shake my head, laughter fading to a soft smile, my voice a whisper of confession. "Just friends." The distance college life has put between us—me with my dance and tutoring, Payson with her RA duties, and Brooke lost in her sorority life—has made these reunions rare. Their presence makes all the difference . . . I've been itching to share all the details with them, but texting just wouldn't do it justice.

"Mmhm, 'just friends,' keep telling yourself that, Milli," Payson teases, an all-knowing smirk playing on her lips.

Brooke gives her a gentle nudge, the quiet between them saying more than words ever could.

I push aside that nagging little voice in my head, trying to convince myself there is no reason to get all worked up about Miles and our recent encounter. Since being at school, whenever we cross paths, we've exchanged smiles, said hi, even stopped to talk about what was going on that day. But now, it feels like something shifted between us last week. I've texted him a few times to check in, but he replies with a casual, "Yes, Mills" or "Yeah, just busy."

His responses only serve to send my mind into a whirlwind of emotions. I can't stop wondering: Are we truly okay? Did he enjoy what happened between us? Does he want to repeat it? Jeez Louise, just the thought of it consumes me all over again.

The tension was palpable.

Those lingering gazes said it all.

The heated touches sent shivers down my spine.

Good god, those touches—his hand on my breasts felt like a page ripped right out of my own novel. It's etched in my memory, so much so it's almost replaced the steamy scenes in my books when it comes to my personal fantasies.

Is it wrong that my mind constantly wanders to Miles, that those moments in the locker room leave me flushed and breathless? Maybe. Logic says we should have been embarrassed, standing there, stripped of all pretenses as well as our clothes. But embarrassment? That emotion was foreign to us. Instead, there was only the electric connection as our gazes met, unflinching, across the bare space between us.

In fact, it was one of the most scorching moments of my life.

Until it wasn't . . .

I try to dismiss the image of Miles abruptly exiting the locker room, a text message transforming his intense, fiery gaze into one clouded with worry. How swiftly emotions can shift—a testament, perhaps, to some unsettling news? The sudden change in his expression, that familiar sinking feeling in my gut, just like whenever I sensed something amiss with Miles. That's what's been gnawing at me this entire week. The unspoken truth of what transpired between us lingers, acknowledged by both, yet addressed by none. Our interactions have resumed to casual smiles on the field, friendly waves across the campus, as if we're attempting to reset the clock. But how do you rewind life, erase moments charged with such intensity?

I missed him, for his touch again, the way his hands felt on my body. But it seems like we have moved past that, or at least, he has. I can't stop replaying those memories, convincing myself we are just friends. This is something more, something deeper.

Just friends, Milli.

Please, do friends actually make out naked?

"Did you get to . . . you know . . . touch it?" Payson asks, her voice teasing as she finishes her leg stretches in the luminous dance studio of our campus. I offer a nonchalant shrug, concealing my burning wish to have felt his muscular, tantalizing cock. Those moments when he was achingly close, when our mutual desire was palpable in every tense muscle and each quickened breath, linger in my mind.

Payson and Brooke groan together, a shared moment of playful exasperation. Payson's smirk grows wider. "I bet that guy is packing like a horse."

If only she knew just how well-endowed he is; he probably outperforms all the guys she's been with. I shake my head once more, deciding to keep certain details of that night to myself. This memory, it's sacred, too intimate to share. It's that bittersweet mix of wanting to spill your heart out to friends but holding back the most precious details. Plus, I dread thinking about how Miles would react if he knew I'd shared our secret. I can almost hear Payson's unfiltered comments the next time we're all together. And just that has me pointing a finger at her, saying, "Don't even." She knows exactly what I am referring to because she pretends to zip her mouth shut, tossing the invisible key to the side.

I rise, my gaze sweeping over the studio—my haven. It's a stark contrast to the one from high school, with its sleek modernity, its walls adorned with colorful costumes and posters, and its dark, polished floors reflecting the streaming sunlight. The familiar hum of music fills the space, wrapping around me like a warm embrace. It was love at first sight, not with a person, but with this place of art and expression.

Some may call it odd, others may not, but as a dancer, most would understand that finding a studio you feel comfortable in and can call home for the next four years is just as important as finding a place to live. And for me, this studio is my sanctuary.

"Well, if you won't spill the beans, maybe I should do some digging?" Payson's words, tinged with mischief, jolt me back to the present.

I turn sharply, my eyes narrowing. She laughs, her eyes sparkling with humor as she steps closer. A flash of jealousy stirs within me, even though I know she's jesting. "Your face says it all," she teases, giving me a friendly nudge.

Before I can even protest, she announces, "Ready for tonight?" I roll my eyes, already anticipating her next words before they even leave her lips. "Not that you really have a say in this—you're coming to the Halloween party tonight."

I release a low groan, despite having assured her earlier in the week that I'd attend—not out of duty, but because it's been forever since I truly last relaxed and enjoyed a party. Given the recent whirlwind of events, especially the complexities involving Miles, a change of scenery seems more crucial than ever.

The thought of dressing up, looking my best, and just forgetting everything for one night is surprisingly appealing.

I nod in agreement, and her face lights up with a radiant smile, probably relieved she didn't have to convince me this time. She's always been the more outgoing one, seizing any chance to go out when she's not tied down with RA duties, which seems like almost every other weekend. She scoops up her bag from where she tossed it on the floor upon entering with Brooke, still buzzing about the SOS message I sent in our group chat last night. She waves goodbye, a casual three-finger salute, and heads out of the dance studio.

"Just ignore her. I'm really excited to see your costume tonight," Brooke says, standing up, her eyebrows dancing with curiosity.

Truth be told, I haven't given my costume much thought, but an idea is forming in my mind. I reply with a half-smile and reach over to switch off the stereo. "Well, I need to focus now. The Hanmann sisters will be here for their dance routine in . . . " I glance at my gold watch, "exactly five minutes."

Brooke pauses, stepping in for a quick hug, her eyes meeting mine with a knowing look. "Just let whatever Payson said roll off your back," she suggests. "She's probably just envious she doesn't have as much drama in her life right now."

I laugh. "You sure about that? She seems to find drama wherever she goes, like a magnet."

"Hey, I know you're talking about me," Payson's voice, half-teasing, half-accusatory, floats back into the studio as she pokes her head through the door, pointing at us.

Brooke and I exchange a knowing glance and walk over to her, laughter bubbling up between us. As we wrap Payson in a group hug, a sense of relief washes over me, easing the knots of worry and tension that had been building up.

"We're always talking about you, Pay," I quip, my lips twisting into a smirk.

She releases her trademark exaggerated sigh, yet her eyes twinkle with mirth. "As long as you're talking about my finer qualities," she shoots back, easing out of our hug.

I give a gentle smile, observing them. My heart fills with a deep sense of gratitude. They've been my steadfast support through every peak and valley, and I'm certain they'll remain by my side, regardless of what the future holds.

Turning my attention back to the task at hand, I clap my hands together, a playful nudge to get their asses moving. "Alright, I've got the Hanmann sisters to coach," I announce, a hint of urgency in my voice.

"Yeah, yeah, we got it the first time," Payson responds with a roll of her eyes, while Brooke just shakes her head, her smile mirroring mine.

As they make their way to the door, Payson casts one last look back, waving with her usual brightness. Brooke, on the other hand, stops, her smile turning tender. "I'm proud of you, Milli," she states, her voice carrying a depth of sincerity that resonates to my core.

"For what?" I ask, genuinely puzzled.

"For everything. College, dance, just . . . life. You're doing amazing. See you tonight," she says, her smile widening with pride. Then, with a final wave, she steps out, the door closing gently behind her.

Left alone, the music softly playing in the background, I take a deep breath. A wave of gratitude washes over me. This life—my friends, this studio, my college journey—it's more than I ever dared to hope for.

"Milli, Milli, you're here!" The Hanmann sisters' voices, tinted with excitement, reach me before I even see their tutus fluttering and ballet slippers tapping against the studio floor. Close behind them, their father, Ben, strides in, a picture of rugged charm.

Ben has always struck me as a blend of literary heartthrob

and a dash of cowboy. His dark green eyes and sandy blonde hair complement his tall, broad-shouldered frame perfectly. He greets me with a smile, his dimples adding to his allure. "Hey there, Milli. Thanks for having the girls come in early today."

I beam back. "It's no problem at all, Mr. Hanmann."

He lightheartedly scolds, "Milli, remember, call me Ben. 'Mr. Hanmann' just adds years to my age."

Our laughter mingles. "Okay, Ben it is."

He hesitates, a hint of nerves in his eyes. "Actually, Milli, can we talk a moment before the class?"

That catches me off guard. What could Ben want to discuss?

I nod, curious and a bit anxious. Ben's unease seems palpable, his gaze intense. He fidgets, fingers raking through his hair. "It's about the upcoming Dazzling Duo Dance," he starts.

That mention stirs a mix of emotions in me. The Dazzling Duo Dance—a renowned mother-daughter competition I'd always dreamed of joining, but never could. Thanks to my mom's disapproval, it remained a dream, watching others participate while I sat on the sidelines.

But that's the past. I focus back on Ben, twirling a curl around my finger to steady myself.

He continues, "Lily and Georgia, they're eager to join. But the thing is, their mom . . . well, she's not around to be their partner."

That revelation hits me. It explains so much—the absence, the unspoken gaps in their stories.

Ben's gaze meets mine, filled with earnest hope. "I was hoping . . . could you . . . would you think about helping them enter the competition?" His voice trembles a bit, but he quickly adds, "You don't have to feel pressured. Regardless, they think the world of you."

His eyes hold a vulnerability, a silent plea hanging between us. The moment stretches, heavy with unspoken desires and expectations.

"So, what do you say, Milli?" Ben asks, his eyes locked on mine, waiting.

Ben's appeal catches me off guard. I'm neither their mother nor a relative. Yet, here I stand, approached to take on a role for the Dazzling Duo Dance that feels both deeply personal and overwhelmingly challenging.

However, the idea ignites a spark of excitement inside me, presenting an opportunity I never thought would come my way, especially given my own past experiences with similar events.

"Ben, helping Lily and Georgia would be a joy for me. They're incredibly important to me, and they've earned this experience." My words carry a dual significance: they hint at the chances I've let slip by in my own life while also expressing a steadfast willingness to embark on this new journey.

Ben's reaction is immediate—his face breaks into a relieved, grateful smile. "Milli, that's wonderful. Thank you. This . . . it means a lot to us." His quick correction and blush add a layer of sincerity to his gratitude.

I return his smile, feeling a surge of purpose. "It means the world to me too, Ben. I'm honored to be a part of their journey."

This is more than just a dance. It's an opportunity to impact these young lives, to be the mentor I've always aspired to be in my dance studio. I want to show them that their dreams are within reach, that they are capable of soaring beyond any limits.

After exchanging a few more sincere, warm words, we go our separate ways. Ben heads toward the waiting room, and I turn to the Hanmann sisters, my heart brimming with enthusiasm. The prospect of the Dazzling Duo Dance fills me with an invigorating energy, ready to pour my passion and creativity into every step of their dance routine.

"You know you looking fucking hot, right?" Payson remarks as I pull up near the Alpha Rho Tau house. The same house, the same throng of costumed students spilling out—aliens, Dwight Schrute look-alikes, all igniting a private chuckle. Skipping this Halloween bash was an option, but that wouldn't be fair to me or my friends. Even if it isn't actually Halloween, students at NorthRidge U. will take an opportunity to party, especially Alpha Rho Tau.

I catch my reflection, my confidence surging in the sexy librarian costume—a short plaid skirt, black glasses, and my strawberry blonde hair in curls. Borrowing these glasses from Luke had been an adventure in itself. Payson had to practically evict him from our dorm after he dared to criticize my outfit. I remember the tension between them, Brooke and I speculating on when they'd inevitably kiss again. It's their life, their choices, even if they're reckless.

Stepping out of the car, we navigate through the crowd, a familiar wave of anxiety washes away as classmates beckon us to the kitchen island. That island—the scene of my second kiss with Miles. A memory tries to surface, but Payson's tug on my hand pulls me into the present. We grab red cups, filling them with beer.

As Payson mingles with other RAs, introducing me and Brooke, I'm struck by one guy, Beckett—Beck. NorthRidge University's pitcher, and a dead ringer for Zach Wheeler. Sports are in my blood, so I can't help but be a little impressed.

Lost in thought, I reach for another beer, the buzz welcome, despite my usual distaste for it. Leaning against the island, surveying the crowd, I hear a voice. "Sexy librarian, or a unique take on a Harry Potter character?"

It's Beck. His confidence reminds me of Miles, that athletic charisma. But this is my night. No Miles. Just fun. I catch Beck eyeing me as I bite my lip, a flutter of butterflies—different from those Miles elicits—stirring in me. "Which do you prefer?" I challenge.

"Definitely sexy librarian," he replies, stepping closer, his gaze leisurely taking me in.

I grin, playing along. "Correct, Beckett." My tone is flirtier than usual, but it's all in good fun.

Tonight is about letting go. College isn't just about campus life; it's about these moments too. And as the evening unfolds with laughter, dance, and harmless flirting, I'm reminded of a quote from my old tutor, *"Milli, just as in dance, where every step tells a story, let your life's journey be choreographed to the rhythm of your deepest truths, creating a masterpiece of authenticity, free from the shadows of regret."*

In that moment, the full weight of those words hit me. I stand there, in the heart of the party's vibrant energy, feeling a profound connection to the truth they convey. Around me, the room pulses with life, laughter, and a kaleidoscope of stories unfolding.

I watch Payson and Brooke as they mingle effortlessly, their laughter weaving through the music and chatter. A warmth spreads through me, a gratitude for them, for the moments we have already shared during our freshman year.

My eyes then find Beck. He is in his element, surrounded by a group hanging onto his every word about baseball. I smile. His passion is palpable, and it reminds me of how each person in this room is following their own path, dancing to the rhythm of their individual truths.

I take a deep breath, letting the energy of the room fill me. It is more than just a party; it is a celebration of us, of who we are becoming in this sprawling tapestry of college life. And as I stand there, I realize I am exactly where I am meant to be—embracing every moment, every experience, and living my truth without any shadow of regret.

CHAPTER 19
MILES

Everything is fine.
Everything is fine.

"Miles!" Harper's voice rings out, a vibrant melody in the sterile hospital room. I catch her gaze, brimming with unbridled excitement. She sits on the edge of her waiting room chair, fidgeting with anticipation as Kins, her ever-present guardian angel in scrubs, checks her vitals. A smile—spontaneous and heartfelt—finds its way across my face. Her enthusiasm is infectious, a bright spark that momentarily stills my heartbeat.

Is she really this excited to see me, Miles Chasen?

Memories flood in, unbidden. Hospital corridors much like these, but lonelier, quieter. My own childhood marred by illness. I remember the silence, the echoing absence of laughter, the mantra my parents repeated: "Rest is best." Friends and stories were replaced by sterile walls and hushed tones.

Harper's world is different. She has Kins, a nurturing presence, and friends like me who bring not just books, but a piece of the outside world, a dose of normalcy. I watch her, admiration and a tinge of envy mingling in my chest.

As Kins wraps up, I move closer, my smile an open invitation. "Hey there, champ. What's the latest from Harper's world?"

Her response is a burst of energy. "Miles, guess what! I made a dragon in art time. The coolest dragon ever!"

I squat down, meeting her at eye level, my interest genuine. "That's amazing, Harper! Tell me about this dragon. Does it have a name?"

Her eyes, wide with excitement, meet mine. "Did you ever have a dragon?"

"Actually, yes," I reply, a smile playing on my lips. "But mine was simply named 'Dragon'."

She giggles, a sound of pure joy. "Mine's 'Flamaraux'. He's red with black and white spikes. Isn't that cool?"

Her laughter tapers off as she contemplates the name I've given my dragon. "Dragon? That's an unusual name," she comments, her nose wrinkling cutely in a manner that brings Milli to mind.

I tap her nose playfully. "Easy to remember, right?"

She nods, a sage in a small body. As Harper dives into tales of Flamaraux's adventures, I'm struck by the resilience and imagination of children. In their world, dragons and art can coexist with hospital rooms and vital checks. I'm here, not just as a visitor, but as a bridge to a world where dragons roam free, a reminder of life beyond these walls.

Kins flashes me a supportive smile as she finishes her tasks. "Dr. Reynolds will be with you shortly," she says, her tone warm and reassuring.

Harper, her small hand gently resting on my arm, gazes up at me, eyes brimming with tales untold, a smile playing on her lips.

A smile strains across my face, but it's a thin veil over the turmoil churning inside. Dr. Reynolds' pending words hang over me like a dark cloud, a haunting echo from my childhood. In those silent rooms, I used to clasp my hands tight, silently pleading, hoping against hope that Dr. Reynolds wouldn't utter the dreaded, "Well, Miles, the scans aren't quite what we were hoping for."

This time will be different. It's become my lifeline, the mantra fueling my week, pushing me through a rigid routine. Every day unfolds with mechanical precision: wake, gym, classes, study, football, eat, study, sleep. It's the discipline I should have embraced most of my time in college, but life, as always, has its twists.

Yet, the routine has been more than a schedule; it's been my anchor, steadying me amidst the chaos, especially after what happened with Milli in the locker room. Walking away from her wasn't what I wanted. She deserves more than a fleeting, heated moment.

Every day is a new tangle in this mess. Milli is everywhere —in class, all over campus, and even at our place, chatting with Luke. The moment I had heard her voice, it was like a jolt. I wanted to bolt out of my room, see her, talk to her. But no, I just lied there, glued to the bed. She had knocked softly, like she was tiptoeing around my mood. I didn't make a sound. She didn't push it. Through the crack under the door, her shadow had lingered; a silent question I'm still not ready to answer. Luke's voice had carried through the walls, tinged with concern. "He's been acting off all week. Doesn't seem like he's well." His words, truer than he knew.

My body is a battleground—stomach churning, head pounding, vision blurring. Is this a long-standing storm I have ignored, or did Kinsley's message cast a glaring spotlight on my reality? Either way, this past week, I craved nothing more than a respite from the storm that is my life.

Plus, that other thing with Milli, it's gnawing at me. We're treading new ground here, in a place we've never ventured before. And Milli seems to just glide through it all. Her smile, which once was like a beacon of light in my world, now only casts shadows of doubt, leaving me wondering if my touch ever really meant anything to her.

My train of thought derails as Harper tugs at my arm, pulling me toward a couple of chairs nestled in the cancer ward. These chairs are like tiny havens in the vast, sterile expanse of the hospital. There's a gentle hum of soothing music and sunlight pours through large windows, softening the harsh clinical edges. Potted plants stand guard, trying their best to infuse some life into the place.

I sink into a chair, propping my chin on my hand, and meet Harper's eager gaze.

"Hey, Miles, did you know something wild about space?" She beams at me.

A smile breaks through my worries. Harper, with only our second meeting, already feels like a balm to my frazzled nerves. She turns a dreaded hospital visit into something almost . . . hopeful. Just being here, making Harper's day a little brighter, gives me a sense of purpose beyond my own tangled thoughts.

Harper fidgets, her fingers playing a nervous dance against her thumb. Then, she locks eyes with me, a torrent of words spilling out. "Kinsley let me explore the hospital library. It was like an adventure!" Her laughter is light, infectious. "Have you been there?"

"Oh, definitely." I grin back. That library was where my dream of being a doctor, a pediatrician, took root. It's where my world expanded beyond the confines of my own health battles.

As she talks about space, her eyes light up with the same kind of wonder that always filled me when diving into medical books or racing down these halls with Luke in my wheelchair.

"Space is completely silent, you know. All those sound

effects in movies are made up. There's no air in space to carry sound."

I look at her, genuinely impressed. "So, space is all quiet, huh? No hospital, no needles, just . . . peace?"

She nods eagerly. "Yeah, we could just float up there, away from all this, and be—Free. Just living a normal life," she adds, her voice a mix of longing and hope, perfectly echoing my own unspoken wish.

I nod, my smile genuine. "Exactly."

Harper shifts in her chair, her youthful energy palpable. "Imagine, Miles, just escaping all this, relaxing without a care about what's—"

"Coming next?" I jump in, my voice tinged with understanding. "To relish the now, without fretting over the future?"

That sentiment hits close to home. I've heard it all before —"Focus on what's ahead, Miles," or "Let's see what the doctor says later, honey." But as a kid, and even now, that future-focused mindset feels like a weight. I often find myself wondering when the other shoe will drop. Here I am, a college senior, excelling in football, acing academics, aiming for med school—yet the nagging thought of impending doom lurks in the shadows.

Keep it together. Everything is okay.

Harper's grin is a ray of light. "Yeah, wouldn't that be something?"

I tap her nose playfully. "The absolute best."

Then, the moment breaks. "Miles, Doctor Reynolds will see you now."

I stand, giving Harper's shoulder a comforting squeeze. She clasps my hand, her small voice filled with sincerity. "Good luck, Miles."

She whips out her Polaroid. "Quick, before you go."

I oblige with a smile. "Of course, Harp."

Her eyes brighten at the nickname, a simple joy that lifts my spirits. Maybe, just maybe, it's the best part of my day.

We snap the photo, and as I turn to leave, I stop. "Hey, Harp."

She looks up, admiration in her gaze. It's a refreshing change from the typical adulation I get for football.

"Show me that dragon later, okay?"

Her enthusiastic nod makes her seem even more endearing.

I point at her, winking. "I'll be waiting for it."

She giggles as I walk away and join Kins, heading toward the familiar room #3. She preps to take my vitals; her approach more relaxed with just me around.

As she wraps the cuff around my arm, she comments, "You know, you really brightened Harper's day."

I can't help but smile. "Seems like I did."

Kins, with her stethoscope casually around her neck, nudges me. "You're in a good mood today, aren't you?"

Am I really handling this well? I've spent the whole week in dread, and now, here in the familiar routine, I'm still playing the part. It's almost easier to wear this mask of calm than to face the storm of fear and uncertainty inside.

Sitting there, lost in thought, Kinsley's routine tasks hum in the background, underscoring my inner turmoil. These moments, so regular yet filled with alternating currents of hope and dread, never become easier.

Kinsley looks up, her voice laced with compassion. "You're so strong, Miles. Always handling this with such grace."

A wry smile crosses my lips. "I guess it's just what I've learned, Kins," I murmur.

She nods, her eyes warm with understanding. "It's a true sign of strength, Miles."

That strength has been my anchor, the one constant

through all this uncertainty. But it doesn't make the weight any less heavy.

Kinsley's voice pulls me back. "Dr. Reynolds will be in soon." I nod, settling into the chair, feeling her gaze on me. She reaches across, her hands enveloping mine in a comforting grip. Her words are gentle, almost motherly. "You've been here before, Miles. Look how far you've come."

I exhale, a tension I didn't know I was holding releases. "You think I can keep doing this?" I ask, more to myself.

Kinsley gives a reassuring smile. "You've fought it before, and you can definitely fight it now."

She leaves, and I'm alone with my racing thoughts. *Fight it now? What the hell does that mean?* My heart pounds, my breath quickens. How can I stay calm with words like that?

Pacing the room, I try to steady my thoughts.

It's all good. Stay strong, Miles.

But those words feel hollow. Maybe Kins meant something less dire, something manageable?

A knock at the door breaks my reverie. "Miles," a voice calls.

Dr. Reynolds steps in, smiling, but he fails to mask the concern underneath. It's a look I know too well, one that's always preceded by unwelcome news. A doctor's smile that never reaches his eyes is a smile heavy with unspoken truths.

Dr. Reynolds gestures to the chair. "Take a seat, Miles," he says, his voice a mix of steadiness and empathy.

I sit, fighting to keep the rising tide of anxiety at bay.

He starts, the weight of his words filling the room. "Miles, the results from your PET scan are in. I wish I had better news." He exhales, releasing tension and his tone softens. "The PET scan revealed some concerning areas, Miles. We need more tests, but it looks like activity in the same area as before."

That "area"—my brain, where I've battled before—suddenly feels like a battleground again.

The weight in the room intensifies, pressing down on me. I inhale deeply, trying to steady my voice. "What's the next step?"

Dr. Reynolds leans in, his gaze sincere. "We're not sure of the severity yet. We'll start with a biopsy. Then, we can plan your treatment. We're here for you, Miles." His reassurance feels hollow.

"Yeah, what's new?" I murmur, more to myself. A whirlwind of thoughts swirl inside. The path I thought I'd left behind now stretches out before me again. What about football, college, the MCAT? My dreams, once within grasp, slip away, the looming shoe finally dropping.

A string of curses slips out, fueled by frustration. *Why now?* My heart races, the room spins.

Everything is fine, I tell myself.

But deep down, I know it's not. Far fucking from it.

CHAPTER 20
MILLI

I just couldn't help myself, you know? I had this gut feeling Miles would be here. He thinks he's all mysterious, but honestly, after watching him for so long, he's pretty easy to read. And man, what a read he is . . .

The way he talks, that effortless charm, he has—just enough to show off, but not too much. His little quirks, the way you can always tell what he's thinking if you look close enough. Those lips, and don't get me started on his cologne —that musky, sandalwood scent. And, of course, there's his body.

It's like my feet had their own plan, dragging me to this lake. I just need to see him with my own eyes, to make sure he is okay . . .

This whole silent treatment thing he's been pulling for a week? Can't stand it. Woke up this morning and thought, *Today's the day, Milli. Time to do something about it.* So, I finished up my stuff and headed over to his place. Figures he wasn't there. Asked Luke, and all he does is shrug and say, "Take a wild guess."

Lake Trout—where else?

Campus is just a half-hour drive, and we're only about ten minutes from where I grew up. I have the afternoon off, so I figured, why not? Might as well drop by my parents' place for dinner, too.

They'd love that.

Deciding to deal with that later, I look over at Miles. My heart's doing this crazy dance, seeing him cast his line, waiting for a bite. Every muscle, perfectly defined, moving so smoothly as he fishes.

Milli, get a grip.

Right, focus. I'm here to check on him. But it's Miles Chasen—Mr. Pickup Truck and Fishing when the going gets tough. I park my jeep, get out, and start walking over. I know, I know—probably not the best idea. Could mess things up even more. But something in me just has to be here, close to him. Maybe even touch him. Or hey, just being a good friend, right? Am I even being a friend now, or is it something more? Does he feel the same?

God, what if this is a huge mistake?

My head's all over the place. Last thing Miles needs is me showing up all emotional, thanks to these crazy hormones.

But here I am, walking closer to him. Heart's racing like mad. It's just us and some old couple walking by. The lake looks amazing—all those trees with their fall colors, and that smell of burning leaves in the air. I wrap my arms around myself, kinda loving the way the wind feels.

Stepping onto the dock, he still hasn't noticed me. I close my eyes for a sec, whispering a little prayer, hoping I'm not screwing this up. Then I open them, take a deep breath, and move closer, close enough to feel his warmth.

"Look who the cat dragged in," I whisper softly.

He turns, his eyes widening in surprise. A heavy silence

falls between us, charged with unspoken words and emotions.

I chuckle nervously. "I guess, more like, look what the tide reeled in." The corners of his mouth turn up.

"What're you doing here, Mills?" he asks.

Our eyes meet, and I swear my knees almost give out. I step closer, the old wooden dock creaking under my feet. My heart's pounding, and I can barely catch my breath.

"Just needed some fishing therapy, you know, to unwind," I reply with a teasing smile.

He arches a brow.

"Like your fishing therapy," I add, trying to lighten the mood.

He keeps looking at me, an amused twinkle in his eyes.

"You know, your thing. Coming here when life gets too crazy," I say.

He laughs, that familiar grin spreading across his face, lighting up the moment. "You don't even like fishing," he says, his grin transforming into a panty-dropping smile.

"Thought I'd give it a shot," I reply, aiming for nonchalance.

Fishing isn't my jam, especially those slimy worms, but if it helps coax whatever's bothering Miles out of him, it's worth a shot. It's a pattern he's had since we were kids—retreating, sulking, trying to escape. But sometimes, there's a limit. He even skipped our tutoring session and, according to Luke, ditched football practice all week. That's just not like him.

Miles' eyes land on mine, and those blue eyes darken with an unabashed hunger, unmistakable. The air between us vibrates with an electric tension, undeniable and charged. His breath, now a warm whisper against my skin, draws nearer as he leans in. Our lips, barely a breath's distance apart.

"Miles," I breathe out, so quietly it's more for me than him.

"You even bring a pole?" he suddenly asks, breaking the spell.

What? It takes a second for his words to register. By the time they do, he's already off, fetching an extra fishing pole from the end of the dock. He hands it to me, our fingers brushing, sending this shockwave down my spine. After everything, all the skin, the heat, the heart-stopping moments we've shared, he still gets to me. Every. Single. Time.

"I guess you knew I'd show up." I chuckle nervously.

Why am I even nervous? Miles and I go way back, but as I cast my line and sneak a peek at him, I wonder if it's not my nerves but his I'm picking up on. There's this tension in him, a heaviness I can't quite nail down. He's staring at the water, lost in thought. It's been only a week since we last saw each other, so is it really me throwing him off? Or is something else eating at him?

I start to fidget, my fingers itching to play with my hair. What was I thinking, coming here? Our friendship could be hanging by a thread because I let my guard down, dared to hope for more with Miles. I should have known better—he's all about football, not settling down. And me? I've still got years of school ahead.

"Stop it," he says, casual but firm.

Next year he could be anywhere, far away, chasing his NFL dreams.

"Milli," he says more sharply, pulling me back from my thoughts.

I'm such an idiot . . .

Milli, don't go there.

"Mills, just stop," he repeats, his grip firm on my wrist, igniting that familiar shiver of sensation through me.

And stop what, exactly?

He flashes that smug look, fully aware of its effect on me. It's the kind of expression that could bring me to my knees, if I ever allowed it. And should that moment come, it would be for one reason, and one reason only.

I'm flustered, confused, a bit miffed, especially after our last encounter. "So, are you gonna tell me what I'm supposed to stop doing or saying?" I snap back, more sass in my voice than I intended.

He just shakes his head, eyes still on the water.

"Is that how you're answering me now?" My frustration's bubbling up.

He shakes his head again, avoiding my gaze.

Milli, remember why you're here.

I set the pole down, crossing my arms. At this point, if I'm annoying him, so be it. He's been driving me up the wall, anyway.

Be the bigger person, Milli.

I'm trying, really. I'm here trying to have a decent talk with him, but man, sometimes he's just so . . . so frustrating. Reminds me of how Mom has to snap Dad out of his zones. I get it now, I really do. And right now, I'd love to give Miles a good flick right on his forehead.

He glances back, that infuriating smug look still there.

I want to kiss it right off his face.

Focus, Milli.

There's another tense pause before he finally says, "You know, I can always tell when something's bugging you. You're about to burst, but can't quite say it."

I narrow my eyes at him, trying to figure him out as he casts another line.

"Like how you play with your hair when you're nervous."

What's he driving at?

"Or your other tell?"

My eyes and brows furrow in confusion.

"Your tongue pushes against your cheek, then you bite it."

He pauses. "You're doing it right now," he points out, his gaze intense as he scans my face, lingering on my cheeks.

I shake my head, an attempt to mask the rush of fluster sweeping over me. Acknowledging it, even silently, feels too vulnerable. So, I pivot away, letting the expanse of water before us take my full attention, my arms remaining defiantly crossed. "Nope, that's not me," I assert, the words aimed more to convince myself than him.

His chuckle cuts right through all my pretending, and damn, it's exactly what I've been missing since I showed up. I sneak a peek over my shoulder, catching Miles dropping his fishing gear and heading my way. I steel myself, ready for whatever he's gonna throw at me, but he catches me off guard, coming up right behind me. His hands find my elbows, and even with the cool air and my sleeves between us, his touch sets off a firestorm inside me.

Get it together, Milli. It's just Miles, for heaven's sake.

But this isn't like those quick, fiery moments we've had before. His touch? It's slow, thoughtful, kinda tender in a way that throws me. As he runs his hands down my arms, I pull them in tighter, aware of how turned on I am. He lets out another one of those chuckles, his breath dancing across my skin, making me shiver all over. Then, he lays his arms on mine, trying to gently open them up. I put up a bit of a fight, though. I'm not quite ready to drop my guard just yet.

He lets out another laugh. "Stubborn as ever, Milli Girl," he whispers, dropping that nickname that never fails to make my heart jump. He tugs me back against him, and I find myself dissolving into his hold, all my resistance fading away despite myself.

Why does he have to be such a puzzle? One minute, he's warm and close. The next, he's distant, leaving me all twisted up inside. I decide to stop overthinking it for once and just let myself rest against him, my head finding the familiar nook of his shoulder. He responds with a gentle kiss on my temple.

What does this mean? Is it just a reflex from our past, or something more?

I'm overanalyzing again, aren't I?

"You're doing it again," he teases, and I snap out of my reverie.

I bite my inner cheek, trying to tamp down the rising tide of emotions. It's more than just this moment; it's a lifetime of feelings, all bubbling up now.

I begin to distance myself, poised to face the tension that's been brewing between us. But as I attempt to step back, he eases his hold. My words are on the brink of escaping when suddenly, my foot tangles with his and my fishing pole. A jolt of panic shoots through me as I instinctively grab onto his shoulders.

The cold shock of the lake snaps me to reality, and I latch onto Miles, his arms instinctively encircling me. His laughter echoes around us, a light-hearted response to the chaos.

Even with the chill seeping into my bones, laughter bubbles up from me, too. The situation, us floundering in the water, hits a note of ridiculousness. I try to muster a glare at him, aiming for irritation.

"Not. Funny," I manage, emphasizing each word with a prod to his chest. But he's quick, capturing my finger and pulling me in until we're flush against each other, soaked and shivering, our breaths mingling.

He gives a nonchalant shrug. "Kinda is, Mills."

I fight the urge to grin, biting down on my lip. This scenario—so quintessentially us—me leading us both into an unintended swim. Any regrets? Absolutely none.

"What happened to your dancer's balance?" he teases, grinning. "What's on your mind, Mills?" he murmurs, his voice a gentle rumble, rich with intimacy. He's always had a knack for reading me like an open book.

My cheeks blaze with warmth, a clear indicator of the inner conflict I'm facing. Caught in the crossfire between the intense memories of what we've shared and the electric tension of now, I'm at a loss for words.

As my gaze drifts away from us, settling on the scene beyond the water, we remain motionless, enveloped by a heavy silence in the chill of the lake. Drenched and shivering, I decide to mirror Miles' earlier demeanor. With a nonchalant shrug, I offer him a dose of his own medicine, mimicking the detachment he had displayed.

He's still grinning a mischievous grin, and despite everything, I feel this urge to close the gap between us. I imagine kissing him, a kiss so fiery and deep it would leave him breathless, yearning for more, his body aching for my touch.

Then Miles snaps me out of it, giving my chin a light pinch, dragging me back to the here and now. Our gazes lock, and in that quiet moment, heavy with all the things we aren't saying, I can feel the undeniable proof of his cock pressing against me. The need to touch him, to wrap my hand around it, is damn near overpowering. Sure, we've danced this close before, felt that electric buzz of wanting the same thing, but right now? The hunger to dive deeper, to really explore that craving, is hitting me harder than ever.

A surge of warmth floods me, and I find myself ensnared by the depth of his gaze. Without fully realizing it, my hand begins to drift toward him, as if pulled by an invisible string. He intercepts it, his features melting into a gentler expression.

There's a hint of pity in his eyes, and it throws me off.

"Maybe we should get out?" he suggests, his voice gentle yet firm.

He leads us toward the dock stairs, and I'm left there,

confused and frustrated. Why is he holding back? It's not like he doesn't want it; that much is clear.

Then my inner voice chimes in. *Milli, just because his body's reacting, it doesn't mean his heart is.* I guess it's true that physical attraction can be separate from emotional connection.

I roll my eyes at myself, trying to rationalize it all. I mean, why would someone like Miles, with all his options, choose me? A dyslexic, hopelessly romantic, nerdy dancer? High school didn't exactly do wonders for my self-esteem.

I mutter a half-hearted, "Mmhm," not trusting myself to say more without breaking down.

Get a grip, Milli. Crushes are just that—crushes. They end, eventually.

So, this is it, I guess. The day I finally get over him. I came here to figure out what's up with Miles, but instead, I'm leaving with even more confusion.

I stride toward the dock stairs, my emotions a whirlwind of irritation and self-reproach. I'm done with this roller-coaster of hope and disappointment. One moment, Miles is there for me, like some kind of fairytale hero, and the next, he's back to insisting we're just friends.

How do you even stay "just friends" after everything we've shared? After all the intimacy, the passion, and those intense moments?

"Hey, Mills, hold up a sec?" Miles calls out, just as I'm making a beeline for my jeep.

It's freaking cold, and, of course, I didn't think to bring a towel. Typical. But really, who carries around a towel in their car when it's 60 degrees outside?

"Mills, stop, please," he begs, his tone soft but filled with an urgency that's hard to ignore. His footsteps squelch on the dock behind me, and then his hand is on my elbow, stopping me in my tracks.

CHAPTER 21
MILES

But logic's always been a bit overrated.

I know I should let her go, but I'm torn. My head and heart are at war, debating whether we should continue pretending nothing's changed between us.

I try to turn her to face me, but Milli's resolute, like a rock. "My stubborn girl," I mutter with a sigh, my emotions tangling up inside me. Logic tells me to keep things under wraps, to prevent any further complications.

But logic's always been a bit overrated, hasn't it, Miles?

"Can I just go, Miles?" she asks, her voice barely above a whisper, still not looking at me.

Letting go feels impossible. She's been my constant in a life filled with chaos.

My Mills.

With everything else in my life up in the air—my health, my future, what Luke might think—it's hard to see what lies ahead. Will I even be around to see it?

"Do what makes you happy, Miles. Just this once," I whisper to myself.

"No, you can't," I tell her, my decision made.

As she turns to me, tears streaming down her face, my heart clenches.

Damn it, Chasen.

Acting on impulse, I scoop her up in a fireman's carry. She starts to struggle, her fists pounding against my back.

Those marks better last.

When I slap her ass, she freezes, stunned. "Did you just slap my ass?" she asks, disbelief in her voice.

The grin that takes over my face is unstoppable. "Yeah, I did. You got a problem with that?" I say, a playful challenge in my tone. Setting her down beside my truck, she avoids my gaze, but I reach for her face. She blocks my hand, so instead, I intertwine my fingers with hers, lifting our hands against the truck. Her sharp intake of breath is all the encouragement I need.

I lean in, bringing our bodies closer, our hands still above our heads. "God, you're so beautiful," I say, and she blushes, her eyes avoiding mine.

I find myself unable to look away from her—the captivating blend of blue and green in her eyes, the way her strawberry blonde hair cascades around her face, and those lips, oh those lips, becoming all the more fucking enticing as she nibbles on them. My gaze drifts down to her chest and I notice how her nipples press against her shirt, betraying her arousal. I inch closer, her breath catching.

Milli's been a force in my life since we were kids, an attraction I've tried too hard to resist. What if this is my last chance to be with her like this? To show her how much she affects me?

Her gaze locks with mine, eyes alight with desire, silently pleading for my next move.

The restraint within me crumbles. I yearn to immerse myself fully in this instant, casting aside thoughts of what lies ahead. As her lips part ever so slightly, I close the distance between us, initiating a kiss that is both deep and fervent, a testament to the intensity of the moment.

Milli

This is unreal.

It's happening again.

I told myself I wouldn't, couldn't, but here I am, getting lost in his kiss, a kiss that feels like it's pulling me under, drowning me in want and need.

And I'm not fighting it.

Lies would be saying this isn't spinning my world upside down, making every nerve in my body scream for more. The cool breeze outside contrasts sharply with the heat between us, my skin tingling where his stubble grazes. I'm clinging to him, drawing him closer, our wet clothes sticking together as if they're trying to merge us into one.

Is this even real?

His scent, a mix of musk and sandalwood, envelops me, intoxicating and oh-so-familiar. It feels dangerously real.

When we finally break apart, he rests his forehead against mine, his thumb brushing my lip. It's like I'm right back where I've always belonged—in his arms. *Home.* My legs wrap around him again as if they've memorized their place. He guides me into his truck, and I slide over as he joins me.

Sitting in his old pickup, I notice the polaroids decorating the interior, capturing snippets of his life. They snap me back to reality. His smug grin beckons me, and his finger motions me closer, setting off a whirlwind inside me.

But there's this internal tug-of-war. Do I let myself fall deeper for him? Do I let him in more than he already is?

His voice cuts through my thoughts. "Come here now, Mills."

As I scoot closer, his hands envelope me. They say big hands mean big . . . oh, not now, Milli.

I should worry about being seen here, in his truck, in this parking lot. But all those steamy scenes from my romance novels are replaying in my mind, courtesy of Miles.

He raises an eyebrow, silently challenging me to make a move.

And damn it, I want to jump his bones.

His hands lift me effortlessly, and I straddle him. My knees lock into place by his hips, and all my doubts dissolve.

"Remember that night by the bonfire?" he asks, his cock pressing against me, drawing a whimper from my lips.

"Yeah," I manage, even as he chuckles, satisfied.

"We're in a Chevy CK," he murmurs, his lips trailing down my neck. The memory of confessing my truck fantasy to him flashes in my mind, and here we are, making it a reality.

"Now what's the hold-up?" His whisper is a siren call.

I could tease, play hard to get, but no. This is an offer I can't refuse. I pull him closer, our lips crashing together in a fervent kiss.

God, he can kiss. It's like he's reading my mind, knowing just how to send me spiraling. He knows his effect on me, and I'm eager to show him mine.

Thank goodness for those romance novels. They didn't prepare me for everything, but they sure gave me some ideas.

His hands, firm and warm, rest on the curve of my back, guiding me closer. "Fuck," he breathes out, a note of raw urgency in his voice.

Suddenly, he shifts us with fluid ease. Before I know it, I'm lying on the leather seat, the cool surface contrasting with the heat of our bodies. Miles hovers over me, an electric current running between us. My breaths come in quick, shallow gasps, my body responding instinctively to his nearness. His lips find mine again, the kiss deep and consuming, igniting a fire within me.

His fingers trace the damp waistband of my yoga pants, sending a shiver through me. I arch instinctively, responding to his touch. He moves his hand down, cupping me gently, and a whimper escapes me, a sound filled with longing and desire.

Miles

This is intense, more than I ever expected. Every time Milli grinds against my fingers, it's a test of my willpower. I never thought we'd be here again, especially not in my truck, while people walk by, oblivious to the fire we're stoking inside.

As I fumble with her leggings, a groan escapes me. "Could these be any fucking tighter?" They're soaked through, clinging to her like a second skin. Milli chuckles, her face lighting up in a way that has me smiling despite the tension.

"You're such a tease," I remark, a playful lilt in my voice as she nibbles on her lip, an irresistible invitation that pulls me deeper into her spell. On impulse, I capture her lip gently between my teeth, our eyes locking in a moment, brimming with electricity. The warmth increasing beneath my hand, still resting on her most intimate of places, urges me to tease further. "Are you ready for me already, Mills?"

Her fluttering eyes and the way she leans into my touch are all the answers I need. The feeling of my hands on her is like a shot of adrenaline, boosting my confidence.

I gently run my tongue across her lips, where I bit. As I gaze down at her lying on the truck seat, I tug at her soaked leggings. I slide them off, revealing her pale pink underwear. "Did you choose these for me, baby? Did you know this would happen?"

Her hypnotized stare is a clear signal of her eagerness. She squirms, her body language screaming for me to take control.

"Miles, please," she pleads softly. My fingers trace her thigh, edging closer to her, until they reach her. She arches in response, inviting more.

"Please what, Mills?" I whisper, pressing my chest to hers, feeling every shift in her breathing.

She pulls me closer, her movements urgent. My body reacts instantly, hard and ready. The thought of being inside her, once a distant fantasy, now feels like an irresistible temptation.

"Don't stop touching me," she breathes out, and my restraint shatters.

If this is how Milli always is, I'm in trouble. I've only had a taste, and already I know I'll never get enough.

My lips gently wander down her neck, my hands on a voyage of discovery, mapping the graceful arc of her knee, igniting trails of goosebumps along her inner thigh. My fingers graze the dampness through her underwear, and I shudder, a tempest of desire and restraint raging within me. A part of me hungers to surrender completely to this storm of passion, yet I remind myself that's not what this is about.

Milli deserves gentleness, and that's what I intend to give her. As one finger slips inside her, she murmurs a soft, "Oh, God," and her body presses against mine. I'm lost in the sensation as she moves against my hand.

"Mills," I groan, withdrawing my finger to trace her, spreading the wetness, her body responding with every touch.

Her legs widen, the urgency of the moment etched in every line of her body. She props herself up, her eyes wide with a mix of awe and lust. It makes me wonder if anyone has ever made her feel this way before.

I want to be the last one to bring her to this edge, to hear her, to see her like this.

As I circle her clit, her reactions grow more intense. "Baby, you're so wet," I say, my voice thick with satisfaction.

She nods, lost for words.

The intensity of our connection in the confined space of my truck is overwhelming, and I'm savoring every second. With one finger inside her, exploring, paying attention to every little response, I ask, "Does that feel good?"

"Yes, yes," she chants, her breath fogging up the windows even more.

No one can see us, but even if they could, I'm not sure I'd care. The thrill, the secrecy, it only adds to the heat of the moment.

"Keep going," she breathes out beneath me, her body a canvas of unspoken desires.

"Do you want me to keep going?" I whisper, my breath warm against her ear. I feel her move restlessly beneath me, a clear sign of her growing excitement. The longing in her voice sends a wave of exhilaration through me.

"Yes, Miles, just—awwh," she tilts her hips, her voice dripping with want, "just give it to me," she pleads.

"Like this?" I ask as I maintain a rhythmic dance with my fingers, moving in and out of her. The truck's cramped space fades into insignificance against the sensation of Milli's tightness gripping me, her wetness an inviting warmth.

"How's this for you?" I slow down, adding a second finger, teasing her before plunging back into her heat. Her sharp cry as I twist my hand sends a wave of satisfaction through me. Her head lolls to the side, her fingers digging into my back.

Those marks she's leaving, they're a reminder, a promise of more to come.

"You like that, Mills? Two better than one?" I press deeper, captivated by her needy sounds.

She manages a breathy, "Yes," her lips trailing over my skin.

"Tell me, in and out, or do you want more?" She shrugs, and I chuckle. "Come on, Mills. I know you've got some wild ideas from those novels."

"Both," she gasps, her words clipped with pleasure. I indulge her, fingers twisting and gliding, her wetness enveloping me. The truck is filled with our mingled moans and the slick sound of desire.

Her hips begin to move in sync with mine, our breaths ragged and heavy.

"Look at me," I command gently, remembering a conversation we once had. "Remember when I said I could teach you some moves? Really get your heart rate up?"

"Yes, yess," she whispers, her movements becoming more frantic. I push harder, lost in the raw sounds she makes.

I had never imagined Milli, usually so quiet, could be this vocal. The thought of what other sounds she could make, with me even closer, drives me wild.

I gently pull back, concentrating on her clit, and before long, she comes undone. Her voice cries out for me, fingers weaving through my hair—a victorious chant, my name from her lips sounding like the sweetest of triumphs.

"Hey, Mills," I call out softly. She's right there across from me, with the windows fogged up, the only sound in the truck is our heavy breathing. Watching her, I notice the rise and fall of her chest, the visible signs of her arousal marking her skin and my fingers. With a deliberate motion, I bring my fingers to my lips, savoring the taste of her. As my eyes meet hers, I see a flash of surprise, her cheeks coloring beautifully. With a smirk, I can't resist teasing, "So, how's that heart rate?"

Her laughter rings out, genuine and full, echoing warmly through the cab of the truck. "Only you, Sunshine," she manages between hearty chuckles. Then, almost as quickly as her laughter came, the atmosphere shifts. The heat of desire darkens her eyes, her hand reaching for me, but I gently stop her. This was about her, about seeing her uninhibited.

But she's insistent. "Let me," she says firmly, pushing me to the other side of the truck. She crawls toward me, hair tousled, her clothes and underwear askew, every bit of her a vision of desire.

I struggle to restrain myself, wanting her in every way possible. She teasingly wags a finger at me, fully aware of my thoughts. Then she's unzipping my pants, her hand wrapping around my cock, a squeeze from her, sending a groan ripping from my throat. The first touch of her tongue is almost too much, bringing me to the brink in an instant.

CHAPTER 22
MILLI

Can you keep a secret?

"Is this really what personal fantasies are like?" I murmur, locking eyes with Miles while sprawled across his lap in his truck. His smirk ignites a flurry of butterflies inside me.

Will this thrill ever dim, even after all that's happened?

It's surreal, like I'm waiting for the universe to pull some prank. That's me right now, teetering between disbelief and this new reality.

This is real, Milli. Embrace it. Find joy in this moment.

Joy encapsulates what I feel, but if I were to pinpoint it, it's utter contentment. He tenderly lifts my chin, closing the distance between us, and my heart accelerates. What kind of spell is this man casting on me? He halts, his smirk morphing into a smug, confident smile, as if he hadn't just turned my world on its head.

"Jerk," I say, my voice laced with laughter as I smack his chest. But he quickly catches my wrist, drawing himself closer, his breath a whisper away from my lips, sparking a wave of anticipation inside me.

He wiggles his brows. "Does it feel like a dream? Like I've flipped your world upside down?"

I pull away, giving him another light smack, even though he isn't entirely off base. It's hard to describe this whirlwind inside me. Like I am floating, untouchable, invincible, not even grounded by the thought of leaving his truck later.

"You mean you've never had a fantasy come true?" I ask, curiosity lacing my voice.

He shrugs casually. "Perhaps I just did."

Wait, does he mean . . . ?

Is he talking about me, or . . . ?

He raises an eyebrow, a mischievous glint in his eye. "And I'm not talking about the truck or this empty lot."

So, he means *me*.

What does this mean for *us*?

For *him*?

Or is he looking for something casual? I'm not sure I could handle just being friends with benefits.

But, before I can spiral further, his fingers gently cradle my chin, his gaze soft and reassuring. "Mills, stop overthinking," he whispers gently.

Me, overthinking? Please, that's definitely not what I was doing.

He looks at my arm on the passenger seat, our fingers touching, then intertwining. "Let's just let this be. No overanalyzing. Just be, baby." A smile breaks through my apprehensions, warmth flooding me at the idea of him calling me "baby" in such an intimate moment. It feels like my entire being has been anticipating that word, ready to ignite at his touch.

I clear my throat, steadying my voice. "I can handle that." I really think I can. Mulling over everything never does anyone any good. Looking to shift the topic, I ask, "Why are all these photos in your truck?" I sneak a quick look at them. I barely got a chance to see them earlier, but his kiss kinda made my world go blurry. It's pretty dark now, but their outlines are still visible.

As he runs his fingers through my hair, he shrugs lightly and says, "I guess I like keeping bits of my life close by—the people who mean the most, the ones who've stuck by me through everything."

There's a subtle change in his expression, a depth I haven't seen before. Is he even aware of it? Or perhaps I'm just lost in a blissful post orgasm and am seeing things differently.

My eyes wander across his truck, pausing at photographs of his family, nostalgic moments with his grandpa, a younger him. A smile naturally finds its way to my face. Among these memories are pictures of Luke, other friends, and, to my surprise, several of me. My heart flutters, touched by the thought that he's kept these snapshots close.

Curiosity gets the better of me, and I pick up a photo. It's Miles and Luke at Emerald Shores, shirtless, fishing rods in hand, smiles wide, living life to the fullest.

I reach for another picture. This time, it's me and Miles. We're lounging on a beach blanket, the serene Emerald Shores in the backdrop, surrounded by a clutter of books— obviously my doing. My hair, a wild cascade of strawberry blonde, is tousled by the wind. Miles' arm is wrapped snugly around my waist, drawing me close as we both beam at the camera. The memory tugs at my heart.

I remember that day vividly. It was part of our "summer's eve" ritual. Since Miles and Luke graduated, we'd promised to make the last day before college start special. That year, after

Luke left us for a spontaneous date at The Southern Way, I found myself alone with Miles, a first for that summer.

Miles' soft cough captures my attention, pulling me from my reverie. I place the photos gently in my lap and pivot toward him. Our gazes lock, igniting a subtle warmth in my cheeks. His eyes hold a spark of amusement as he observes me.

"Enjoying the stroll down memory lane?" he teases.

I giggle, unable to contain my joy. "I love this picture of us," I admit with an easy smile.

He takes the photo, eyes lingering on it. "One of my best summers," he says, a hint of nostalgia in his voice.

Curious, I ask, "Because of the beach?"

He shakes his head, his nonchalance not fooling me. I lean in, almost as if to catch every word. "No, because of you."

"Me?" I look at him, searching for confirmation in his eyes.

He chuckles, the laughter carrying a note of nervousness yet undeniably charming. "Yeah, that summer? When Luke ditched us for that girl he met at The Southern Way?"

I nod in acknowledgment. "Our first time flying solo, wasn't it? And what did we decide to do with that freedom?"

Before he can continue, I interject, my tone light and teasing, "Read."

He laughs, a genuine, full-bodied chuckle. "Yep, you wanted to read to me."

A smile blooms across my face, reflecting the memories sparkling in his eyes. "I really did that, didn't I?" My lip catches between my teeth, and his eyes soften, a glimmer of desire shining through, undoubtedly making my panties wet again. Not that they had much opportunity to dry, considering our situation at the lake and the incredible climax he led me to.

He chuckles again, this time more softly, brushing a strand of hair behind my ear with such gentleness. "Yeah, you did. And it wasn't just cute, it was . . . peaceful. No one's ever done that for me before," he shares, his voice infused with a mix of warmth and sincere gratitude.

I give him a shove, telling myself it's to keep things light. Because the way he's looking at me, the gentle touch on my face, it's getting too intense. It's definitely not an excuse to feel his chest against me. But then he grabs my arms, pulling me closer, his breath hot against my cheek. Right then, all I can think about is closing that last bit of distance between us.

But I hold back, not wanting to rush whatever's unfolding between us. Clearing my throat, Miles' eyes narrow, but he leans back slightly, giving me some space.

"So, are you going to share what's been happening with you?" I inquire.

He attempts to maintain a composed facade. "I'm not sure what you're referring to."

I move to sit across from him. "Come on, Sunshine. I know something's off." He looks away, that nervous habit of his a dead giveaway. There's a silence, his fingers running through his hair in a move he just mirrored on me.

He sighs. "It's nothing. Just school and practice, you know?"

But I'm not buying it. I've known Miles long enough to see there's more. I came here to find out what's up, and I'm not leaving without answers.

"I know you better than that," I say lightly. "Come on, spill."

He chuckles, a bit strained, but it's a start. Humor's our way of easing tension, and it's working its magic.

His eyes find mine. "When did you get so good at reading me?"

I shrug playfully. "I've always been good at it."

He shakes his head, a small smile on his lips. As I'm

about to speak, I decide against it and instead hold his hand, offering silent support.

He looks down. "Can you keep a secret?"

A pang hits me. What's so heavy that he's this hesitant? I refrain from pushing, offering a pinky promise instead. His pinky links with mine. He starts to pull away, but I keep our hands together, giving him the space to open up in his own time.

"Honestly, I am stressed," he finally says, sounding exhausted.

I squeeze his hand reassuringly, showing him he's not alone.

"But that's not all," he continues after a pause. "It's my future. That's what's really eating at me."

The weight of his worries is palpable. I stay silent, giving his hand another reassuring squeeze. I'm here, no matter what.

"You know, what do I want in a future? What does the damn future even look like? What if what I want in my future doesn't align with what others want? What if I can't have a fut—"

I press my fingers to his lips, locking eyes with him. "Hey, the future? We don't just walk into it. We shape it, Miles."

His expression shifts to one of surprise at my declaration. Yet, it stands as an undeniable truth. We are the sculptors of our destinies, not mere pieces on another's chessboard. It's up to us to define our desires, not be dictated by others.

His eyes soften, a vulnerability emerging before he whispers, "I . . . I want to be a doctor."

That catches me off guard, but in a good way. Doctor Miles Chasen? That's a thought.

He drags his fingers through his hair, tugging at the ends as if clinging to them for support, and exhales sharply. "Fuck, admitting that shouldn't be so difficult."

"Being a doctor is your dream?" I ask him.

He nods, his gaze darting around, avoiding mine.

"Why's that so hard to say?" I probe gently.

His head snaps to me. "Mills, you know how it is. My dad's been grooming me for the NFL since forever. It's like I'm set to disappoint everyone." He sighs heavily. "I can't bear to think of letting them down."

I just listen, holding his hand, letting him pour out his heart.

"How do I tell them I don't want the NFL life? I can already see my dad's dream for me shattering."

His dad's dream, not his. But I keep quiet.

He starts again, "It's not like it matters. I don't even have a—" He stops himself, swallowing the rest of his sentence.

My heart sinks. *What's he holding back?* He pulls away, glancing at me. "We should go. It's late."

I'm torn. Do I hug him? Offer some words of comfort? As his hand slips from mine, the silence grows heavy, filled with all the things left unsaid.

I hesitate, wanting to reassure him, but he cuts in, frustration in his voice. "I don't even know if I can be a doctor. I've missed so much, wrapped up in football, our study sessions . . . I haven't even started on the MCAT." I hear the regret in his words, the yearning for a different path. "I thought this was my year. To end football on a high, enjoy my last college days . . . "

I give his leg a supportive squeeze, my heart aching slightly that I'm not part of his "perfect year." Pushing aside my feelings, I lean back, thinking carefully about my response.

"You know, life's full of surprises," I say, trying to ease the tension. "Sometimes the best years are the unexpected ones, where we roll with the punches."

Miles offers a small, grateful smile, the stress in his shoulders easing.

I sense he needs some space, that easy smile of his fading. As much as I want to be his go-to person, he'll come to me when he's ready, just like he did today. Eager to leave things on a lighter note, I reach for the passenger door, throwing in a bit of humor. "You sure you're cut out for med school?"

He raises an eyebrow at my comment. So, with a smirk, I tease, "I mean, can the hospital handle your charm? Might be a health hazard for the patients, right?"

His laughter rings out, a sound that lifts me up, making me feel like I'm soaring. "I'm charming, huh?" He shakes his head, still smiling. "Only you, Milli Sutton, could turn a serious moment into something light-hearted."

I step out of his truck; the breeze catching my hair as I lean back in through the open window, grinning. "Well, someone's got to keep you grounded, Mr. Future Doctor." With a wink, I add, "See you around, Sunshine."

CHAPTER 23
MILES

"Alright, everyone," Professor Huggins starts, his voice ringing through the classroom. "I hope you're all set for the stats assignment. And remember, finals aren't far off. Think back on all the work we've done this term."

Around me, there's a chorus of groans and a few sarcastic, "Oh yeah, like we could forget."

My phone vibrates. Milli's name flashes on the screen, sparking an instant smile, even though she's just a couple of rows ahead.

MILLS

Nailed that last assignment, right, superstar?

A quiet laugh escapes me as I steal a glance at her. There's a twinkle in her eyes when she turns slightly, catching my gaze. But it's the way she's absentmindedly biting her pencil that really draws me in, stirring a familiar warmth inside me. Flashes of those lips. Those teeth . . . on my cock . . . flicker in my mind.

Not the time, Miles. Focus.

Easier said than done when it's Milli. I try to refocus as Professor Huggins drones on. "These assignments are key for your final exam, so I hope you've kept them."

I hear some classmates mutter about tossing their old homework. I quickly type a response to Milli.

MILES

> Aced it. And this one's a surefire A+. I've got a fantastic tutor, you know? She's incredibly skilled . . . and I'm not just referring to her tutoring sessions.

After I send the message, she glances back at me again. It's become a ritual in every class, from the very first day to now, almost like a dance we've silently agreed upon. As I catch her eye, her cheeks flush with color. It amazes me, the ease with which I can affect her, especially considering everything that's transpired between us.

Professor Huggins' voice fades into background noise as I think about Milli's relentless organization skills. Those tutoring sessions, her insistence on keeping everything in order. Seemed excessive at first, but it's paying off now.

Cam nudges me, whispering, "You still got all those assignments, right, Chasen?"

The urge to roll my eyes is strong. I want to say, "Yeah, Cam, but they're not for your last-minute cramming."

Instead, I simply give a nod, holding back my real thoughts. Being a mentor is about leading by example, even when it reminds me of my own freshman days—those times lost in parties, neglecting assignments, learning lessons the hard way.

I've been keeping my distance from the wild campus life, the parties, and the chaos. Luke's been in the thick of it but hasn't bugged me about joining in. I've got enough on my plate, especially after opening up to Milli about my real ambitions.

Telling Milli about wanting to be a doctor . . . it felt right. I don't know why I ever hesitated in the first place. She's always had this way of pushing me forward, making me believe in my own dreams. With her, there's no looking back, only moving forward.

"Miles, you can't just stand there all the time." Milli nudged me toward the little kid's football field just a few blocks from our house. Mom was busy with a client, and Dad was in a super important meeting with his agent. So, it was just me at home, well, with Amilia, our housekeeper/nanny. She took care of me whenever my parents had to leave the house suddenly.

I sighed a lot today, like a gazillion times. Milli saw me leaving my house, and her parents were cool, so they didn't care if she came with me to the field. It's our hangout spot, where Luke and I go after school or on the weekends.

But today felt weird. I was in remission, still kind of weak. I could feel it in how I walked, picked up the football, and did my normal stuff that used to be easy. I knew coming back wouldn't be super easy, but I also thought maybe things would be a bit like before. And as I stood in the same spot for the fifth time that week, I knew Milli was right; I needed to move.

"That's it, Miles. One step at a time. One throw at a time." Milli's cheering words bounced around in my head and all over my body. The next thing I knew, my feet were moving, and when I peeked behind my shoulder, Milli was one step behind me. Her pretty smile was all the cheering I needed to keep going until I made it to the middle of the field.

Milli jumped up and down in her tiny pink and bright yellow tutu, wearing pink leggings and her old rainbow shoes. She looked like a colorful and pretty rainbow. It made me feel happy and gave me the energy to keep going.

"You can do it, Miles! I'll be right here cheering for you. No take backs!"

My phone dings, snapping me back to reality.

MILLS

I need to meet this amazing tutor of yours.

A smile breaks through, almost against my will.

MILLS

Pretty?

MILES

More beautiful than anyone I've ever seen.

MILLS

Smart?

MILES

The brightest.

MILLS

What else is there to know about her?

She's the one who's stolen my heart.

"Hey, Earth to Miles!" Cam intrudes, leaning into my phone's view. I angle it away, keeping my messages private. Cam sighs, frustration clear. "Dude, I know something's going on. I haven't spilled anything to Luke, have I?"

I mean, he's got a point, but also, like, give me my space.

I lift the folder of assignments, waving it. Facing Cam again, I say, a bit irritated, "They're all here."

He pats my back. "You're the best, man."

I look at him, half-joking, half-serious. "Don't get used to it. I'm not your forever safety net." I'm hit with the reality of my own uncertain future.

Everything's fine, Miles.

I've been pushing all those gnawing worries to the back of my mind. Since that intense talk with Dr. Reynolds, life's just been me drifting from one day to the next. Diving into schoolwork and football has kind of been my hideout, especially when those biopsy results are hanging over my head.

And Milli, she's been solid—like a rock for me, especially after all that went down in my truck.

Guilt shouldn't be part of the equation, yet it clings to me, unwelcome but persistent.

Those lips.

Those soft whimpers.

The pleas.

God, her pussy was practically begging for my touch, saying, "This might be your only chance." But shit; after that moment with Milli, I'm just getting started. I knew she had her fantasies, and I wanted to show her the real deal, taking pages out of those so-called "romance" books and teaching her how a guy can really take care of a woman.

Miles, be careful with what you start.

My mind's been a battlefield since then. I've shared part of what's going on, but not all of it.

Do I tell her about the doctor's words? Maybe. But Dr. Reynolds didn't seem overly worried, and I don't want to cause unnecessary panic.

As Cam and I get ready to leave, I sneak one more look at Milli. There's a tightness in my chest every time I see her. Is this what love feels like? Falling for your best friend can't be this simple, can it?

She's chatting with Brooke, but then she turns and beams at me. Cam's gaze flickers between us, but before he can comment, I hold up a hand. "Don't even start."

I quickly finish my text conversation with Milli.

MILES

She is my whole world.

With that, I pocket my phone, carrying a sense of hope as I walk away.

I might be crossing a line, but I don't care. The truth is, Milli's become my world, in more ways than one. She's been my rock, my go-to, supporting me through thick and thin. But what happens after graduation? The future's this big, uncertain thing, and it's got me tied up in knots.

I've got feelings for Milli, real ones, and they're not going anywhere. But all these what ifs keep swirling in my head.

What's our future look like?

Is there an "us" to even think about?

Sure, Stoneton and NorthRidge aren't worlds apart. We've managed the distance alright, but what if I end up at Harvard or Penn? And what if . . . well, what if I'm not even here a year from now?

Stop it, Miles. You're fine. Just fine.

Yet, something inside me is shouting that it's not that simple.

Cam throws me a knowing look. "Told you, man, from day one, you're in deep," he says, squeezing my shoulder before heading out. "Catch you at practice."

"Get ready to kiss the ground, Leif!" I shout, earning a cheeky wink from him. As he disappears, my attention snaps back to Milli. She's wrapping up her chat with Brooke, and like magnets, we're drawn together without even thinking.

I prop myself against a desk, flashing her my best grin. "Ready to ace that final, Baby Sutton?" I catch a glimpse of the shy Milli peeking through, but it's swiftly overshadowed by her signature sharp retort.

"Better question, are you?" She throws back, her eyebrow lifting in a fun challenge.

I shoot her a wink. "With you as my secret weapon? We're talking about smooth sailing."

She blushes, then asks, "We still on for our tutoring session?"

"Wouldn't miss it," I reply, eager for any moment with her.

She laughs softly, shaking her head at my enthusiasm.

"Milli, you coming to practice?" Wyatt peeks in, breaking into our bubble.

I try to keep cool, even though I don't like the way he's eyeing her. Does he know she's off-limits?

Does she know, Miles?

"Give me a sec," she tells him, turning back to me. I move away from the desk, expecting maybe a hug. But with Wyatt still lingering, I decide to make a statement. I gently cup her chin, turning slightly, and press a kiss to her cheek, letting it last a little longer than normal. Let him, let everyone know she's mine.

All I'm sure of is that I can't let chances slip by. It's like the universe is finally tipping in my favor, you know? That guy, always showing off what was just out of my reach, but now, it's like he's signaling, "Go for it, now or never."

Our eyes meet, locking in a moment charged with unspoken words. His eyes widen slightly, though whether from surprise or something else, I can't discern. As the distance between us grows, a silent, intense connection lingers with Milli. My jaw tightens involuntarily. Just as I'm convinced she'll leave without another word, she edges closer. Her whisper a feather-touch in my ear. "Jealousy is not your style, Sunshine."

She draws back, and our faces hover in a breath's space. Her gaze pierces through my confusion right before she drops the revelation. "Wyatt's gay."

Wait, what?

He's gay? That's fucking a curveball.

His eyes, his gestures, they didn't hint at that.

Then, with a twist, she kisses my cheek, her tongue teasing the corner of my lips. A gentle tap on my shoulder, and she's off, with a skip in her step, reminiscent of Dorothy's carefree jaunt in *The Wizard of Oz.*

I watch her move toward the door, catching her glance back and wink. It ignites a fire in me, a wild urge to chase after her, toss her over my shoulders, and have my way with her.

Punish her for making me think there was something more going on between her and Wyatt.

For teasing me with that delicious tongue of hers, leaving a trail of unsaid promises.

"Move it, Chasen! Push! Run!" Coach's voice thunders across the field. Clutching the football, my heart drums with adrenaline. The freshly cut grass under my cleats feels like a solid launching pad as I hunker down behind the center, my breath fogging in the chilly, late-fall breeze.

As sweat beads on my forehead, I survey the field, eyeing the defensive line. The opposing team, their gear like battle armor, zeroed in on me with fierce determination.

Snatching the snap, my thoughts race. A gap in their line winks at me, a narrow chance for precious yards. I lunge forward, my cleats tearing into the lush grass. The cacophony of teammates and colliding gear envelope me, yet my focus is laser-sharp on propelling the ball forward. My cleats thud rhythmically against the turf as I dodge past defenders, my agility defying expectations. Known for speed, today, I feel an unmatched synergy with the game, each stride deliberate and exact.

The cheers from my teammates grow louder as I break into the open field. The autumn sun casts long shadows on the field, and the end zone appears distant, its painted grass a shimmering gold in the afternoon light. My heart races, and the weight of the football in my arms is almost insignificant compared to the challenge ahead. This is my moment to feel like I'm not going anywhere, and I am fucking determined to seize it.

The defenders are closing in on me, desperation driving them to make the tackle. But I have a burst of speed left in me. With one final push, I extend the football toward the end zone, breaking the plane of the goal line and scoring the touchdown.

Celebration erupts around me as my teammates mob me, offering pats on the back and joyful shouts of pride filling the air.

"Damn, Chasen, where's that been all season?" I hear Luke say.

Not really sure, but it feels damn good, even though this killer headache is trying to ruin the whole practice. The throbbing behind my eyes is like a drumbeat, getting louder with every move. It's like my head's got its own little concert going on, and I'm not sure if I'm the drummer or the audience. But hey, the thrill of that play is still there, even if it's mixed with this annoying pain.

"You better play like that with the Panthers' Game coming up," I hear another teammate say.

Coach's stern expression melts into a proud grin as he approaches. "That's how you run the ball, Chasen!" he bellows, his voice thick with pride.

Basking in this triumphant moment, I know this practice is a turning point. I'm ready to take on any challenge that'll come my way. What I feared in the doctor's office is nothing. My confidence soaring higher than ever before, I grab Luke by the helmet, throw it off, and mess with his hair as I say, "Fuck yeah."

He chuckles and says, "Easy, man, you still have a few practices before the Panthers' Day game."

I flash a cocky smirk. "Your jealousy is talking, Luke."

He rolls his eyes. "In your dreams, Chasen. I haven't been the one struggling lately."

After a light shove, he trots toward the sidelines for a drink. I follow, my cleats imprinting the well-trodden grass, a cool breeze playing with the leaves. It is another typical day on the field, marked by the familiar rhythm of teamwork and friendly jibes.

Staggering to take a break, my foot catches on an unseen divot. The world spins, vision blurring into darkness. As I fall, Milli's figure becomes a fleeting blur, her voice a distant echo from the dance practice.

Silence descends like a veil over the field. My heavy breathing fills my ears, my heart pounding like a drum, the sky above me blurs into chaotic disarray.

"Shit, Chasen, you okay?" Gunner's voice cuts through, laced with concern.

Resisting the urge for drama, I push myself up, opting to sit. Bad move. The sudden movement sends a spike of pain through my head.

Gunner is at my side in an instant. "Easy there. I'll get you some water."

Coach's voice, firm, joins in. "Get his damn water, now."

Closing my eyes briefly, I hear Milli's anxious voice. "Miles! Are you alright?" Her presence is a temporary solace, but my head throbs mercilessly. I wince, pressing my temples.

"Hydration. How's it been, Miles?" Coach's voice is sharp, yet caring.

I nod, trying to sound convincing. "Good. I'm fine, Coach. Just tripped over the grass."

But did I really just trip? My inner voice probes, doubting.

Coach's gaze is knowing; his experience as our unofficial "field doctor" telling him there's more to it. He's always pushed me, knowing my past, and for that, I'm grateful. But right now, his scrutiny feels too intense.

I stand, resolved to prove I'm alright. Hands on hips, I offer a bold smile to all—my teammates, Coach, Luke, Milli, even a couple of the dancers. Their apprehensive gazes, tinged with a blend of pity and unease, grate on me. Why does every little setback trigger these sympathetic stares?

They care, Miles.

"How about we skip the deathbed stares and get back to practice?" I say, grabbing my helmet.

The murmur of voices dies down, practice picking back up, but Luke and Milli, they're still there, hanging back. Their faces are all twisted up with concern, kind of like how they looked when I dropped the bomb about my cancer. You can almost touch the tension coming off them, their eyes darting over to me, full of questions and worry.

Normally, I'd lighten the mood with a joke about hide-and-seek, but today, their worried glances hold me back. I try to ease the tension. "Let's not start hide-and-seek here on the field, okay?"

They manage small smiles and shake their heads. It's a minor gesture, but it eases my headache a bit, calms my hands, and clears my vision.

I make a mental note to hydrate more and pick up electrolytes later. As practice continues, we all refocus, the drill consuming the next hour.

It's only afterward, checking my phone, that I see a missed call from Dr. Reynolds.

CHAPTER 24
MILES

*It's just a kiss, Milli,
not a life commitment.*

Thursday Night:

One Missed Call: Harborview Regional Medical

Message: Miles, this is Dr. Reynolds' office. We have your biopsy results. Please call us back to schedule an appointment.

Friday Afternoon:

Two Missed Calls: Harborview Regional Medical

Message: Miles, Harborview again. It's important we speak with you. Call us back when you can.

Saturday Morning:

One Missed Call: Harborview Regional Medical

Message: Miles, please return our call.

Sunday Afternoon:

One Missed Call: Harborview Regional Medical

Message: Hey Miles, Kinsley here from the clinic.
We've been trying to reach you. It's vital we discuss
your appointment and biopsy results. Your health is
our top concern. Please call us at (303)-245-7980.
We'll arrange a time to talk with Dr. Reynolds.

As I sit, struggling to steady my breathing, my phone lies abandoned in my hand. Suddenly, the doorbell disrupts the silence.

Who the hell is here on a Sunday night?

Crossing the living room, I swing open the door, revealing Milli. Dressed in a "just give this girl a book" cropped top and form-fitting yoga pants, she's a picture of casual beauty. Her hair's in a dance-practice bun, and she sports a pair of black-framed glasses, giving her a charmingly intellectual air.

My very own sexy tutor.

Leaning against the door frame, I catch her eyes roaming over me. Clearing my throat, her cheeks color, and I can't help but smile. Her gaze is as exhilarating as a game-winning touchdown.

"What's up, Mills?" I ask casually.

She lifts a white plastic bag. "Brought you something— Gnocchi soup, your favorite. Figured you could use it."

Hearing that, my stomach rumbles, and we share a laugh. "Weren't we meeting at the library in an hour?" I ask.

She shrugs nonchalantly. "Thought we might study here tonight." Her gaze briefly flickers behind me, no doubt searching for Luke.

"He's out with a . . . " I begin, but she jumps in, "Girl, right?"

Typical Luke and his ever-present girl pursuits.

"You know him too well," I say.

She chuckles. "Hard not to with Luke." She shifts, a playful sass in her stance. "So, are you letting me in, or do I freeze my ass out here?"

Damn, that tone of hers.

Focus, Miles. Tutoring first, fun later.

Or, maybe a bit of fun first to clear the mind?

Discreetly adjusting myself, I catch her eyes drifting south, a hint of mischief in her look.

I chuckle, stepping aside. "Come on in, mi lady."

She saunters in, heading for the kitchen, throwing over her shoulder, "Don't start with the gentleman act now, Sunshine."

I move around the kitchen island with a wink. "Just watch how polite I can be."

She catches her lip between her teeth, a gesture that ignites a raw urge in me to taste it myself.

I pull out a chair, a hint of command in my voice. "Sit, will you?"

Her lips curve into a knowing smile, her gaze sending my mind racing back to that night in my truck. Climbing into it now, I'm torn between feeling like I'm betraying my grandpa's memory and reliving the most exhilarating night of my life. Every time I'm behind the wheel, all I can think about is her.

Her soft moans.

Her quiet whimpers.

The feel of her, warm and responsive, against my fingers.

"Miles, you still with me?"

I snap back to reality, noticing Milli's playful gesture, the same one I've used on her before. Now I'm the one lost in thought.

When did I start revolving around a woman?

But then, it's always been Milli, hasn't it?

I close the distance between us. Her eyes, curious and expectant, follow my every move. Instead of spelling out my intentions, I tug her closer by her waist. She gasps, and I know I've caught her off guard.

I edge in, so close I can almost taste her. We're right there, on the brink, teasing each other without a word. She runs her tongue over her lips, like she's daring me. Fuck, it's hard not to dive right in and see how far we can push this game. But I'm curious, you know, about where her limit is— and mine.

I pull her in tighter, our breaths getting all tangled up together. And just when she's about to shut her eyes, thinking I'm gonna kiss her, I switch gears. I grab her waist and launch into a full-on tickle attack. Her eyes snap open, all wide and shocked, then she gets it. I wasn't aiming for a kiss. Not just yet.

She tries to pull away as I tickle her, her laughter mixing with a look of defiance. She declares, "Off-limits, Miles!"

I cock an eyebrow, throwing her own game right back at her. "Oh? Seemed like fair game last week, didn't it?" Her cheeks light up with a blush, but she's quick to throw on her armor again.

"Yeah, well, that was then," she shoots back, all sass and fire.

I take a step closer, watching her retreat till the kitchen island stands like a fortress between us. But I've got a plan to breach those walls, to get past her teasing guard.

Her gaze follows my every move, anticipation building. I make a bold step forward, and she quickly moves around the island, her backpack swaying. I shake my head, her lip bite driving me crazy. I want to leap over the island, whisk her away, and show her that she wants it just as much *now*.

As her lips relax into a smug grin, I see it as my cue. But as I step forward, she retreats. Matching her movements, I pivot, closing the gap between us until we're face to face.

Our eyes meet, a silent understanding passing between us. My hands gently find her waist, and she leans into the touch, her eyes reflecting anticipation, as if she's fully immersed in the moment.

Without thinking, I hoist her up onto the island. She reacts in a flash, her legs wrapping around my waist as a thrill zips through me. I keep my hand firmly on her waist, her legs drawing me in, inch by inch.

In our encounters, I often take the lead, but now, I'm curious to see Milli assert herself. I wonder if she'll voice her desires, if she'll embrace that newfound confidence she's been exploring.

Milli slips off her backpack along with her black glasses, setting it aside with a meaningful look. She motions for me to come closer, but the counter is a barrier. Keeping my hands on her, I slide her to the edge, bridging the distance between us. Her eyes widen slightly in surprise, and she instinctively reaches up, her hands finding a comfortable place around my neck.

Milli

His fascination with countertops puzzles me, but I don't mind, especially when he tenderly lifts my chin with his knuckle and thumb. His voice, a whisper of temptation, breaks the silence. "Are you sure you don't want me to touch you now?" The tension, thick from our playful exchanges, hangs in the air.

My heart races, desire coursing through me. A part of me yearns to take control. He led last time, and while his dominance thrills me, there's a growing urge within me, a craving to express my own desires. But before I can act, he leans in, capturing my lips in a kiss that's tender yet charged with emotion. We break apart, foreheads touching, sharing a breathless moment.

"God, do you know how many times this week I've wanted to do this?" he confesses softly.

A smile dances on my lips. "Probably as much as I did," I admit, closing the gap again, this time initiating the kiss. His hand finds its way to my hair.

"Kissing you is like breathing," he murmurs, his words trailing shivers down my spine. My heart dances with excitement, yet I tread carefully. Deep emotions have a way of sparking rash admissions.

Just enjoy the moment, Milli.

Miles' lips find mine once more, blending urgency with longing. His hands grip my hips, drawing me nearer. The light material of his athletic shorts doesn't conceal much, and his low groan, murmuring, "Mills," fans the flames of desire inside me.

He bites my lip. "No bra today, Mills?"

His observation, both casual and intense, is spot on. The rush from tutoring to dance practice left no time for such considerations and, by his heated gaze, I can tell it was the right choice. The spontaneity of my visit suddenly feels even more thrilling.

I let out a soft laugh, but it's quickly transformed into a gasp, then a moan, as Miles lifts my shirt, his fingers tracing a path along my skin. A wave of heat flushes my face, my breaths quickening.

He lifts my shirt higher, baring me entirely. A soft curse escapes him as he looks at me, awe and yearning intertwined in his expression. My head tilts back, lost in the torrent of sensation washing over me.

"Goddamn, I thought I had my fill, but seeing you

now . . ." he murmurs, pulling my shirt off in a fluid motion, discarding it.

Under the bright kitchen lights, clad only in yoga pants and quirky socks, I might have felt exposed, but Miles' gaze, full of sheer admiration, leaves me feeling nothing but empowered and cherished.

Standing there with Miles, I've never felt more exposed, yet so electrified. The previous times we met, shadows and dim lights shielded us, but now, in this blatant visibility, there's an exhilarating thrill. He grips my ass firmly, sending me to the brink. A smirk curls my lips; I arch an eyebrow in silent challenge. I thought I'd be the one steering us tonight, but damn, the way he takes charge—it's a whole new level of hot.

His touch dances between pain and delight, nails gently pressing in, then caressing away the very traces they create, sending ripples of pleasure through me.

God, I hope those leave marks.

Those romance novels and fantasies? They were just rehearsals. But with Miles? It's like I'm ready for the main event.

He presses his hips into mine, his hardened length creating just enough friction to elicit a needy whimper from my lips. Miles swallows the sounds with a guttural groan of satisfaction.

He pulls back, breathless. "Fuck, Mills, who knew you had such sexy little whimpers in you?"

I'm tempted to retort, "You could've heard them ages ago," but the words never leave my mouth. Instead, I remain silent as his hands glide down my exposed back, over my hips, and gently curve over my stomach. His thumbs tease my hardened nipples.

"More, Miles, please," I find myself begging. It's like I'm

living in one of those steamy scenes from my books, and I'm the star.

He complies, rolling my nipples beneath his skilled fingers, then pinching them firmly. He plays me just right. "You like this, Baby Sutton?" he teases, and I know he's just making me admit it.

Our eyes lock, and I'm nodding, breathless.

"Keep going, Mills? Like how I'm playing with your tits?" he asks, and I can only gasp, "Yes." He pinches my nipple, sending a throbbing pulse straight to my clit.

"Think I can make you come from just this?"

Once, I might've laughed off the idea. But with Miles, suddenly anything seems possible. "Try me," I challenge, our eyes still locked.

He chuckles lightly and then claims my mouth again, our tongues tangling in a fiery dance. I pull him closer until my breasts press against his rock-hard chest. Every inch of our bodies is touching, and still, it's not enough. I want us naked again. I want him inside me. I'd let him take me right here on this counter, where I could let him replay it in his mind every time he passed by, or I could revisit the memory every time I came to visit him and Luke at their house.

Reminding him, us, just how freaking good it is between us.

Reveling in the intense connection between us, Miles tightens his grip on me, rolling my nipples between his fingers while our lower halves keep grinding against each other. At this point, I'm amazed I'm still on the counter with the fervent dry-humping we're engaged in, my hips moving in sync with his every thrust. We both look down, captivated by the sight of our bodies sliding against each other.

"Fuck, Mills," he pants, his breaths ragged. "You feel incredible." He's all over me, and I'm caught up in the intensity of it. His hands, his mouth, his everything—it's overwhelming in the best way.

My head falls back as Miles takes my right breast into his mouth, sucking with the kind of hunger that ignites my desire. I watch as he continues to lavish attention on my breasts. Using his teeth, he pulls at my nipple, and our eyes connect. With a wet pop, his tongue darts out, trailing all over my nipple, and I let out a low whimper.

"Don't stop, please," I'm practically whimpering. It's like every nerve in me is on fire, and he's the only one who can put it out. I'm dripping wet, on the edge of ecstasy, feeling the pulsing waves of pleasure building within me. It's the combination of grinding against his hardness and the hot, wet sensations on my nipple that drive me wild. His strong hands cup my ass to keep me in place as he continues to thrust against me, his cock brushing against my clit with each roll.

"Y-yes," I breathe out.

As he keeps grinding into me, he slams his hand against the island counter next to us, a guttural exclamation escaping his lips. "Jesus."

He kisses my bare neck and collarbone, mapping out my jaw before biting my ear. Every muscle in my body tightens with that, my hips moving instinctively as he hits my clit over and over. Then we fall together right over the edge. Him clothed, me, half clothed—my breasts on full display, moving in sync with my panting, all red and rosy from him sucking on them.

As the waves of my climax wash over me, Miles tightens his grip, anchoring me in the storm of sensation. He lifts his gaze from where it's been buried in my neck, watching me unravel under his touch.

"Goddamn, Mills," he breathes out, a note of wonder in his voice. His eyes are fixed on me, drinking in every shudder and moan as if he's memorizing this moment. And I think, if this is how

I melt under his touch, clothed, what more could happen with nothing between us?

Exhausted, I lean into him, my body slackening with fatigue and satisfaction. His arms are the only thing keeping me standing. I rest against him, my fingers lazily twirling strands of his hair, still feeling the aftershocks coursing through me.

Amid our usual playful exchange, he quips, "Can we do that again, maybe a few times over?"

A genuine, deep laugh bursts from me. I'm still shaking my head when my gaze drifts to the noticeable bulge in his shorts, silently calling out to me. The urge to touch him, to taste him once more, is overwhelming. Once is far from sufficient with Miles; it's a craving that seems insatiable.

But before I can act on my desires, he shoots me a look loaded with amusement. "So, about that tutoring session?" he asks, his tone a blend of jest and eagerness.

I lift my head, trying to steady my breath. My gaze drifts to the obvious tension in his shorts.

"But—"

"Mills," he cuts in, his voice a blend of desire and restraint. "As much as I want you, right now, we can't risk Luke walking in. You're worth more than sneaky hookups." He runs a hand over his face, frustration etched in his features. "I want you freely, all over this house, not just hiding in a room." He sighs, a wistful look crossing his face.

I try to lighten the mood, biting my lip suggestively. "Check my bag."

He chuckles. "That's your first thought after I talk about wanting you everywhere?"

I let out a giggle and give a casual shrug, catching how his gaze clings to every motion I make. "Why would you want my shirt back when I can tell you're enjoying the scenery?"

He shakes his head, though I catch the subtle lift at the corner of his mouth. "I do enjoy the view," he admits softly, extending my bag toward me. "Your bag, m'lady."

I push him teasingly, catching as his eyes drop to my chest. Deciding to push a bit further, I say, "Now, how about my shirt?"

He raises an eyebrow, holding my shirt just out of reach. I decide to play to his weakness, knowing well how men, even those in my novels, can be so predictable. I trace a finger over my breast, and his eyes are instantly glued to the movement. It's almost too easy. As I tease myself, he's captivated, one hand holding my shirt, the other lightly resting on my waist. Seizing the moment, I quickly grab the shirt from him.

As his gaze locks with mine, a sly grin takes over his face. "Gotta say, using your assets like that? Not disappointed at all," he says, a chuckle in his voice.

I slip my shirt back on, and he gives me a puppy-dog look. It's adorably familiar, a tactic I've seen since we were kids. Luke used to get away with everything using that face, but when I tried? "Milli, no means no," was all I got.

I take my bag from his hands. "That look won't sway me, Miles. Besides, every time we're together, I walk away pretty satisfied."

I can sense his grin even as I rummage through my bag. When I finally look up, there it is—that classic, trouble-making smirk of his.

He corners me. "Just 'pretty satisfied'? Not the best ever?"

I shoot back a casual shrug. Who knows what's next for us, but a girl can dream, right?

He studies the book I've pulled out, squinting at the title. Stepping back, he gives me some breathing room, though I'm craving the opposite.

"What's this?" he asks, eyeing the book.

"It's 'MCAT Prep for Dummies'," I reply, all nonchalant.

He lets out a laugh. "Yeah, I see that. But why?"

I shrug again. Miles has dreams, big ones, and he's only shared them with me. So, in my role as tutor, best friend, and whatever else we are, I'm here to help.

He waits, expectant, as I hop off the counter and head for the soup. "Look, you want to be a doctor, right? I'm here to help. In every way," I say, waving my hand vaguely. "You deserve someone rooting for you, pushing you toward that dream."

I can see it in his eyes—the realization of the support I'm offering him.

As I start setting up for dinner, he asks, "But 'For Dummies'?"

I chuckle, the sound bubbling up effortlessly. "We're both navigating blind when it comes to the MCAT, aren't we? Best to start somewhere." Before he can formulate a response, I quickly add our familiar rule, a twinkle in my eye. "And remember, our usual deal—no take backs."

His laughter fills the room, a sound that warms me to the core. He comes up behind me, his hand wrapping around my waist. His breath tickles my ear as he says, "I'm no dummy, Mills. I'm going to be a doctor. But thank you."

He plants a kiss on my temple, a gesture so simple, yet it sends my heart into a frenzy. *It's just a kiss, Milli, not a life commitment. But oh, what a kiss it is.*

CHAPTER 25
MILES

"Ready for that play we've been drilling, Miles?" Coach's voice cuts through the tension, his eyes probing mine for certainty.

I nod, fiercely determined. It's etched in my brain—this play, this moment, right before Panthers' Day. This isn't just any game; it's the one where I prove to my dad, and to myself, that I've got what it takes.

Back on the field, I assume my position, feeling Jensen, our center, sizing me up with a glance.

My affirmation is on the tip of my tongue when suddenly, my vision wavers. I shake my head, clearing the blur, heart hammering in my chest. Hands trembling, I reach out, calling the snap with a voice that betrays my nerves. "Hut, hut, hike."

The ball snaps into my hands, a familiar and comforting weight. I drop back, adrenaline spiking as I scan for an opening. The defenders close in, but I'm locked in—this play is ours. But as I'm about to pass, disorientation hits like a tidal wave. The ground rushes up, and I'm on my back, pain throbbing in my head, my body a vibrating mess of sensation.

Miles, get up. This isn't the time to falter.

Struggling against the pain, I force my eyes open to a blurry figure leaning over me. It's Luke, those damned questioning eyes looking down. Anger flares within me, an urge to lash out.

"You good, man?" Luke's hand extends, pulling me up.

As teammates hover, worried, Coach's voice breaks through. "Get back out there, now!"

Luke gives me a supportive slap, nodding toward the field. "You heard him, let's move!"

Returning to his spot, Luke's questioning look lingers. My heart's a wild drum in my chest, but I muster a nod, pushing past the pain.

"Perseverance over pain," I whisper to myself, a mantra to overcome the struggle. Despite my dreams of medicine, I can't forget the football field and my dad's faith in me. Each moment counts.

Dad's eyes meet mine from the sidelines, tapping his head —our silent signal. I jog back into position, focus sharpening, heart rate steadying.

Fifty seconds, Miles. Make it count.

I line up behind Jensen, his reliability a rock in these final, crucial seconds.

Our rivals are set, their determination a mirror of ours. The stadium is an echoing cauldron of noise, the weight of expectation heavy on my shoulders.

Inhaling deeply, I ground myself. Raising my hand, I signal the snap. The ball hits my hands, and the world narrows to just the field, the players, and the end zone ahead. This is our moment, the culmination of every challenge, every victory. Now, it's all about this play, this snap, this chance.

Gripping the ball tightly, I watch the clock count down the precious seconds. Determination surges through me, each tick fueling my resolve. The stadium pulses with life—a symphony of cheers and palpable support. With adrenaline coursing through me, I execute Coach's meticulously planned play.

The snap is perfect, the scramble intense, and the pass—a stroke of genius. The ball lands in the receiver's hands, igniting the crowd into an uproar of triumph. Touchdown! The stands are alight with our victory.

Dropping to my knees, I offer a silent thanks skyward before touching the ground, whispering to myself, "We did it." My teammates swarm around, lifting me in a victorious whirl. Amidst the dizzying celebration, my eyes find Milli racing onto the field with the dancers. When I'm finally back on solid ground, my balance wavers slightly.

Milli's grip on my arm is firm, her smile as radiant as ever. "You okay?"

Better than okay, now that you're here.

I drape an arm around her, eliciting a soft giggle. Her blush, a perfect match for her strawberry blonde hair, sends my thoughts spiraling. Wondering what it would be like to give her a playful tug as I take her from behind, pumping into her mercilessly. I can't help but imagine she might enjoy it, perhaps even get turned on by it. I mentally file that away as something to explore with Milli at a later time.

We start toward the sidelines, where Coach, the Suttons, and my parents await. Dad's grin speaks volumes of his pride.

Luke, casually draping his arm around Milli and Payson, jokes, "Hell of a game, right, Chasen?"

I nod, my mind echoing Dad's usual advice about focus and resilience on the field. Milli's reassuring squeeze on my hip pulls me back from my thoughts. Her silent support means the world to me.

The last week has been a whirlwind of emotions

surrounding Milli. Do I confess how I feel, or let things flow naturally? For now, I return her smile with a knowing wink.

Luke releases Milli, focusing on Payson. I keep Milli close, her presence calming amidst the impending lecture I know that's coming from my dad.

But right now, all I crave is the simplicity of ending this day. To retreat back home, wash away the game's sweat and strain in a hot shower, then dive into my study materials for the looming final exams and MCAT prep. And perhaps, just perhaps, bring Milli back with me.

With Luke out for the night, the possibilities unfold in my mind—the two of us under the shower's cascade, sharing her favorite strawberry ice cream, maybe drawing her a bath that I know she's been longing for, and then just unwinding together, lost in each other's arms.

When my gaze drifts back to Milli, it's like she's reading every thought. Her eyes, deep and knowing, meet mine, and the way she bites her lip sends a wave of excitement through me.

But reality checks in. The awkward interruption from someone's cough breaks our moment. Reluctantly, I let go of Milli, both of us feeling the loss. I just want to grab her, kiss her damn mouth, show everyone, including our families, that she's mine.

But is she really mine?

Right now, certainty eludes me, but frankly, it doesn't matter. What I do know, with every fiber of my being, is that I'm deeply in love with her. And that's enough for me to want to continue this journey we're on; wherever it may lead.

Mrs. Sutton's invitation to Glasshouse pulls me back. Her knowing glance between me and Milli says she's onto us. I agree to join, telling them I need to shower first, and the longing in Milli's eyes tells me she's right there with me, in memory and desire.

Just then, my phone buzzes with a text from her.

MILLS

Need help in the shower?

Her message ignites a spark within me; *this girl.*

An hour into the evening at Glasshouse, and it's clear things won't be any simpler than the post-game family chat.

"So, you're tutoring Milli?" Mrs. Sutton asks, her eyes flicking between my mom and Milli, sharing a knowing smile. Great, so this is how the evening unfolds.

Glasshouse is buzzing tonight, a mix of post-game celebration and the usual crowd. I catch

Milli's eye; she looks as surprised as Luke does by Mrs. Sutton's question. We hadn't planned on announcing our tutoring sessions, but secrets don't last long in our families, especially with my mom's knack for sharing news.

Luke's face is a storm of emotions—annoyance at being out of the loop and the protective brotherly concern. He's always been wary of me and Milli together.

The cat's out of the bag now, so I play it cool. "Yeah, she's been helping me with a class." The table chuckles, but Luke's confusion is evident. "Since the beginning of the semester," I add, cutting him off before he can probe further.

He's visibly irked, questioning Milli directly. "Are you okay with this?" She shrinks back a bit, her shyness on full display.

I can't stand how he's treating her—like she's some damsel in distress. "Why wouldn't she be okay with it, Luke?" I interject.

His shrug appears nonchalant, yet his voice carries a

definitive edge. Just as I'm gearing up to respond, a soft touch on my calf stops me. Milli. Beneath the table, her foot, snug in a Converse, strokes my leg, easing away the irritation. It soothes the storm brewing within me.

Milli straightens up, confidently addressing Luke. "Yes, I'm fine tutoring Miles." I return her support with a covert foot rub, acknowledging her strength in standing up for herself.

Mills and I have this under control.

But do you really, Miles?

Milli's smile is grateful, but before Luke can reply, my dad chimes in. "A solid C in that class is fine, Miles. Remember the real dream."

I nod, appeasing him. "I know, Dad. But I still want to finish strong academically."

The conversation drifts, but Milli breaks the silence, praising my recent academic success. I'm grateful, even as her foot leaves my calf. She finds a new way to comfort me, positioning her feet around mine, a gesture reminiscent of our more intimate moments.

Lifting my head, Milli winks at me. This type of support is both surprising and incredibly welcome. I'm used to relying on myself, especially during tough times at the hospital. But Milli's presence, her subtle gestures of solidarity, they're changing the game for me. Depending on someone else is new, unnerving, yet incredibly reassuring.

As I try to reconcile these feelings, I realize Milli isn't just standing up for me. She's showing me a different kind of strength—the kind that comes from letting someone else in.

My phone vibrates just as I notice our moms, huddled together, exchanging those knowing glances and whispers like they're plotting the next chapter of a daytime soap.

Pulling out my phone, another missed call and message catch my eye.

"Miles, we need to hear from you. Ignoring calls isn't helping, and avoiding treatment is not an option."

Dr. Reynolds had hinted at a treatment plan, but the reality of facing it head-on is another story. I'm not ready to confront that yet. My focus has been on the game, the class with Milli, and the MCAT prep. Plus, there's something about being with her that just lifts me up. Each glance, each smile, she sends my way feels like a jolt to the heart, a reminder of what I want to hold on to for as long as I can.

I lock my phone, trying to shake off the unease. The table buzzes with football talk, and Luke's absorbed in his phone. The moms are still in their world, now showing Milli something on Mrs. Sutton's phone—probably discussing gala dress options. Milli's polite nod doesn't mask her disinterest.

Leaning back, I take a casual sip of my beer, letting my mind wander. I imagine whisking Milli away from this mundane chatter, longing to be alone with her. She catches my gaze, her eyebrow raised, a hint of mischief in her smile. I can't help but grin back, the thoughts in my head growing hazier with each sip of beer.

She doesn't verbally rise to the bait but instead bites her lip, tongue darting out seductively over her lips. It's a private show just for me in the midst of this oblivious crowd.

I'm utterly hooked on her. Milli's energy is electric, irresistible—I've always been magnetized by it, and I'm certain I always will be. She winks and turns back to the conversation, leaving me with a grin of her own and a head full of thoughts.

She's playing a tantalizing game, and I'm all too willing to play along. And, later, when she stealthily slips into mine and Luke's place, the night unfolds with a passion that's hard to forget. That moment when her soft whisper, saying my name, echoes in the room; it imprints itself in my memory, a tender yet intense reminder of our connection.

CHAPTER 26
MILLI

An hour into the rehearsal, I observe Lily and Georgia in the dance studio, their mix of frustration and determination almost endearing. "Let's try again, girls," I say, injecting some cheer into the atmosphere.

My mentor, Jen, and Mr. Hanmann watch with keen interest from the edge of the room. They've been a constant presence since the preparation for the Dazzling Dance Duo competition began.

Ben is capturing every moment with his phone, a symbol of his unwavering support and love. Watching him, I'm reminded of my own dance journey, how my parents were present but seemingly more focused on Luke's aspirations than mine. It hurt, of course, but it also drove me to forge my own way, not for fame, but to deepen my passion for dance and share it through teaching.

I guide the girls through the routine again, striving to balance enjoyment with precision. "One more try, as if the judges are watching," I softly suggest, kneeling to their level. I explain that this run-through is for the competition video, sparking a light of understanding and renewed concentration in their eyes.

Their final performance earns enthusiastic applause, with Ben's cheers ringing the loudest. Witnessing their growth and expression in dance fills me with a profound sense of happiness.

Coaching these young dancers goes beyond choreography; it's about fostering confidence and finding joy in movement. Dance has always been my safe haven, a place to be my true self, and my goal is to extend that sanctuary to others.

Jen's hand on my shoulder brings me back to the present as the Hanmann sisters leave. "You did great, Milli," she says with genuine pride. Her words strike a chord, especially coming from her. It's a validation I've craved, different from the casual encouragement of friends and family.

Jen's hug is comforting. "Happy tears only in my studio," she jests, lightening the moment. Her comment makes me laugh through the emotion.

I gather my things, lingering a bit in the now-quiet studio. Opening my laptop, I'm greeted by a message from Ben, the video attachment ready to be uploaded. His words of gratitude bring a smile to my face, and I get to work, uploading the video for the judges to see.

This is more than just a dance competition. It's a step in my journey as a mentor, a future dance coach, a step toward realizing my dream of owning a dance studio. As I hit "Submit," I'm filled with a sense of purpose and anticipation for what lies ahead, not just for the Hanmann sisters, but for myself as well.

"God, that feels incredible." The words slip out in a moan as Miles' hands masterfully knead my calves. We're nestled together in the grand clawfoot tub situated in the bathroom he shares with Luke—a detail of their home I've always been fond of. The idea of a shared bath gave me pause at first, mindful of Luke's presence, but as fate would have it, he's out with someone else. And really, the allure of relaxing alongside Miles, coupled with the enticement of bubble baths and strawberry ice cream, proved irresistible.

His reply to my moan is teasing, laced with innuendo. "Keep making noises like that, and I'll have to share something even more incredible," he jests, his wink loaded with promise.

I join in the banter, positioning my foot against his solid chest, sensing his muscles flex beneath my touch. He puts on a show of being wounded when my toes playfully squeeze his chest, but the laughter in his eyes tells me we're both enjoying this.

Moving closer, the water rippling around us, I'm acutely aware of the growing intensity between us. Our interactions have always been a dance of desire and restraint, each encounter bringing us closer to a line we haven't yet crossed. Sitting astride him now, the physical manifestation of his hard cock pressing against me, I'm both exhilarated and apprehensive. Crossing this threshold will change everything, a fact we're both keenly aware of.

His hands grip my waist firmly, a perfect balance of desire and control. "Baby, you're driving me crazy," he whispers, his voice strained with a cocktail of emotions. His vulnerability, so raw and open, strikes a chord deep within me.

Whispering close to his ear, "Maybe that's exactly what I want."

His response is immediate, a blend of hunger and intensity in his eyes as he lifts me from the tub, guiding me to the edge with an urgency that sends a pool of wetness between my legs.

We stand there, soaked and breathless, the tension between us electric. Instead of guiding me to the bedroom, Miles gently pushes me against the tub, asking me to brace myself. As he kneels, the sight of him—so powerful, yet so devoted—lifts my leg to his shoulder.

His lips trace a path upward, each kiss planting a shiver of excitement through my veins. My skin blossoms with goose-bumps, marking the thrilling impact he holds over me. My heartbeat accelerates, thundering against my ribcage, while my fingers weave into his hair, clutching softly yet eagerly.

"Better hold on, baby," he whispers with a knowing smirk, moments before his lips meet the most sensitive part of me. The touch of his tongue is both gentle and assertive, a perfect dance of sensation that nearly lifts me off the bath's edge.

But Miles is just getting started. His hands grip my hips, and he teases me with his tongue before dipping a finger inside and slowly bringing it out as lips seal over my clit. He brings me to the edge before pulling back.

Again and again.

Over and over.

Sweat mingling with bathwater, I am so turned on that I can't see straight. I tug at his hair, begging for more. And that is when he slips his tongue inside of me, his thumb circling my clit. The sensation is too much. I buck against him as the brightest lights explode before me and a cry escapes my lips. I rock against him as I ride out every last bit of pleasure.

And he stays right there.

My arms are tingling.

My legs are tingling.

My head is spinning.

When my breathing calms, he lifts his head; mouth glossy with my desire. His lips turn up the tiniest bit, and he just watches me as if I am the only woman to ever exist. As I finally catch my breath, Miles' expression is a mix of satisfaction and awe.

"If anything ever happens to me, I just want you to know I'm the fucking luckiest guy in the world," he says, his voice a tender murmur.

He pulls me into his arms, and in that embrace, I feel like the luckiest person alive, wrapped in the warmth of a moment that feels like this thing between us could last forever.

CHAPTER 27
MILLI

No, Milli, she's just your plus one.

"Okay, what do you think of this one?" Payson twirls in her gala dress, seeking approval while I'm half-lost in a romance novel. "Milli, are you even paying attention?" she huffs, her impatience clear.

I glance up, masking my indifference. Dress shopping isn't high on my list, but I'm intrigued by the idea of visiting Whimsical Words & Pages downtown. Last weekend at Glasshouse, my mom and Mrs. Chasen had their picks for me, but I'm set on making my own choice. I informed my mom recently that I'd be selecting my dress solo, a small assertion of my growing independence.

This gala at NorthRidge University feels different for me this year. It's not just an event for the inner circle of Coach Kreft anymore; I'm part of it, an equal, not a tag-along.

Payson's reflection catches my eye, and I offer a noncommittal, "I like it," noticing her frustration.

She's been changing outfits for a while now, and Brooke, draped in an olive green gown, chimes in, "Why the fuss over the perfect dress?"

I exchange a knowing look with Brooke as Payson deflects with talk of fixing her nails for the gala. She bites her lower lip as Payson casually shrugs, then turns toward me, her back to the mirror, waving her hand vaguely. "No, no. No reason, none at all."

She's not being entirely honest. For one, she's avoiding eye contact with me and Brooke. Two, she's nervously fiddling with her fingers, as if she's examining her chipped nails. Then she adds, "I should really get these fixed before the gala, right? It is a black-tie event, so I need to be in tip-top shape."

Brooke, now with her hand on her hip, raises an eyebrow in Payson's direction. She's clearly trying to mimic Payson's stance to grab her attention. "Out with it," Brooke demands, and Payson lets out another little huff as her eyes dart between mine and Brooke's.

"Seriously, I'm going solo," Payson finally admits, and I roll my eyes. That's such a Payson response—always into fashion and the dating scene, much like Luke with his flings. They're both a little crazy but have no intentions of getting serious in the future.

I contemplate the fleeting nature of such interactions. They lack the depth and excitement of something more meaningful—like what I have with Miles. Speaking of him, my phone pings with a text from him.

MILES

Mills, you gonna show me your gala dress or what?

As Payson and Brooke continue their discussion, I reply to Miles, curious about how he knew of our shopping plans.

MILES

Saw Payson leaving the locker room. She mentioned it.

I shake my head, amused yet not surprised. Payson's a cheerleader at heart, but hardly a football strategist.

MILLI

Do you think the coach caught her eyeing some of your teammates?

In that moment, it's as if I can hear his hearty laugh as he responds.

MILES

Wouldn't put it past her.

So, the picture? Dress color?

Hold on, you have no choice but to tell me. I am your date, after all.

We clearly need to coordinate.

The mention of him as "my date" stirs a flutter in my heart, yet I strive to moderate my enthusiasm. Despite the joy I find in our moments together, the unresolved mystery of our future direction lingers.

Milli, you're already in love, my inner voice chides. But I push that thought away. Yes, we've crossed physical boundaries, but the emotional stakes are higher and more complicated. I'm enjoying the here and now, not ready to confront the possibility of unreciprocated feelings.

"Who's been occupying your thoughts so much lately?" Payson asks, looking at me with curiosity.

I briefly look up from my phone, pausing for a moment. Closing my messages, I straighten up in the chair, mirroring Payson's evasive nail inspection with a casual shrug.

"Milli, seriously?" she half-laughs, her irritation barely masked. "I want details."

Rising to meet her challenge, I confront her directly. Brooke, meanwhile, watches us with an amused yet exasperated expression. It's clear she thinks we're both skirting around the truth for no reason. Payson could drop it, but my own curiosity is piqued. I wonder who she's been secretly seeing, as it seems I'm not the only one navigating clandestine meetings.

Technically, it's no secret I'm tutoring Miles, but the full extent of our relationship remains our own.

Payson, visibly wrestling with herself, finally relents. "I might have a date," she concedes before quickly retreating to the dressing room, leaving us with a mystery.

Brooke and I exchange a look and a chuckle at her minimal disclosure.

"Now it's your turn," Payson calls out from her changing cubicle.

Browsing through the selection, my fingers brush against a pastel pink dress. It embodies elegance, featuring a sweetheart neckline that whispers sophistication, echoing the vision I shared with Mrs. Chasen. Fashion usually isn't my battleground, yet the prospect of seizing Miles' complete attention at the gala is irresistibly alluring. The thought of him, impeccably dressed in a suit, and undressing him later, has my thighs clenching.

"Milli, we're waiting." Payson's voice cuts through my daydreams.

I need to deflect. I grab the dress and head to the fitting rooms, maintaining my facade. "Just busy with tutoring on campus," I reply, slipping into the dressing room. "Mrs. Raker's got me booked solid. Between studying, classes, and dance, tutoring's pretty much all I have time for."

It's not a complete lie.

Inside the fitting room, the dress envelops me like a second skin, accentuating every curve.

Gazing in the mirror, I'm surprised at how stunning I look. This dress isn't just a choice; it is a statement. Biting my lip, I envision Miles' reaction, his eyes gleaming with unmistakable desire. The thought alone sets off a wave of excitement within me.

I quickly snap a photo, capturing just the dress and my bare feet.

MILLI

What do you think of the color?

Waiting for his response, a flutter of nerves unsettles me. Just as I'm debating whether to change out of the dress, Payson's exasperated voice pierces the air. "What are you doing here?"

I gently nudge the fitting room door open. Peering out, my eyes land on Miles, who's casually chatting with Payson. He looks effortlessly handsome, as always, in simple jeans and a white t-shirt, topped with a shacket that highlights his body.

I push the door wider, intrigued by Payson's tone. It's not like her to snap at Miles. And there's Luke, casually draping his arm around her, though she seems less than pleased.

Their sudden closeness puzzles me. Have they always been this way, and I just never noticed?

My thoughts are interrupted by Miles' voice, asking, "Where's Milli?"

I quickly try to close the door, not wanting to eavesdrop. But then Luke echoes, "Yeah, where's Milli?"

Cam, ever the instigator, teases, "Miles, why are you so curious about Milli's whereabouts?"

I roll my eyes, knowing Cam's penchant for stirring up drama. This is not the time or place for it, especially in this upscale boutique. I silently plead for a change of subject, wishing they'd focus on the gala instead of on me.

Miles responds, attempting to deflect, "Honestly, whenever Payson's around, I find myself asking, 'Where's Milli?' Those two are always together."

Payson's sigh echoes my own eye roll. Miles' cover might be smooth, but Payson and I are far from inseparable these days. We're both on our own paths at NorthRidge University, seeking our own discoveries.

"Suree . . . " Cam sarcastically says, only adding to the tension.

The conversation shifts, thanks to one of the freshmen that Miles mentors as he says, "Regardless of who anyone's looking for, I need to snag a damn suit before Coach Kreft gives me a hard time about it again."

"Take it easy, Gunner," Cam says.

Then, Miles chimes in, "Don't pay any attention to the dweeb, Gun. We're in the right place. Just follow my lead."

Letting Miles take charge seems like the best choice. If I were in their shoes, I'd follow Miles' lead without a second thought, every single time.

As I stand there, caught in my own thoughts, I notice Payson has slipped back into her fitting room, leaving Brooke engrossed in her phone. My eyes drift toward the men's section, where Miles and Gunner are browsing through an array of formal wear. Despite my intention to focus on my own dressing, I find myself inexplicably drawn to observing them, especially Miles.

He's effortlessly picking out shirts, handing selections to Gunner while choosing some for himself. Just as I'm about to pull back, Miles turns, catching my gaze. His eyes sparkle with mischief, and a familiar warmth floods my cheeks. His grin, coupled with a knowing wink, sends my heart into overdrive, leaving me slightly unsteady.

I chastise myself silently. *Milli, focus. You're in a dressing room.* My resolve wavers as a hand suddenly halts the door's closure.

"Shit," I mutter under my breath, fully aware of who it must be.

I let out a resigned sigh and peek out, immediately greeted by the sight of Miles' athletic frame. Those arms have been a source of both comfort and excitement for me, time and again. As he stands there, his presence is almost too much to take in. I'm drawn out of my shell, a side of me he's unknowingly nurtured.

"Can I help you?" I ask, trying to sound nonchalant.

Miles leans in, his voice a low murmur. "I want to see what my *date* is wearing."

I retort with a raised eyebrow, "Date? I thought Brooke was my date."

His laughter momentarily breaks the tension, a sound that always brings a smile to my face, making my toes involuntarily curl in delight. As quickly as the laughter comes, Miles shifts to a more intimate tone, leaning so close I feel the warmth of his breath on my ear. I risk a quick glance around; everyone is absorbed in their own world, oblivious to our hushed conversation.

"No, Milli, she's just your plus one," he whispers, his breath tickling my ear.

I ponder the distinction. *Isn't a date and a plus one essentially the same?*

Catching my uncertain gaze, Miles' eyes hold a depth of meaning. "There's a distinction," he says gently. "Choosing a plus one might conclude the evening with a void, a lingering question mark of 'what might have been,' echoing in the silence. But a date," he pauses, ensuring each word lands with precision, "a date is an adventure that leaves you with an insatiable desire, a thirst for the depths of connection we've just begun to explore. And baby, I promise, by the end of our evening together, you'll be wanting more."

My eyes momentarily widen. *Did he really just say that? And so effortlessly?* Goodness, talk about igniting a blaze within me and putting every romance novel I've ever read to utter shame.

With a final tap on the dressing room door frame, Miles leaves with a wink, his words resonating deep within me. My heart pounds like a relentless drum, its rhythm echoing through me for the rest of the day.

CHAPTER 28
MILLI

Taking a deep breath, I steady my nerves, whispering to myself, "You look stunning, Milli. Just breathe." Slowly, I open my eyes, and the reflection in the closet mirror makes my heart race with excitement. The image staring back is a bold, new version of myself, one I've never fully embraced until now.

Clad in the soft, pale pink dress from last week's boutique visit, complemented by delicate gold earrings and my hair in gentle curls, I have a surge of confidence. This look, so different from my usual style, embodies a new chapter—one where I feel irresistibly attractive and empowered.

I lift my dress, revealing my white Converse sneakers—my little act of rebellion hidden beneath the elegant fabric. They're a secret nod to my true self, comfortably tucked away from critical eyes. Glancing at the stack of books next to them, cherished gifts from my former tutor, I smile, feeling a perfect balance between the bold new Milli and the girl I've always been.

"Done admiring yourself?" Payson's voice snaps me back. She's ready to go, her tone lighthearted, yet impatient.

I suppress an eye roll.

Can't a girl savor a moment like this?

I remember the last time Payson had a hand in my look—it was a blend of trouble and thrill. Tonight, she's outdone herself with the finishing touches—hair, makeup, even my lingerie. It's a daring choice, but wearing it makes me feel liberated, as if it was made just for me.

"You look incredible," Brooke says, her hand on my shoulder, her reflection full of admiration in the mirror. I grab her hand, feeling the silent encouragement I need to embrace this new look fully.

"Alright, let's go," I say, grabbing my jacket and wristlet, ready to take on the night.

Arm in arm, Payson, Brooke, and I stride through the dorm hall, drawing curious glances. Tonight's gala at Gridiron Glory Hall is an exclusive event, and our glamorous attire stands out amidst the typical Sunday evening of studying and dorm life.

As we step outside, a crisp autumn breeze envelopes us, carrying the promise of change. I pull my jacket closer around my shoulders, disentangling my arm from the girls as we make our way to my jeep. There's a tangible buzz of excitement in the air, anticipation building for an evening that feels destined to be unforgettable.

Miles

"Hey, Miles, it's Dr. Reynolds. We're reaching out for the last time. We get it; this is a lot for you to take in.

We've done everything possible on our side. Remember, you're in charge now; you're an adult, and the decision about your treatment rests with you. We're hoping you'll decide what's best. Please, when you're ready, give me a call back."

"Fuck, this is the fifth time this week they've fucking called me," I mutter to myself, a simmering frustration brewing as I listen to the voicemail. His words reverberate through the phone, casting a shadow of dread over me. There it stands, stark and undeniable—my health, my decision. It's a burdensome realization, grappling with the fact that the choice rests solely on my shoulders.

In a moment of annoyance, my phone slips from my grasp, landing with a soft crack on the bathroom vanity. "Perfect, just what I needed," I groan, spotting a new crack on the screen. As if I don't have enough on my plate.

My reflection in the mirror looks back at me, a mix of anger and helplessness in my eyes. I try to steady my racing heart, gripping the counter as if it's the only thing keeping me grounded. This tremor in my hands, it's like my body's betraying me, revealing the turmoil I'm fighting so hard to hide.

I slam my fist against the countertop, a wave of frustration washing over me. "Fuck, get it together, Miles. You've got to pull it together," I whisper to myself, trying to muster some semblance of control.

Tonight's gala is more than just another event. It's my senior year, the year when everything's supposed to fall into place. My future, my career, it all feels like it's hanging in the balance. I need to show up, not just for my dad or the NFL scouts lurking in the shadows, but for a cause that's bigger than all of us.

Splashing water on my face, I try to wash away the frustration, the fear, the uncertainty. "You can do this, Miles. It's showtime," I tell myself, trying to drum up some enthusiasm.

As I step out, my eyes instantly find her—Milli. She's making her way to the bar, probably for her usual Shirley Temple. I can't help but smile; she's always been so predictable in the most charming way. Payson and Brooke are somewhere in the crowd, but it's Milli who holds my gaze.

The woman who effortlessly has my heart in her hands.

She's stunning tonight, in a pale pink dress that makes her glow, her hair down in a way I haven't seen for ages. She looks like a dream. My fingers itch to touch it, to feel its softness, to pull it, just to hear her response.

I watch her, my heart skipping a beat as she casually twirls her hair, a telltale sign of her nerves. But she has no reason to be nervous, not looking as breathtaking as she does.

Then, I notice the Converse on her feet—those special ones from her tutor. Classic Milli, blending elegance with a touch of rebellion. She catches me looking, our eyes locking in a moment of silent understanding. She turns away, but not before giving a twirl and a bow, like she's the star of her own show.

I laugh, the tension and worries of the past hour melting in her presence. She's heading my way now, and I move to meet her, eager for just one dance, one moment where it's just us and nothing else matters.

As we come face to face on the dance floor, everything else blurs into the background. I lean closer, my voice a soft murmur. "You look like a dream, baby." I observe the gentle shift in her eyes as she processes my words. And I truly mean it—she's breathtaking. Amidst all the uncertainties surrounding us, they seem insignificant now. What counts is here and now, with Milli in arm's reach, tangible, real—someone I can immerse myself in.

But our moment is short-lived. Luke's voice cuts through our bubble, and she tenses up. I give her hand a reassuring squeeze, trying to ease her worries. It's just Luke, after all.

Reluctantly tearing myself away from Milli, I head toward my father, each step weighed down by the burden of his expectations. The thought of facing him, knowing what he wants from me tonight, tightens a knot in my stomach.

Cam's hand lands firmly on my back, jolting me back to the present. His gesture, simple yet grounding, redirects my focus to the here and now—the gala, its purpose, and the community it supports.

In moments like this, I'm reminded that life isn't just about the game on the field or the battles within. It's about something far bigger, more meaningful. We're here not for personal glory or to settle internal conflicts. Tonight, we're part of a collective effort to make a real difference, to bring a ray of hope into the lives of those fighting battles much harder than any football game.

Navigating through the crowd, I let my eyes roam over Gridiron Glory Hall. This place, steeped in memories, is like a vault of my college life. I remember my first walk through these doors as a wide-eyed freshman. We'd heard stories from our parents about these events—Dad and Mr. Sutton, immersed in the football world, always talked it up. But nothing prepared me for the sheer opulence of it all.

The hall exudes a kind of elegance that's hard to put into words. Those chandeliers, cascading light from above, always cast a warm, golden glow over everything, making the whole place feel like a scene from a classic film. I recall being a bit star-struck by the servers in their crisp uniforms, ferrying drinks and gourmet appetizers around.

The gold tablecloths glittering under the lights add to that sense of grandeur. And there, always at the center of it all, is the sign: "A Touchdown Against Breast Cancer." A powerful reminder of why we are all there, a beacon of hope in the fight we are all part of.

Every visit here has felt like a journey into a world where elegance meets purpose. I know these experiences will stick with me long after I leave NorthRidge University.

Distractedly, I mutter, "Mmhm," to Cam's comment as he pats my shoulder and moves on. Spotting my dad across the room, I give him a subtle nod toward the bar. He seems reluctant but joins me, anyway. We order beers, and while I know Coach wouldn't mind, I can almost hear Dad's gears grinding in disapproval.

"You sure that's wise, Miles?" Dad questions as I take a swig, the cold beer a small comfort against the unease his presence stirs in me.

I just shrug, leaning back against the bar. The familiar buzz of pre-event chatter fills the air, a tapestry of anticipation and excitement. My gaze drifts back to Milli. She's still with Payson and Brooke, looking like a radiant beacon in the crowd. Dad's voice fades into background noise as I catch her eye and she flashes that smile—the one that always sends my heart racing.

"See Coach Lockhart over there?" Dad's words pull me back. I nod, following his gaze to the unmistakable figure of the NFL coach. Dad's texts, always laced with reminders of the looming Panthers' Day game and the scouts' watchful eyes, echo in my head. I get it, Dad—no need to hammer it home.

"Maybe we should go say hi," he suggests. Milli's watching us, her playful salute morphing into concern. I reassure her with a smile before agreeing to Dad's plan.

As we start to move toward Coach Lockhart, Milli stands up, all mock-serious, then winks at me. I grin. Her little gestures, her unspoken support—they mean everything.

But then, Dad steps squarely in front of me, blocking my

view of her. His eyes lock onto mine with an intensity that's rare for him. "Don't even think about it, Miles," he says, and I realize he's not just talking about approaching the coach. He's seen the exchange between me and Milli, and his warning is clear.

The full weight of expectation and my own aspirations crash into each other. This evening isn't just about the dazzle of the gala, the game of football, or the noble cause of breast cancer awareness. It's a microcosm of the greater challenge I'm facing: charting my own course amidst a sea of external expectations.

Dad's words cut through my thoughts, his voice firm. "Your focus needs to be here," He taps his temple, emphasizing his point about football. "No time for distractions, especially not girls."

But he doesn't get it. Milli isn't just a distraction, she's . . . well, she's Milli. But in Dad's world, where my life orbits solely around football, she's invisible. Our talks never veer away from the field, each conversation a reminder of the path he's carved out for me.

Stealing glances at Milli over Dad's shoulder, I see her concern, her gestures trying to lighten the mood. She's my solace in this whirlwind, yet here I am, trapped in a conversation I don't want to be in. Dad's light tap on my face snaps me back, and I catch the alarm in Milli's eyes. I quickly reassure her with a hand on Dad's, signaling that it's alright, he's just trying to make a point, not hurt me.

"Let's go see Coach Lockhart," I suggest, steering the conversation back to safer waters.

His smile, that proud, football-focused grin, makes me wonder. What if I shared my real dream with him, my ambition to be a doctor? Would that smile fade? Would his love or regard for me change?

These thoughts swirl in my head, filled with doubt. What if I never get to pursue that dream? What if . . .

Shaking off the wave of anxiety, I remind myself to focus on the now. Tonight is about something bigger than my personal struggles, and I need to keep it together, at least for now.

Milli

I can't shake this nagging feeling that Miles needs an escape right now, a break from the weight of expectations. It's something I resonate with, caught up in my own whirlwind of midterms, tutoring, and dance commitments. And the Hanmann sisters! Their success in the dance competition has been a bright spot in my hectic schedule.

But just as I'm contemplating how I might offer Miles that much-needed respite, the evening's agenda takes over. "Please make your way to your tables," announces a voice over the microphone. Clutching another Shirley Temple, I navigate toward my assigned seat.

At the table, I spot Brooke, my parents, the Chasens, and Luke . . . and, wait, is that Payson next to Luke? That's unexpected. Could she be the one Luke was talking about? My curiosity is piqued, but my mom's not-so-subtle side-eye at Payson suggests she's less than thrilled with this pairing.

As I sit down, neatly adjusting my dress, I feel Miles' eyes on me. He's looking dapper in his suit, his hair styled just so, giving off that irresistible aura. And then there's the color coordination—our attire matching in shades of pale pink. It's a small detail, but one that makes my heart flutter.

I try to keep my expectations in check, though. Flirting with Miles is one thing, but deciphering what lies beneath is another. Yet, when I lick my lips and hear his low groan, I can't help but giggle at the fun of teasing him this way. A way

I have always imagined, but never thought would be a reality and, now that it's happening, I don't want it to ever end.

As I'm about to take my seat, I feel a sudden, bold grip on my ass, making me jump. I turn to see Miles grinning that mischievous grin of his.

"What a tease," I whisper, trying to keep my composure as he leans in, his breath warm against my ear. "Takes one to know one," he retorts with a wink.

The night progresses with speeches and recognition of the cause we're all here for. The gala is more than just a social event; it's a platform for change and support. As volunteers commit to helping, I'm not surprised to see Miles' name among them. His dedication is a given, as deep-rooted as his connection to the cause.

Then comes the moment for a volunteer speaker. The room buzzes with anticipation, and I lean over to Miles. "Any idea who's speaking tonight?" His response is laced with that smoldering look that sets my nerves alight.

Before I can react, the announcement comes, "Miles Chasen, come on up."

He stands, leaning close to me, his words sending a thrill through me. "Guess we just found out, huh?" I roll my eyes, but inside, my heart races with excitement.

I hear the familiar giggles and whispers from our table corner. Our moms have been eyeing me and Miles ever since I sat down. Their glances are too telling; they see us as a couple, decked out in matching attire and lost in our flirtatious world. But they don't know half of it. They'd probably be thrilled if they did, though. It feels like they've secretly hoped for this all along, and now that it's happening, their excitement is almost palpable. And Luke's glares? I just shake my head and bite my lip, letting them slide off me.

Miles makes his way to the front, and I let my eyes linger on him, admiring every confident step.

"Looking at something?" Brooke teases, nudging me gently.

I try to suppress a laugh, but fail miserably. Why hide how Miles makes me feel?

She leans in closer, her voice a whisper of knowing. "I always knew something would spark between you two in college."

I roll my eyes, but inside, I'm agreeing. Brooke's always had a keen sense for these things.

As the room falls into a hush, Miles takes the mic, and a hushed, "Shit," slips from his lips, breaking the silence. "Public speaking isn't my forte," he confesses, triggering a wave of laughter across the room. He stands there, slightly awkward but utterly charming, admitting his reluctance about speaking tonight. "When Coach Kreft asked me to speak tonight, my gut reaction was a flat no. Why me, of all people? I'm not the guy for this job," he shares.

But then his tone shifts, growing more reflective. "It took me just a few hours to change my mind and call Coach back. I realized this night means more to me than most probably realize. It's not just about Coach Kreft's wife and her fight—it's about what it means to each of us, personally."

Miles fidgets slightly, his gaze drifting down before his eyes find mine across the room, locking in a moment of silent encouragement. "I thought this was just another athlete's obligation at first. But then, I understood its deeper meaning, particularly for someone who's battled cancer."

The room falls into a stunned silence, a collective intake of breath filling the air. This revelation, though known to some, is a bold admission in such a public setting. I swell with pride, knowing this is a defining moment for Miles.

His voice wavers but doesn't break. "It felt like the end of the world. But really, it was a lesson in strength, in overcoming. And tonight, I see that same resilience in all of you."

Pausing, Miles draws in a deep breath, his presence commanding yet vulnerable. "Life throws curveballs. Some we think we can't handle. When I faced cancer, I was filled with fear, anger, and was lost in uncertainty. But it was then I found my resilience, the indomitable spirit within me."

His words, heartfelt and sincere, resonate with everyone. "This evening is about more than just raising funds. It's a celebration of our shared humanity, our collective resilience. We stand together, united in our struggles and triumphs."

Pride swells within me, bringing tears to my eyes. This is the Miles who will make an incredible doctor, the Miles who's more than just a football player. He's a survivor, a fighter, and, in this moment, a beacon of hope and strength for everyone in the room.

He steps down from the podium, but instead of returning to our table, he detours somewhere else. Concern flickers in my heart, urging me to follow, but I'm momentarily halted.

"Milli, what's going on with you and Miles?" Luke's voice cuts through my thoughts.

Surprised, I meet his gaze, a hint of defiance in my eyes. Gone is the shy, reticent Milli. With newfound confidence, I retort, "What about you and Payson?" My eyebrow arches challengingly, throwing him off balance.

Without waiting for his response, I pivot on my heel, striding toward the bar where Miles has found refuge. Our eyes meet, a silent understanding passing between us. He's seeking an escape, and I know exactly how to provide it.

CHAPTER 29
MILES

"You okay?" Feeling Milli's soft touch on my arm, a sense of calm washes over me. The speech

I just gave was a raw, unscripted dive into my past, something I never planned to reveal, but it felt right in the moment. I wanted the room to understand the true essence of this event, not just as a social gathering or a football talk, but as a support system for people like me who have faced life's toughest battles.

The constant buzzing of my phone with messages and calls I've been deliberately ignoring now feels like a pressure valve about to burst. It's as though everything I've been holding back is yearning to break free, to be acknowledged and confronted.

In Milli's presence, the storm of worries and doubts that usually plague me momentarily quiets down. I glance at her, offering a light-hearted wink and a reassurance. "I'm perfect now." Her gentle touch as she wraps her hand around my arm and rests her head against it ignites a complex cascade of emotions within me. These feelings, deeper and more intricate than anything we've shared before.

You love this girl, no two ways about it.

But these intense emotions bring a sense of vulnerability. The fear of rejection, the uncertainty of our future, and the risk of misinterpreting her signals loom over me. I'm trying to stay in the moment, enjoy our current connection without overthinking. But it's tough not to ponder what all this might mean for us.

As I take another sip of my beer, I softly let go of her hand from my arm. I notice a quick shadow of disappointment in her eyes, but it swiftly changes into a seductive bite of her lip that always drives me wild. In response, she grabs the opportunity and pulls us toward the dance floor, initiating a carefree twirl. The vibe is easygoing, encouraging me to cheekily tap her ass. This surprises her, and she turns around with a defiant look.

Milli turns, her eyes challenging me. "Sunshine, keep touching my ass like that tonight and see what happens," she teases in a low purr.

"Show me, pretty girl," I coax with a grin, twirling her effortlessly, our moves a perfect match with the rhythm of the others around us. As she comes back into my arms, it's like we're two halves of a whole, my hands finding their spot on her lower back as if they belong there. "How did you know I was in the mood for dancing?" I ask, the words wrapped in the warmth of our closeness.

With a sly grin, she responds, "Because who wouldn't want to dance with the best?" Her confidence is infectious, and I laugh, genuinely enjoying this moment.

I pull her even closer, our bodies almost merging into one. Whispering near her lips, I confess, "I am incredibly lucky." The surprise on her face shifts to a look of awe, as if she can't believe I've vocalized my feelings. But I mean every word—I am lucky to have Milli in my life.

The beat shifts, dropping into that slow, haunting rhythm of "Fade Into You" by Mazzy Star, and it's like a signal just for us. Without thinking, I pull Milli closer, till I can almost hear her heartbeat mingling with the music. Everything else just . . . fades away. It's just her and me, in this bubble where the glares and whispers of the world can't touch us. This dance, this moment—it's ours alone.

With Milli's hand gently climbing up my arms to encircle my neck, I respond by wrapping my arms around her waist. Our gazes lock, a wordless conversation unfolding between us, filled with unspoken emotions and questions.

The dimming lights cast a soft glow around us, enhancing the intimacy of our dance. The formalities of the event have given way to a more relaxed and sociable atmosphere, with guests mingling and enjoying themselves.

In a fluid motion, I spin Milli, bringing her back against my chest. As we sway to the music, her head rests comfortably on my shoulder. My hands, starting from her waist, explore the contours of her body through the fabric of her dress. It's a silent declaration that she's with me tonight, a subtle message to anyone who might be watching.

Her body pressed against mine sets off a torrent of thoughts. She's all ease and trust, eyes shut, lost in our dance, and it's downright mesmerizing. Leaning in, my breath hot against her ear, I can't help but murmur, "You got any idea the restraint it takes to not fucking sweep you away at this moment?" My arms pull her closer, hands spreading across her stomach, our fingers lacing together. A quiet moan slips from her lips, and the feel of her, so close, has me on high alert.

I half-joke, "I'm tempted to just scoop you up and end the night on our terms."

Milli's response, her eyes sparkling with a mix of challenge and curiosity, is unexpected. "Then why don't you?" she teases.

The idea is tempting, but the setting isn't right for such a move. So, I lean in and kiss her neck gently, a small gesture of affection that makes her melt into me.

"Why did you do that?" she asks.

I turn her to face me, cupping her face tenderly in my hands. "Because it's you, Mills." It's a moment of pure truth, revealing the deep place she occupies in my heart. Yet, despite the yearning, I find myself pulling away, catching the confusion flickering in her eyes. It tears me apart, this inability to just whisk her away, to declare to the world she's mine—especially not here, under the scrutiny of prying eyes. It wouldn't be right to her.

Heading back to the bar, I finish my beer and adjust myself, but fail. I step out into the cool night, reflecting on the evening's unexpected twists. It didn't end as I had initially imagined, but dancing with Milli was more than enough.

Milli

Standing at his doorstep, I hesitate, my hand poised to knock. I'm not sure I should be here, outside his house, still in my dress from the gala. Dropping Payson and Brooke off at the dorms, something urged me to come, to show Miles tonight's feelings weren't one-sided. But doubt creeps in. What if he didn't want this, didn't want me? My hand falters, hovering in mid-air.

I'm about to retreat when the door swings open. There's Miles, looking slightly disheveled, as if he's been lost in thought, his keys in hand. He's casually dressed in shorts and a Panthers shirt, and I'm struck by the realization that he was about to leave.

Is he going to see someone else?

Confusion and panic set in, but he reaches out, his hand gently grasping mine. "Wanna come in?" His voice is soft, inviting.

My thoughts whirl, but before I can give them a voice, I'm already inside; the door closes sharply behind me. We stand face to face, wrapped in a heavy silence. Miles stays motionless, not attempting any of his usual quips or gestures to lighten the mood. It's just us, completely alone, and the space between us is thick with all that's left unsaid and the emotions we've kept at bay.

His breath is unsteady, mirroring my own, and his eyes find mine. "Why did you open the door?" I manage to ask.

"Why were you about to knock?" he counters.

"I asked you first."

"I was coming to find you."

"Well, here I am."

His fingers brush my cheek, prompting me to close my eyes briefly, savoring his touch. "Here you are," he echoes softly.

My eyes open to his intense gaze, and I'm overwhelmed with a desire to be impulsive, to give in to the heat between us. His hands glide down my body, gripping me in a way that sends waves of heat through me. The proximity of his body, the obvious arousal beneath his shorts, only heightens my own needs.

His hands find their way into my hair, gently tilting my head back. His lips hover over mine.

"Mills, you sure about this?" Speechless by his question, asking for my approval instead of just taking it, I simply nod.

"Speak it, Milli. Let me hear you say it."

"Yes, Miles," I confirm, as heat pools in my core. His dominance, evident in every aspect of his life, is intoxicating. I'm the one he's chosen to share this side with, to explore this intensity.

"You going to tell me why you were going to knock on the door?" he probes.

After a moment, I confess, "Because I wanted to see you."

It's not the whole truth, but it's not a lie, either.

He raises an eyebrow, questioning. "Anddd," he prompts.

I playfully push him, saying, "Do you really need me to spell it out?"

His grin is contagious. "Absolutely."

Gathering my courage, I look him dead in the eye. "I knocked because I came to get what's mine."

His eyes light up with a brief flicker of surprise before a deep, intense gaze takes over. And, good god, my heart seems to leap right out of my chest, my entire being buzzing with want. To have him closer to me, much closer.

"And what is that, Mills?"

Under different circumstances, I might have withdrawn, but with Miles, it's like I'm infused with a newfound boldness. It's always been this way with him. Everything leading up to now just fits—it's as if all the pieces have fallen perfectly into place. No second-guessing, no doubts. I want nothing more than to be right here, with him.

"You," I say, the simplicity of the word heavy with all the unspoken feelings and the significance it carries for us both.

Miles' expression softens initially, then shifts to a smug grin. "You saying you want me, Mills?" he teases.

I nod, shedding my reservations, embracing the confident side of myself that Miles always manages to bring out. Right now, I just want to turn off my brain, forget my responsibilities, and lose myself in this moment with him.

CHAPTER 30
MILES

H.O.L.Y. Geez Louise

When she whispers, "You," it's as though the rest of the world just disappears. Suddenly, it's just us, enveloped in our own universe where the pull between us is palpable, impossible to ignore. This moment is what I've been holding out for, and now that it's arrived, there's no way I'm letting it pass us by. Throughout this semester, Milli has evolved from merely a friend to my cornerstone, constantly there, her support unwavering, cheering me on and even helping me navigate the complexities of the MCAT. Our connection has always been profound, yet it feels as though we've recently transcended to an entirely new depth of intimacy.

In a swift motion, I lift her up, her legs instinctively wrapping around my waist in a perfect fit. Her hands find my neck, her skin tingling with goosebumps under my touch. The intensity of her breathing tells me all I need to know about her desire. Her wanting this. Wanting me.

I grin, keeping the mood light as I whisper, "About fucking time." Her chuckle—that smile of hers—it's unforgettable. Milli has always been a permanent fixture in my life, and right now, I can't imagine a future without her in it. I want to savor every second of this, to lose myself in her.

Our lips meet in a kiss that's both tender and full of promise. Gently, I carry her to my bedroom with this new, electric undercurrent between us. I'm keenly aware of how significant this moment is. It's a crossing of a threshold, both physically and metaphorically. Our eyes lock, and there's a shared understanding that what we're about to do is more than just physical—it's the culmination of years of friendship, trust, and unspoken attraction. This isn't just about passion; it's about two people who've been orbiting each other finally colliding in the most intimate way possible.

We are meant to be here together at this moment, with fate guiding our path.

Milli

Pressed against the wall in Miles' dimly lit bedroom, the soft glow from the hallway paints shadows across our faces, and I catch my breath. His name escapes my lips, a whisper lost in the space between us.

"Miles." My voice is barely audible, our lips a mere breath apart.

He searches my eyes, his gaze softening. "Are you sure? Is this what you really want?"

My heart races, words faltering. "I don't want to risk our frie—"

"I know, baby," he interjects gently, his lips meeting mine in a kiss full of promises. Desire ignites as his tongue meets mine, our bodies pressing closer. "My cock is dying to be inside that sweet pussy of yours." His voice is rough, lips grazing mine.

H.O.L.Y. Geez Louise. A cascade of emotions floods through me. I've seen many sides of him—his confident swagger, his tender heart, and now, this intoxicating blend of dirty talk and raw desire.

"Please," I find myself whispering, my voice dripping with a need I can't and don't want to hide. This is Miles, after all. My childhood friend, my first crush; the center of my world. My experiences pale in comparison to the way he's looking at me now, filled with a mix of curiosity and questions.

"Fuck, Mills," he breathes out, his gaze intense. "Who was it?" But I dismiss the question with a shake of my head.

"It's not about them," I tell him, holding his face gently in my hands. "This moment, with you, is what truly matters."

He looks at me, still uncertain, and I fight the urge to growl in frustration. We've been building up to this moment for weeks, skirting around our growing attraction, and now it's within our grasp. I want it more than ever.

I softly plead, "Make me feel good, Miles."

Without a moment's delay, he pushes me against the wall, his hand softly yet assertively holding my chin. His kiss is passionate. His touch, both urgent and caring, sweeps down my back, grounding me in the present moment with him.

"Need to get this off," he murmurs, fumbling for nonexistent buttons on my dress.

I guide his hands, unzipping my dress myself. It pools at my feet, revealing the delicate pink lingerie I'd debated wearing. Miles' gaze devours me, igniting a feeling of being deeply desired, that I want to etch into my memory forever.

"God, Mills," he whispers as he closes the gap between us. Lifting me once more, he presses me against the wall, his eyes searching mine. "Is this for me?"

I answer with a shrug, his familiar grin spreading.

His fingers find their way above the waistline of my panties as they move back and forth, teasing me, savoring me and, god, is his touch killing my own patience.

His fingers fall lower, so frustratingly close to where I need them that I whimper into his mouth. "Needy, Mills?"

"Yes," I admit, unashamed.

His hand is so big, he palms my ass perfectly, squeezing it before he slips his fingers under my panty line again, this time grazing over my entire pussy like it's a reward for being honest with him. I lean back, my head hitting the wall.

"Such a soft pussy, Mills," he hums against my throat as his mouth trails over it. "You're ready for this, aren't you?"

I let out another needy whimper, overwhelmed by how long I've waited for this moment. His finger halts its motion, and a groan of frustration escapes me. Our eyes lock in a moment of shared vulnerability. He exhales heavily, his forehead resting gently against mine.

"Mills," he begins, his voice tinged with uncertainty. I respond with a reassuring stroke on his hand, yet the combination of his hesitant tone and the look in his eyes set my heart galloping behind my ribs.

"I-I can't believe it took me so long to realize," he whispers, a confession that barely escapes his lips, "my feelings for you."

His words leave me speechless. My mind races, but before I can fully process his words, his lips tenderly caress my collarbone; a flurry of shivers ripples through me. His eyes meet mine once more, now imbued with a tenderness and depth that was absent when we first stepped into the room. Anticipating the weight of his next words, I briefly close my eyes, savoring the warmth of his breath as it intermingles with mine.

"I love you, Milli Sutton," he says, and time seems to stand still.

My heart leaps, skipping beats as those long-awaited words wash over me.

Miles Chasen loves me? The realization hits me like a

thunderbolt. Is this the heart-swelling, soul-stirring euphoria that the heroines in my romance novels experience when their love is declared? That overwhelming surge of joy and disbelief, where every page of fantasy seems to pale in comparison to reality? Because right now, my heart is in my throat, my emotions are a whirlwind, and I feel like I'm living in the most breathtaking chapter of my own love story.

He exhales a mixed sigh of sadness and regret, a sound that tugs at my heartstrings. Opening my eyes, I'm met with the depth of his blue eyes, conveying emotions far beyond words. "I'm so sorry it took me this long," he starts, his voice heavy with regret. "And it doesn't matter if you feel the same because I had to tell you—"

I gently place my finger on his lips, silencing him. He closes his eyes, and the resignation wrenches my heart. "Look at me, Miles," I implore softly. There's a moment's pause, but I firmly guide his chin, needing his gaze to meet mine. "Now." Even with his eyes closed, the hint of his familiar smirk emerges, perhaps in response to my uncharacteristic demand.

Leaning in, our foreheads touch, a silent communion. My hands cradle his face, a tender anchor as our eyes finally lock. "Sometimes we don't get to choose who we love, baby. It's often right there, hidden in plain sight. I think falling in love with your best friend is like discovering a new layer in a familiar song—it's been playing softly in the background all this time, and suddenly, it's the only melody that makes sense. It's when the heart makes its choice, silently and surely, even before the mind catches up, uncovering a harmony in a tune you thought you knew completely."

His gaze softens, reaching into the depths of my soul. "I love you, Miles," I breathe out, our lips finding each other in a kiss that feels like both a confirmation and a commencement of something new. As we part, I lock eyes with him, my heart laid bare. "I always have, you know."

His laughter, light and filled with relief, envelops us, before his eyes blaze with an unbridled desire, sending a wave of warmth cascading through me. His touch becomes more fervent, his fingers exploring my clit, each movement stealing my breath. "Tell me what you want, Mills," he breathes into the charged air.

"Everything, I want everything," I breathe out, the words barely a whisper. "Me too, baby, me too," he replies, his voice a blend of deep yearning and a pledge for the future.

His fingers work magic, stirring a storm inside me. His touch, his scent, everything about him is overwhelming right now. A finger slips inside, slowly working its way deep. An unexpected gasp escapes from my lips, but I'm ready for him. I have been my whole life. He keeps his mouth close to my ear. "Are you clenching on my finger already, Mills?"

I swivel my hips as he strokes inside of me. "More," I beg. "God, please more."

"That's it, Mills. Ride my hand."

As he continues, my head tilts forward, resting in the crook of his neck. His movements are rhythmic and deliberate, the sensation intense. I cling to his shoulders, surrendering to the overwhelming pleasure. My legs tighten around him, holding his hips to give my clit a bit of friction as he works inside of me. Heat and pressure coil in my lower belly. He strokes his fingers once more and my response is intense, a climax that shatters me, leaving me clinging to him.

Miles' voice is a husky whisper, laced with an emotion. "Seeing you unravel, Mills, it's . . . it's something else," he murmurs, his touch gentle yet stirring as he helps me regain my composure. Our lips barely touch, a fleeting connection that leaves me wanting more.

"I can say you are much better than any of my book boyfriends," I admit, a breathless confession.

His chuckle vibrates against my lips. "Damn right I am better than any of those."

As my strength ebbs, he tenderly adjusts my lingerie, steadying me on trembling legs. Not giving him the chance to stop me, I drop to my knees, palm grazing his body until they land on his thick thighs for support.

Miles towers above, concern etched in his features. "Mills, you don't have to—"

"I am," I assert with a decisiveness that even takes me aback. This seems to stir something profound in him; his eyes shift, growing darker, a hunger mirrored in his look.

My fingers grab the side of his shorts, then I move them down, and his cock springs up in all its glory. He really does have a beautiful cock. I have only seen one other cock in my life, unless you count porn, which Payson made me watch on a dare in high school. The head is thick, all big veins, red and angry. I lower my head and swipe my tongue across the precum decorating the tip. I flick my tongue back and forth before slowly bringing his cock into my mouth an inch at a time until the warm texture hits the back of my throat, making me gag for a second.

And I know he likes that, knowing he didn't stop the first time I gave him head in his truck. If anything, it made him more turned on. I feel his balls tighten as he lets out a hiss and I can't resist a smile.

His grin, the one that unfailingly unleashes a storm of butterflies in my stomach, lights up his face as he murmurs, "Absolutely fucking perfect, Mills." Right then, his words aren't just an expression of love; they empower me, make me feel powerful, sexy.

Miles, he's everything I've *wanted.*

Everything I have *needed.*

My movements become quicker, more fervent. He reaches out, gently placing a finger under my chin, lifting my face toward his. "As much as I love your mouth on my cock baby, not right now. Right now, I want you. I want to show you how much I love you."

My heart flutters uncontrollably. It's the kind of moment every romantic soul pines for—to hear, to feel, to experience. And now, it's my reality. I've been longing for this closeness with Miles, and here it is, unfolding before me.

He peels off his shorts all the way, revealing his delicious ass. And, goddamn, I just want to sink my teeth into it as he moves toward the bed.

This man . . . he's breathtakingly . . . *mine.*

Effortlessly, he lifts his shirt over his head, casting a knowing glance toward the bed. His bed.

A fleeting thought crosses my mind about its past, its history with others.

Milli, focus. He's just poured his heart out to you.

As if he can sense the tumult in my thoughts, he reassures me, "Never, baby, this bed, us, it's a first."

A timid smile finds its way to my lips, because honestly, what woman wouldn't be moved by such words, especially given how many vie for Miles' attention? My eyes drift to the scar above his navel, a mark that somehow makes him even more attractive. It's a symbol of his bravery, a testament to his resilience against whatever life throws at him. He doesn't let it define him; instead, he wears it openly, a display of pride rather than something to hide. And there's something incredibly appealing about that kind of confidence and self-acceptance.

"Mills, stop eye-fucking me and get your ass on my bed." I gracefully make my way toward his bed. Miles swats at my ass in passing, a mischievous glint in his eyes.

"Your ass; it's irresistible to me. Every time I see it, I just have to touch it," he says, half-joking, half-serious.

I give a shimmy, adding a teasing sway to my hips. His

groan of appreciation follows, mingling with my laughter as I settle onto the bed. I take a seat on the edge of his bed as I say, "It's a nice ass, isn't it?"

Miles closes the distance between us with a confident stride, positioning himself between my legs. His charisma is palpable.

He claims ownership in a lighthearted tone. "Mmhm, *my* ass." Gently lifting my chin, his lips meet mine in a tender, wanting kiss. His hands find their way around my bra and, with a single flick, it unclasps. A hooded gaze meets his eyes and there's nothing but heat in them. Heat, lust, and need. "God, these tits." His neck cranes back with a tortured groan. He eyes the ceiling for three beats before bending down on his haunches, heels to ass, and those deep blue eyes level with mine.

The air shifts again as he approaches me and takes me in a selfish kiss. He bends to my height as he works his lips down my collarbone and chest. His tongue swirls around my nipple, his throat rumbling in a groan before he slips it in his mouth. He sucks, making my back bow, and when he repeats it on the other side, I'm all but falling off the edge of his bed and into his lap.

"Come here," he beckons, his voice slightly roughened. He draws me closer, urging me to straddle him on the floor. He grabs my ass, sucking my other breast harder.

A moan escapes me. "You might just make me come again, just like this," I breathe out, half in disbelief.

His smile is felt more than seen as he gently rocks me, creating a delicious friction. "What can I say? I'm just that good." he murmurs, his voice rich with desire but also cocky.

He's got a point.

He tugs at the waistband of my panties with his, then lets it snap back against my skin. The sensation sends a wave of goosebumps cascading down my spine. In a second, I am thrown on his bed. Gracefully, he gently eases my panties down my legs. There I am, bare and open, my hair fanning out, while Miles stands, holding my underwear on one finger. "Goddamn," he breathes out.

He moves onto the bed confidently, casually tossing my panties aside. His smirk, as he catches my gaze following his every move, is filled with playful arrogance.

"Enjoying the view, Mills?" he teases.

Oh, if he only knew. I've always enjoyed watching him— on the football field, lost in thought during tutoring sessions, or even absorbed in his medical books.

In the brief time I've known Miles intimately, one thing has become crystal clear: he wasn't exaggerating when he said he knows how a real man should treat a woman. I'm witnessing it firsthand. He steps off the bed and retrieves a condom from his nightstand, opening it deftly with his teeth.

"Can I?" I ask, sitting up and moving toward him on the bed.

He raises an eyebrow. With a shrug and a smile, I reach for the condom, his readiness evident. Carefully, I roll it onto him, feeling the pulse of his excitement under my touch. Our hands meet, his guiding mine in a rhythmic motion, his eyes closing momentarily in pleasure.

He gestures toward the bed, signaling for me to move back. I obey, crawling backward. But instead of assuming a conventional position, I turn around, presenting myself on all fours, facing the headboard.

He laughs lightly, giving my ass a playful tap. "Mills, what are you doing?"

I glance back at him, our eyes locking. There's a spark in his gaze, and my cheeks warm with a blush.

"I thought . . . maybe you'd like this," I say, my voice tinged with shyness. "It's what I've read about, and I wanted to try something new."

He gives me another gentle slap, igniting a thrilling sensation. "I like anything with you, but I prefer seeing your face, that beautiful face I love so much," he says, climbing onto the bed behind me.

Oh, my heart. Will it ever feel normal hearing him say those words? Sure, we've exchanged I love you's as best friends, but this, this is entirely different.

He wraps one arm around my waist, the other caressing my front, pulling me up against him.

His breath is warm against my ear. "Let me see you, Milli Girl." His hand trails down, igniting a fire within me, making it difficult to move.

His movements bring us closer, his length sliding against me. He kisses my neck tenderly. "Ready for this, Mills?" he whispers.

I nod eagerly, feeling his chuckle vibrating through me. Gently, he guides me onto my back, following my lead. Our legs intertwine as he positions himself, the moment charged with anticipation. We pause, our breaths and gazes locked, understanding the significance of this step. Finally, he shifts, entering me carefully. A gasp escapes me as I adjust to him, my toes curling.

My voice is barely a whisper. "It feels . . . too big."

"Baby, you got this," he assures me, confidence lacing his voice. As he gently caresses my clit, a moan escapes my lips. His movements are tender, coaxing me to relax. "Just breathe, Mills. Deep breaths," he guides me.

Following his instruction, I inhale deeply, allowing my body to yield. Gradually, he moves, and I feel the fullness of him, a sign that he's completely within me.

His low groan breaks the silence. "Shit, y-you, feel amazing, Mills," he murmurs, his voice filled with wonder. His query echoes in my mind as I try to ignore the sharp stretch.

"This live up to your book expectations?" He chuckles with light amusement.

I smile despite the intensity of the moment. Always the book jokes.

He checks in. "Still okay?" I nod. The pain is more of a dull ache now, that delicious pinch of being too full.

"Good," he responds, then moves his hips and thrusts fully inside, his body splayed over me, pinning me to the bed. His hands travel down my arms until they reach my hands above my head, intertwining our fingers. He holds himself up to not crush me, but I can feel how hard he's breathing. He begins to move with pace and it feels insanely amazing. So incredible. So big. So warm. It's beyond what I ever imagined sex would be like with him—so real, so profound.

He whispers near my ear, "Mills, this was supposed to happen between us, you know that?"

His words blur into the background as I match his movements, lost in the rhythm.

"Fate wanted this for us, no matter the future," he continues, one hand leaving mine to explore further, heightening the sensation.

"M-Miles," I stutter out, barely a whisper.

"Mmm," he responds, a soft hum vibrating in the air.

He suddenly pulls out, the emptiness hollowing my stomach before his hand removes itself from my clit as it opens my legs, putting one on his shoulder, giving himself a better angle before he guides himself back inside of me. We both groan as he fills me. He slides in easier this time, my body ready and willing to take him.

His hand anchors my hips while he fills me over and over again, placing kisses on the inside of my ankle as it rests on his shoulder. He plays with my clit. He squeezes my tits. Then he bends forward, folding my leg into my chest as he uses the leverage of the bed to fuck me into the mattress.

And. Oh. My. God.

I'm at his mercy, and he's not holding back, sweat beads on his brow, our skin sliding together as my hands search for something to hold on, my nails digging into his back.

"Too good, baby," he murmurs. He snaps his hips to thrust again as he brackets my jaw with a single hand and kisses me roughly, his tongue sweeping into my mouth. His body falls onto mine as our movements change.

It's less frantic.

We sync into a rhythm, our kisses unfolding slowly, exploring deeply. His forehead touches mine, his hands roaming, cherishing every inch of my skin. My fingertips dig slightly into his lower back as he moves with me, in harmony.

Our eyes lock.

It's intimate.

Right now, it's only us, everything else dissolving into insignificance.

"I love you, Milli Girl," he whispers, his nose gently brushing against mine. A tear escapes me, a reaction to the tender familiarity of that nickname, reserved only for our most heartfelt moments. He meets my tear with a soft kiss, and I embrace him fully, our bodies intertwined in perfect harmony until we both are coming.

We're touching and stroking; we both ease back down, and when Miles pulls out of me, I've never felt so empty, losing that connection. He plays with my hair as he lays at my side, watching me with appreciative and longing eyes.

"So perfect," he murmurs, his voice a gentle caress.

"I love you," I breathe out.

His smile feels like a tender touch against my skin, and I come to the realization that tonight has surpassed every hope and expectation I ever had.

CHAPTER 31
MILES

Have you ever surfed on a crest of euphoria so exhilarating you wished never to come down? That was me, last night, as Milli's "I love you's" washed over me like a relentless, joyful tide.

She loves me. It's surreal, and as I gaze at her this morning, her dreams fluttering behind closed eyelids, strawberry blonde strands caressing her face, I vow to cling to this high. Her bare skin whispers secrets under the covers, and I'm lost in this moment.

Her eyes flutter open, a lazy, affectionate smile playing on her lips. "Watching me sleep, Sunshine?" she murmurs.

I gently brush her hair aside. "Problem, Mills?"

Her gaze, hazy and perfect, locks with mine, and it feels like home.

"Yeah, but I did my fair share of watching too," she admits, laughter in her voice, remembering how long it took for us to calm down, to let sleep take us. I tickle her, rejoicing in her laughter, in the lightness she brings to my world on a day like today.

Today's Panthers' Day. The day my whole year revolves around, the day scouts come hunting for talent. Usually, it's a day that weighs on me, but with Milli in my arms, all that pressure seems trivial.

"Creeping on me, Mills?" I joke.

She stretches, an adorable yawn escaping her. "Takes one to know one," she retorts, her laughter fills the room, a sound I've missed amidst the stress of the past months. I carefully pin her down, tickling her more, her protests mixing with giggles.

When we finally settle, breathless, I feel like the fucking luckiest guy alive. My phone buzzes, intrusive and untimely.

"Your other booty call?" Milli teases. I tickle her in mock retaliation.

"No need. I've got one right here." Her pretend shock quickly transforms into that bold, confident expression I have come to love.

As much as I want to know what last night meant to us both or where it's leading, this feeling, this moment with Milli, I don't want to question it. Not now. With college, football, and MCAT prep all demanding my attention, I'll have time later to navigate this. For now, I'm content to take it one step at a time, just as I've always done in life.

Checking the time, it's only 5:30 am. That's barely five hours of sleep, but every moment was worth it. Every second with Milli is worth it.

Pussy Panthers

CAM

It's game day, fuckers.

GUNNER

Hell yeah it is!!

DEVON

Game time, boys.

LUKE

Easy now. Some of us are still charging up.

I shake my head, knowing Luke's antics all too well. His text from last night didn't surprise me—he wasn't coming home, which, in Luke's world, meant another adventurous night out. He often jokes about his "good luck rituals" that include being deep inside some random female.

I quickly type a reply, eager not to miss any more seconds with Milli.

MILES

Go back to bed.

CAM

Nah, too much adrenaline. Can't sleep.

Selfie in the gym.

LUKE

Dude, relax.

GUNNER

You are lifting right now?

DEVON

And at fucking 5:30 am? Who does that?

CAM

It's game day, baby. It's what I do.

With an affectionate roll of my eyes, I set my phone aside and turn back to Milli. Gently, I pull her into my arms, our bodies fitting together perfectly. "Spend the morning together?" I suggest, an eyebrow playfully raised.

She laughs, soft and sleepy, it's pure music as she nestles

in closer. "Need to ask, do you?" she shoots back, her grin lighting up the whole room.

The morning unfolds in a blissful rhythm—wrapped up in each other's arms, sharing warmth and whispers. We linger in the shower, letting the water cascade over us, and later, we sit down for a hearty breakfast, laughter and light conversation filling the air. As we part, Milli teases with a twinkle in her eye, promising a special reward if tonight's game goes well. Her words add an extra layer of motivation, as if I needed another reason to give it my all on the field tonight.

"Miles, this is no time for setbacks to shadow your dreams, our dreams. The sweat and grind you've endured to get here, to break into this league, it's monumental. Hang in there a bit longer, and you'll see —it's all going to pay off." My father's words anchored me as I nodded, absorbing his conviction. "Remember, pain is transient, a mere visitor. But pride, that's a constant companion. Football tests your spirit just as much as your physical strength."

He laid a hand on my shoulder, a reassuring weight, then smacked my helmet, a silent cue to rejoin the fray. It was a nudge to confront my fears, to push past the shadows of post-cancer anxiety. I shook off the last of my nerves and strode back onto the field; his gaze followed me through the grid of my helmet. He clapped, a signal clear as day— it was my time to shine, to live up to the faith he'd placed in me. I flashed him a smile, a silent promise, and he mirrored it back. His hand tapped his temple a few times, and he mouthed the words I've come to live by, "It's go time."

Looking back as an adult, I see the truth in my dad's words. Football, like fighting cancer, is a battle of the mind. It's about laser focus—locking onto that ball, reading your opponents, syncing with your team. Cancer is similar. You've got to cling to hope, even in the depths of pain.

Decision-making in football is split-second, strategic. In cancer, it's choices about treatments, bracing for their fallout. And tactics? Football's got its plays, but cancer . . . you need to really know your enemy, anticipate every side effect.

Pressure, that's something else. As a kid, it was proving myself on the field, living up to my dad's sacrifices. Motivation? In football, it's pushing through the toughest drills, the longest seasons. In cancer, it's about the people around you, their support fueling your fight, making you believe in a comeback greater than any setback.

Dad's words cut through my thoughts, a lifeline in my mental storm. "It's go time, Miles." It's like a jolt of adrenaline. I've faced worse; I beat cancer. I can handle this.

I'm ready to fight, to come out on top.

Dad's hand is heavy on my shoulder pads. We're staring down the field, the tunnel mouth framing our view. It's not just the crowd, my team, or our rivals out there. There are NFL scouts, sizing me up. Dad's trying to ease my tension, but it's locked in there, deep. The crowd is wild, their "Let's go, Panthers" banners a blur. My stomach twists. The pressure's never been this intense. It's not just Dad, not just the scouts. It's everyone's hope for me, Miles Chasen, to clinch the Panthers' Day trophy.

I feel Dad's hand again; a firm tap. "Leave it all on the field, Miles. Shine." It's meant to inspire, but it's another weight on my shoulders.

I turn, give him that practiced, reassuring smile. "I've got this," I tell him. And myself.

But am I ready? Really ready?

There's no time to dwell on the week's pain—the headaches, muscle aches, blurred vision, swollen feet. I know what they mean, but I won't let them follow me onto the field. In that moment, the world fades. It's just me and the game. This is where I push my limits, where my mind and body are tested to their extremes. The crowd fades into a distant roar, my pain and fear dissolving into the background.

It's go time.

I step onto the field, the November chill a welcome slap against my skin. My cleats crunch satisfyingly on the grass. The announcer booms my introduction, and the stadium unfolds before me—a sea of faces, a buzz of excitement.

The crowd chants my name, a rhythmic, energizing call. It's electric, lifting me up. The colors, the sounds, the crisp air—it all converges into a single, vivid moment. Energized, I'm ready to dive into the game under the bright stadium lights.

"Ready for this?" Luke's slap on my shoulder jolts me back to the moment. Over his shoulder, I catch Milli's gaze.

My girl.

She's a vision in her Panthers' dance outfit, a stark contrast to the usual due to the weather's whims. She's stunning, the tight white leggings with our team's logo and a dusting of glitter complementing her sleek black zip-up. Her hair, pulled back in that signature bun, accentuates her striking features, making her look like she's just stepped off a fashion runway. Through my helmet, I flash her that grin I know she loves, and our eyes lock.

"I am now," I reply, the words ringing with a truth that goes beyond this week's struggles. I'm filled with an unshakeable belief in tonight's victory, envisioning our team's ecstatic collision post-game. And then there's Milli. I see her in my arms, the night stretching out before us with promises.

One more tap on my helmet, a personal ritual. "Come on, it's go time," I murmur to myself.

Milli's wink and the heart she forms with her hands realigns my focus. That's all it takes.

Our pregame huddle is a fortress of determination. Coach's game plan unfolds, his voice a blend of command and inspiration. I'm soaking in every word, visualizing the plays. Around me, my teammates' faces mirror the intensity; a silent chorus of nods with each of Coach's directives. The energy is tangible, an electric current connecting us all in this sacred pregame ritual.

As Coach concludes, rallying us with his final words, the huddle bursts with renewed vigor. We disperse to our positions, the green expanse of the field sprawling before us, the stadium a colossal presence. The distant roar of the crowd serves as a constant reminder of the stakes, of the eyes fixed on every move we make.

On the field, adrenaline is my pulse. The game unfolds in a whirlwind of precision and chaos, our strategies coming to life. Faces blur, movements synchronize; it's a dance we've perfected over endless rehearsals, now fueled by the raw energy of the moment.

Amidst the fervor, a realization dawns—this is my final Panthers' Day game. No more camaraderie with my team, no more Milli's sideline cheers, no parents in the stands, no Coach's fiery encouragement. This chapter is closing, with only a few weeks left, our eyes set on the Grey Bowl in January.

Football, under Dad, Coach, and teammates' urging, became more than a game; it's been a journey of thrill and relentless adrenaline. From childhood dreams to this defining moment, nostalgia already begins to seep in. This is the motivation I need to pour everything into tonight.

Lined up, I signal, "Hut, hut, hut." The familiar cadence echoing. The stadium vibrates with anticipation. The ball snaps; the play erupts into motion. Opponents charge, and my instincts take over. My mind races, scanning, calculating.

Memories flash through—endless practices, sweet victories, stinging defeats, bonds forged, Coach's guidance, the roar of the crowd. This game, like many before, becomes a microcosm of my football journey. Each play is a page in the story that has brought me to this moment. The adrenaline courses through my veins, and a fire ignites within me. This may be my last Panthers' Day game, but I'm determined to make it one to remember.

Milli

Tonight is Miles' night to shine, and shine he does. His passes are a spectacle, each one a thread in the intricate tapestry of his skill. This isn't just about completing passes; it is about commanding the game with a maestro's precision, making every throw a statement.

Miles isn't just a player; he is a leader, an electric force rallying his team.

The way his teammates sync with him, you'd think they are all parts of a well-oiled machine. His decision-making is sharp, his moves calculated, with turnovers a rare sight. And those four touchdowns? Each a testament to his prowess, sending the crowd into a frenzy.

The vibe in the stadium is tangible, igniting the air with excitement. The opposing defense is in turmoil, desperately trying to match Miles' every step. This isn't just a game; it's a testament to Miles' extraordinary talent.

But it is more than just the game that has me on edge. I watch our parents in the stands—my dad on the brink of tumbling off the bleachers in excitement, Mom deep in conversation with Mrs. Chasen. Mr. Chasen, somehow always managing to be right in the action on the sidelines, is fixated on Miles, his intensity unmistakable.

From my spot with the dancers, I see Miles' response to his dad's familiar, pressure-inducing tactics. The tension is almost tangible. I know the burden Miles carries, the dreams he is expected to fulfill.

The game resumes, and Luke playfully smacks Miles before the team regroups. The clock is ticking down, the final minutes of the game upon us. He is in his element, his voice cutting through the charged atmosphere. Every game this season has been a nail-biter, but this is different. This is the culmination of everything.

Miles positions himself behind the center, his voice cutting through the tension as he barks out the next play. As he readies himself to throw, there's a collective inhale from the crowd. However, he throws everyone for a loop, opting to run instead. The anticipation skyrockets as he dashes down the field—40 yards, 30 yards, 20 yards. The air is thick with excitement. Then, with just 10 yards left, a defensive player delivers a bone-crushing hit from the side. The impact is pinpoint, sending Miles airborne, his head meeting the unforgiving ground before he crumples, motionless.

The stadium, once alive with cheers and excitement, is swallowed by an unsettling silence. The distant hum of the crowd is replaced by the echoes of concern. My gaze shifts from the still figure of Miles on the field to the faces in the stands—a sea of worried expressions, furrowed brows, and exchanged glances.

It's as if time slows down. The internal battle between my instincts and restraint continues. Run out there, check on him, my mind urges, but my feet remain rooted, paralyzed by the intensity of the moment.

Luke beats everyone to Miles, squatting down beside him. The rest of the team gathers, creating a close-knit circle around their downed teammate. The look on their faces is a blend of worry and disbelief, a sharp departure from the usual celebration after a victory.

I catch sight of Mrs. Chasen; her face marked by apprehension, her eyes locked on the unfolding scene. The stadium lights cast a somber glow over the field, underscoring the seriousness of the situation.

Meanwhile, the medical staff rushes onto the field, their urgency evident. It's a scene I've witnessed in countless games, but this time it feels different. It's personal. Miles isn't just a player; he's . . . my Miles.

My best friend

My biggest supporter.

My confidant.

My everything.

My mind wanders through the reel of memories Miles and I have built together—our childhood, the wins, the losses, and the silent connection that stretches far beyond the football field. In the stillness of the stadium, it's as if the echoes of our laughter, our teasing exchanges, and the shared experiences are playing like a distant melody, bringing us to this moment.

The tension is thick, and all eyes remain fixed on the unfolding drama. The outcome of this night, once full of promise, now hangs in a delicate balance.

The medical team works with meticulous care, their actions both deliberate and swift. Miles remains motionless. The subdued whispers of the crowd blend with the distant buzz of anxious discussions, weaving an atmosphere with collective unease.

I shift my gaze between the medical team, the clustered players, and the anxious faces in the stands. Each passing second feels like an eternity.

As the medical team evaluates Miles, they gently lift him

onto a stretcher. The sight of the ambulance rolling onto the field elicits a collective gasp from the stadium. Mrs. Chasen covers her face as tears carve silent trails down her cheeks. Nearby, my parents stand by her, my mom's comforting arm around her shoulders, my dad offering words of reassurance.

In my head, I chant a silent mantra: *Everything will be okay. Miles has to be okay. He's always been the strong one.*

He's my Miles.

My eyes drift to Mr. Chasen. He's a statue of contained emotion, his eyes steadfastly following his son's journey to the ambulance.

As the ambulance departs, its sirens slicing through the tense quiet, the stadium is enveloped in a surreal calm. Moments ago, it was alive with the vibrancy of the game. Mr. Chasen's stoic demeanor reflects the silent solidarity of those around him, a wordless chorus of hope amidst the worry.

The ambulance shrinks to a speck in the distance, and a subdued sigh seems to sweep through the crowd. Wyatt, standing next to me, wraps an arm around my shoulder, offering a comforting squeeze. It's a gesture of support I didn't know I needed, and I lean into the warmth of his embrace, grateful for the silent solace.

Luke, typically a pillar of strength, locks eyes with me. In that brief exchange, a wordless understanding passes between us. We're both shaken, grappling with the unexpected turn of events. The close-knit group of players slowly drifts apart, a shared burden of concern weighing heavily on each of us.

I scan the sea of faces in the stands. Mrs. Chasen, encircled by supportive figures, embodies a mix of vulnerability and fortitude in her distress. My parents share a glance, an exchange that speaks volumes.

As the crowd begins to disperse, the usual post-game

chatter and jubilation give way to a collective reflection, a pause in the rhythm of life. We are all suddenly reminded that life can throw the most unexpected and challenging curveballs. And if there's one person who embodies the spirit to face them head-on, it's Miles.

CHAPTER 32
MILLI

This isn't your fault.

Mrs. Chasen's gaze flits around the hospital waiting room, her voice trembling. "Where's Miles? They said he'd be here, at Maple Valley Medical." Her eyes, wide and searching, move from one face to another, desperate for any news of her son.

I stand, taking in the chaos of the hospital. Doctors dart between rooms, nurses rush past, and the air is thick with the anxiety of waiting families. The hum of hushed conversations and the rhythmic steps of pacing feet fill the space. Something's not right.

I try to calm myself. *Don't jump to conclusions, Milli.* But the what ifs crowd my mind. What if Miles is seriously hurt?

Stop, he's fine. He has to be.

Mrs. Chasen's whisper breaks through my thoughts. "What if it's back?" Her fingers grip her husband's arm like a lifeline.

Back? My heart races, piecing together unsaid fears.

A nurse approaches, her expression apologetic. "I'm sorry, ma'am," she says gently. "I can't release information without proper authorization."

"But please," Mrs. Chasen's voice cracks with desperation, "he was hurt at his football game. I just need to know he's okay."

The nurse offers a comforting word. "We'll update you as soon as possible."

I sink into a chair, its hard surface matching the tension I feel. Suddenly, the doors swing open, and familiar faces rush in. Luke, my parents . . . After Miles was whisked away in the ambulance, I remember hugging Wyatt goodbye, his promise to follow, and the understanding look from my parents before I dashed from the stadium. I had to be here. Miles needed me.

Their faces are etched with the same worry that's gnawing at me.

"We got here as quick as we could," Dad says, and I believe him. The game, the victory—it all seems so distant now.

Luke dashes to the nurse's desk, urgency in his voice. "Where is he? Is he okay?" His questions tumble out. Dad gently pulls him back, guiding him toward the Chasens.

Mom's eyes meet mine, brimming with tears. She hurries over. "Sweetheart, are you holding up?" Her voice quivers.

I nod, fighting to keep my emotions in check. I'm usually good at this, but not today. Not with Miles in the balance.

The nurse's voice cuts through the tension. "Let's take a moment, everyone."

Mrs. Chasen's frustration boils over. "How can I breathe when I don't know what's happening with my son?"

She confronts the nurse, her finger pointed in accusation. "You've told us nothing! He could be . . . " Her voice trails off, choked with emotion.

"I understand, but—" the nurse is interrupted.

A new voice joins in, calm yet authoritative. "I'm Dr. Patel, overseeing Miles. Let's discuss this privately."

We move to a small conference room, the atmosphere is consumed with worry. Dr. Patel's gaze sweeps over us, lingering on those not directly related to Miles. I'm about to suggest we leave to give the Chasens space when Mr. Chasen speaks up.

"They're family. Please, tell us what's happening with our son." His voice is firm, underlined with a father's concern.

Dr. Patel starts, "Miles experienced a seizure at his game. It was minor, but we're keeping him for observation."

"Minor?" Mr. Chasen's voice is strained. "A seizure is never minor."

Dr. Patel inhales deeply, searching for the right words. "The situation could have been worse, but fortunately, we acted promptly. We've administered anticonvulsants to prevent any more seizures, and Miles is now resting. However, we've observed some signs that warrant close monitoring over the next few days."

Mr. Chasen's frustration is palpable. "What do you mean by 'concerning signs'? You're the doctor here, you should be able to explain!"

My dad's hand on his shoulder is a silent plea for patience. "Let the doctor speak, Drew."

Mr. Chasen exhales a heavy breath, nodding for Dr. Patel to continue.

Dr. Patel proceeds. "Miles experienced what we classify as a minor seizure. Upon his arrival, we conducted several tests and there are more we need to perform to fully understand his condition."

Mrs. Chasen's voice is a whisper of worry. "More tests? What are you looking for?"

"We observed a significant fever and Miles was holding his head in distress. We plan to perform a CT scan to investigate further. His blood pressure was unusually high, and his oxygen levels were concerning," Dr. Patel explains, his tone measured. "These symptoms contributed to his seizure, but there's more to it . . . "

The pause in his speech heightens the tension. Mr. Chasen urges him to continue, anxiety etching his face.

Dr. Patel sighs, the weight of the news evident. "We contacted the school for Miles' medical history as he wasn't previously registered in our system. It appears he has been under Dr. Reynolds' care for the past month, receiving specific treatment."

Mrs. Chasen's hold on her husband strengthens, her eyes welling up with tears. "What kind of treatment? I thought we had put all of this behind us," she utters, lifting her gaze to meet Miles' dad.

I fight the urge to spiral into worst-case scenarios. *Stay grounded, Milli. It might not be as bad as you think.*

Dr. Patel shifts. "We're still waiting for the full details of Miles' treatment plan with Dr. Reynolds. The school provided some information, but we need the complete records to understand the context of his recent health issues," he says, aiming to reassure us despite the many unanswered questions lingering in the air.

As the reality of the situation dawns on us, it hits like a tidal wave of shock and disbelief—Miles' cancer could be resurfacing. This fear, once a distant shadow, now looms ominously. Each clear check-up had been a beacon of hope, but now, doubt creeps in. Had he been hiding this all along? His recent stress, the unspoken words in his truck, the troubled look during our video call . . . were these silent cries for help that I had missed?

The room is suspended in a tense silence. Dr. Patel tries to navigate this emotional minefield with care. "I know this is hard," he says gently, "but let's not jump to any conclusions. We're doing everything we can to gather the necessary information and determine the best way forward."

Mr. Chasen rakes his fingers through his hair in frustration. "I just need to know what's happening with my son. We can face anything, as long as we know."

Dr. Patel nods in understanding. "We're working on getting Miles' full medical records as quickly as possible. Meanwhile, we're conducting all the necessary tests to get a clear picture of his current health."

Mrs. Chasen's eyes brim with tears, her grip on her husband's hand tightening. "After everything we've been through . . . the thought of him facing this battle again is unbearable."

The room feels like a storm cloud of mixed emotions—fear, hope, uncertainty. I'm rooted to my chair, the gravity of the situation pressing down on me. The thought of losing Miles, the heart and soul of my world, is paralyzing. His laughter, his smile, his touch, his very presence are irreplaceable treasures in my life. The mere thought of a future without him twists my heart into an unyielding knot.

My mom's hand on my shoulder brings a small comfort. Her touch seems to say, "We'll get through this." But the reassurance feels hollow. Not until we know for sure about Miles' condition.

In the stifling silence, it's as if a heavy shroud has been draped over us, its weight unbearable. My heart goes out to Miles and his family; our lives, once so ordinary and carefree, have been upended in an instant.

I push back the guilt that starts to creep in. *This isn't your fault, Milli,* I remind myself.

Mrs. Chasen's voice breaks the silence, determined yet fragile. "I need to see him. I need to be there for him."

Dr. Patel rises. "Let's keep it to the immediate family for now," he suggests.

The Chasens follow him. Mrs. Chasen's tears are a silent

testimony to a mother's love and fear. The door closes, leaving the rest of us enveloped in a solemn hush.

My mind races, struggling to process the news. Luke, pacing restlessly, looks like he's fighting his own demons. It feels surreal, like a bad dream that refuses to end.

"When did you last see Miles?" Luke's voice quivers.

"This morning," I whisper back, my voice a fragile thread. We were entwined in each other's arms, silently wishing to stay cocooned in bed all day. And now, I can't help but wish we had. Maybe, just maybe, things would be different.

Luke wrestles with his own sense of guilt. "I should've seen the signs."

Dad's voice, gentle yet firm, interrupts his self-reproach. "Luke, this isn't on you. We had no way of knowing."

"But what if we overlooked something?" Luke's voice cracks with the strain of unanswerable questions.

Inside, I'm tormented by similar thoughts. Were there signs I ignored, too caught up in my own life to see his struggle?

Luke's fist crashes down on the conference table, sending a tremor through the room as he exclaims, "Shit, I should have seen it coming. Fuck. The signs were all there. He's been off at practices, and even in a few games, but he chalked it all up to fucking hydration issues."

Dad shakes his head, our voice of reason. "We can't lose ourselves in what ifs. Our focus now should be on supporting the Chasens."

Luke's nod is weighted, his eyes shadowed by doubts and fears that reflect our shared apprehension.

"How about you both head home now? Grab something to eat, take a shower, try to rest," Dad suggests.

Mom, sensing my inner unrest, adds softly, "Maybe diving into your book tonight might help, Milli?" She nudges me gently, trying to offer some solace.

I muster a small smile. "Yeah, maybe."

But the truth is, reading is the last thing on my mind. How can I possibly concentrate on a book when Miles is here, suffering and possibly facing the same nightmare from his past? I yearn to rush to his side, to hold him close. I want to be there for him, tell him I love him, reassure him that we have a future together. I want to stand by him, just as I did before, every step of the way.

Feeling my mom's gentle nudge, I'm pulled back from my thoughts. After sharing a heartfelt embrace with both my parents, I nod toward the door. Luke and I exit the hospital, stepping into an uncertain future, unaware of what the coming hours, let alone days, might bring.

"Oh my goodness, Milli, are you okay?" Payson's worry washes over me as she hurries over the moment I enter our room.

Brooke follows closely, her eyes filled with anxiety. "Tell us he's going to be okay," she pleads, enveloping me in a hug alongside Payson.

The dam of my emotions finally breaks. I've been holding back a sea of feelings, trying to remain strong in the hospital, but now, in the sanctuary of my room with my closest friends, I let the tears fall. "I just . . . I don't know," I admit, my voice choked with tears.

"Oh, Milli," Brooke murmurs, her arms tightening around me.

"Let's sit down, okay?" Payson guides us gently to my bed.

We huddle together, a comforting trio. "The whole thing was just so shocking," I confess, my voice trembling. "Seeing Miles get hurt like that, being rushed off . . . it's unreal."

"And they don't know what's wrong?" Payson asks.

"They're keeping him for observation," I reply, my heart heavy. "But they haven't figured it out yet. They're missing some details about his medical history."

I bite my lip, holding back the fear that Miles' past battles might be resurfacing. It's not my place to share his deepest secrets, even with my best friends.

Payson's eyes widen. "But what if it's serious? How could they not have all the info?"

Brooke, ever the voice of reason, chimes in. "In emergencies, they have to act fast. I'm sure they're doing everything they can."

"I just wish I had more information," I manage between sobs, with tears rolling down my face. The guilt is relentless. "Was there anything I could have done to stop this?"

"No, Milli," Payson insists, her voice firm as she cups my face in her hands. "You can't think like that. You couldn't have known."

But the doubts linger.

"You couldn't have known," Brooke reinforces, her hand soothing my back. "Let's not jump to conclusions. We're here for you, and we'll be there for Miles and his family, no matter what."

I nod, finding a shred of comfort in their unwavering support. "Thanks, guys. I really need you right now."

"We're always here for you, Milli," Payson says with a warm smile.

The room falls into a comforting silence, their presence a balm to my troubled heart.

Payson, suddenly energized, heads for our DVD collection. "I think we need a distraction," she declares, her voice taking on a lighter tone.

She selects *Legally Blonde*, our go-to movie for tough

times. Despite the heaviness in my heart, I can't help but smile at the thought of our movie night ritual.

Payson answers a call, stepping out for privacy, leaving me and Brooke alone.

Brooke's gaze is knowing. "What's on your mind?" I prompt, sensing her hesitance.

She takes a deep breath, sitting closer. "Mills, I've seen how you and Miles are together. Especially at the gala. There's definitely something more between you two."

I stay quiet, caught in a storm of emotions inside my head.

Brooke continues, "Even your brother, preoccupied with football and the NFL draft, would notice if he wasn't so focused on his own stuff. And Payson . . . she's got a sixth sense for these things."

Her words hit close to home. My relationship with Miles is complicated, and yet, Brooke sees right through it.

"I know. I can't keep it inside anymore," I admit, my voice a whisper. "You've always known, haven't you? The way I feel about Miles." Brooke and Payson have seen the unspoken truth in my eyes long before I found the courage to voice it, at least to him.

I love him.

Brooke nods gently, her gaze never leaving mine. "We've seen it, Milli. The way you light up around him, the way you talk about him. It's always been more than just friendship."

I nod, my emotions making the words feel heavy. I confess in a hushed tone. "I love him, B."

Brooke pulls me into a tight hug, her warmth enveloping me as I break down into sobs. "I know you do, honey," she murmurs, her voice soothing. The reality of confessing my love for Miles out loud, right when his health hangs in the balance, overwhelms me.

"Let it all out, Mills. We're here for you, no matter what,"

Brooke reassures me, rubbing my back gently. In this maelstrom of uncertainty, I'm not alone. With my friends by my side, I find a little more strength to face whatever comes next.

Brooke's hand remains steady on my back as I try to compose myself. "I'm just so scared, B," I admit, my voice quivering. She squeezes my hand, encouraging me to continue. "All I want is to be with him, to support him. I need to be by his side, to reassure him that I'm here, that he's not alone."

A heavy sigh escapes my lips as I think of Miles' family dynamics. "His dad . . . he's caught up in his own dreams. And his mom, she's loving, but I know I can support Miles in ways that are different, unique to what we share."

Support him like I did all those years ago.

Brooke nods, her expression one of understanding. "I get that, Milli," she says, her voice gentle. "But remember what we promised before college? We vowed to embrace our journey, to grow and not lose sight of who we are, despite the challenges. This, sweetie, is a challenge, maybe one of the hardest ones you've ever faced," Brooke says, her voice tinged with empathy.

Her words take me back to those carefree days filled with laughter and dreams, to the time we made a pact. We promised each other that no matter the chaos, we'd always find reasons to laugh, to love, and to chase our dreams.

"It's important, Milli, that you don't lose yourself in this," Brooke says, pulling me back to the present. "You need to keep moving forward."

I manage a smile, acknowledging her wise counsel. The thought of balancing my own life with what's happening to Miles feels overwhelming, yet I recognize the truth in her words.

"Promise me, okay?" she presses, her eyes earnest.

Nodding, I make a silent pledge to do my best. It's a daunting task, balancing the different parts of my life, especially with my heart being pulled in various directions.

Payson rejoins us, her eyes hint at unshed tears, but we choose not to probe. She playfully holds up *Legally Blonde*, her eyebrow arched in a way that lightens the mood.

"Gal Pal Fête," I declare, my spirits lifting slightly with the familiar term.

Together, we rearrange our beds into a makeshift king-size retreat. As we get comfortable, Elle Woods' adventures begin to play, offering a momentary escape from the realities we face.

However, the respite is short-lived.

My phone vibrates, and even before I read the message, a feeling as if a band is tightening around my ribs makes it hard to breathe, as if I already know what it's going to say.

LUKE

They got his medical history from Dr. Reynolds—his cancer is definitely back.

CHAPTER 33
MILES

"What do you mean, he can't play anymore? Don't you understand how vital this year is for him? Scouts, opportunities . . . " My father's voice cracks the air, each word a hammer to my already fragile state.

I blink slowly, the world around me a blur. His voice, though, cuts through the fog—unmistakable, unavoidable. It's Dad. I rest my head back, trying to find comfort in the rhythm of my breath.

Inhale. Exhale. Inhale. Exhale. Focus, Miles.

My eyes flutter open again, this time a little clearer. Dad's standing there, toe-to-toe with Dr. Reynolds, his face a canvas of frustration and fear. "This could destroy everything we've built!"

His voice booms, echoing off the sterile walls, each word a jolt of pain through my head, a stark reminder of the reality crashing down on me.

This can't be real. Not now, not like this.

I clear my throat, desperate to drown out the pounding in

my skull and the rising tide of my dad's anger. My mind is a whirlpool of confusion—hospital, IVs, pain. Why am I here?

You know why, Miles. You've always known.

As if on cue, Dad's eyes lock onto mine, and he rushes over, his hand gripping mine in a vice-like hold. "Thank God, Miles, you're awake."

Dr. Reynolds has a melancholic smile that feels more like pity than relief as he approaches. "Good to see you, Miles."

Inhale. Exhale. Inhale. Exhale. Stay calm, Miles.

"How are you feeling?" Dr. Reynolds' voice is soft, cautious.

Like I'm on death's doorstep. The pain, the aches, the rawness in my throat—it's all too familiar, a haunting echo of the past.

I manage to nod, my throat a raw scrape of pain. Dad releases my hand as I reach for the water, his touch fleeting, leaving a void. I understand his true concern—not for me, but for the future he envisages, the NFL dreams he harbors for me. It's suffocating; I'm living his dream, not mine.

"I feel like I've been run over," I say, the words rough and hollow.

Dr. Reynolds chuckles softly, a hand on my shoulder. "With your condition, that's not surprising."

Condition. That word hangs heavy in the air, a truth I've dodged for too long.

As if he's reading my mind, Dr. Reynolds shakes his head, his eyes briefly meeting mine before dropping to his clipboard. Just then, a voice pierces the tense silence.

"Oh my God, you're up. You've been asleep for days." My mom's voice trembles as she rushes to my side.

Days?

Confusion etches my features, deepening as my dad chimes in, his voice heavy with concern. "Miles, you've been here for a week."

A week?

A whole week lost to this haze? The realization hits me like a freight train.

Dr. Reynolds breaks the news gently. "You had a minor seizure during the game last week. The hit was hard."

A seizure. The words echo in my mind, piecing together the fragments of that day. The collision, the spinning world, then nothing but darkness.

"A seizure?" My voice is a scratchy whisper, barely audible.

He nods, his face lined with empathy. "Yes, and it led to some complications. You've been drifting in and out since then."

My mind reels, struggling to grasp the reality of a week slipping by unnoticed. My thoughts are a whirlwind, but they're interrupted as Kins steps up, adjusting the IV with practiced ease.

"You're fortunate to be awake now, Miles. We've all been quite worried." She offers a gentle smile.

Surveying the room, the sterile walls, the anxious faces of my family, their concern weighs on me, tangible and heavy.

"And now?" My voice is frail, laced with uncertainty.

Dr. Reynolds leans in, his voice a blend of reassurance and seriousness, but he's cut off by my dad's deep sigh. "Son, the cancer's back."

The news doesn't stir me; it's an old shadow, one I've felt lurking. Dr. Reynolds and I exchange a silent look, an acknowledgment of a truth unspoken to my family. I close my eyes, fighting the surge of emotion, refusing to let it overwhelm me. When I open them again, everyone's eyes are fixed on me, seeking answers I don't have.

Fuckkkkk.

I'm swimming in a fog of doubt. Every wish, every plan for what's ahead feels blurry. Why bother setting dreams in motion? Why imagine a tomorrow when this sickness throws a shadow across everything *again*? The room's thick with worry, a tangle of love and fear that's just too much. How do I offer up hope when I'm knee-deep in my own questions, my own dark thoughts?

And Milli, what about her?

How is she coping with all of this chaos? The thought gnaws at me. She must be struggling, maybe even resentful. A lone tear escapes, trailing down my cheek. Only a week ago, we were basking in the joy of confessed love, seemingly untouchable in our little slice of heaven. But then, as if on cue, fate cruelly snapped its fingers, deciding I'd had my share of happiness. "Enough, Miles," it seemed to say.

The weight of guilt twists in my gut, the secret of my condition now laid bare. They deserved the truth, but the burden felt too heavy, too dark to share when I couldn't even face it myself.

"I'm sorry," I murmur, piercing the tense quiet. My voice fractures, heralding the tears teetering on the edge. "I didn't mean to pile on more for you to fret about." In a silent exchange of looks, my parents' expressions meld understanding with apprehension. They reach for my hands, their touch a quiet anchor in the storm.

But it's not long before Dad's familiar resolve surfaces. "Miles, we've overcome this before. You're a fighter. You'll show everyone what you're made of, on and off the field." It's like being seven again, back in a hospital bed, Dad's encouragement morphing into those motivational speeches, urging me back to health.

How naïve to think he'd react any differently.

Mom's eyes linger on Dad for a moment before turning to me, her voice soft yet firm. "Honey, what's most important now is getting you healthy again. Back to your *normal* self."

Normal. That word stings more than it should.

I am normal. I'm just . . . me. My mind races, yearning to escape this room, to find peace in my own space, with Milli, to somehow return to the joy of our Panthers' Day game victory.

I shake my head, trying to focus, to heed Kinsley's advice on breathing through the chaos. But it's a losing battle when Dr. Reynolds interjects.

"Miles, we need to keep you here another day for observation. Then you can go home. But," he pauses, his gaze flitting between me and my parents, "with your cancer returning, we need to discuss treatment options."

His eyes lock with mine, an acknowledgment of my stubborn refusal to face this sooner.

If only I hadn't delayed. Could I have prevented this?

Regrets won't help now, Miles.

"The silver lining," Dr. Reynolds continues, "is that we're dealing with a benign form this time, not as aggressive as before."

Somehow, this doesn't feel like relief. The words "brain cancer" still hang heavy, malignant or benign. It's a loop of fear and uncertainty, a cycle I thought I had escaped.

Dr. Reynolds' voice softens, attempting reassurance. "This means we have a fighting chance with a less aggressive treatment plan."

Just like before, right? And yet, here I am again, facing down the same beast in a slightly less ferocious form. The optimism in his words feels distant, unreachable. I close my eyes, tuning out the hopeful murmurs. They're just echoes in the void of my frustration and fear.

"I'll start preparing your treatment plan," Dr. Reynolds says, breaking the silence. "We're in this together. You're not alone."

But I've heard it all before. As my parents go over the details, my mind wanders, caught in a tempest of anger and despair. It feels like a vicious cycle, a harsh echo of a previous fight I believed was behind us. The idea of a "less aggressive" cancer doesn't soften the blow; it's a harsh reality, shrouded in the same fear and ambiguity.

CHAPTER 34
MILLI

This isn't about Miles.

Life can feel like a maelstrom sometimes, everything moving at lightning speed, and you're just there, fully immersed in the thrill of it all. But then, without warning, something slams into your world, a hurdle or a twist of fate, and suddenly, time drags. It's been three weeks since I found out Miles is battling cancer. Three weeks of silence from him. Three weeks of a void where he used to be.

He's shut everyone out.

Including me.

WEEK ONE

Utter silence. Not a word from him. Nothing.

WEEK TWO

I was pounding on his door, frustration and pain churning inside me. "Miles, just let me in," I begged.

I had thought, hoped, that when he came home, I'd be the one he'd reach out to. That he'd ask for his favorite gnocchi soup or just my presence. But a whole week slipped by before I even knew he was back, and I was fuming. Luke hid behind "bro code" as an excuse for not telling me. But that's no excuse, not when the man I love is wallowing in his room, refusing treatment, succumbing to whatever twisted fate he thinks he's been dealt.

As I stood there, knocking until my hands turned red, tears streaming down my face in the biting cold, I pleaded softly, "Miles, please, just open the door for me."

"Go away, Milli," came his muffled reply. It took everything in me not to shout back, to tell him he was being foolish. But I didn't. Instead, I let my hand drop and drove back to campus, sinking into my own pit of despair.

WEEK THREE:

"Dammit, Miles," I yelled, pacing in his and Luke's living room.

Luke quickly vacated the premises when he saw the determination on my face. I was on a mission, fed up with the silence, the waiting. My friends had nudged me; even my mom had advised me to let Miles hit his own bottom, to let him find his fight. So, with a heavy heart, I slammed my fist onto the kitchen island one last time and walked to his bedroom door.

Resting my forehead against the cool wood, I whispered, "Miles, fight this. If not for me, then for yourself. You're meant for greatness, for the title of Dr. Chasen, for a life filled with love. Don't let your demons win."

We all have our demons, but it's up to us whether we let them consume us or if we stand and fight. When Miles offered no response, I knew it was time to step back, to let go.

In the library, surrounded by books and silence, I'm

supposed to be lost in my studies. But my thoughts? They're miles away, stuck on him. Today should have been another tutoring session with him, but he's a no-show, again. Despite promising myself that it was time to step back, to let go, I find myself unable to detach.

I understand Miles too well. He lets problems simmer, especially when his world crumbles in an instant. But like before, he needs support, and I can't just stand by and watch him sink into despondency. He needs a wake-up call to remind him that giving up isn't an option. There's too much love for him, too many people who need him around.

I want him here.

I want him in this world.

I want him in my world.

Books hastily packed away, I sling my bag over my shoulder, my mind made up. Week four, and here I am, still caught up in his turmoil, still fighting for him despite the frustration and the advice to stay away.

My jeep roars to life, cutting through the quiet afternoon. The familiar streets pass in a blur as I pull up outside his place. Pausing, I take a deep breath.

This is the right move. I have to believe that.

Stepping out, I approach their door with resolve. My hand hesitates before knocking, questioning my decision.

You're already here, Milli. No backing out now.

Luke answers, his expression etched with resignation. And, I get it, I do. He's another voice in the chorus telling me to let Miles be, to let him work through this alone. But how do I do that? How do I just let the person I love flounder without trying to help?

"Hey, is Miles around?" I ask, trying to sound casual.

Luke nods, motioning toward the living room. "Yeah, he's in there. Come on in."

The house is in disarray—dishes, clothes, beer bottles. Miles is on the couch, a picture of defeat. Our eyes meet, and he quickly looks away.

Last week was bad, but this is worse.

Luke mumbles something about needing to leave, then leans in close. "Hope you know what you're doing."

So do I.

And then I'm alone with Miles, the silence thick between us.

Before I can say anything, he speaks up. "Aren't you tired of showing up here?"

His words sting, but I can see the pain behind them. He's lashing out, looking for a target for his frustration.

But I'm not backing down. "Here's your homework," I say, slapping the stack of papers onto the table. "You've been missing class, so I brought this over."

He dismisses it with a shake of his head, then stands, beer in hand.

Is he drunk?

"Thanks, but I'll pass," he states, with an air of indifference.

Luke's parting words echo in my mind. Maybe this is the moment to let him figure it out. But that's not who I am. I'm not one to walk away easily, especially not from Miles. He's facing a monumental challenge, and harsh words won't deter me. I'm here, ready to fight for him, even if it means fighting with him.

I grab the papers from the table, determination fueling my steps as I follow him into the kitchen. Pushing the papers into his hands, my frustration boils over. "Do you seriously think I've spent every Sunday this semester helping you just to watch you fail?" My voice is sharp with alarm. "You're mistaken if you think I'm going to let you throw all that effort away, Miles."

He turns, his expression a cocktail of surprise and annoyance, and then there's a smirk. It's not the one I fell for. It's tainted, bitter. "Not like you didn't get anything in return."

His words stop me dead. Confusion and hurt swirl inside me.

"What are you talking about?" I demand, my voice rising.

He lets out a cynical laugh, raking his hands through his hair, and turmoil is written all over his face. He's a shell of the Miles I know, the pressure from his dad about getting back into the game weighing on him even though he hasn't been near a football field since that fateful night. He's been trapped in this house, in his own head.

"You got to sleep with Miles Chasen, the one and only," he retorts, reaching for another beer. The house is littered with them; he's drowning himself in alcohol to numb the pain.

His eyes meet mine. "You got what every girl wants, didn't you, Milli Girl?" The nickname stings, used in such a context, far from the sweet moments it usually signifies.

How can he say that? How can he be so cruel?

His expression darkens, his message clear and cutting.

Do I mean nothing to him?

I remind myself he's not himself, but my patience is wearing thin.

"I don't need your help," he says, his words like shards of glass. "I don't want your support," he continues, each word a hammer to my heart. "I don't need *you*." The final blow. "Just . . . leave," he mumbles, turning away to drown himself in a movie, in his misery.

The words cut through me, leaving a sting that's both physical and emotional. My eyes threaten to betray the pain with tears, but I refuse to let him witness the depth of my hurt. Swallowing hard, I muster every ounce of composure I have, masking the inner chaos.

With a heavy heart, I cast a final, scathing remark over

my shoulder, "I didn't take you for a coward." It's a parting shot, laced with disappointment and a tinge of sorrow, as I step away from him, from us, into an uncertain future. I cling to the one thing I know for certain—the promise I made to Brooke weeks ago, a promise that guides me forward.

"Didn't expect to see you here," Wyatt remarks as I scan the dance studio, our eyes meeting. He's got that signature hip sway going, his expression clearly asking, "What's going on?" And yeah, it's 11:00 pm on a Sunday, and here I am, in the dance studio, a place I've avoided for weeks.

To anyone looking in, I'm still the same Milli—always cheerful, buried in books, tutoring, dancing. But inside, I'm unraveling. This semester, once a highlight, is now spiraling downward.

I remember this one time, Payson and Brooke practically dragging me to class. I was just . . . out of it, emotionally drained from my efforts with Miles. Trying to support him the way he needs feels like running on empty, and honestly, it's embarrassing.

I do sound pathetic, don't I?

Thanks for the reminder, inner critic.

Everyone's been saying the same thing—I can't let one guy mess with my head, derail my future. But Miles isn't just "one guy." He's the man I love. But after our last conversation and now, sitting here in the dance studio, my refuge, I'm questioning if it's all worth it.

People come into our lives for reasons we can't always understand. They appear, leave us pondering their purpose. Miles is like that—not just a fleeting presence, but a significant part of my life, intertwined with countless memories, laughter, tears. But everything feels different now.

It's as if Miles has his own chapter in the book of my life, and I'm trying to decipher if he's meant to teach me something vital, or if I'm just clinging to what's no longer meant to be.

Was it ever meant to be?

His words still haunt me. *"You got what every girl wants, didn't you, Milli Girl?"* It feels like my heart shatters all over again.

But I need to remember, I am strong. I won't let his words define me.

Wyatt steps in front of me, snapping me back to the present. "Alright, beautiful, what's on your mind?" He drops his bag nonchalantly and grabs my hand, pulling me to stand with him.

"Smooth move, am I right?" His wink is enough to draw out a laugh from me. Imagine Wyatt, in his spandex shorts, a flashy tank top, and hip-hop shoes, oozing confidence and style.

I shake my head, still smiling, but the smile fades as he loosens his grip, allowing me space. He gently lifts my chin, our eyes connecting. "Milli Sutton, are you letting someone else's problems steal your happiness?" he asks.

Is that what I've been doing?

My eyes flick away from his searching look as he says, "Remember, I swore one day I'd get to the bottom of what's been bugging you."

Wyatt's waiting for me to say something, but my mind's racing. What if Miles just keeps falling? What if he vanishes from my life for good?

The mere thought squeezes my heart, and a tear slips down my cheek.

However, Brooke's advice rings in my ears, a reminder not

to get lost in all this chaos. And yet, here I stand, betraying my own vow, utterly absorbed by Miles' problems.

Wyatt senses my distress and pulls me closer. "How about we dance it out?" he suggests.

Is this his way of drawing me back into the world of dance, of helping me let go of Miles' hold on my mind, even just for a moment?

As he leads me onto the dance floor, his hand playfully slaps my ass. I chuckle, a part of me comparing it to Miles' touch, but then I stop myself.

This isn't about Miles.

And my brain finally gets it—about time. This moment? It's all mine for the taking. A chance to rediscover myself amid the chaos.

As Wyatt and I glide across the dance floor, effortlessly matching each other's steps, a moment of separation has us glancing at our reflections in the mirror. In that instant, a jolt of realization strikes me—it's time for things to change.

Our dance continues, and I'm drawn to the little things—how Wyatt's movements mirror mine, the thrill of our spins. The mirror captures this seamless connection, a visual echo of our easy rapport.

This dance floor epiphany crystallizes something crucial: I need to end this semester on a high. With winter break looming and the spring semester around the corner, it's vital to finish my freshman year at NorthRidge with strength and positivity.

I'm chasing a sense of pride when I look back on this year. I envision a year-end gathering with my closest friends, sharing our achievements, and setting new goals for the upcoming year. I don't want their perception of my year to be clouded by a singular focus on a guy, whether he's a childhood crush or my best friend. I want to be remembered for more than that.

More importantly, I don't want the tough times and sadness to overshadow all the good moments. Watching Wyatt channel his inner Kevin Bacon, another epiphany strikes me: I need to reclaim my joy. If I've been encouraging Miles to keep pushing forward, it's time I heed my own advice. I need to shake off this funk and embrace the happiness I deserve.

"That's the way, Milli," Wyatt cheers, his encouragement acting like a balm to my burdened shoulders.

I shut my eyes, allowing the harmonious beat of our steps to anchor me. With every inhale and exhale, the dense fog of grief begins to clear. It's astonishing how dance, much like getting lost in the pages of a romance novel, offers an escape from the real world, tearing down walls and granting a momentary reprieve.

For now, Miles fades into the background of my thoughts. The music envelops me, each beat a step toward liberation. I can rise above the challenges weighing me down.

As Wyatt twirls me, the world becomes a blur of joy and motion. I can find happiness without Miles. I've done it before. When he was in college and I was still in high school, I carved out my own joy. Things were different then, but I made it work. I don't need a relationship or guy to be happy; maybe this is the universe's way of nudging me to let things unfold as they should.

Stepping out of the dance studio, will I still feel this happiness? I can't be sure. But one thing is clear: I have my own battles to fight, my own path to forge. It starts with getting back into dance practices with the Hanmann girls, helping them ace their upcoming competition.

Wyatt dips me, drawing out a smile that feels liberating, a stark contrast to my morning with Miles. His bear hug envelops me, and as I close my eyes, tears of relief and happiness trickle down my cheeks. "This is what you needed, Milli," he whispers.

And he's right. This is exactly what I needed.

Wyatt's words resonate within me, heralding a shift in perspective I know will extend beyond these walls.

"Honey, I get it, trust me. But sometimes, when you love something deeply, you have to let it go. If it returns, it's meant for you. If not, it was never yours to begin with."

I pull him into another hug, absorbing the wisdom in his words. He continues, "Finish this semester strong. Make amends with the Hanmann sisters and Ben. Win that competition. Then, Milli, take a break for yourself. Rediscover who you are. Find joy. Achieve the goals you set as a freshman. And most importantly," he steps back, eyes meeting mine, "fall in love with yourself all over again." He playfully taps my nose, adding, "You don't need someone else, especially not a guy wrapped up in his own problems, to feel loved or weighed down. Miles will sort himself out. Believe me, I know. We eventually get our act together, especially when it's about someone we care about."

With that, he grabs his bag and heads for the door. Glancing back, he blows a kiss my way, sparking a laugh from me.

As Wyatt's advice lingers in my thoughts, I cue up Mandisa's "Stronger" on the speakers and let myself dance. The notion of taking a break, of rediscovering and falling back in love with myself, starts to lighten the burden on my shoulders. With each dance step, I embrace the journey of finding inner happiness.

The dance studio becomes more than just a space for practice; it turns into a sanctuary where the rhythm guides us and our shared passion for dance ignites. It's not just about perfecting routines anymore; it's about rediscovering my love for dance, for self-exploration, and the sheer joy of living in the moment.

As the music envelops me and I'm reminded of the power of stepping back, taking a breath, and dancing into a new chapter of life. Grateful for friends like Wyatt, I realize that sometimes the best way to move forward is to take a moment to pause, reflect, and dance your heart out.

CHAPTER 35
MILES

"You realize this couch isn't your permanent address, right?" I reluctantly drag my gaze from the TV to meet Luke's, his eyes piercing with an unspoken plea. But it's a lost cause. A month has dragged into a year in my mind, and I'm knee-deep in self-pity. So what if I am? Life's dealt me a lousy hand with cancer—maybe not the exact same kind as when I was seven, but just as life-altering. Football's out, school's a blur, and studying for the MCAT or finals feels like a joke.

Why bother with what's beyond my reach now?

"You could still hit the books, Miles."

Silence swallows the room, punctuated only by the TV's distant murmur. I shift on the couch, Luke's words like weights. I just want him to back off.

"Yeah, I hear you," I grumble, avoiding his gaze. Everyone's got an opinion on how I should cope. But it's my dwindling life, and I'll face it my way.

Luke sighs, frustration ruffling his features. "I'm not saying it's easy, but you need a new focus. Moping here changes nothing."

He doesn't get it. He didn't see those pitying faces in the hospital, echoing since I was seven, whispering I'm a disappointment. Dad won't see me in the NFL, Mom will tell clients she's busy with her "sick" son.

Again.

He's not staring down a future that's a shadow of what he dreamed. What if I beat cancer, and it comes back? A third, a fourth time? I can't put everyone through that, not to mention my own terror.

A bitter laugh escapes me. "Find something else? Like what, Luke? This isn't some minor injury. It's not just going away."

His expression tightens. "I know it's hard. But this doesn't define you. There's life beyond football, beyond the NFL."

The same spiel Dad's been giving me. *"Control your future, Miles. Face this battle. You'll bounce back, prove them all wrong."*

Exasperated, I say, "Enough, Luke. I get your concern, but I'm not looking for a coach."

The truth? I'm lost in this new reality. Every dream seems unattainable, and I'm suffocating under the weight of what's to come. But the gloom is relentless.

Luke stands, his anger palpable. "If not for yourself, do it for Milli."

Her name strikes me with a force that stops me cold. I've been pushing her away, her of all people, the one I least want to see me in this state. Yet the remorse for sidelining her eats at me. She's been my steadfast support, my anchor, and the thought of facing this battle alone terrifies me more than I dare to acknowledge.

"Milli deserves better than to be dragged into this shit," Luke murmurs, his voice echoing in the room.

I let out a heavy sigh. Ironically, keeping her at arm's length may inflict more pain than drawing her close.

"She's seen too much of my struggles already," I whisper,

eyes glued to the floor. "It wouldn't be right to heap more onto her load."

Luke looks at me, his expression one of gentle understanding. "Miles, carrying burdens together can make them easier to bear. She cares about you, you know."

Luke's words halt me. I turn, facing him as he says, "You must think I'm daft to have not noticed how you and Milli are around each other." He shakes his head. "You two have always been thick as thieves, but this semester, with you two together constantly, the romantic spark is unmistakable."

He really thinks that, doesn't he?

His eyes land on mine, understanding and brotherly. I'd expected maybe disappointment or surprise from him about me and Milli evolving into something more. But no, he's just calmly accepting it, as if he knew all along.

Before I can ponder over Luke's take on my complicated "situationship" with Milli, the door bursts open. The freshman trio enter with their usual flair. Cam's beaming, Gunner's got a case of beer, and Devon looks awkwardly out of place. They turn their collective gaze from Luke to me, a silent communication passing between them before they chorus, "Let's go."

Raising an eyebrow, I stay put. Cam sidles up, then suddenly jerks back, waving a hand in front of his nose. "Damn, Chasen, you stink! Been skipping showers, huh?"

Their laughter fills the room, and despite myself, I crack a smile. It's somewhat true, but I'm not about to admit it. These guys, showing up out of nowhere, clearly in on some plan I'm oblivious to, is frustrating. Our last encounter was post-hospital, their pity-filled glances still fresh in my mind. It was like reliving childhood again—being the odd one out, only now, it's adults who look at me like I'm fragile.

Approaching them, I reach for a beer. *Why not?* But Cam slaps my hand away, and Gunner hides the case.

"What the hell?"

Cam nods at Luke, now standing with the others. "No beers until after today," he declares.

Confused, I look at them, unanswered questions hanging in the air. They just shrug, leaving me standing there, as they start belting out our pregame anthem. It's odd, and this "after today" thing only adds to the mystery.

Cam claps my shoulder, grinning. "Hang in there, Chasen. It'll make sense later."

I shoot them a skeptical look but decide to let it be, because honestly, I don't wanna fight, nor do I have anything to lose. Luke gives me a reassuring nod, and I find myself going along with whatever they've planned; the mystery of the beer and the "after today" rule lingering intriguingly.

Cam and Gunner head for the kitchen, likely to hide the beer from me. Devon's busy on his phone, probably scrolling through football memes. Luke stands firm, his eyes alight with determination for whatever they have up their sleeve.

A part of me yearns to break free from the past month's dreariness, to do something, anything. Perhaps it's the electrifying atmosphere or just sheer boredom with my routine, but a compelling urge within me wants to explore this unexpected path. So I excuse myself to shower and get dressed.

"Brace yourself for some action, Chasen," Cam announces an hour later.

I'm feeling somewhat human for the first time in weeks. I grab my coat, and we head to Luke's truck. Climbing in, I feel their collective gaze on me.

Luke asks, "Ready for this?" His tone is more inquisitive than assertive, leaving me unsure.

I respond with a noncommittal shrug, my lips sealed.

The drive is filled with chatter about our football team's upcoming Grey Bowl game. After my hospital stint, they won the crucial game, securing a spot in the Bowl. Listening to them, a voice inside suggests I should feel upset about missing out. No more field adrenaline, no more crowd roars. But, surprisingly, I don't feel that pang of regret. Perhaps the break from football, a first in years, has shifted something in me, or maybe it's a change in perspective I'm still trying to understand.

My thoughts are interrupted as we pull into the hospital parking lot. Confusion grips me. I lock eyes with Luke in the rearview mirror, my look clearly asking, "Why here?"

Before I can voice my thoughts, Cam slaps my shoulder, jokingly saying, "Ready for some excitement?"

Anger bubbles inside me. I had pictured a light-hearted evening, maybe at the indoor golf range, but this? A surge of frustration washes over me. I haven't been back since my last appointment, after which I firmly chose my couch over further treatment.

I meet Luke's eyes again, shaking my head emphatically. No way am I going in. But he just nods toward the entrance. My gaze follows, and there, through the glass, I see her.

Harper.

"Miles, Miles, Miles!" she mouths, her words lost but her enthusiasm visible as her breath fogs up the cold glass. A swirl of annoyance at Luke grips me, even as I'm thankful. I'd made Harper a promise, one I hadn't fulfilled.

Instinctively, I wave back. Her smile infectious, pulling one from me too. Despite my strong resistance, my feet start moving toward her, propelled by an unknown force. I shoot Luke a questioning glance. How did he know?

He simply shrugs. "Don't shoot the messenger."

I frown slightly, still piecing it together, but before I can dwell on it, they're waving off, Gunner teasing, "Beer's waiting for afterward."

"Save some for me!" Cam calls out.

I can't help but grin, shaking my head at their antics as they drive away. Here I am, walking toward the one person who, right now, seems to light up in my presence.

CHAPTER 36
MILES

"Did you know? Earth's the only place where water exists as solid, liquid, and gas!" Harper exclaims as I enter. "It's all about our position relative to the Sun, the atmosphere, and temperature dynamics." She takes a breath, still riding the wave of her excitement.

Is it my return that's got her so animated, or just her passion for our planet? Either way, since I've sat down, that oppressive weight I've been carrying vanishes—just like that, evaporates as she speaks.

I take a moment to really look at Harper. She's changed since I last saw her—thinner; her once full cheeks now slightly hollowed. Her hair, once long, is now buzzed short. I remember my own experience all too well.

Life's a relentless roller coaster—one moment you're riding high, the next, you're blindsided by something like brain cancer. It throws everything into perspective—your health, your relationships, your priorities. What really matters—family, friends, the simple joys?

Harper's transformation speaks volumes. The specifics of

her cancer are unknown to me, but the changes in her appearance suggest a fierce battle. Yet, it's her spirit that strikes me the most—her energy, the fierce determination in her eyes, even with her new haircut. She's a beacon of strength.

A sarcastic voice in my head chides me. Maybe I could find that same strength if I faced my future head-on. I brush the thought aside as Harper catches me looking at her. She blushes and averts her gaze, a hint of embarrassment, possibly annoyance, flashing across her face. Without thinking, I adopt my usual deflection tactic—turning away, arms crossed, head tilted.

"So, this is the game plan now?" I ask.

She turns back, her voice soft yet audible. "You were staring."

Those three words hit hard, sending a pang through me. I drop my arms and face her directly. Her cheeks are a deep shade of red, her effort to hold back tears evident. She doesn't want her vulnerability on display.

I should've been more sensitive. Having been in her shoes, I know the weight of those stares, the wondering, the longing to be seen as just another person.

Not now, brain. Not the time for introspection.

Harper turns away, her body language signaling a retreat, but as I stand and lean toward her, the reality of her emotions becomes clear—tears streaming, her face flushed, her small frame trembling.

Damn it, Miles.

I wish I could hug her, but the IVs and tubes make it impossible. Instead, I brush a tear away with my thumb. "Harp, do you know why I was staring?"

Her eyes meet mine, their hardness melting away with the nickname, yet filled with a silent anticipation. I gather my thoughts. "I was staring because, despite everything, you're still Harper. Your strength is inspiring. It's not pity I feel; it's admiration."

Those thoughts echo inside me, a reminder of my own battles.

"I don't see a patient," I continue, my thumb gently catching another tear. "I see Harper, the fighter with fierce eyes, ready for whatever comes her way."

She inhales sharply, managing a small smile. "You really think that?"

I grin. "Absolutely. I wouldn't say it if I didn't mean it."

I move to sit next to her, but a voice interrupts. "Miles?"

Kinsley pauses in the corridor, her face etched with perplexity. She assumes I've come for a consultation. I shake my head, indicating Harper. Kinsley understands—I'm here for her, not me. She moves off, disappointment fleeting in her eyes.

I pivot back to Harper, her eyes radiating curiosity, searching deeply.

The voice in my head taunts, *Whose fault is that, Miles?*

I'm about to speak when Harper cuts in. "You can't lie to me."

I exhale, a reluctant smile creeping onto my face, one I wish wasn't there but can't help. Harper's laughter, so genuine and free from life's burdens, draws me in, melting away the layers of ice that have encased my emotions since my last football game, since my time in the hospital. In Harper's presence, the walls I've built around me start to crumble.

"Can you keep a secret?" I ask.

Without missing a beat, her playful assertiveness shines through. "I'm the queen of secrets," she declares with a grin.

Her giggle breaks through, bright and catching, loosening the tension in my shoulders. My face eases into a smile, and a wave of peace sweeps over me. She looks my way, her eyes alight with interest. I hesitate, then something inside me pushes me to move forward.

Just say it, Miles. Let it out.

And I do. I unload everything—my tangled feelings for Milli, my shift from chasing NFL dreams to pursuing medicine, the cancer battle—it all spills out in a torrent of words to a seven-year-old.

I pause, realizing the absurdity. She's just a kid. How can she grasp the complexities of my life?

But Harper, with startling directness, says, "Get the heck over it."

What the fuck? Did she really just tell me to get over it?

I shake my head, trying to reset. When I look at her again, her gaze is piercing, unwavering. I'm tempted to walk away, but then I hear a voice behind me, firm yet gentle, "Listen to her." It's not a suggestion, but a command.

Feeling my frustration simmering to a boil, I take a deep breath.

Sitting here with her feels like talking to my own father, but instead of at our dining room table or on the sidelines of a football field, we're in the hospital's cancer wing.

I glance away, avoiding her probing look.

Get it together, Miles.

"Yeah, easier said than done," I mutter, my irritation clear in my voice. Harper's eyes shift past me, nodding slightly, as if confirming something with Kinsley. The silent exchange leaves me pondering the dynamics at play.

Harper then stands, skillfully maneuvering her IV stand, and gestures for me to follow. I rise, abandoning my seat to trail behind her. We leave the familiar ward behind, our footsteps echoing in the corridor. Side by side, we approach the hospital's large windows, the world outside reduced to a miniature scale beneath us. The holiday lights glow warmly in the hallway, their colors dancing against the walls, contrasting the sterile environment we've left.

We round a corner, and Harper's whisper cuts through the silence. "There's something I want to show you."

Recognition dawns as we traverse the new corridor. We've entered the children's cancer wing, a place teeming with my own memories. It's not just any hallway; it's a timeline of my life—marked by pain and laughter, triumphs and setbacks.

This is where Luke and I shared moments of joy in my darkest times.

Where Kinsley and I sought refuge in simple games.

Where Milli's calls brightened my gloomiest days.

Here, I began to carve out my own path, distinct from my father's expectations.

Now, I'm engulfed in a whirlwind of emotions. Is my return here fate or just another cruel joke by the universe? I wouldn't be surprised either way.

Abruptly, I freeze, my gaze fixed down the corridor. Harper continues on, undeterred. The glass windows lining the hallway offer glimpses into the lives of the children, each room a story in itself.

I spot a child, a mirror of the younger me, who once occupied a similar space.

A child clinging to hope amidst the relentless barrage of grim news and medical verdicts.

A child, each day a renewed vow to fight for life.

A child longing for a future, just like I once did.

And here I am, the complete antithesis of that fighting spirit.

A wave of guilt washes over me, settling heavily in my gut. Subconsciously, my hand rubs my stomach as Harper looks back, her eyebrows arched inquisitively. "You coming, Miles?"

I straighten up, mustering a facade of composure to

mask the turmoil within. No, I won't let my guard down. Not here, not in front of Harper, not amidst these other kids.

I quicken my pace to catch up with her. We move from window to window, my heart lodged in my throat. Each child's story strikes a chord.

We're back where it all started, but this time it's *different*.

Children of various ages fill the wing. The youngest, mere infants, radiate innocence and curiosity. Toddlers toddle, their laughter echoing through the halls. The older ones, though young, wear expressions shaped by their battles—a mix of resilience and hard-won joy.

Walking beside Harper, I'm struck by a sense of connection with these kids.

Miles, this isn't just history repeating.

I stop outside a room where a young boy named Ralph, about three years old, is absorbed in playing with a toy car. His parents are there, supporting him. The window is a mosaic of stickers, drawings, and messages, each marking a milestone in his journey against Acute Lymphoblastic Leukemia.

"He's not expected to make it past five," Harper says, her voice tinged with sadness.

Before I can fully grasp the gravity of Ralph's situation, Harper guides us to another window. Inside, two girls, Adenly and August, both Harper's age, mirror her vibrancy. Their window is adorned with symbols of shared adventures, highlighting a deep bond among them.

I was supposed to pop in, say hi to Harper, and leave. Not confront all this. Not today.

Harper waves at the girls, and their grins mirror my own. In their eyes, I see my younger self—thrilled by the novelty of a new face, a break from the routine judgments and treatments.

As they play, Harper leans in, her voice a hushed revelation. "They're my cousins."

Her words jolt me. *Cousins?* My mind races, trying to piece together this unexpected twist in Harper's story.

Seeing Harper's cousins, both battling cancer just like her, weighs heavily on me. This girl, already locked in her own fight for survival, now bears witness to her family enduring the same.

I try to refocus on Harper, but it's fucking hard. Her usual aura of strength has dimmed under this new burden. It's as if a dense, heavy cloud has descended upon us, the earlier energy now overshadowed by a tangible sense of shared struggle.

Her gaze holds a resilience that goes beyond her tough exterior, a silent declaration of, "Yes, life's tough, but we're tougher."

We stand there, wordlessly sharing a bond. Cancer, family, the intricate web of it all—we're both navigating these choppy waters. Our shared understanding speaks volumes.

"The doctors say they might make it to ten, but after this year . . . " Harper says, her voice trailing off. She shrugs, a fleeting sigh escaping her. For a moment, she drops her guard, but just as quickly, she's back to her strong self. It's heartbreaking, this facade she's forced to maintain. If only I could shoulder her pain, fight her battles for her.

Running my fingers through my hair, a pang of realization hits me. Here I am, wishing I could fight for Harper, yet I've been avoiding my own battles.

She leads us to the end of the hall, stopping outside the last room. My eyes land on the glass window, emblazoned with "Harper" in rainbow-bold letters. This is her world.

Her window is adorned with doodles, stickers, and mementos of her journey. Among the cheerful display, a collage of Polaroid photos catches my eye. Each snapshot, featuring Harper with family, friends, and even Kinsley, tells a story beyond these hospital walls. It reminds me of the collage in my own truck, a collection of meaningful moments. It's as if fate guided me here today.

I'm drawn to the photos of us—our first meeting, our subsequent visits. Harper wanted to capture each day, not just for herself, but to share these memories with the world.

Her eyes meet mine, shining with gratitude. "Remember how I said I wanted to capture every day?" she asks, her voice filled with pride.

I nod silently, struggling to keep my composure.

"Well, it wasn't just for me," she continues, a bittersweet chuckle escaping her. "When I got my lymphoma diagnosis, the doctor gave me a bleak prognosis. It hit hard, but I decided if my time was short, I wanted to make each day count, not just for me but for my parents, too."

A lone tear traces Harper's cheek. "These photos, the people in them—they're what keep me fighting. They're daily reminders of the love and friendships I'm blessed with, including ours, Miles."

Her words stir something profound in me, rendering me speechless. My truck, the photos within it, the reasons behind them—Harper and I, we're reflections of each other, sharing similar struggles in our unique ways. Fate, I realize, played a role in bringing us together. Initially, I questioned it, but sometimes embracing fate is more meaningful than fighting it.

Harper's hand rests over her heart, a gesture that speaks volumes. "Things have gotten worse recently. The cancer's spreading, and now, I'm down to less than a year," she reveals. "Maybe God's given me this time for a reason," she muses, holding a picture of us. "Perhaps to see you again, or to spend more time with my family." She puts the photo back, her resilience shining through. "I've fought every day, and I'll keep fighting."

Her quick movement to hide her emotions catches me off guard. How does such a young soul manage such composure?

Harper's gaze returns to the window as she concludes. "I wanted to show you the battles we face here. We're all fighters, making the most of each day. Unlike some of us, you have the luxury to look beyond just a week."

"Me?" I respond, taken aback and slightly bewildered.

"Yes, you," she affirms, her cheeks tinged with a faint blush.

"What do you mean?" I urge her to elaborate.

After a brief pause, Harper confesses, "I saw your treatment plan."

Surprise registers clearly on my face.

"I-I accidentally found it while looking for my own records," she explains. "Miles, you've got a chance to stand up to this. You can have your dreams, repair things with Milli. Football might be out of reach, but there are other ways to stay connected. School can be on your terms."

Her words strike me with the intensity of a revelation. Harper, facing her own daunting challenges, is encouraging me to confront mine. It's a stirring call to action, urging me to face the battles I've been avoiding.

"Thanks, Harp," I murmur. If she can face her challenges with such fearlessness, then maybe, just maybe, I can find the strength to confront mine as well.

Meeting her gaze, I see a look of deep accomplishment in her eyes, as if she's understanding the significance of her actions for the first time. It's a moment brimming with joy and pride, and it's almost overwhelming to witness.

Harper isn't finished yet. She looks at me, her young voice earnest. "I know it's super hard," she says. "But you get to pick how you deal with it. You can let it be the boss of you, or you can be your own boss, even with it around. Fight for the life you want, Miles. You're not just a passenger in your fate."

Whether I'm ready to face the uncertainties of my future or not, Harper's insight rings clear: I can meet this challenge head-on.

Again.

She reaches out to poke me, missing slightly and tapping my abdomen instead. It's a gentle nudge, but it reinforces her inspiring message. She gazes up at me, her eyes filled with a fierce determination. "You don't have to let fate be the boss of you. You can be like a superhero and fight it!"

Despite her small stature, Harper packs a mighty inspirational punch. Her conviction is infectious, leaving me with a newfound sense of resolve to take control of my own destiny.

CHAPTER 37
MILES

"What do you mean you don't want to play in the NFL, Miles?" Dad asks, his intense gaze locking with mine across the dining table.

I let out a heavy sigh, absently pushing around my green beans, steeling myself for the conversation ahead. My fork slips from my hand, clattering loudly on the plate and drawing all eyes to me.

Well, this is it.

I interlace my fingers, pushing my plate aside and resting my hands on the table. Looking around, I see the faces of my steadfast supporters—my parents, Mr. and Mrs. Sutton, and Luke. The absence of one person, though, feels glaring. Milli, who could have made this easier, is not here, and I know it's on me to handle this. Part of me wishes the Suttons weren't here for this, but seeing everyone's expectant looks, I feel it's right to address this now, with everyone present.

My eyes drift to our Christmas tree, twinkling behind Dad. There's Milli's handmade ornament from the year I was battling cancer. That ornament, and the memories attached to it, make my chest tighten. I've let things go wrong with Milli, and her absence now is partly my fault. Luke and his parents sense the reason behind her absence, too.

Staring at the ornament labeled, "Warrior," I gather my thoughts, then meet Dad's gaze again.

You're a warrior, Miles. This is your fight, I tell myself silently.

With a deep breath, I start to unravel my truth—the early knowledge of my cancer, my newfound desire to pursue medical school over the NFL dream, and my treatment plans. After I finish, a heavy silence descends on the table. I immediately regret exposing all this in front of everyone. Luke then breaks the silence with a light chuckle and ruffles his hair.

"Didn't see that coming from you," he comments, giving my back a light tap. "You sure know how to talk when you're fired up."

I give him a quizzical look. Seriously? I just laid out my entire life, and he's cracking jokes?

Luke squeezes my shoulder, realizing his mistake. "It was just a joke, man."

I nod, shifting my focus back to Dad. His gaze locks onto mine with piercing sharpness, yet there's a moment when his demeanor softens, revealing a trace of capitulation. He briefly closes his eyes and lets out a deep sigh, one that carries a hint of disappointment.

Well shit, did I just make a mistake choosing this path over the one we had always envisioned since I was young? But inside, a reassuring voice counters, *No, Miles. You're doing the right thing. This is your life, your choice.*

I bolster my resolve, determined to stand my ground for my future and my dreams. Oddly enough, it was a seven-year-old's wisdom, Harper's, that spurred me into action these past weeks. Her influence has been a surprising catalyst. Motivated by our encounter, I immersed myself in studies and it paid off—I aced all my final exams.

I used to think the thrill I felt was exclusive to football, but the rush of pride and empowerment after completing Professor Huggins' exam was something else. It pushed me to go further, to keep striving. I ended the school term on a high note and even made it back to the football field, supporting the team as they prepped for the Grey Bowl.

Looking ahead, I'm focused on the spring. That's when I'll take the MCAT and make serious strides toward starting medical school in the fall. I've come this far on my own, not letting fear, future uncertainties, or my treatment schedule hold me back.

"Why'd you keep this from us, Miles?" Dad's voice cuts through my thoughts, his finger pointing accusingly between him and Mom.

As if confessing this would have been easy. His reaction, maybe shaded by the recurrence of my cancer, makes the NFL dream seem even less important now.

"Do you really think this was easy for me?" I spit out, the frustration boiling in my voice. "Confessing I don't want to play football? It's far from simple." My hands fly up in exasperation. "Fuck."

"Miles Chasen, watch your language," Mom scolds from across the table, her arms folded in disapproval. I meet her eyes briefly before returning to Dad's intense gaze. "Choosing to become a doctor over an NFL player wasn't a walk in the park," I continue. "Especially knowing how much you wanted that for me."

Dad looks confused. "Me?"

I let out a heavy sigh, feeling the tension at the table. Everyone's watching us, like they're spectators at a high-stakes game. But this isn't a game; it's more intense, more real.

"Yes, you," I affirm.

Dad's expression becomes gentler, a glimmer of comprehension momentarily crossing his features before he conceals it. He speaks again, his tone more tender; the sharpness of anger dissipates. "It was our dream, Miles."

My heart sinks. This is harder than I thought.

Suddenly, Mom reaches out to Dad, trying to ease the tension. "Maybe we should—"

But Dad cuts her off, standing abruptly. "No, we'll talk about this now. He brought it up, so let's deal with it."

The anger resurfaces in his voice.

I straighten up, steeling myself, refusing to let my feelings show. If he wants to confront this issue, to make it a spectacle in front of everyone, then I'm ready.

What did I expect? I hoped for understanding, but that seemed too much to ask for.

"Listen, I've got to straighten something out," Dad begins, his hands weaving through the air between us. "This journey, it's always been a partnership. From your very first breath, through every trip to the hospital, I've been there, steering you, convinced I was doing what's best." He takes a moment, his gaze drifting toward the glass doors before snapping back to mine. "The NFL isn't what's bothering me, Miles."

It's not? That takes me by surprise.

With a rueful laugh, he continues, "If you're thinking the NFL is what's got me riled up, then you really don't understand me."

"What's the problem, then? Why are you so worked up?" I push for an answer.

He shakes his head, glancing toward Mom, who's biting her lip, clearly holding back.

My frustration bubbles over. "Can someone just spell out what's happening here?"

Finally, Dad opens up. "I'm upset because you've spent

your life making me think this was your dream, Miles. I supported you in football because I believed it was what *you* wanted."

I shake my head firmly. "No, Dad. You pushed me toward the NFL because you had to give it up."

Dad throws up his hands. "Yes, I did—because of you, Miles."

That revelation hits like a sucker punch. I'm reeling, struggling to process his words, feeling a mix of shock and betrayal.

What do I even say to that? *Thanks for being honest, finally?*

He sighs, regret in his eyes. "I shouldn't have said that."

"Maybe it's time for dessert," Mrs. Sutton interjects, perhaps to lighten the mood.

"Yeah, great idea," Luke and his dad agree, quickly leaving to get dessert. But I'm not sure I'll stick around for it.

Dad starts pacing, and my tension rises, my hands clenched tight.

Mom stays seated, watching us. She gives me a knowing nod, as if acknowledging that this conversation between me and Dad is overdue.

I wonder, though, can we really just move past this? Have I shattered his NFL dreams for me?

Dad stops pacing and comes over, placing his hands on my shoulders. Then, unexpectedly, he pulls me into a hug.

Okay, what is happening?

It's a genuine embrace, not a celebratory hug or one borne out of spite. Just a father hugging his son. I can't help but return it, feeling a rare comfort in his arms.

When he steps back, his hands cup my face, and our eyes meet. "Miles, listen carefully, alright?"

I close my eyes, and, despite my best efforts, a tear escapes.

So much for keeping it all together.

He brushes the tear away with his hand and says jokingly, "You had a little something there." I smile—his attempt to lighten the mood is exactly what I need right now. But the smile quickly fades as the gravity of the moment sets back in.

"Miles, you've only got this one life, and it's yours to live," he says earnestly. "You know better than anyone how quickly things can change. Your cancer battle scared the hell out of me. The thought of it coming back? Even worse. But here's what I need you to understand: football was a big part of my life, sure, but you and your mom, you're my life. You always have been. I loved that football was something we shared, a way to escape the tough times and something that brought you joy."

He lowers his hand but keeps the other gently on my cheek, his touch now moving to his chest and then mine. "This life we have, it's about being father and son, about supporting and loving each other, no matter what. The NFL doesn't matter to me right now, Miles. You do." He continues, "I'm here to support your dream of becoming a doctor. I want to help with your treatment, be there for you through it all."

I chuckle. "That's a bit over the top, Dad." We all laugh, including Mom, who's been quietly watching.

"But you get what I'm saying, right?" he asks.

I nod, understanding fully.

"I'm sorry if I ever made you feel pressured about the NFL. That wasn't my intention. I just want you to be happy, healthy, and fulfilled in this life, whatever that looks like."

I notice the moisture in his eyes, a rare sight. "Something in your eyes, old man?" I tease, and he hastily wipes his eyes.

Mom joins us in a big group hug, a warm, comforting embrace. Looking over Dad's shoulder, I see the Suttons smiling at us through the glass doors. The moment overwhelms me with a wave of emotion.

I've done it. I've opened up to them, and it feels like a massive weight has been lifted.

But as I start to relax into this newfound acceptance, I pull back slightly. "You really mean all that?" I whisper, needing reassurance.

Mom leans in, her forehead touching mine and Dad's, reaffirming our bond. "Absolutely, Miles. We're here for you, in every way. Even if it means helping you win back a certain someone's heart."

Every part of me is screaming to run to Milli right now. I need to apologize, to explain how sorry I am for everything—for pushing her away, for not being there, for all the hurt. I want to tell her that I need her by my side, more than ever, as I gear up to fight cancer again. I want to show her that I can be better, that I'm truly sorry for being such a jerk, and that I can love her the way she truly deserves.

But just as I'm about to act on this urge, Dad gently steers me back to the table, his hands firm on my shoulders. "Let's hear more about the MCAT, son."

In spite of the rush of emotions and the urgency I feel about Milli, I smile at my dad. Sitting down, I start to share my plans, my aspirations to become Dr. Chasen. In this moment, surrounded by my family, I'm grounded by their support and love, even as part of me longs to make things right with Milli.

CHAPTER 38
MILLI

That's the thing about life—it's about pushing against the odds.

"Milli, are you ready?" Wyatt calls out, his voice bouncing off the walls of my dorm room, brimming with anticipation.

"Time to hustle, girl," Payson adds, stepping out of the bathroom in her robe, her hair cocooned in a towel. A mischievous glint sparkles in her eyes. "Brooke and I are your personal cheer squad today. And who knows, maybe we'll catch the eye of a charming teacher or a striking single dad?" She strokes her chin, pretending to ponder, her look teasingly faraway.

I smirk at her antics, even as I mentally picture Mr. Hanmann, the epitome of her "single dad" daydreams. Shaking my head, I focus on my bag, excitement for the dance competition bubbling within me. "You're going to love the Hanmann sisters' performance. They're absolutely breathtaking."

Payson's laugh is lighter than usual, filled with genuine admiration. "Of course they are. They've got the best teacher."

Her words widen my smile, filling me with a warm, proud

glow. I've watched those girls transform under my guidance, and I can feel it—today's the day they shine.

As I sling my dance bag over my shoulder, I catch a glimpse of myself in the mirror. Suddenly, Payson's hands rest reassuringly on my shoulders. Our eyes meet in the reflection, a moment of unspoken understanding passing between us.

"You're going to be incredible, Milli," she says softly, her hands briefly cupping my face in a gesture so tender it almost brings me to tears. "I'm so proud of you, especially after everything last semester. You're still here, stronger and more fabulous than ever."

She leans in, her cheek brushing against mine. "Remember our pact before college? You might have strayed a bit, but you didn't lose sight of what's important—your goals, your growth."

I nod, moved by her words. Her faith in me is a beacon, especially when I reflect on the tumult the past few months have been.

January has arrived in a flash, and with it, a mix of excitement and challenges. Juggling my studies, the dance competition, and the persistent thoughts of Miles have been a test. The mention of his name still sends a tremble through me, echoing memories of what was and the possibilities of what might have been.

Despite everything, I not only aced my classes, but all my students I tutored excelled brilliantly in theirs, too. It's a quiet triumph for me. As for the Hanmann sisters, they're absolutely dazzling on the dance floor, a testament to our collective dedication and effort.

Christmas passed in a blur. I steered clear of the usual holiday gatherings, particularly the Chasens' dinner. The mere thought of encountering Miles there was overwhelming. Did I consider keeping our tradition of exchanging gifts on Christmas Eve? Absolutely. But then, Miles left his present at my doorstep. Jerk. Imagine waking up on Christmas morning to find his gift waiting just outside my room, challenging every bit of my willpower not to cave.

What's more, he couldn't have chosen a better gift—a bouquet of books. It was as if he had a direct line to my heart, each book a perfect match for my literary tastes. I was struck by the depth of thought he put into it. It wasn't just about the books; it was about his understanding of my passion for narratives that weave tales of romance and adventure. It was a perfect gift, in its unique, book-lover's way.

And yes, I did reciprocate with a gift of my own. Tradition is tradition, after all. But whether he appreciated the custom-engraved "Dr. Chasen" stethoscope as much as I appreciated his gift, well, that remains a mystery.

"Milli, pick up the pace or we're going to miss it!" Wyatt's voice echoes down the hallway just as I'm stepping out of my dorm room. There he stands, effortlessly cool in tight black leather pants and a half-zipped sweatshirt emblazoned with our school's Panthers logo. Shaking my head with a smile, I close the door behind me and head toward the front entrance of our dorm building. "I'm coming, I'm coming," I call back, certain that he's either grinning or shaking his head in amusement. His concern is a constant, comforting presence.

We hop into my jeep, and as I fire up the engine and fling my bag into the backseat, I notice him shooting me an inquisitive glance. "What's with that expression?" I inquire, reversing out of the parking space.

"Just checking in. You ready for today?" he asks, rummaging through his bag.

His question irks me a bit. Why would he question my preparedness? After the chaotic close of last semester, I've hit the ground running this time around, meeting my goals early on. I give him an eyebrow raised in subtle skepticism.

"It's just a question, Milli," he says, hands raised defensively.

"But, why ask? You've seen me at every rehearsal. You know I'm prepared," I reply, a hint of frustration in my voice.

He lets out a long sigh. "I get it, and being there for you has been important to me. But I needed to make sure you're truly okay, considering there's just a handful of us in your corner."

But what he doesn't realize is that during the break, I had a heart-to-heart with my parents, particularly with my mom. Our relationship had grown distant over the semester; we weren't close to begin with, but we had never been so far apart. When I saw her over the winter break, I couldn't hold back my emotions. She assured me that everything would be okay, and I believed her. I realized that I could rely on her, even though I hadn't wanted to in the past. So, when I received her text this morning and her call last night, both expressing her pride in me, it meant the world. "*I am so proud of you, Mill. I always have been. I may not always show it or say it, but I am truly proud of you, as is your dad. I'm immensely sorry you haven't felt our support and I'll keep apologizing. We love you and can't wait to see where your dreams take you, including at this competition. Can't wait to see you kick some Sutton ass.*" Hearing her use the word "ass" made me laugh; she's never been one for swearing.

It had dawned on me that one obstacle, in the form of my best friend's situation, even if I did love him, was that I shouldn't allow my entire world to come crashing down. I understand that regardless of where mine and Miles' path leads from here, my focus needs to be on the present, not on a future that might never be.

"It's nothing," I insist, sidelining the lingering thoughts of Miles. There's a surge of thrill coursing through me, yet in the stillness, my mind wanders, touching on the void left behind.

Snippets of his current life have reached me. He's come clean to his family about his dream of becoming a doctor and has embarked on a treatment journey. Even with the space between us, my pride in him swells—for confronting his cancer head-on and pursuing his aspirations.

That's the thing about life—it's about pushing against the odds, just like Henry Ford said about airplanes taking off against the wind. It's a lesson I learned early on, and it's what keeps me going.

Wyatt places a comforting hand on my thigh, his touch easing my tension. I'm grateful for his unwavering support. Smiling, I focus on driving us to the competition. We arrive at the Rhythm Haven Center, a building adorned with vibrant banners and dance graphics. The nerves finally hit me.

This is it, Milli. Your moment to shine.

Inside, the place buzzes with activity. Young dancers and their moms are everywhere. I feel a pang for the Hanmann sisters, missing this experience with their mom, but I know our routine will make up for it.

As we head for the check-in table, Wyatt places a hand on my shoulder. "This is your moment. Own it. I'll be in the auditorium cheering you on."

I hug him tightly. "Thanks for being here. I couldn't do this without you."

He smiles warmly. "Always, Milli. Always."

With a final wave, I enter room 5, ready to give my all for the Hanmann sisters. Their bright, eager faces greet me, and I'm filled with a sudden surge of confidence. Today, I'm going to make them proud, no matter what.

CHAPTER 39
MILES

"Miles, you look like you're about to pass out. Nervous?" Luke observes as we park outside the Rhythm Haven Center. I stop my hands from their anxious dance, giving my thighs a reassuring pat.

This feels like déjà vu, akin to the time I told my dad I wanted to pursue medicine instead of the NFL.

Calm down, Chasen.

I'm here to support Milli, albeit from a distance. She probably won't even notice I'm here. And if she does? Well, I can always slip away if she's uncomfortable with my presence.

After giving my legs one last encouraging slap, I push the truck door open, brushing off Luke's concern. "You coming or not? I can't sit in your freezer-on-wheels any longer."

He chuckles and follows me out as we head into the auditorium, finding ourselves in seats uncomfortably close to the stage.

Great, front and center. Just perfect.

But hey, at least I won't miss any of the competition. The only downside? There's a high chance Milli will spot me here.

I'm surprised to see the Suttons and my parents among the crowd. Milli has confided in me before about feeling overlooked by them, yet today suggests a turning point, perhaps a move in the right direction. It warms my heart to see them here for her. She's worthy of their backing, just as any child merits encouragement from their family. I offer them a friendly wave before taking my seat.

Mrs. Sutton greets me with a knowing smile. "Good to see you, Miles. Milli will be happy you're here."

I'm not so sure about that, but I offer a friendly smile, anyway. "Yeah, just here to support Milli," I say, which is genuinely true.

While Luke chats with our parents, I take a moment to appreciate the auditorium. It's an impressive venue, conveniently located near campus. The high ceilings are adorned with elegant chandeliers, casting a warm glow over the comfortably arranged seats. The walls display a tasteful mix of art and history, adding to the charged atmosphere of anticipation.

Suddenly, a voice booms from the stage, announcing the start of the Dance Duo competition and welcoming everyone. The moment the curtains sweep aside, performers flood the stage—trios, duos, a vibrant mosaic of talent. My gaze darts across this spectacle, instinctively searching. Deep down, I feel it—Milli knows I'm here. It's that inexplicable pull, like an unseen hand drawing you to someone in a crowded room.

It's always been there.

Suddenly, her head pivots our way. Caught in the harsh wash of stage lights, I find myself frustratingly unable to discern her thoughts. Is she glad I'm here? Annoyed? It's a mystery, lost in the brightness. But no time to ponder; the show is shifting gears, the spotlight dancing from group to group, revealing the enthusiastic dance instructors.

I squint through the dazzle, trying to interpret Milli's

expression. It's like piecing together a puzzle in pitch darkness—impossible. Regardless of the uncertainty chewing at me about Milli's feelings, the room is charged with an infectious energy. Each group parades their distinctive charm, igniting the auditorium with a dynamic pulse.

In this whirlwind of excitement, I find myself on edge, awaiting Milli's moment in the limelight. With each introduction, the knot in my stomach tightens, my mind buzzing with questions about the Hanmann sisters' performance, and crucially, how Milli will react to my unannounced arrival.

"Presenting NorthRidge University, let's hear it for Milli Sutton and the Hanmann sisters!" The crowd's enthusiasm bubbles over, chants of "Go Panths, Go Panths," filling the air.

Milli nudges the girls, encouraging them to wave to the audience. As they sweep their hands through the air, our eyes meet. It's a moment filled with an intense connection that has always sparked between us, both undeniable and enduring. It's a mute exchange, laden with our common history and unsaid feelings, a heart-to-heart that transcends words.

In that brief, wordless exchange, my feelings for her resonate loud and clear.

I have always loved this woman. How could I let her think any differently?

At first, Milli looks surprised, her gaze flickering away from mine to her parents. I'm momentarily concerned that she might be uncomfortable with my presence, but then her eyes find mine again, and she offers me the faintest of smiles. My heart practically somersaults in response.

Sure, things between us are a bit uncertain, but that small smile from Milli? It means the world to me. As the curtains draw to a close, the room falls silent. Then, Mrs. Sutton's voice drifts over, "Did you see that, Miles? I was right. Milli's happy you're here."

I can't help but smile, though I'm cautious not to read too much into it. Perhaps she was just pleased to see her parents.

But then again, could it be a combination of both?

That thought stays infused with a deep sense of hope.

Milli

Just breathe, Milli. In one, two, three, there you go. Out, one, two, three.

I can't believe it. Just when I am juggling enough stress, ensuring everything is perfect not only for me but also for the Hanmann sisters, he has to show up. My palms grow sweatier, my heart races just a bit faster. I shouldn't be this nervous just because he's here, right? I shouldn't feel the need to impress him, but somehow, I do.

Before I can get too caught up in thoughts, I hear the announcement, "Milli, you and the Hanmann sisters are up next."

Great.

Okay, Milli, just breathe. In, one, two, three. Out, one, two, three.

I follow that rhythm, making my way to the back of room 5, where I gather the girls. "Ready to go win that prize?" I ask. Their faces light up, excitement palpable, as they grab my hands and we head backstage.

I squat to their level, squeezing their hands. Lily and Georgia grasp the bottom of my leotard skirt. "I'm glad you're doing this with us," Lily says.

I beam at them. "Me too, sweetie. Ready to show the judges what you've got?"

Their nods spark a surge of enthusiasm within me. Taking a deep breath, I close my eyes, slowly letting it out. That's when I hear, "Please welcome to the stage, the Hanmann Sisters."

Kissing each of their heads, I guide them to the stage. As they move, Georgia looks back at me.

I mouth, "You got this," giving her a double thumbs-up.

She grins and skips to the center of the stage. As the lights dim, I catch Miles' gaze. The butterflies inside me go wild. It's not just his look—it's the tiny fist pump and smile that accompanies it, a gesture I haven't seen in ages.

The stage descends into darkness, and the opening chords of Rachel Platten's "Fight Song" start to play, marking the beginning of our performance. As the lights gradually brighten, revealing us on stage, Lily and Georgia begin to move in sync with the rhythm. A rush of adrenaline courses through me; it's my cue to join them, to showcase our collective strength and determination despite life's distractions.

Empowered by this thought, I glide smoothly to stage right. The lyrics of the song amplify around us. "This is my fight song, take back my life song, prove I'm alright song, my power's turned on." Each line reinforces our resolve, mirroring the strong spirit that we embody.

I'm entirely focused on each step, every gesture we've perfected over countless rehearsals. As the music fills the auditorium, our routine flows with precision. Lily leads, setting our pace, and we follow. We move in unison, our dance a perfect symphony of twirls and spins, each motion speaking to our unity and hard work.

The energy on stage vibrates through the crowd. The Hanmann sisters' faces are alight with joy, excitement in every step. Together, we bring our routine to vibrant life, infusing each movement with our passion and perfectly synchronized steps. The audience is captivated; the atmosphere buzzing with their excitement and appreciation.

In the heat of our performance, I briefly catch Miles' gaze. He watches closely, his eyes radiating admiration and encouragement. That fleeting connection fills me with a surge of confidence and determination, his presence providing an unexpected boost. Re-energized, we continue our routine with heightened passion and vigor. As my part comes to a close, I execute a final elegant twirl and gracefully exit the stage, leaving Lily and Georgia to shine.

Backstage, the moment has arrived for a special addition to our routine. I glance at Mr. Hanmann. "You ready for this?"

He looks nervous but nods, his attire perfectly chosen for the occasion. His agreement to this last-minute addition to his daughters' performance speaks volumes of his dedication as a father. He's poised and ready, and I have no doubt he'll be fantastic on stage.

"Alright, it's showtime," I say, feeling the energy as the song's beat signals Mr. Hanmann's entrance. He's the first dad to join the performance today, a pleasant deviation from the norm of moms dancing with their children. His impact on his daughters makes this moment all the more special.

The audience's reaction is immediate and enthusiastic as he steps on stage. Cheers and applause reverberate through the auditorium, welcoming Mr. Hanmann as he confidently joins his daughters. It's a heartwarming scene—a father dancing with his girls, a sight that captures everyone's attention.

Their routine unfolds seamlessly, with Mr. Hanmann synchronizing flawlessly with Lily and Georgia. As the performance reaches its climax, the audience's enthusiasm grows stronger. It evolves beyond just a dance competition, transforming into a moving testament to family bonds and unity. The happiness in the girls' eyes and the evident joy on Mr. Hanmann's face are clear for all to see.

When their dance ends, the applause is thunderous. Mr. Hanmann, beaming, embraces his daughters. After congratulating them on stage with high-fives and a teasing, "Not too shabby, Ben," to Mr. Hanmann, we make our way backstage, then out into the lobby, where everyone waits for the announcement of the winners.

As I stand there, trying to calm my racing heart, a familiar voice suddenly says, "That was amazing, sis." Luke's arms wrap around me from behind, lifting me off the ground in a tight hug. "You kicked ass out there," he adds, his voice filled with pride.

I close my eyes, soaking in the moment, when another voice adds, "That was truly incredible to watch, Mills." My heart misses a beat at the sound of that voice—Miles.

Miles, Sunshine, my best friend. The one whose absence has created such a deep void in my life, the one I've missed more than words can say. All the emotions I've been wrestling with come rushing to the surface. My heart feels like it's cracking open, each fissure a reminder of how much I've yearned for this moment, for him.

I steel myself, fighting to keep my emotions in check as I gently touch the ground and turn to face him. His deep, expressive eyes meet mine, eyes that have always communicated more than words ever could.

Stay focused, Milli.

Just then, the announcer calls, "Could we have Milli Sutton and the Hanmann sisters on stage, please?"

Luke's hand rests on my shoulder, nudging me gently but firmly. "Sis, go on. It's your moment," he says encouragingly.

Again, the announcement: "Milli Sutton, please come to the stage."

Me? Wait, did we win? Excitement bubbles up inside me, a mix of disbelief and sheer joy.

Before I can hurry off to find Georgia and Lily, a hand grasps my waist, halting me. In that moment, everything narrows down to just him and me.

Miles reaches out, gently tucking a strand of my hair behind my ear. Despite my initial impulse to pull away, I'm frozen, captivated by the closeness of our encounter. His breath caresses my skin, triggering a chill to ripple down my spine. "I'm so damn proud of you, Milli Girl," he whispers gently.

His voice, the warmth in his use of my special nickname, the genuine respect shining from his gaze—it all wraps around me, igniting a conflict within: an impulse to pull him into a fierce kiss or to push him away with a slap.

I catch myself; there's a tangled web of unresolved issues lying between us. This isn't the moment for old flames to rekindle, not with the scars of the past still tender. I muster a small smile, offering a measured, "Thanks, buddy," while lightly tapping his chest.

Oh, that chest. It feels like tapping into solid strength.

Focus, Milli.

His face changes, a flicker of confusion crossing it, likely thrown off by my restrained reaction.

Did he really think things could go back to normal so easily?

Shrugging off the intense moment with Miles, I redirect my focus and stride toward the stage. This is my moment, and I'm determined not to let anything, especially my complicated emotions for Miles, overshadow it.

Quickly, I scoop up the Hanmann sisters, still basking in their father's embrace, and we dash hand in hand toward the front of the stage. The audience, still buzzing from the energy of the performances, watches us with anticipation. My eyes catch sight of a woman approaching with a check so enormous it nearly dwarfs me. The excitement of holding it, feeling the tangible proof of our victory, thrills me. But more than for myself, I wanted this victory for Lily and Georgia. This win isn't just a personal triumph; it's a stepping stone for their future in dance.

They deserve this and so much more. Such moments reinforce my dream of opening my own dance studio to create opportunities and inspire others. The impact I've made in these girls' lives is immeasurable, and I know it's an experience I'll carry with me forever.

As Lily and Georgia grasp the oversized check emblazoned with "CONGRATULATIONS ON YOUR UNLIMITED DANCE LESSONS FROM K - 12," my heart swells with pride. They now have the freedom to choose their dance journey, a wonderful opportunity for them to learn from the best.

As I'm about to step down, allowing the girls to bask in their achievement, the announcer, with a playful chuckle, draws my attention. "We have something for you, too, Milli." A woman, perhaps a few years older than me, steps forward, presenting me with a plaque. "Outstanding Achievement Award for Best Duo in Dance Teaching," it reads in elegant silver letters. The applause from the audience washes over me as I accept the plaque, a mix of surprise and deep gratitude flooding through me.

This moment signifies more than just a personal accolade; it's a recognition of my dedication to teaching and nurturing a love for dance. Reflecting on the hours spent choreographing last semester, guiding these young beginners, and watching their growth, this award feels like a validation of all those efforts.

Standing there, with Lily and Georgia glowing beside me, I realize this award celebrates our collective journey; how dance can transform lives, instill confidence, and forge unbreakable bonds.

As the event slowly winds down, encircled by proud parents, students, and encouraging supporters, I'm immersed in a sensation that transcends the thrill of the night. This occasion isn't merely another checkpoint in my career; it's a profound validation of my dreams and ambitions.

Clutching the plaque tightly to my chest, I descend from the stage. The dream I've harbored for so long, of opening my own dance studio, now seems closer and more achievable than ever. Turning to look at Lily and Georgia's radiant smiles, my heart fills with renewed determination. I'm more inspired than ever to guide, teach, and revel in the magical realm of dance, ready to tackle any obstacles that lie ahead.

CHAPTER 40
MILES

"Milli, today you shined like the brightest star in the sky." My mom beams from across the table at Glasshouse, her smile so warm and genuine it's contagious.

"Honey, you were simply breathtaking out there. I'm already excited for your next performance," Mrs. Sutton adds, her eyes locking with Milli's. There's a newfound bond between them, a connection running deep and meaningful. Watching them, a wave of happiness washes over me, proud and thrilled for Milli.

Around the table, our little circle of support—myself, my parents, the Suttons, Brooke, Payson, even Wyatt—are all gathered, celebrating Milli. We've been here, immersed in laughter and conversation for over an hour, yet beneath my joy, there's this undercurrent of restlessness, an eagerness to have a moment alone with Milli.

There's so much I need to tell her. I've made mistakes, big ones, and even if she can't see me as a friend or more, I have to live with that. It's a tough pill to swallow, accepting that maybe I don't deserve her after everything, but it's a truth I need to confront.

Throughout the evening, as we chat and share stories, Milli and I keep exchanging glances. She tries to be subtle, but I catch every quick smile, every fleeting look. It's as if she's just as eager to talk to me as I am to her.

Then, out of the blue, Payson throws a curveball. "Hey, Milli, think Ben would be up for a date?" she blurts, nonchalant, sipping her mocktail with all the finesse of a seasoned socialite.

Milli nearly chokes on her drink, shooting me a baffled look that screams, "Seriously?" I stifle a chuckle—leave it to Payson to drop such a bombshell, especially with our parents right there.

Mrs. Sutton gives Payson an eye roll, but before Milli can respond, Luke chimes in with a playful jab. "Payson, can you give the guys a break for just one second?"

Payson, quick as ever, retorts with a sassy comeback, and I lose it, laughter bubbling out of me. Her words leave Luke dumbfounded, his expression priceless.

I decide to step in, clearing my throat to grab everyone's attention. The table falls silent, all eyes on me. Great, this is not how I planned to steal the spotlight.

I didn't mean to create this pause for a grand declaration, but now that I have their attention, maybe it's a sign. I should say something to Milli, right here, right now.

Collecting my thoughts, I focus intently on her. Our shared history rushes back to me—the echoes of laughter in this very restaurant, the nostalgia of our childhood adventures, the electric thrill of our first kiss, the tremble in our voices during our first whispered confessions of love. She returns my gaze, her lips curving in a tentative smile, but then her expression shifts, morphing into something else, a mix of emotions I can't quite decipher.

Damn, this is hard. My nerves kick in again, and I run a hand through my hair, second-guessing myself.

Should I just keep it simple? Congratulate her and leave the rest for later?

No, Milli deserves more. She deserves the truth, my feelings, all of it. Maybe not here, in front of everyone, but I need to say something, even if it's just the start.

Here goes nothing.

Standing up, our eyes meet across the table, reigniting our connection. "I'm not usually one for big speeches," I begin, my voice resonating with sincerity, "but Milli, today you've outdone yourself. You were absolutely incredible."

Her eyes soften, encouraging me, but the next words get caught in my throat.

"You know, seeing you today, it struck me how naturally this comes to you. Your knack for teaching those kids, it's nothing short of remarkable. The way those girls were captivated by every word, the way they look up to you—it's clear you're making a real difference in their lives. Your performance today was just another proof of your talent. You've always been goal-oriented, Mills, and you're smashing every single one of them. Cheers to you for nailing it today. I'm really glad I could be here to witness it."

The table goes silent, absorbing my words. In that moment, I reflect on my own journey—the treatments, the challenges, and the resilience to face each day with determination. It's a blessing to be here, to celebrate Milli's success and share in this moment.

As the table bursts into applause and congratulations, my focus stays on Milli. In a private exchange, her lips part slightly, sending a jolt through me. Her eyes flutter toward me, and there's a silent understanding, a spark of something more.

She shakes her head, that familiar, heartwarming smile

lighting up her face. It's not just her smile that catches me; it's the gleam of amusement in her eyes, a light I've missed for too long. This simple, unspoken exchange fills me with a comforting sense of relief, affirming that, regardless of what's left unsaid, we're going to be okay.

This recent break almost shattered me. The irony isn't lost on me—the distance between us during her high school years and my college days didn't hit as hard as it does now. It's true, they say, absence makes the heart grow fonder, and our experience is a testament to that adage.

The table buzzes with lively conversation, yet I sink deeper into my chair, champagne in hand. I'm engaged in the dialogue, but my attention often shifts to Milli, exchanging secretive smirks and teasing looks. Her sporadic flirty moves only amplify the excitement growing inside me.

In a quiet space, away from the bustle and the crowd, I'm longing for the opportunity to not just reconnect, but to open my heart to her, to apologize sincerely, to express how deeply I want her—more intensely than my next breath, more fervently than my aspirations of being a doctor.

CHAPTER 41
MILLI

"You really thought I'd let this night end without a goodbye?" I rib Miles, catching him by his pickup truck outside of Glasshouse. He halts, releasing the car door handle, and pivots to face me. His typical aura of confidence seems to falter, revealing the less assured, more vulnerable side I know so well.

An impulse to envelop him in a hug surges within me, longing to bridge the gap of our unspoken feelings. Yet, I resist, wagging my finger. "Not so fast, Sunshine. Tonight's about celebrating me, right?"

His trademark smirk, always so disarming, is in full effect tonight. It's unfair, really. I'm trying to maintain my composure, but inwardly, I'm yearning to ask if we can just move beyond all the barriers. Whether as friends or possibly more, I crave having Miles back in my life, in the spot he's always belonged.

Approaching him, he gestures toward the restaurant. "You seemed pretty wrapped up in there, and sure, it's your night. But shouldn't you be enjoying it inside, not out here?"

"What if I said I prefer it out here?" I counter, knowing he can't resist a good challenge.

But instead of engaging, he gives another nonchalant shrug. "You'll freeze in that outfit," he says, his tone serious but his eyes betraying a deeper intensity.

Closing the distance, I question, "What's wrong with my outfit?" I glance at my ensemble: a brown leather skirt, a white bodysuit, topped off with Converse—a chic tutor look, only missing my reading glasses and a hair bun.

He appears conflicted as I lessen the distance between us, his hands repeatedly diving in and out of his pockets, his foot rhythmically tapping on the snow-dusted ground.

"Your outfit's fine, Mills," he says tightly, a hint of strain in his voice. My provocations are reaching him, gently nudging him to break through this overwhelming tension that envelops us.

Milli, hold your ground. You're owed an apology, and so much more.

I'm acutely aware of this, and it's the reason I halt my advance. Despite our complicated relationship, Miles' gaze holds a rare intensity, a depth I've seldom witnessed.

Feeling empowered by his look, I close the final gap, bringing us mere inches apart. Our breaths mingle, our hearts seemingly beating as one.

I meet Miles' gaze just as he asks, "Is this a test, Mills?" His question cuts through my thoughts. His arms wrap firmly around my waist, a grip I could escape from but choose not to. I can't deny it; the closeness feels right, feels needed.

Feels like home.

With his arms securely around me, every inch of me recognizes this is where I'm meant to be.

His gaze drifts momentarily over my shoulder, then descends to the curve of my neck, drawing in a deep breath. I shut my eyes briefly, bracing myself. But soon, I find there's no need for defenses; his embrace shifts, his hands moving to my upper back, transforming his hold into one of comfort and safety. His touch, both strong and gentle, encircles me like a protective cocoon.

And god, it feels amazing.

Being in his arms once more, feeling the closeness of his presence, simply existing together in this moment—it's all I could ask for. The emotional toll of the recent weeks hits me with full force—my heart pounds, my palms sweat, and tears I've valiantly held back now threaten to spill.

My emotions cascade when he softly says, "I missed you, Milli Girl." His voice, tinged with pain, tugs at my heart-strings.

Miles tightens his hold, and my emotions spill over. "I—I missed you too," I manage to say, my voice faltering as I bury my face in his neck, holding onto him like he's my lifeline, terrified of losing this connection again.

Stay strong, Milli. You can do this.

It's not easy, maintaining composure while longing for an apology from someone who means so much. The challenge of hearing about him through others, the regret of not being there when he needed me most. But now, those concerns fade, overshadowed by the raw, undeniable truth of our rekindled connection and mutual longing.

Gradually, I steady my emotions. Miles' gentle circles on my back easing my turmoil. Raising my head, I meet his gaze, my eyes still shimmering with tears. What do we say now? How do we move forward? Have we ever really stopped being friends?

Reading my confusion, Miles' hand cradles my neck and jaw tenderly, his thumb tracing calming patterns. I instinctively lean into his touch, finding a momentary peace.

"Hi, Mills," he whispers, the simple words laden with unspoken emotions.

I let out a small, tearful laugh. "Hi, Miles," I reply, a sense of relief washing over me.

His smile, warm and inviting, sweeps over me, and a blush rises in my cheeks, intensified by the chilly air and this electrifying moment. His gaze drifts to my lips, and the urge to pull him into a kiss is almost unbearable. It's as if he's in tune with my thoughts, but then again, he's always had an uncanny ability to read me.

He brushes a stray lock of hair from my forehead, tucking it behind my ear. His hand then curls around my neck again, drawing him closer to me. I can feel the warmth of his breath tantalizingly close to my lips. My eyes flutter shut as he whispers, "Can I kiss you, Milli Girl?"

I reopen my eyes, finding his alight with a softness that stirs my soul deeply. For a moment, we're lost in each other's gaze, the world around us fading away. Finally, succumbing to the moment, I reply playfully, "Is it going to be worth it?"

He shakes his head, that familiar, charming smirk on his lips. My heart flutters, my knees feel weak. And before I have a chance to react further, he bridges the gap between us.

Our kiss is intense and soul-stirring—our lips moving in harmony, our breaths intermingling, the familiar dance of long-suppressed desire. It's more than just a physical connection; it's an outpouring of everything we've left unsaid, a culmination of our pent-up emotions and the deep connection we've always shared.

The sensation is breathtaking—his lips pressed to mine, the intertwining of our tongues, the harmonious sounds of our mutual pleasure, his hands exploring my body with a familiarity that stirs deep within me. Yet, amidst this intense connection, I find myself pausing. As much as I long for this, for him, and yearn to return to what we once had, I can't dismiss the thoughts racing through my mind. He was the one who distanced himself. I'm determined not to fall back into old patterns; he needs to show that he's fighting for this, for us.

It's about learning to flow with fate rather than against it.

Life often sees us exerting immense effort to control our destinies, as though sheer will can alter the course that fate has seemingly set. We resist, we struggle, and we strive against life's flow, convinced that our determination can change our predestined paths. Yet, in this relentless struggle, we sometimes miss the beauty that emerges when we let go, when we surrender to life's natural rhythm.

When we finally release our tight hold on life and allow things to unfold, that's when the magic truly happens. We begin to see how effortlessly the pieces of the puzzle fall into place, guiding us on a path that feels just right, leading us to unexpected joys and moments of bliss.

Miles looks at me, a trace of confusion in his eyes, as he tries to understand why I've stopped our kiss. He leans in, his forehead resting against mine for a fleeting second before pulling away, a look of emptiness crossing his face. "God, what was I thinking? That shouldn't have happened. You might think that's all I'm after. Tonight, it seems like I'm not thinking straight. Milli, you should've stopped me—"

But then, it's my turn to quiet his doubts, my lips meeting his once more. I let the kiss deepen, savoring the moment, allowing him to unwind and let go of the tension that had previously seized him. As he relaxes, his hands settle on my waist again. I ease back slightly, just enough to meet his eyes, seeing the hint of his familiar smirk returning.

"You're quite the charmer," he says, a trace of admiration in his voice.

With a casual shrug, I respond, "I'm aware," mirroring his smirk with one of my own.

His playful squeeze elicits a gentle chuckle from me. Our intimate sphere fades into obscurity—the distant sounds of conversation, the cars departing the lot, all seem inconsequential. It's just us, here and now, the connection between us intensifying with each heartbeat. The warmth of his nearness, the locking of our gazes—it's like looking at the one constant in my life, my ally in every moment of joy and adversity. I finally release the words that I have been yearning to escape, the words I've longed to say to him once more.

"I love you."

He pauses, his eyes briefly widening, a flicker of surprise or perhaps realization crossing his face, before he exhales slowly. My heart teeters on the edge of uncertainty, silently begging for him to echo the sentiment. Just once more, to hear those words that mean everything. Surely, after the journey we've navigated together, after all the laughter, tears, and silent understandings, it can't be too much to ask for.

As I'm caught in this whirlwind of thought, Miles' lips meet mine once more, setting off a torrent of emotions. His words, tender and heartfelt, brush against my lips. "God, I love you too, Mills. That feeling never faded, not since the first time I admitted it. I've been caught up in a battle against fate, doubting if I was ever enough for you. With my illness, I feared being a burden, that a future with me would be too much. I thought you deserved someone healthier, stronger, someone who could offer you everything."

Yet he fails to see—with or without his illness—he's always been the one for me, my steadfast constant, my future.

A smile breaks across my face, our lips still intertwined. "Miles, stop resisting it. You've always been my future," I say, laughter lacing my voice. "Haven't you realized? I've always had a crush on you."

His tickling evokes a laugh from me. "Oh, I knew," he responds with a tease.

I draw back slightly, injecting a lighthearted note into my voice, "You did?" followed by a soft push against his shoulder. "Why didn't you say anything?"

He stands there, hands casually rubbing the back of his neck. "Would I be a jerk if I said I liked seeing you react to every wink and blush at every touch?" A smirk plays across his lips.

This endearing, yet maddening man.

It's charming in a way, but also frustrating. If he knew all along, why the silence?

"I kept quiet because I didn't want to jeopardize what we had," he admits, shrugging slightly. "Obviously, that wasn't the best plan. Just look at us now."

Drawing closer, I wrap my arms around his neck, leaving past crushes behind as they seem inconsequential now. "So, what's 'now'?" I ask, his arms encircling my waist and effortlessly lifting me, my legs naturally wrapping around him.

As he carries me toward his truck, my back pressing against the cool metal, a shiver of both chill and memory runs through me. It's only been months, yet it feels like an eternity has passed. Our foreheads touch, and he releases a deep sigh.

His admission, laced with regret, hangs heavily between us, underscoring the depth of our connection and the complexities of his journey. "If you can forgive my stubbornness over the past month, maybe longer," he starts, his voice echoing with remorse. "I was foolish, not handling things the way I should have. My cancer diagnosis, the pressure about the NFL, the end of my college football dreams—it all hit me hard. But that's no excuse for the pain I caused."

His sigh is exasperated, revealing the struggle to express these burdens. I run my fingers through his hair, encouraging him to continue. Bottling up feelings can be so damaging; they tend to sneak up on you when least expect it, causing more harm than good.

He gives a gentle squeeze at my side, his expression turning earnest. "I know I was wrong for shutting you out, for ignoring the help from those who cared. It was a real ass move, and I get that. But I swear, Milli, I won't do that again. Hell, I'll even let you kick my ass, maybe even give me a good spanking." He winks. Yet, his eyes hold a commitment to making that particular scenario a reality, and hopefully, it might come soon. Although, just to clarify, he'd be the one doing the spanking, not me.

"But I'm making you a promise, Milli—no more shutting you out. I'll be open, honest, let you in, especially now as I face this fight with cancer."

The sincerity in his eyes is unmistakable. A shiver of anticipation runs through me at his words, but then he continues, "Falling for you, Mills? It's like I stumbled upon a hidden treasure in all our good times together. It totally took me by surprise, but it's the best kind of surprise. You know, I never really got to choose who I fell for. It was always you, sneaking up on me, weaving your way into my heart when I least expected it. Being in love with someone who gets me completely—that's us. Every inside joke, every late-night heart-to-heart, it's all turned into something more. Something deep and exciting. It feels like all those laughs and tears we've shared have just knitted us closer, in a way that's super comfortable but also completely new and thrilling."

He leans in closer, his voice dropping to a whisper. "And . . . I want to be able to say I love you as many times as I want to and . . . I want to fuck you, hear those sweet whimpers and moans of yours, whenever, because, I can."

"Say that again," I prompt, a mix of playfulness and depth in my voice.

He wiggles his eyebrows as he says, "What? That I want to fuck you when I can? Wherever and whenever? Hear those sweet soun—"

I quickly silence him, placing my hand over his mouth. "Not just that part."

He looks at me, a soft smile playing on his lips. "Oh, you mean when I said I love you? Because I do, Mills. I really do, so damn much."

His declaration resonates deeply, and for a moment, I'm rendered speechless, caught up in the emotion of it all. But then, finding my voice, I respond with our characteristic playful banter, "So you think you can handle all of this, Sunshine?"

He replies with confidence, "I've been ready for you since day one, Milli Girl." In that instant, everything falls into place. The laughter, the love, the journey we've been on—it's all led to this moment, and I can't help but feel like it's exactly where we're meant to be.

The sound of applause suddenly interrupts us, drawing our attention. Turning toward the source, our friends and family are gathered, all eyes on us. Our dads are shaking their heads in mock disapproval, while Wyatt sports a wide grin. Payson and Brooke are chatting animatedly, their faces lit up with joy as they glance my way. I return their smiles. Then, I notice our moms in their own little circle, thrilled; their laughter and chatter a sign of their happiness.

Luke's voice cuts through the air. "Put my sister down, you Neanderthal!"

Chuckling, I shake my head. Miles, undeterred, calls back to Luke, "I just got her back. She's not going anywhere, Sutton. Not now, not ever," he whispers the last part, sending a wave of joy through me.

I can't deny it; I'm completely smitten.

He turns to me, his grin infectious. "Seems like they're pretty happy for us."

I nudge his shoulder, laughing along with him as our family and friends head back into the restaurant, leaving us to our moment once more.

Leaning in, Miles asks in a teasing tone, "Ready for the real celebration tonight?"

I raise an eyebrow, joining in the banter. "Is that a challenge, Sunshine?"

He shrugs nonchalantly, but his eyes are alight with excitement and anticipation. "Guess you'll have to wait and see, huh, Mills?"

I smile warmly at him. "I love you, Miles Chasen."

He nudges me back, responding, "I know."

I retort, "Hey, you're supposed to say it back."

He sees right through my act, leaning in to plant a soft kiss on my lips. Pulling away, he affirms, "And I love you too, baby, more than you could ever imagine." The sincerity in his voice wraps around me like a warm embrace, confirming that everything we've been through has led us to this perfect moment.

Milli

"Challenge accepted, baby," I declare with a grin. The thrill was in my veins even before we stepped out of the restaurant. I always knew I'd be ready for whatever challenge Miles threw my way. It's our thing, isn't it?

"God, Mills, you have no idea how long I've been craving this—to touch you again, to hold you in my arms, to claim you as mine," he breathes out, his voice a low, seductive rumble as my back presses against the door of his house. His words fan the flames of a fire already raging within us.

Damn, he's just so sexy in these moments, completely and utterly mine.

The reality still feels like a dream—I mean, Miles Chasen, my lifelong best friend, now my lover.

God, I am the luckiest woman ever.

He hoists me up effortlessly, and my legs encircle his waist. It feels like our own unique dance, and I wouldn't change a thing. Chills dance across my skin as our lips unite. Our hands lock together, guiding us to his bedroom. Falling onto his bed sends waves of nostalgia crashing over me, memories of our first time here enveloping me.

That day seems like a distant memory, yet it's as vivid as if it were happening right now. I watch, lips parted, as Miles strips off his clothes—jeans first, then shirt, in that effortless way that's so him. Watching him now, touching him, being held in his embrace, I'm struck by the realization that there's no need to worry about the future, no need to ponder his thoughts afterward. I can just be in the moment. I can relish this time with him, now and always.

Because he is *mine*.

Isn't it just incredible? Knowing he's mine?

"Nope, because, baby, you're mine," he declares, his tone deep and possessive as he hovers over me.

Did I really just say that aloud?

He gives me that smirk, the one I love so much, and says, "Yeah, you did, and I'm dying to hear it again and again. Might even rival 'I love you' as my favorite phrase."

My eyebrow arches, my hands exploring his sculpted back, his firm form. I teasingly comment, "So, 'you're mine' gets you going, does it?"

His reply is cut short as I quickly silence him with my

hand, suggesting, "How about less chatter, more . . . catching up?"

His grin is wicked as he kisses me, starting from my jaw, making his way down to my neck, playfully teasing, before continuing his journey with soft kisses. His gaze locks with mine, and he whispers seductively, "I'm all for that, and so much more, baby."

A thrill of anticipation surges through me, my toes curling in delight. And oh, he promises so much more than just words.

〜√√√♡⌇〜

"So, what's next?" I whisper, my head resting on Miles' chest, still basking in the afterglow of our intense passion—was it the third or fourth time? I've lost count, but it hardly matters. With him, I could go on forever.

He draws me closer, wrapping me in his arms. As he tenderly brushes my hair back, he suggests, "Ready for round five?"

I give him a light nudge, teasing back, "You know that's not what I meant."

He feigns a hurt look before turning serious. "For now, we live life on our own terms."

But what does that really mean?

I shift slightly, propping myself up on his chest, our eyes locking.

What's the game plan? The future looms ahead—my freshman year wrapping up, and where does Miles stand in all this? His medical aspirations, his cancer treatment . . . We've danced around the future for so long. How can we dream of a forever without facing these questions?

He seems to sense the whirlwind of thoughts in my head.

Gently, he lifts my chin, his kiss landing softly on my lips. It's a comforting, grounding gesture, a silent promise we both understand and treasure.

Bringing our faces close, just inches apart, he offers, "How about we take it one day at a time? Embrace a little uncertainty. Does that work for you, Mills?"

His words, somehow, click into place. It feels right, easing into the future rather than rushing to solve it all at once. Everything seems destined to fall into place, just like us.

I smile, feeling his thumb caress my chin. "As long as I'm part of your everyday, I'm all in for that plan."

His eyes soften. "You're my constant, Milli, and I know it took me a while, but I get it now. I can't imagine a day without you, or not telling you I love you."

I beam, feeling like the luckiest person alive. Miles Chasen—he's not just a name, but my personal jackpot. His laughter, light and soft, fills the room as he gently repositions us, leaving me lying on my back.

With a twinkle in his eye, he teasingly inquires, "Now, where did we leave off?" That question marks the beginning of our new adventure together, unfolding in the most incredible way imaginable. Seriously, it's the best. Here we come, round five.

BONUS *scene*

Discover the next chapter in
Miles and Milli's adventure!

Scan Here!

for all the romance things!

For the readers who enjoy their
fictional men like their drinks   spicy!

@authorcharlicotner

Acknowledgments

Hey lovely readers,

First off, big virtual hugs for picking up this book! Writing it was like being on a rollercoaster of emotions, and knowing you're here for the ride makes everything worth it.

A heartfelt shoutout to my family for their endless encouragement and coffee. My children, you're my inspiration with your laughter and sweet interruptions. To my other half, you're the real-life romance that keeps the dream alive. Thanks for putting up with the late nights, the plot rants, and for being my forever plus one.

A huge thank you to my editor, Chelsea. You've polished my chaos into something beautiful and kept me on track.

And to everyone who's been a part of this journey, you're all awesome. Now, let's dive into this adventure together with Miles and Milli, and remember, love always finds a way.

- Charli Cotner